PETROS MAKRIS grew up in Cyprus and was educated at a private high school in Nicosia, where he excelled, and won the school's three prestigious prizes.

He was once a carpenter's apprentice, a farm worker, a clerk and a waiter, before he turned his attention later to higher education.

He became among other things, a Chartered Accountant, and a Chartered Secretary, and whilst working full time as a Senior Regional Manager he did a Master's degree (in Social Ethics), which he followed up with a PhD.

He has previously published many articles and written a number of short stories. *The Apostate* is an imaginative and inspiring thriller about contemporary issues.

THE
APOSTATE

PETROS MAKRIS

SilverWood

Published in 2014 by the author
using SilverWood Books Empowered Publishing®

SilverWood Books Ltd
30 Queen Charlotte Street, Bristol, BS1 4HJ
www.silverwoodbooks.co.uk

ISBN 978-1-78132-285-7

British Library Cataloguing in Publication Data
A CIP catalogue record for this book is available from
the British Library

Set in Bembo by SilverWood Books
Printed on responsibly sourced paper

Part One

I

Manila 2001

When Hamid arrived in Manila, The Philippines, he went straight to the hotel to check in, and left without unpacking his suitcase; he was on a mission. He asked the way to the Golden Mosque and when he arrived he hung around and struck up conversations with other worshippers. He soon asked if any of them knew of Maalik, who he described as an old friend whom he hadn't seen for many years. To his surprise they all said that they knew him.

'He usually comes here around 6pm,' one of them said. It was already 5.30pm, so he decided to wait. When Maalik arrived, the man pointed him out. Maalik was of medium height, wore Western-style clothes, had thick black hair and was clean-shaven. Hamid went straight up to him and introduced himself, saying that he was a friend of Abdul Hassan and that he would like to have a chat somewhere quiet.

'Don't tell me... He has a job for me,' said Maalik.

'How did you know?'

'The moment you mentioned his name I knew something was up. Let's go. There is a quiet café nearby where we can talk freely.' They strolled down to the café and ordered two coffees.

'So what does the old warrior want me to do?'

Hamid looked around and hesitated.

'If you feel uneasy here, let's finish our coffees and take a walk,' Maalik suggested.

'Yes. I would feel happier that way.'

Quickly finishing their coffees, the two men paid and left the café.

'We go back a long way, Abdul Hassan and me,' Maalik explained. 'We fought the Russians, you know; kicked the old Ruskies out. And we'll do the same with the infidels that we have now in Afghanistan.'

They walked and talked for an hour or more. Hamid brought Maalik up to speed, and reiterated Abdul Hassan's instructions: take two babies from Parenting4U; preferably one from a very wealthy American family and one from internationally famous Americans, if there are any. That was the best way to collect the large ransom money.

'We needn't concern ourselves with the ransom,' Hamid added. 'All that matters is for us to carry out Abdul's instructions. Getting all that information before the event without arousing suspicion will be difficult, I imagine.'

'I know where to start: the chauffeur to the CEO of Parenting4U – a Mr Wang. He is a balding, flaccid old fool who likes to boast a lot about his clever daughter who also works there. She has a little boy who she is bringing up by herself. She is a single mum.'

'That's your leverage, then,' commented Hamid. 'Remember, everybody is dispensable; even you and me. I hope you will do a clean job; let's have no collateral damage.

Hamid explained that he had to inform Abdul Hassan when to arrange for the transporters to come over, as he was only a messenger. He told Maalik that they would come prepared, with money and passports, and would leave the country immediately after the abduction. He imagined that security at the airports and ports would be tight once the news got out. Maalik agreed and said he'd speak with the transporters once they had arrived. He would arrange everything for them in due course.

'Is there anything else you need to know?' Hamid asked.

'No. Just give me some time to organise things. Meet me at the café at the same time in two days. I hope to have a plan in place by then.'

When they met, Maalik confirmed that he had a team in place to carry out the operation, and that he had tracked the movements of Mr Wang's daughter. The plan was to take her son hostage in her house, and threaten to kill him if she did not do as she was instructed.

'I will offer her a considerable amount of money to begin with, and if that doesn't make her cooperate I will threaten her son's life. That should do it.'

'You need inside information, Maalik. You must get the appropriate documents for each baby, and they must be American,' Hamid reminded him.

'I understand, but with an operation like this there may be casualties and we may not get exactly what we want. The place is like a fortress; we have to convince her to help us get in. She must provide us with the babies' locations and documents in advance, without realising that we are planning to abduct them. She is high up in the organisation and has security access to everything. She's our best bet,' explained Maalik.

'Good. I can see you've been busy. I hope you haven't aroused any suspicions by being pushy.'

'You worry too much, Hamid – we have hardly started. Give me three more days to set everything in motion. Meanwhile, you had better get the transporters over here. I want all of you to come to the mosque at the same time, and I hope by then to have everything in place for the operation to go ahead at a moment's notice.'

'Very well, I will see you then. Goodnight. May Allah be with you.'

With that, Hamid, having taken out his expenses from the $30,000 that he brought for the operation handed over the balance to Maalik, and they went their separate ways.

Hamid went straight back to the hotel and called Abdul on his cellphone. He told him to dispatch the transporters right away, and that when they arrived they were to go straight to the safe house organised by Maalik. Three days after the phone call, they were to be waiting at the main entrance of the Golden Mosque at 6pm.

II

Maalik continued finalising his plan. It was simple, but rested entirely on the forced cooperation of Miss Loo Wang. He would enter her house and hold her and her son hostage until she agreed to provide them with the information and documents on all the babies at Parenting4U who were two or three months old. They would then choose two and ascertain their location. If they were inside the complex they would use her to get to them. After that they wouldn't need her assistance any further. She was disposable, as were her son and parents. He was ready to set his plan in motion.

That night he watched Loo Wang's house and gained entry under the pretext of being a businessman connected to her employer. He then told her outright that he would pay her $10,000 if she would provide the information and documentation he wanted. As he expected, she was outraged. He tried several times to convince her that it was in her best interests to accept his offer, but she refused. Maalik became impatient; he took out his gun and told her that if she screamed or did anything stupid he would shoot her and her son dead, and then would tell his people outside her parents' house to kill them too.

'Cooperate and you all live. Refuse and you all die. What we are trying to achieve is for the greater good. It is the will of Allah, and with your help nobody will get hurt,' Maalik stressed.

But she was adamant and still refused. Only when Maalik stood over her sleeping son, pointing the gun at his head, did she agree. He told her what information he needed and that he would be back the following evening at the same time. He warned her that if she set a trap for him he would gladly die for the cause, and his associates would track her down, no matter how long it took them, and kill her and her entire family in revenge. 'My advice to you is to take this money and cooperate.' He gave her the $10,000 and left.

Maalik was not absolutely sure she would do it so he decided to take further precautions. The following night, rather than return himself, he sent an associate to her house to collect the papers. 'Just ask her for the papers and leave,' Maalik instructed. 'Make sure you are not being followed, and put the papers in a plastic bag. Meet me at the café, but remember we have never met.'

The associate went to her house as planned. Loo opened the door.

'I have come for the papers,' he said. She turned around and picked up a large, bulky envelope from a nearby table and handed it to him.

'This is what you wanted. Please leave me alone now. If any of you come here again I will report you,' Loo warned.

Not wishing to be there longer than necessary, the man thanked her politely and left. He didn't notice anything suspicious so he went straight to the café and handed the envelope to Maalik. Maalik thanked him for doing well and told him to leave, so that they would not be seen together. He opened the envelope, looked inside, and was satisfied that she had done as asked. He breathed a sigh of relief and phoned Hamid to arrange another meeting.

When they met later that evening Maalik told Hamid that he was making good progress; he had obtained the necessary details of five suitable babies and needed Hamid to identify which two to abduct.

'What are the babies' backgrounds?' Hamid asked.

'There are twin boys and a sister who must come from an extremely rich family, as they each have a $30 million Child Trust Fund in Swiss bank accounts. There is a three-month-old girl with a $10 million trust fund, and two African American babies with a $5 million trust fund each.'

'We'll concentrate on trying to take one of the boys, and the girl with the $10 million trust fund. That should satisfy Abdul. Where are the babies kept?'

'According to Loo, they are all with their surrogate mothers in apartments in the company's complex, except for one of the twins and the girl, who are both in a private hospital on the outskirts of the city.'

'Is there something wrong with them?'

'I don't know,' answered Maalik. 'If you want that information I'll have to pay Loo Wang another visit. As long as it's nothing serious we will attempt to take them from the hospital – I think it may be easier as the Parenting4U complex is heavily guarded.'

'You must go and see her again and find out what you need. I hope by then the transporters will be here. Once the two babies are in their hands they will disappear, and your role in this ends,' said Hamid.

'I understand. It's getting late now and I must go. I'll speak to you again, hopefully tomorrow night.' Maalik bid him good night and left.

Loo Wang was not pleased to see Maalik again the following evening. 'You said you'd leave me alone once I gave you the information you required. Please stay away from here,' she said.

'I need more information. Tell me why the two babies are in hospital and when they are coming out. You are in the clear. No one will know you gave me this information, I promise, and I'll make sure nobody bothers you again. But I warn you; if you don't, the consequences for you and your family will be dire – I don't need to spell it out.'

Being terrified at the thought, and feeling utterly helpless, she said, while sobbing, 'The two babies had a bad case of measles and had to be hospitalised. They will be out in two days – on Friday at about 4.30pm.'

'Who will take them back to the compound? Will they be under guard?'

'Their surrogates, an armed guard and a driver will go and collect them.'

'Thank you. That wasn't so hard, was it? I assure you, this way nobody gets hurt. Mind you, if you say anything to anybody now, or at any time in the future, you and your family will all be as good as dead.' With that, Maalik left.

Loo Wang knew very well that whatever they were planning was going to be an atrocity, and she felt awful thinking about it. However, from her own family's point of view she was sure she had done the right thing. Then she remembered the money they had given her. I had to do it to save my family; I didn't do it for the money. I will burn it, she thought to herself. I'll burn the lot, and that way I will both cleanse my conscience and destroy the evidence.

III

Maalik got everything he required and started to mull over his options.

Option one was to ambush the car taking the babies back to Parenting4U, but since the guard was armed there would most likely be casualties and a high risk of failure. Option two was to wait until they were back in their apartments within the complex, but then they would have to somehow get past the security guards at the two sets of checkpoints, and the armed guards patrolling the whole complex, grab the babies from their apartments, and then get back out again. This option had a much higher risk of fatalities and failure. Option three was to snatch the babies from the hospital before they were due to be released. He knew that the hospital was not as secure as Parenting4U, and as it was out of town it would be easier to get away. This, he reasoned, had a much lower risk of casualties and a very good chance of success.

On balance, he favoured the third option and decided to go ahead with it. He needed to assemble a small team of two men, including himself, and two women. He would telephone the hospital a few minutes before they arrived and say that he was from Parenting4U, and that one of their teams was passing by the hospital and would pick up the two babies then instead of at 4.30pm. They would turn up and enquire if Parenting4U had already informed the hospital of the early pick-up. If that didn't work then they would take them by force, shooting anyone that got in their way. To be convincing, they would need to wear the company's logo. No markings would be needed for the stolen car, as the company did not identify its cars for security reasons.

He phoned Hamid and told him to have the transporters in place, ready to collect the babies and dash off straight to the airport. Hamid confirmed that they would be. As he was not going to see him again, Maalik told him that it had been a pleasure working with him and wished him a successful journey back. Hamid did the same and told him that he would pray to Allah for everything to go well. He then told him that if he was ever in the area back home, he should pay him a visit, and finished with, 'Allah is great.'

By Thursday night everything was in place. Maalik phoned Hamid and told him that his plan was finalised and would be executed at 12 noon. The transporters were to check out of their safe house on Friday morning and go and wait in the car park of the supermarket at the main crossroads interchange, not far from the airport. The moment they arrived with the babies at the car park he would report his location to the transporters via mobile phone. Maalik was pleased with himself: everything was done and everybody knew exactly what to do and where and when to do it.

At 11.45am the following day, Maalik drove his team to the hospital. The two women who were dressed as nurses, together with the man who was dressed as a guard, went upstairs to the reception desk.

Maalik stayed behind in the car. He was going to phone at exactly 11.50am and say that he was phoning from Parenting4U, that a team of theirs was passing by, and that they should get the babies ready for them by 12 noon so that they could pick them up. They were to send on any paperwork later if it was not ready.

One of the imposters, a nurse, approached the receptionist and told her that they had come to pick up the two babies, Jonathan and Masha, and that the office at Parenting4U should have telephoned and requested them to be ready.

The receptionist looked at her quizzically and said, 'This is rather irregular, isn't it? Anyway, we haven't heard from Parenting4U. If you wait here a minute, I'll phone them and get confirmation.'

'Surely there is no need. We are here already anyway,' said the other nurse.

Just as she finished talking, the phone rang. The receptionist answered. The three intruders held their breath and prayed it was Maalik. They concealed a sigh of relief as they heard her say, 'They are already here.' She hung up the phone, asked them to wait, and phoned through to the ward to get the babies ready and brought down. They sat down and waited – it seemed like ages.

The man couldn't take his eyes off the receptionist; at one stage she disappeared behind a door and he got up immediately and went and rang the bell. To his relief she came straight back and he enquired how much longer they were going to be. As he spoke they saw the babies being brought down the corridor towards them by two nurses and an armed guard. There was a tense moment when the man saw them; he put his hand in his pocket and grabbed the gun that Maalik had given to him. He gave the receptionist an inquisitive look and was about to pull his gun out, when she said, 'Your company insisted on a 24-hour armed guard.'

They took the babies, went down, and got into the waiting car. The car pulled away, they coolly congratulated themselves for doing so well, and then headed to the pre-arranged rendezvous.

The transporters, two women and one man, took the babies – who were surprisingly subdued – and split up. Farouk and Leila took the girl, while the other woman, Alima, took the boy. They took separate taxis to the airport. The couple were to fly to Jakarta and the lone woman to Karachi. There they would change passports and fly to Kabul.

They estimated that by the time the abduction was discovered, they would be in the air. As a further confusion and delaying tactic, Maalik was going to telephone Parenting4U and say that the Taliban, together with Al-Qaeda, had taken the babies but that they were safe, and Parenting4U was to wait for instructions for their safe return.

IV

Abdul Hassan, the man who had given Hamid the instructions, lived in a mansion in a northern province of Afghanistan, not far from Hamid's village. He was a middle-aged warlord who controlled the local opium trade, among other things.

Almost all the people who lived in the village were peasants, living in ramshackle buildings, and did not always have sufficient income for a ready supply of food, so they more often than not felt the miserable pangs of hunger. In desperation, some resorted to growing poppies for opium – a dangerous occupation, as it was strictly controlled by ruthless regional warlords like Abdul Hassan. The whole province had no infrastructure of any description: no economy, no public services, no law and order, and no proper justice system. In fact, at the time this was true for most of the country.

Abdul Hassan had flowing grey hair, a deeply-lined, clean-shaven face, and he spoke with a compelling, harsh and rasping voice. His callous nature struck fear into the hearts of both his enemies and his friends. As a young man he had fought against the Russians, whom he hated with a vengeance. In later years he had worked behind the scenes in the fight against the Americans, the British, and the other invaders from the West. He viewed them all the same: arrogant infidels forever meddling in the affairs of Muslim countries under the guise of democracy and human rights.

At the turn of the millennium, ten years before Osama Bin Laden was killed by US Navy Seals, Abdul Hassan had regular meetings in his mansion with three close associates from the Taliban and Al-Qaeda, to discuss joint strategy and operations. Jamal Niazi was a young Taliban lieutenant from central Afghanistan. Sayed Afridi, also from central Afghanistan, was an Al-Qaeda senior commander. He had direct connections to, and dealings with, Osama Bin Laden, who contributed funds to their operations. However, Sayed conveyed the impression, in recent times, that he was disgruntled with Bin Laden because he was losing control of the other regions. Finally, there was Mohamed Sadat, a Taliban leader from a northern region of Afghanistan.

With the exception of Abdul Hassan, the men dressed in traditional Afghan attire, had long black beards and wore white turbans. Abdul's attire was European in style. As a teenager he had spent a number of years at a private boarding school in England. He had got used to wearing European clothes, eating roast beef with Yorkshire puddings, and drinking tea with milk. He spoke impeccable English.

It was during one of these meetings that they had started working on the plot to abduct two babies from Parenting4U for a $10 million US ransom. The background to the case, and how Hamid had got involved, together with the mentality, planning and logic of those involved, is revealed by some of their discussions.

Jamal argued that they should instead massacre as many children as possible in order to create terror in the West, and thus convey their message of stopping at nothing to rid their country of the foreign invaders. The fact that they were children didn't bother him; in his eyes they were just another bunch of infidels.

Abdul Hassan's eyebrows arched as he listened to Jamal; a massacre was foolish and fruitless, he thought. He stressed that the kidnap plot would be far more effective; it would demonstrate again, to the Americans and the other invaders, that they could strike anywhere they chose, and they would also collect a huge ransom. Jamal gave an uneasy nod. Sayed agreed and said that in his opinion that was definitely more beneficial. Abdul's gaze moved to Mohamed, the fourth member of the group, who nodded his support for the kidnapping and ransom plan.

'Let's formulate our plan. It's a long way to Manila and some careful planning is required. Any time spent in planning is time well spent,' said Sayed.

The three others muttered their agreement. Jamal then asked, 'Do you know any of our brothers in that area whose support we can enlist?'

'Unless any of you have any better contacts, I suggest my old comrade, Maalik Khalid, a Muslim extremist from the Philippines. He fought with me against the Russians and we have stayed in touch ever since. He is an educated man, speaks good English, and he is committed to the cause,' said Abdul.

'Where is he now?' Mohamed asked.

'He will be easy to find. He hangs around the Golden Mosque in Manila,' Abdul answered. 'We could send a courier there with money and instructions to plan the operation. I'm sure he will be delighted and will do whatever is necessary. I suggest we use $30,000 from the joint operations fund.' Funds came in for both the Taliban and Al-Qaeda from all over the world, under the guise of contributions towards the resettlement of innocent Afghans displaced by the fighting and for other humanitarian work.

'Who do we send on such an important mission?' Sayed asked.

'I have in mind Hamid Ali, our local teacher,' Abdul replied.

'Can we trust him for this mission?' enquired Jamal.

'Yes, I trust him implicitly. He knows a lot about my activities and he has never disagreed or disapproved. He is well-educated; a scholarly man who is well spoken and can outwit inquisitive officials. What else can I tell you about him? Oh yes, he is also a vizier for the province. He is a tall, smart man in his late thirties; he has a short beard and wears suits when he travels to Kabul on official business. If we are all in agreement, I will get in touch with him and tell him to get ready to leave,' said Abdul.

They all nodded in agreement.

'I'll update you on the situation at our next meeting, here as usual. As always, do not speak to anybody about this,' Abdul reminded them.

They knew not to cross Abdul. Anyone who betrayed him would be hunted down and killed like a dog.

The next day Abdul paid Hamid a visit. The moment Hamid saw him he knew something was up. The notorious opium trader and warlord did not make house calls for social reasons. Hamid was in awe of him and knew that whatever Abdul had come to ask him to do he would not be able to refuse; he had a wife, a daughter and an older sister to think about. No one said 'no' to Abdul Hassan.

Abdul took his time to explain everything to him in detail. He was to find Maalik, who usually hung around the Golden Mosque in Manila, and give him his instructions. He must only deal with Maalik, nobody else must know, and he must not part with the money until Maalik confirmed that the operation was feasible. It might take a few days while Maalik evaluated the situation, so he should be prepared to stay there for as long as necessary.

Hamid's eyebrows arched with intrigue as he listened in silence to Abdul's determination and enthusiasm, feeling uneasy about the feasibility of such a plan. However, he thought it would be unwise to challenge anything coming from Abdul Hassan.

For security reasons the instructions were verbal. Maalik was to abduct two babies of American parentage – one very rich and one, if possible, with famous parents. He must also get proof of their identity: DNA profiles, birth certificates, Child Trust Fund details, and any other relevant documents. These documents were crucial for the payment of the $10 million ransom. The success of the project was assured by his contact, with whom the deal was struck, Abdul explained, and as soon as they brought the babies safely to him, he was going to handle it.

'How will Maalik identify the babies?' Hamid enquired.

'He will know. He knows how to extract information from people, don't worry yourself about that,' Abdul answered. 'Also, tell him that a man with two wives will come in due course and they will need safe accommodation for a few days. They will take the babies and bring them over to Kabul. You, Hamid, will collect the babies from the transporters and bring them to me. The transporters will come prepared with money and forged passports. Maalik's involvement ends when he hands over the babies.'

After taking a few moments to absorb the details, Hamid said, 'I'll need to arrange to take a few days off from school and from my other duties, otherwise my sudden absence will arouse suspicion.'

'Yes, do that. You will need to go next week,' Abdul said. And he bid him farewell, praising Allah.

As instructed, Hamid arranged his time off and booked his flight to Kabul. Two days before his departure, Abdul paid him a final visit. He gave him the money and said, 'Guard it with your life. The success of the mission depends upon Maalik receiving the money, but take your expenses out of it first. He needs it to bribe people and to pay his own expenses. Also, the three transporters will be Mr Farouk Ibrahim and two women, Leila and Alima, who are supposedly his wives. They will pretend that they are all there on holiday; you will have to let me know when they have to be there. Will you remember all this?'

'Yes, I will. Is there anything else?'

'There is nothing else you need to know. Stay there until it's all done. Goodbye. The mighty Allah is with you.'

'Allah is great,' Hamid exclaimed as Abdul was leaving.

Hamid thought over the plan; it posed an enormous risk. The logistics were difficult and the odds were stacked against them. The whole plan could end in disaster. Like it or not, he was involved, but on reflection he was untroubled. This was his chance to carry out the will of Allah. He was no longer a remote spectator; he was on a mission to create jihadist events himself.

…and he did. He did as he was told; he carried out Abdul's instructions to the letter. Fortuitously, he was very impressed with Maalik; he carried out the operation like a professional and true jihadist. You can admire a man like that and make him a friend for life, Hamid thought. When he left Manila for Afghanistan after the abduction, he was quite pleased with himself and was looking forward to reporting back to Abdul Hassan.

V

New York

The phone rang, waking up Edward and Greta in the middle of the night. They both realised at once that something bad had happened since nobody would call at such an ungodly hour for any other reason. At the other end of the line was Damien Jones, the CEO of Parenting4U, who, after apologising for disturbing them at such an hour, proceeded to tell them the dreadful news. His voice was filled with distress.

'There has been – how am I going to tell you this? I wish...' he hesitated. 'I wish I didn't have to... Terrorists have abducted two babies and one of them is your Jonathan. I am so sorry, Edward. We are doing everything we can to track them down.' The words came out in a rush and it took a moment for their meaning to sink in.

'How could this happen?' demanded Edward. 'I thought the compound was impenetrable! Are you *certain* it was Jonathan? Do you know who took him and why?'

'The two babies were taken from a nearby private hospital, where they were being treated for measles. They were guarded by an armed guard 24 hours a day, but the abductors tricked the staff into releasing the babies. I've been told by the abductors that the babies were taken by the Taliban and Al-Qaeda supporters. They also told me that they will telephone with ransom demands.'

'*The Taliban and Al-Qaeda abducted our baby?*' Edward repeated. 'My God! What exactly do they want? What did they say?'

'A man speaking with a thick accent phoned and said: "We, the Taliban, together with Al-Qaeda, have got the two babies. Stand by for the ransom demands." I quickly asked "What do you want?" There was interference on the phone, the phone then went silent and after a moment he said something that sounded like "ask" and then "mum" or "mums". Or maybe he said "their mums". Then the connection went dead. I was so shocked and upset I didn't fully understand what he said; now I'm not even sure he was talking to me then.'

'What did he mean? It doesn't make sense.' Edward was starting to get over his initial shock. 'Have you told the police?'

'With your permission I will alert the police now. You should be aware that the police will not negotiate directly with the terrorists, whereas you may wish to,' said Damien.

'The first few hours are the most vital in these situations,' Edward said. 'And time has already been lost, during which the terrorists may have covered their tracks and got away. The only way to proceed is with negotiations. Please alert the authorities to the abduction and let them know that we are willing to negotiate. I'll be on the first available flight to Manila. Please keep me informed of developments – I'll have my mobile phone with me at all times. If the terrorists contact you before I arrive, let them know that we are willing to talk.'

Even listening to only one side of the conversation, Greta had got the gist of the situation and its seriousness. Edward quickly filled in the details as he dressed.

'We need to contact the American Embassy in Manila. Both babies are American citizens so we must alert them immediately,' said Greta.

'I'm not sure they should be involved,' Edward mused. 'I'd rather pay whatever the kidnappers ask and get our baby back. However, the embassy staff may have useful information on the Taliban or Al-Qaeda operatives and suspects, and they could provide the police with vital information to assist in tracking them down.'

'I'll call Matthew at the CIA,' Greta said. 'But that will have to wait until it's a more reasonable time to call. We can ask his advice and take it from there. He specialised in terrorist threats emanating from home and abroad.' She got out of bed and also started dressing. 'We must get our baby back. We have the money; whatever it takes, we'll get Jonathan back.'

Matthew was appalled to hear about the abduction when Greta called with the news, and was very surprised to learn that they had babies at Parenting4U. He asked Greta what the terrorists wanted, and she told him that they had apparently told the CEO of Parenting4U "to ask mum" or "their mums" or something, and that they would be back in touch.

Matthew was silent for a moment, bewildered. He had known Greta for a long time and was naturally concerned about the safety of her and her husband's baby. He told her that the Agency was not aware of any active Taliban or Al-Qaeda cells in Manila, or in the Philippines for that matter. He assured her he would do whatever he could, and would try and find out about the situation from the US Embassy.

When Matthew called the embassy in Manila, his source confirmed that he was also not aware of any local Taliban or Al-Qaeda cells. Unfortunately there were many connected organisations, plus isolated individuals, moving around, any of whom were capable of conducting a one-off atrocity such as this. The Manila agent felt it would be very unwise to negotiate with the abductors, as they were unlikely to negotiate in good faith.

Matthew called Greta and relayed the news. He stressed that they should get all the authorities working together: the embassy staff, local police and government agencies.

Edward then called Damien at Parenting4U to find out if any further progress or contact had been made. There hadn't been, and he continued with his arrangements to leave for Manila.

Greta said, 'This situation is way beyond our experience or understanding. The only thing I care about is the safe return of Jonathan, so we will just have to pay the ransom and hope the kidnappers keep their word.'

'I agree, honey. We have no experience in these matters. I will arrange for a large sum of money to be available to hand over at a moment's notice. I would rather that than let the police try to recover our baby by using force. I think we should take an experienced negotiator – can you call Matthew again and see if he can recommend someone?'

Greta called Matthew again and told him that they had no further information but they wanted his advice on the best course of action. Matthew told her that he was leaving for the airport soon, as he had to return to Afghanistan, but that he would still try and help. He advised them to wait for further information, such as the ransom demand, and then to try to negotiate, but draw out the negotiation conversations to allow the security forces to locate the kidnappers by tracing their calls. She then asked him if he knew anyone who had previous experience in such a situation; someone who could go with Edward to assist him and the authorities. Matthew knew of several people who he thought would be able to help, and recommended an experienced hostage negotiator called Fred Nicholls.

Greta was desperate to go with Edward but, after talking it through, she reluctantly agreed that it would be better for her to stay in the US and speak regularly with him on the phone. As soon as the negotiations were finished and their baby had been handed back, she would join him in Manila.

Edward spoke to his bank to arrange to have immediate access to $10 million, which he passed off as a deposit for a deal. This was not uncommon for him so no questions were asked by the bank.

Fred Nicholls called shortly after Edward had finished talking to his bank. Having spoken with Matthew, the negotiator had agreed to drop everything and assist Edward and Greta. They had a brief discussion about where they would meet in Manila, exchanged contact details, and agreed to leave discussing a strategy until they met face-to-face.

Edward kissed Greta goodbye and left for the airport.

VI

Greta had been working for the CIA for some time. When she joined the Agency she had been in love with Edward, a man of outstanding good looks who stood out in a crowd. Of Italian descent on his mother's side, Edward was tall with black hair, and had an intellectual-looking face, with sharp brown eyes. He was even-tempered and had a genial, relaxed manner. At an early age he had shown an aptitude for computers, and as soon as he had finished his Master's degree at Harvard he had started his own IT company, winning the acclaimed "Young Entrepreneur of the Year" prize two years later. When his company grew, at home and abroad, he had to travel all over the world.

Before Greta had married Edward, she had been Greta Faraday, the elder daughter of Senator John Faraday from Baltimore. She was of Irish descent on her father's side, had dark hair and blue eyes and came from a well-to-do family: her father, besides being a senator, was a wealthy man. By the age of twenty-one she had graduated from Stanford with a First in Law. She was a tall and beautiful woman, who was always dressed smartly and had been prepared to put the hours in at work. Keen and ambitious, she had been determined to do well in her chosen career. Even after she married Edward, she had continued to work with the same determination and enthusiasm.

Matthew was a senior colleague. Although they had worked in different departments, their work had brought them into close contact at times. She respected him greatly, and would occasionally call him and discuss intricate problems with him. He was a man of few but precise words, and would cut to the chase.

She had first met Matthew when she joined the Agency, around the same time as he had done. During the early part of her career she had done well on the promotion scale, keeping pace with Matthew.

Matthew was a tall and rather large and imposing young man. When he started working for the Agency he was engaged to be married to a tall and attractive Swedish girl. He was full of drive and enthusiasm and had conveyed the impression that he would reach the top of his chosen profession quickly. He had taken his work very seriously, coming across to his colleagues as sombre and stern, not at all jovial and easy going. However, he also had a reputation within the Agency for being forthright and approachable, and people appreciated the fact that they knew where they stood with him. He had continued with his hard work, rising to ever more senior positions in the Agency.

Everything had been going well for him, until his wife died from cancer at the age of thirty-six, which had utterly devastated him. Since they had had no children, he had buried his sorrows in his work in an attempt to ease the pain. He had joined the Counter Terrorism Unit and served with distinction at home and abroad. He had soon been acknowledged as the top expert on many aspects of National Security. Because of his expertise, he had even been seconded to the White House for a while. There he had been held in high esteem, and had been consulted by people more senior than him, including, on more than one occasion, the President himself.

Part Two

I

When Edward boarded the aeroplane for Manila he was in a state of severe anxiety. He sat in his seat poker-faced, staring out of the window. How did it all go so wrong, he kept on asking himself. On both previous occasions that he went to Parenting4U he was very impressed with the security and everything. Perhaps Tracey King was right; the turbulence was an omen. No, of course not, he thought, as he recalled the time he met her on the aeroplane the first time he went to Parenting4U.

It all began a long time ago for Edward and Greta Everest. Edward knew all along that his wife did not want to have and bring up children the normal way; she considered conceiving, carrying and giving birth abhorrent. They both wanted to have children that were genetically theirs. They had agreed that they would investigate a 'nurturing' company, which actually raised children to an agreed age. These organisations had sprung up in several countries around the world. Though controversial when they first appeared, demand for their services had meant they soon spread, and the controversy gradually died down. All the prospective parents had to do was provide the ova, the sperm and the money. It was 'labour' free but costly, and a remote way of having and bringing up children.

So one day Edward, on his way back from a business trip to Hong Kong, made a detour and went to Manila. While he was boarding the aeroplane, he overheard some of the conversation between two crew members.

'We're going to have a VIP on board today,' a stewardess said.

'Who is it?' her colleague asked.

'Tracey King.'

'Really? Isn't she gorgeous; please may I attend to her?' The young air hostess asked anxiously.

'No, you can't. You know the rules; only senior crew are allowed to do that.'

Edward walked on, found his seat and settled down; it was the aisle seat of three on the left-hand side, in the business class area. He was going to find out as much as he could about a 'nurturing' organisation called Parenting4U. It was the most famous of that type of organisation in the world, and considered to be the best. Having spoken briefly to Mr Jones, the Chief Executive Officer, he had made an appointment to see him in person.

A few minutes after Edward sat down, a beautiful, blonde, smartly dressed woman came and sat next to him in the middle seat. The seat by the window remained empty. She was Tracey King, the VIP that the airhostesses had been talking about; a US chat show hostess who was as famous as any Hollywood celebrity. VIPs were always offered an aisle seat by the airline but Tracey preferred a middle seat – as long as the seat by the window was vacant. Edward introduced himself and said that he was pleased to meet her in the flesh, so to speak, as he felt that he already knew her from her show. After the introductions they carried on talking and were amazed to find that they were both going to Manila for the same purpose. Tracey told him that she had already been to Parenting4U and had been very impressed with their state of the art technology, security and everything. Edward was pleased to hear that and told her that he and his wife had chosen it because they thought it was the best in the world.

In due course, after take-off, the cabin crew started to serve a variety of drinks. Tracey accepted a glass of champagne that was offered to her. Edward opted for a glass of whisky on the rocks, and they carried on talking about surrogacy, Parenting4U and other subjects.

When they ceased talking, Tracey turned around, leaned towards the window and stared at the vast void of the cosmos and sensed an eerie feeling as she wondered about the events she was going to set in motion at Parenting4U. Her partner in New York was at ease with it and thought that in some respects the Vatican was not moving in the right direction in a modern world. Nevertheless, Tracey was resigned to the fact that it was in conflict with Catholicism, their faith. It was her purgatory but it had to be done.

Edward resumed thinking about the questions he had in his mind to ask Mr Jones. He had done a lot of research via the Internet but he wanted to see it "in the flesh" and hear it "from the horse's mouth". He would convey everything he learned to Greta when he returned home to Washington DC.

The company's mission statement read: "To provide a confidential service to parents; delivering healthy children using the latest embryology techniques, and raising them in a sophisticated, safe and healthy environment, from conception to the time they are handed over to their genetic parents.' Edward wanted to see some evidence of how the company implemented this.

After the birth of a child, the company carried out various tests, including blood and DNA tests for confirmation that the right ova and sperm had been combined. Copies of all the verification documents were supplied to all relevant parties. The organisation kept the originals for future reference and matching purposes – if it ever became necessary.

At one stage Edward said to Tracey that, according to the website of

Parenting4U, they held the surrogate mothers in high esteem, but that he wondered how they were treated and what happened to them afterwards.

'They certainly do hold them in high esteem,' Tracey replied, 'because they form the foundation of all their services; without them the business would cease. Apparently, they recruit women in their late teens or twenties, and some remain there until their late thirties or even early forties. Some choose to become professional surrogates and have multiple children during their time with the company, while some move on to become professional nannies. You can request the option to have another child later with the same surrogate if you want to, but in the end it is up to the surrogate to accept or decline the offer.'

'That's interesting. I do hope their financial benefits are not short-lived; I mean that they last longer than the duration of the pregnancy.'

'Yes they do; they are paid a good salary on a monthly basis, and at the very end of their contract, if they have fulfilled their obligations, they receive a lump-sum bonus which is equivalent to a year's salary. It's an incentive for them to do their best and to stay on until the end of their contract. It also helps them to accumulate some money for the future after they leave the company. It's all in their contract of employment.'

'I see that you are well informed.'

'Once agreement is reached by the surrogate, the company and the client,' Tracey continued, 'the surrogate becomes an employee of the company and is allocated first an apartment, and later on a house with a garden and some sporting facilities, depending on the wishes and the finances of the client. The surrogate becomes a single mother, bringing up the child, or children, of the same family together; no father figure is provided I am afraid. Having all the children in one place is expedient for the parents if and when they visit.'

Within half an hour, the airhostess reappeared; she was very attentive to their VIP passenger. 'Excuse me, Miss King,' she said. 'Would you like another glass of champagne, or is there something else you would like?'

'No, nothing, thank you.'

'What about you, sir?'

'No thanks,' Edward replied, and turned round and asked Tracey if they had already found their surrogate.

Tracey was glad to impart the information that she had gleaned from her previous two visits.

'We have; she is Russian. They recruit them from all over the world, but mainly from the Philippines, China, India, Pakistan and Turkey, as well as from some African countries. They aim to have a variety in order to satisfy the preferences of their large clientele. Besides variety in ethnic origins, the company employs women of different religions: Christianity, Hinduism, Islam and many others.'

Suddenly the seatbelt sign appeared on the aeroplane screens and a stewardess requested that passengers should put their seatbelts on as there was some turbulence ahead. After that their conversation stopped; it seemed to have come to a convenient end.

II

Soon after, the aeroplane started to bounce in turbulence, and some passengers looked around nervously. Edward did not think much of it; he closed his eyes and carried on deliberating about Parenting4U. The trembling continued; it was gradually getting worse and the flight became bumpy. The turbulence was intensifying; the plane was bobbing up and down, and was tossed from left to right. Tracey felt as though she was riding a butterfly and was getting distressed. Edward was not perturbed. Various small items were hurtling around in the fuselage, and some passengers started screaming. In spite of the requests from the crew to stay calm, as there was nothing to worry about, the expressions on the passengers' faces told a different story. The turbulence and commotion inside the plane continued for an eternity – or so it seemed.

As though things couldn't get worse! All of a sudden the aeroplane went through an air pocket and dropped a few thousand feet in the space of a few seconds. The voice of the captain was heard quite clearly. 'Oops!' and was followed by, 'We ran into some bad weather; we're going through some fast-moving cumulus clouds, but there is no need to be alarmed. We'll soon be out of the storm.' To him that was nothing unusual but to the passengers the aeroplane seemed to be out of control; that was it, the end!

Some of them were frightened out of their wits; Tracey was petrified. She grabbed Edward's hand, leaned hard on him and said despairingly, 'As our loved ones are not with us, do you mind putting your arm around me and holding me tight? I am so scared. I don't want to die...alone.'

Edward gave her a surprised look, but obliged. He was sympathetic but not alarmed, and said in a soft voice, 'Tracey, listen to me. We are not going to crash. I've travelled considerably and encountered turbulence many times; this is just another.'

Tracey, who already felt that she was a sinner on account of her partner, said to Edward in a trembling voice, 'A thought just occurred to me; could this be an omen that we shouldn't be going down this route? To have children by using Parenting4U, I mean. I am Catholic, you see.'

Edward chuckled. 'No, I don't think so, Tracey. Forgive me for saying this, but I think your mind is conjuring up all sorts of scenarios because of the terror of the storm. There isn't anything paranormal about it; it's just a coincidence. I am a Catholic too and so is my wife. We have considered the issues and decided that we have no choice; it's either this or no children. I don't think bringing life into the world this way is a sin.'

The aeroplane was gradually becoming steady; Tracey breathed a sigh of relief, regained her composure and relaxed. She then said, 'I am sorry. You must be right.'

It was extremely important to Edward and Greta that their children were raised in a happy and emotionally secure environment, and that they were well-educated. The company's website stated: "The children's upbringing is based on the latest scientific methods for stimulating their intellectual, psychological and physical development."

The company encouraged input from the parents and had flexible agreements which covered a wide range of options: discipline, education, sport and other activities, periodic reports, religious education, and visits by the genetic parents. The options were there for parents to choose from; alternatively, they could leave some or all to the company.

All these, and raising the children up to eleven or eighteen years, added up to a lot of expenses. The company required two bank accounts in Geneva, Switzerland; each supported by an agreement. The first was between the genetic parents and the bank but was also linked to Parenting4U. It was for a designated trust fund for the child. A lump sum, $1 million minimum, would be deposited in this account on birth, and the child would inherit it when he or she reached a specified age between eighteen and twenty-one years. In the unfortunate event of the child's death before the fund was claimed, it became refundable in full, and with interest calculated to the date of repayment, to the parents or another designated party on presentation of proof of death.

The second bank account and agreement related to the relationship between the company and the client, and was to cover the company's expenses. A lump sum could be deposited in that bank account, and a regular payment to the company would be set up. The first payment would be made after successful implantation and conception by the surrogate was confirmed, the second when the child was born, and then once per year on every birthday until the child was handed over to its genetic parents and the contract concluded.

When they arrived at Manila airport and collected their luggage, Edward said goodbye to Tracey and hailed a taxi. He asked the driver to take him to a nice restaurant for something to eat. Tracey was staying overnight at a hotel, as her meeting was the following morning.

III

Edward then took another taxi to Parenting4U and, despite being expected, he had to produce identification at a checkpoint before he reached the main office building. The receptionist, who was a charming Filipino lady, apologised to him and explained that it was a necessary evil of maintaining high security.

He brushed it off and said, 'I am impressed! It shows how seriously you take security.' She then asked him to sign the register of visitors, before inquiring if he was familiar with the company's work.

'Well, I do know about your procedures, surrogates and financial requirements, but I still have some points that I hope to get clarification on today.'

'I am sure you will,' she said. She then looked down at her computer screen for a moment and said, 'We've arranged for you to see Dr Chew, the Head of Fertilisation and Implantation, who will brief you on the company's relevant procedures before you see Mr Jones, the Chief Executive.' She looked around as a white-haired man came through a side door and she introduced them. Dr Chew was tall with white hair; he stooped with age and walked with a cane.

As they started walking, Edward heard the noise of a helicopter approaching and looked at Dr Chew inquisitively.

'Oh! It's one of our clients; some fly to Manila in their private jets and then hop on a helicopter to come here. Some even bring their bodyguards with them. Personally, I think that's unnecessary as the security in and around the complex is excellent,' Dr Chew said.

Edward acknowledged with, 'I see' and followed Dr Chew down a short corridor and into a neat, moderate-sized office.

'Please, have a seat. I have been asked to fill you in on anything you would like to know about our fertilisation and implantation procedures before you go and see Mr Jones.'

'I have been trying to find out as much as I can about the company. What I am not clear about are the initial stages of the facilitation, and the possibility of multiple births.'

'The first thing we do is to obtain confirmation that the sperm and the ovum to be used in the conception are provided by the client. You will appreciate that some clients prefer to have these procedures carried out in their home town at recognised fertility clinics; they are all listed on our website. They then send to us the frozen genetic material, along with DNA profiles for both parents for subsequent matching with the child's DNA profile. Alternatively, the parents go to the nearest fertility clinic and, after having any necessary treatment, they plan their visit here to coincide with the time for ovulation. Once they are here we take over. Finally, clients may come here from the beginning, and the company will carry out any necessary treatment and procedures; but it requires a longer stay within the complex.' Dr Chew paused and looked at Edward.

'We would most likely choose the second method; I would like my wife to also come and see your facilities.'

'Excellent. I am sure she will be very impressed. With regard to your concern about multiple births, I want to put your mind at rest. We only facilitate twins, and that's only if a client wants twins. Some clients prefer having one child by one surrogate and another by another, instead of having twins. In any case, either way there isn't much difference in our charges. Embryology has been perfected for some time now and in the last few years we, here at Parenting4U, have specialised in only transferring one embryo into the womb. Our success rates are still the best in the world.'

'Glad to hear it,' said Edward.

'Is there anything else you would like to know before I take you to see Mr Jones?'

'No, that's all, thank you.'

Damien Jones was of mixed parentage; he looked partly European and partly Filipino. A thin, nondescript man in his early forties, he welcomed Edward with a smile and said 'I hope I haven't kept you waiting too long.'

'No. Dr Chew was very helpful.'

'Was there anything specific you wished to ask me?'

'Sure. I want to know a bit more about the surrogates: who actually pays them and when do their services begin and end?'

'They are our employees and are paid by us. Their employment begins on signing the contract and ends when you take possession of your child or children, which may be at any time after a successful birth, but no longer than eighteen years.'

'I believe you have surrogates from a number of different nationalities and religions. Is it possible to specify a particular type of surrogate? I am sure my wife would prefer a Catholic surrogate. As you might know it's against our religion to enter into these arrangements…but we won't go into that.'

'I understand,' replied Mr Jones. 'And yes, it is possible. We take the wishes of our clients very seriously. We aim to bring up their children as though they themselves were doing it.'

'What kind of contact do parents have with their children while Parenting4U is contracted to raise them?'

'Again, that depends on the parents and is laid down in the agreement. For example, they may wish to be present when the child is christened, cuts a tooth, takes the first step, or is circumcised. Some parents take their children on holidays, or have them at home during holidays, whereas others do not want to know much or anything at all until they take them from us. Some are so busy they just cannot spare the time and attention that young children need. Much better that those children are raised here, by a company like us, where they get the attention and stability that promotes a healthy and productive attitude. Everything is covered in the agreement, and if you require any clarification you are welcome to contact us with further questions. Our forms are available on a computer disc, a USB device, or we can open a computer account for you and you can access them with your computer.'

'I'll take the device please, and have a look at it on my laptop on the aeroplane.'

'It's straightforward: you can fill in all the sections one by one, or ignore sections and leave the arrangements as default. There is also an option for multiple forms, i.e., if you want to have more than one child. You will appreciate that the agreements have to be legally binding in three countries: the Philippines, the client's country and Switzerland. We simply ask our clients to fill out the sections as they require, and then submit the form to us. We then evaluate their requirements and calculate the costs.'

'We are thinking of having two children; presumably I will need to fill out the form twice?'

'The form can be saved and then you can create a duplicate copy, changing any details if you have different requirements – for example, if the first child is a boy and the second a girl – and then submit both forms.'

Edward glanced at his watch. 'Is there anything else I should know?

I have to be at Manila airport to catch my plane at 5.30pm.'

'Not unless you have any further questions? And I'll call my secretary and tell her that my chauffeur is to take you to the airport.'

'There's no need to do that. I'll get a taxi.'

'But I insist,' Damien said. 'At this time of the day it may be difficult to get a taxi.

It's no trouble.'

Damien then asked his secretary to call his chauffeur. He arrived within minutes and was introduced as Mr Wang.

On the way to the airport, Mr Wang took a convoluted route that allowed Edward to see much of the complex before leaving its grounds. He was an affable, fat fellow in his fifties who liked to talk. He took the opportunity to show off by telling Edward about his daughter Loo, and how proud he was of her because she was very clever and had studied medicine in London. She had specialised in IVF and embryology, and had been headhunted by Parenting4U. Both he and his daughter were very happy and honoured to be working for Parenting4U.

IV

During the flight home Edward had plenty of time to reflect on what he had learned from his visit. He certainly was impressed with the size and security of the complex; it must have covered many square miles, and the guards patrolling the grounds were armed. Everything had looked clean and tidy: the parks, the streets, the people and the children. Everywhere he had looked there had been an appearance of affluence – not much of a surprise considering that children of some of the most influential and wealthy people in the world were born, lived and brought up there. The whole place also conveyed an idyllic and relaxed atmosphere. He felt pleased that his children might grow up in that sort of environment. What a contrast to the noisy and rather dangerous city that he was going back to, he thought. Perhaps that was why Mr Wang had taken him on a mini-tour of the compound before heading straight to the airport; so that the image, and contrast, would be fresh in his mind.

Edward was used to flying around the world on long-haul flights on business, and used some of the time to work during the flight. He pulled out the USB device that Damien had given him and started working on the agreements; sifting through, ticking boxes and answering questions.

A couple of hours later, having completed what he could on his own, he started thinking about the need for a trust fund for each child. Wealthy parents took the opportunity to set up huge trusts for their children to avoid inheritance taxes, and also hedge against the possibility of losing all their wealth before their children inherited it. Wealthy spouses with surplus funds, and no pre-marital agreements, might also put large amounts into their children's trusts to avoid the other spouse getting it in the event of a divorce. But that would never happen to us, Edward thought. Since he had already accumulated quite a lot of money, he decided to be very generous to his children from the beginning and set up a $30 million trust fund for each, which they would inherit on their twenty-first birthday.

He arrived home in Washington in the evening. The house was empty apart from the domestic staff, which meant that Greta was still in Boston. He went to his study, sat down and telephoned her.

'Hello, honey. I just got back home,' he said.

'I am so pleased you are back, darling. Was the flight all right? You must be so tired.'

'The flight home was fine, but I am tired. It's been a long day. I've got so much to tell you. When are you arriving? I'll pick you up at the airport.'

'Sorry, darling, but I've got another meeting to go to. I'm on my way there now. I don't think I'll be back until Sunday afternoon. We can talk about everything then.'

'All right, honey. I love you. Bye.'

'Bye, darling. I love you too.'

The following morning Edward woke up late. After a good breakfast he went to his company's office in town. There he opened those letters that were marked as personal, and carried on with work as usual. He then looked at his work schedule for the following few days, which as usual was full of meetings.

He had started his software company, EverSoft Corporation, soon after finishing his Master's Degree in software engineering and business management at Harvard. After a few difficult years in the beginning he had won a contract with a US government department, and it had taken off from there, with orders flooding in from home and abroad. The growth over the five years since had been phenomenal, and the profits had soared: first $5 million, then $30 million, and currently over $70 million per annum.

Once the company's success was assured, he had proposed to and married the woman he loved: Greta, the beautiful and dynamic daughter of a US senator. It had been like a dream come true.

But success had brought with it a lot of responsibility and hard work, or perhaps it was the other way around. Every year that went by, he had to work harder to keep the business successful. He had to keep competitors at bay and he had to keep the momentum going.

His unwavering enthusiasm for work, to keep advancing instead of resting on his laurels, had led to his continued and enduring success – that's what his father would have said. Even as a child, Edward had been encouraged to work hard and plan ahead. "Work hard, plan your life, and do the right thing, son. Then everything will fall into place," his dad had used to say to him. "There is no such thing as luck, son. All that there is is hard work, bravery and imagination. Luck is allied to the brave. You have to be brave to be an entrepreneur; but if you work hard enough, you will almost certainly make money. Money will give you power and open doors for you, besides providing for your family. It's money that makes the world go round. The harder you work during your early life, the easier your later life will be. But there will be failures in your life, mark my word, there will be some, son. Don't fall at the first hurdle: learn from it and move on. Let failure be a lesson to you, not the epilogue of your life. We build our strengths and character in times of despair, son. Be prepared, not only for success but also for failure."

He looked at his watch and realised it was time to meet his friend and business associate, John Meredith, for lunch. They had been best friends for many years, ever since they had met at Harvard. John's wife was called Sam, and they had two children, Paul and Gillian. Their wives also got on very well together.

V

The next day Greta called and asked Edward to pick her up at the airport at 12 noon. Edward was very pleased to hear her voice again. Every time one of them went away for work, which they both did quite often, he always looked forward to seeing her again. He still loved her as much as he did the day they got married, and missed her, especially at night.

When Greta came through arrivals she rushed towards Edward and gave him a big, welcoming smile. He responded in the same way, and thought how very lucky he was to have such a beautiful and wonderful wife.

Having picked up her bags, they went to the car and headed to a restaurant they knew, not too far from the airport. Greta said that she was tired from the flight, but was looking forward to hearing about his findings from his visit to

Parenting4U. He told her all about it, and that he was very impressed with everything there: the people, their approach and practices, and the security around the whole complex.

Later he said, 'You can't believe who is also having a baby at Parenting4U.'

Greta thought of saying, "Is it a guessing game, darling?" but being too tired just inquired with a 'Who?'

'Tracey King; she was sitting next to me on the flight to Manila.'

'That's interesting. I wonder who the father is.'

Edward was not surprised by that comment. Tracey King's partner was a woman, Stella Mancuso. Tracey was very famous, but so was Stella; she was a soprano who sang all over the world. They were an icon to lesbian women in the whole world.

'I think the father is the black tenor, Keith McNally. Well, she didn't actually name him. I deduced that from what she was saying about the sperm donor. Apparently both women are strong believers in biodiversity, and by not having a white baby, like themselves, they believe they are contributing to biodiversity.'

'How bizarre!' Greta exclaimed.

'Well, in their opinion the greatest strength of life lies in its capacity to diversify; without it, it would have become extinct. It's as though life discovered biodiversity in order to perpetuate itself. There is something to be said about the theory, don't you think?' asked Edward.

'I beg to differ. Strictly speaking, being Catholic, I do not believe in evolution. Life did not "discover" biodiversity, darling, God bestowed it on it; that's what I think.'

'By the way, I had lunch with John yesterday and told him of our plan. I invited him and Sam to come to dinner on Saturday, if it's all right with you.'

'Of course it is. I will also invite Martha and Timothy, and Bernard and Ellie. NASA let Bernard have a few days off and he is down here with Ellie – until the following Monday, I think.'

VI

The guests arrived at about 7.30pm, and after the usual welcoming pleasantries they all had a drink before sitting down round the table for dinner. After the starter, Greta turned to her brother Bernard, who was sitting to her left, and said, 'Bernard, Edward and I have decided to have children.'

'Really? I knew you would change your mind,' he said, sounding pleased and excited. 'How many months are you?'

'No, Bernard, I haven't changed my mind, and I am not pregnant. We are going down the surrogacy and fostering avenue.'

By the time she finished the sentence their guests had turned in unison and were listening and looking at her. Ellie, who was sitting next to Bernard, asked if it was too early to say congratulations.

'Yes, it is, I'm afraid,' answered Edward.

'Anyway, it's about time,' Martha, Greta's twin sister, said. 'Our Gemma will be four in June, and she will be going to school full-time in September.'

'It's a good start and a great step, Greta. I know how you feel about having babies and bringing them up,' said Sam. 'We used to talk about it when we were in college together and you *hated* the idea.'

'Well, if you feel so strongly about it, then you've chosen the best way forward,' said John, Sam's husband.

'Yes, I'm ashamed to admit that I do feel like that,' said Greta. 'Just the thought of it, a foreign body living inside of me, makes me shiver. Aside from that, how can you fulfil your potential if at the height of your physical and mental wellbeing you are stuck in motherhood? That's not very fulfilling; well, not for me anyway.'

'Hasn't that route been condemned by the Vatican? And if you don't mind me asking, you, being a close-knit Catholic family; how do you feel about that?' Timothy, Martha's husband, enquired.

All the others around the table gaped for a moment, and then Edward said, quite casually, 'We see no problem there; we're dealing with it as best as we can, Timothy.'

'I'm glad to hear it. Personally, I believe there is no room in today's society for some of our Christian canons. In fact the majority of Christians view their faith as an irrelevance to today's society. When we go to Mass on Sunday and find the church nearly empty, personally I am disillusioned and saddened. I think we are witnessing the beginning of the end of Christianity as we know it. True, we want to remain Christian but that's because we are horrified at the thought of being something else. None of us is a truly practicing Christian, whereas all Muslims are. That's one reason why Islam is becoming an overpowering force in the West,' Timothy said with a sombre expression.

'Yes, regrettably that is so. A large proportion of Christians has become apathetic about faith and the Muslims have not. Still, as long as they do not ram Islam down our throats we needn't worry,' declared Greta.

'Why don't we change the subject?' John suggested. 'Is it true that NASA helped the US military put a geostatic neutron bomb over Teheran?' he asked Bernard.

Bernard, who worked as a scientist at NASA, said, 'No, we won't change the subject, and I don't know anything about a geostatic bomb. Even if I did, which I don't, I couldn't tell you, as it would definitely be classified.'

'Okay, Bernard, no need to get testy,' said John. 'I just read something recently in an obscure military magazine. It's probably just wild speculation.'

Bernard turned to Greta and asked, 'Where are you going to do it?'

'The Philippines – the company is based in Manila,' she replied. 'It's called Parenting4U, and it's been in existence for a number of years. They have been very successful, had no problems and no adverse publicity of any kind. Edward was there last week and he was very impressed.'

'Yes, absolutely,' confirmed Edward. 'I was impressed with the whole place and the people I met and spoke to. People from all over the world have their children raised there. The compound is very large; it is really a multi-ethnic town in its own right. The children there grow up knowing that all humans are equal, irrespective of race, faith, colour and so on. That's so important these days.'

It seemed as though the subject was exhausted, but the brief silence was broken by Timothy. 'Have you found a surrogate mother or do they, the company I mean, provide one?'

'The company employs the surrogate,' said Edward, and went on to explain that they recruited them mainly from poor countries, but that they were treated and rewarded very well. Some became professional surromums and stayed with the company for ten years or more. By then they had saved quite a bit of money and were still young. So they could return to their own country to get married and raise their own children. Surrogate motherhood had become a profession and was no longer considered a stigma.

'Do you really think so?' Timothy asked.

'Sure I do,' replied Edward.

'This is just another way of exploiting the proletariat, the poor and the vulnerable,' sneered Timothy.

'Look here, Timothy, I won't have any of your leftist, outdated, Marxist psychobabble!' Greta exclaimed.

Even Martha, his wife, added, 'Don't be so ridiculous, Timothy.'

'Let me explain. In the beginning there were the Greeks, then came the Romans, and after them the Europeans—'

'What on earth are you talking about?' sniggered John.

'Just let me explain,' repeated Timothy. 'They all conquered and enslaved people. They used them to do their jobs; farming their lands, fighting their wars and bringing up their children. In order to do that, they had to bring them into their countries, their homes, as slaves. The Greeks and the Romans had them, and Western Europe started the slave trade and sold us the blacks to do our dirty work. Now we in the West transfer our horrible jobs abroad, to the poor and vulnerable. All of our and Europe's dirty manufacturing has been transferred to China, India and other countries in the Far East. In essence, they are our "slaves" now. We discovered a new weapon: remote enslavement by trade.'

'I don't see it that way at all. We are not imposing anything on them. They are not "slaves": they are not owned, they cannot be bought and sold or treated like property. It's their choice whether to do something or not,' said Edward.

'I agree,' said John. 'They are free people.'

Greta frowned, but decided to ignore Timothy's cynicism. She was used to his outspoken and left wing views.

Next to Bernard, Martha had buried her head in her hands, so he decided to try and diffuse the conversation. 'Why don't you focus on the positive side, Timothy? The businesses that you're talking about in China, India, the Philippines and other places are legal. In fact, we are helping them raise their standard of living by exporting our jobs to them, at a great cost to our workforce. Many jobs have been lost to the Far East, I dare say.'

'I don't disapprove of what Edward and Greta are doing, I'm just pointing out the ugly side of capitalism,' said Timothy.

'Don't talk to me about capitalism,' said John. 'Look at what happened to our financial system not so long ago.'

'Not just our financial system but the whole world's,' added Edward.

'And to think that the very people who stabbed capitalism in the back were in fact the bankers; people who owe their existence to capitalism. It's poetic justice,' said Timothy, sounding pleased that the capitalists had scored an own goal.

They had finished dinner by then and moved to the drawing room for after dinner drinks. The conversation continued to flow. Timothy was still taking centre stage with his affinity for indulging in potentially controversial debates. This time it was about minority rights: how the West had been granting rights and special privileges to minorities, willy-nilly, to please them.

'Such as?' enquired Edward.

'There is a wide variety of them, ranging from colour, invalidity, ethnicity and even religion I might add. There are a lot of things you cannot say now because they may be considered inflammatory or offensive. More specifically, positive discrimination at work: some positions are earmarked for blacks and other minorities,' Timothy explained.

'Not to mention anti-discrimination laws for gays, the aged and the disabled,' John chipped in.

'Have you noticed that in a busy car park, almost invariably the only empty spaces you find are marked for disabled people? It's just overdone,' commented Sam.

'What gets my goat are ethnic and religious minority demands. Why do we have to appease them? I'm no racist but why do they have to have privileges? We don't need their primitive ways and thinking. Haven't they heard of, "When in Rome do as the Romans do?" The next thing that we'll have, here in the US and in the West, is Sharia law. Mark my words, it *will* happen before long,' Timothy stated.

A chorus of protests followed.

'The majority of Americans would rather *die* than put up with Sharia law,' Greta said unequivocally.

'Since we've granted so many other rights and privileges to minorities, why not grant Sharia law as well? It's not that infeasible, you know,' Timothy argued. 'All the Western governments do is give in; out of fear of upsetting the extremists.'

'You never hear Buddhists complaining. Do you know that in some European country, I think Norway, Muslims have more rights than the natives themselves?' commented John.

'I'm sorry but I think I've heard enough about the subject for one night,' said Martha.

After that a few less controversial topics of conversation sprang up, keeping everyone engrossed until they realised the lateness of the hour.

The first to get up was Martha. 'Look at the time; it is gone midnight, and we told our babysitter that we wouldn't be late,' she said.

One by one, Greta and Edward's guests finished their drinks, and then the couples began to depart with promises to meet up again soon.

The last to leave were Bernard and Ellie. 'It was such a lovely evening. Thank you for inviting us,' said Ellie. 'I hope to see you both again soon.'

'Likewise. It's been a pleasure,' Greta replied. Turning to face Bernard, she said, 'Keep in touch.'

'I will,' he promised. 'By the way, have you told mum and dad?'

'No, I haven't; but I will after it's all done, maybe in a year's time. I don't want dad to keep on at me. I told Martha not to say a word.'

'I understand. I won't say anything to them either. Goodnight, and thanks for tonight.'

'Our pleasure. Good night,' said Greta.

VII

The following week went by as usual, except that they did not stay late at work, leaving them with more time together in the evening to work on the agreements with Parenting4U. After dinner every evening they would go into the drawing room and work for a couple of hours, dotting the i's and crossing the t's. Fortunately they were both generally in agreement on how their children should be brought up: Catholic, disciplined and intellectually stimulated.

'The first thing to decide on, darling, is whether we want to have the same surrogate mother for our children. We need to allow one to two years between the first and second child,' Edward said to Greta.

'I would rather we had both our planned children more or less at the same time.'

'But that means that we must complete two sets of agreements now, and we'll need two surrogate mothers, unless we use one and have twins by having two embryos implanted. However, I've been told that the costs won't be much less.'

'In that case let's have two surrogates,' Greta said. 'That way we get it all over and done with in one visit to Parenting4U.'

'What about the names of our children?'

'We must name them in the agreements. The moment you decide the sex of your child, you must also provide a name. I would like our son to be called Alex; my father's name,' stated Edward.

'Yes, of course, if that's what you like, darling. And we'll call our daughter Emily. I am so excited and happy that it's finally happening. I do not want to die childless, and for me this is the only way. I will be a mother without being a mother – if you see what I mean.'

'I understand.'

They finalised each section carefully and moved on. In particular, when they came to the section dealing with the children's education, Greta said that Mandarin would be a more useful language for their son, and Edward agreed. On many occasions during his business trips to the Far

East, he had wished he could speak an oriental language. They also put football, piano, chess and swimming for their son, and for their daughter they put French, piano and ballet. Under the section dealing with religion they ticked Roman Catholic, and for going to church they selected "once or twice a month".

For the section that dealt with guardians, in the event of the death of both parents, they chose Greta's sister and brother-in-law. The two siblings got on very well and would do anything for each other.

Another section to which Greta paid particular attention was the surrogate's own religion and breastfeeding. She said, 'Edward, you know how I feel about religion. In fact, the three things that please me most about my existence are: I am a Catholic, a woman and an American. I know our faith does not approve of IVF and surrogacy but, if it's possible, *our* children should have Catholic surrogate mothers. Also, they must be breastfed until they are about fourteen months, just like I was.'

'Okay, that shouldn't be a problem. We also need to discuss the trust funds.'

'I thought you were going to deal with that.'

'Yes I am, but I would still like to hear your thoughts. I was planning on $30 million for each child, to be received at twenty-one.'

'That's a lot of money to part with so soon; are you able to raise all that in one go? Let me contribute, darling,' said Greta.

'Thank you, honey, but honestly there is no need for you to pay any of it,' said Edward. 'The trusts have to be set up now and the money deposited in a Geneva bank account for each baby once conception is confirmed. If the child dies, God forbid, before it reaches the age of twenty-one, then the money will be paid back to us with interest on production of the death certificate. All the trust money that the children receive will escape death duties, and since the company is doing well I might as well secure our children's future.' He smiled. 'We will still have money left; more than we'll ever need anyway.'

'That makes a lot of sense, darling.'

The last section they had to go through together dealt with progress reports.

Greta leaned back on her chair and after a long moment she said, 'This section is giving me a headache. In fact, I don't want to know anything at all, except that it's all going well. Going through the agreements has made me realise, even more, just what is involved in raising children, and I have done all the upbringing I can by filling the forms out. I feel as though I have laid down the foundation for a good upbringing and a good life for our children until they are eleven years old.' She turned towards Edward, almost in tears, and said, 'I am sorry, darling, but I can't do any more than that. The whole idea of something growing inside my body, giving birth and rearing gives me nightmares. I am really sorry for saying all this – you must think I am a horrible woman.'

'Of course not, honey, I know how you feel. I understand. I imagine many other women feel the same; that's probably one of the reasons why these parenting companies have become so popular and successful within such a short time.'

'Thank you for being so understanding – I couldn't have a better husband if I searched the whole world.' Greta smiled and took a deep breath, letting it out slowly before adding, 'In any case, if at some time in the future we wanted progress reports, we could ask for them then.'

By the Friday after the party they had gone through both sets of agreements several times and were happy with everything, but they were still in need of clarification on a few points, which Edward was going to discuss with Damien Jones on the phone on Monday. He asked Greta if she could think of anything else that should be considered and discussed with Damien. 'As a matter of fact,' she said, 'I just thought of something. Can you ask him if our children can be born by caesarean section? I do realise that it's not nature's way, which in general our faith insists on.'

'Is that really necessary?' asked Edward, sounding rather surprised.

'Yes, I think it is. Sometimes there are complications during labour. And a caesarean saves the mother from all the pain and suffering of childbirth,' explained Greta.

'We also need to arrange for both our children to be born more or less at the same time, and of course there is the question of the timing of our visit to Manila for the sperm and the ova. We can either do it all through an approved fertility clinic here and have it sent to Parenting4U, or we can use only some of the services of a fertility clinic and at the right time we fly to Manila for the extraction of the ova, etcetera. I imagine you will want to see the place yourself, honey, and that way we don't have to spend too much time in Manila,' Edward said.

'I do want to go and see the place where our children will be born and grow up. And as soon as you get clarification on the outstanding points, I will make an appointment for us with the nearest approved clinic to go and start the process.'

VIII

At the first visit to the fertility clinic which was recommended by Parenting4U, Greta was told that she needed to have a special hormone treatment; a series of injections in order to stimulate her ovaries to produce more than one ovum. This was to safeguard against any setbacks from genetic abnormalities in fertilised embryos, or failed implantations of healthy embryos. After adequate stimulation of the ovaries with the treatment, a final injection had to be given at night to cause the eggs to finish developing. Having planned and done all this, the timing of her ovulation had been determined and they needed to be in Manila in the middle of July. That was just a few days away.

Edward did not need any treatment as the clinic had established that his sperm count was good. However, he was advised not to have sex for two to five days before collection, as it affected sperm quality.

'If we go next month, July, and conception takes place then, our babies will be born the following April: we will be parents then. Wow!' said Greta.

'Wow indeed. Have no doubt, honey, with a bit of careful planning and patience we'll get there,' Edward reassured Greta.

That evening, when they retired to bed, Greta lay awake for hours reflecting on what they were going to do. She was determined to have children but not to bear or bring them up herself. She was horrified by the thought of bearing children – she considered it a form of torture – and she was too busy to bring them up properly. She was convinced the psychological and physical pain she would suffer would be too much for her. It was either Parenting4U or no children. Since there were people who were willing to take on that anguish for her, why not let them do it? I am not lazy, she thought. I work hard, I do what I am good at, and I enjoy it. The next ten years or so will be the most important and fulfilling of my career. That's when I'll realise my potential. Bearing babies, changing diapers and bringing up children would take that opportunity away. Nothing will make me change my mind, she reassured herself.

Edward was very pleased with Greta's enthusiasm and speed. He promptly phoned the company and spoke to Damien.

'Can you be in Manila by this Sunday?' Damien asked.

'Sure. Absolutely,' Edward replied enthusiastically.

When Edward told Greta, she was delighted. She was looking forward to visiting the company's head office and to seeing the whole complex. 'I need to *see* that they provide the best facilities and place for our children to be brought up. I want to be sure that they will be physically secure, grow up in a healthy environment and be intellectually stimulated,' she said.

'From what I have seen, I am sure that you will be satisfied,' Edward assured her.

They never stopped thinking or talking about their plans; they talked in the house, on the way to the airport, and in the aeroplane to Manila. The more they talked the more it reinforced their conviction that they were doing the right thing – both for their children and for themselves. At one point Greta said, 'It's like partial adoption, isn't it, Edward?'

'What do you mean?' he asked.

'Well, look at it this way: we let our babies be brought up by others but only for a specified period of time, and we attach detailed conditions to how they must be brought up. We are effectively supervising their treatment and upbringing,' she explained.

'That sums it up beautifully, honey.'

'Martha told me that we will miss seeing them grow up, especially when they are little. Up to two and three years old, they are like little angels. You would be amazed by the things they come up with.'

'Like what?' Edward enquired.

'Well, when Gemma was about three, Martha was telling her that before she was born she was inside her tummy. Gemma turned around and asked, 'How did I get there?' And some other child on the same topic said to her mum, 'Why did you eat me?''

Edward laughed, then said, 'Amazing, and logical to a three-year-old.'

'After the age of four, they become crafty and wilful apparently, but they are still cute. Unfortunately, we won't see any of that; it can't be helped. It's similar to the old days for the upper classes; they didn't see them grow up. They had their children brought up by governesses in a nursery in a remote part of their grand houses. Their parents only saw them for a few minutes a day, if that, and then they were packed off to boarding schools at a very early age. Their parents didn't, in fact, bring them up. They had no real influence on their upbringing or on their treatment at the boarding school either, except for sizeable monetary donations for an expellable offence I suppose, whereas we will.'

'By laying down the way we want our children brought up,' Greta continued, 'we remain in charge. The company conforms to our wishes. Since they carry out regular inspections and assessments of the nannies' performances, those surromums must strive to fulfil their commitments and comply with their clients' instructions. There is also the incentive for them to do well because, if they don't, they won't receive the performance bonus at the end of their employment. At Parenting4U both the children and their surromums are treated very well. I feel quite happy from what I've learned about them.'

IX

When Edward and Greta arrived at the offices of Parenting4U, they were taken straight to Mr Jones' office. After the introductions and a brief discussion, Damien told them that it was possible to arrange for the children to be born more or less at the same time. 'In fact,' he said, 'the company is in the process of securing agreements with two sisters, Dolores who is twenty-one, and Marissa who is eighteen. They could be your surrogates. I would like you to meet them later today.'

Both Mr and Mrs Everest said that they would love to. Damien told Miss Wang, who had arrived from the clinic, that he wanted them back in his office in the afternoon in order to meet the sisters who might become their surrogates.

By about 4pm everything was done at the clinic and they were taken to see a typical house where children grow up. On their return Miss Wang confirmed that everything had gone well; they had collected some healthy-looking ova and had a good supply of many motile sperm – sperm capable of fertilising an egg.

Back in Damien's office they were introduced to the two Filipino sisters. The two girls were all smiles – not at all nervous. After the introductions and a long discussion about their past, present and future plans, Greta was satisfied that the two sisters would be ideal for them. She looked at her husband, who seemed pleased with everything the girls had said. He nodded his approval and Greta turned back to the girls with a smile. 'I think you will be just right for having our children,' she said.

Damien, who had been listening to the conversation, looked at his watch. 'If there is nothing further to discuss, then the girls can go and we can carry on.'

Both Edward and Greta thanked the girls and said goodbye to them.

After the girls had left Greta said, 'I am very satisfied with both girls.' She looked at Edward.

'Me too. They are ideal for us.'

'I am glad to hear that,' said Damien. 'In that case, I will proceed with the girls' contracts as your named surrogates. That concludes the business for today. I will see you both tomorrow to discuss the results of today's procedures.'

The following morning they met with Damien as arranged. He told them that the results were very good. Edward and Greta again expressed their delight with everything and at being fortunate enough to have Dolores and Marissa as surrogates for their children.

'Since we've finished with everything here, we can catch a flight back,' Greta said.

'Unfortunately we cannot delay our return,' Edward apologised. 'But our time here has worked very well from our point of view. We are very impressed with the security, the thoroughness, the state of the art clinics, the housing and all the amenities for the children, not to mention your hospitality,' he added.

'Thank you. You are very kind,' replied Damien. 'We try to excel in everything; that's why I believe we are the best in the world.'

'Judging from what we have seen and heard, you are,' agreed Greta.

By the time they arrived at the hotel it was just after noon, so they decided to have lunch there. Despite the delay, Mr Wang, who was taking them to the airport, insisted on waiting for them.

On the way to the airport, both Edward and Greta admired the scenery that they hadn't been able to see on their arrival, pointing out to each other anything that seemed exceptionally interesting. Sometimes they asked Mr Wang what something was and he would answer in his usual jovial manner. They were curious to know what nationality Mr Jones was, as he didn't look entirely Filipino, so Greta asked Mr Wang about him.

'You are right, ma'am, he is only half Filipino; the other half is Welsh – his father I think. He grew up in Cardiff and went to university there. He is very clever, a good businessman, and above all he is a very good and honest man. He has been the CEO of Parenting4U for about ten years now.'

On arriving at the airport, they thanked Mr Wang and said goodbye to him.

During the flight home Greta said to Edward, 'What a successful visit! The only thing left now is to hear that the girls are pregnant with our babies.'

'Everything worked out perfectly,' Edward agreed. 'Before long we'll know. Time will fly, you'll see.'

'Yes, I suppose it will. It always does, especially when you're busy, and believe me we are going into a very busy period at the office. From now on, there will be nothing else on my mind, just work and us, you and me, darling.' Greta smiled. 'It's as though a huge weight has been lifted off my shoulders. And now it's done. I do appreciate that you agreed to this, Edward, and I love you even more. Thank you, darling. Thank you so much.'

'I love you too, honey, and no need to thank me; I wanted to do this as well. It liberates us from the chore of bringing up children.' He chuckled. 'Who knows, we might not have been very good at bringing them up anyway.'

Satisfied that they were doing the right thing, they both slept for most of the remaining flight.

X

The following week, Greta was the first to go to confession and ask forgiveness for her sins. As expected, Father Mahoney was not at all understanding or sympathetic. What he disapproved of most was the fact that they had not talked to him first before going ahead with their plans. In the eyes of the Catholic Church it was a mortal sin, no matter what the circumstances were.

'I know, but I'm psychologically incapable of bearing children, Father,' Mrs Everest mumbled. 'And I don't want to die childless.'

Father Mahoney continued, 'Our benevolent Lord listens and forgives, but you must repent and make a firm resolution not to sin again, and through the sacrament of penance you will be granted absolution.'

Greta declared her sorrow, recognised the severity of her sins, and committed herself to do her penance of Hail Marys. Afterwards, Father Mahoney imparted absolution, and she left. A few days later Edward did the same, and he too had to do a sacramental penance.

From then on time flew, as Edward had predicted. They went about their jobs more intently than ever. One evening after work, Edward answered the house phone to hear Damien's voice.

'Damien, great to hear from you; do you have news for us?'

'Yes I do, and it's excellent news, Edward. Let me be the first to offer my congratulations: you and your wife will soon be the proud parents of three babies—'

'Did you say *three*?' interrupted Edward.

'Yes, three: Dolores is going to have twin boys, and Marissa will have your girl.'

All Edward could think was, Oh my God.

'Tell me, Edward; are there twins in your or your wife's family?'

'Yes, in fact my wife is a twin herself.'

'Well, that explains it,' said Damien. 'You'll want to keep the other baby I'm sure… Won't you?'

'Of course, we certainly will! Greta will be overjoyed.'

'I was certain you would. I'll send you another agreement then. You will also have to set up an additional Child Trust Fund, Edward.'

'Of course, I understand. We'll speak tomorrow.' Still dazed, Edward hung up before Damien could say goodbye.

By the time Greta returned from work Edward had come to terms with his surprise and couldn't wait to tell her the news.

'Good heavens!' she exclaimed. 'There have been twins in my family for generations, but twins from a single IVF embryo are so rare; it must be God's will that we have three children, Edward.'

The following day Edward called Damien: he confirmed that they would be keeping the third child and asked if the two boys were identical twins. Damien assured Edward that they were definitely identical twins and said that there was no need to return to Manila, as the additional agreement could be dealt with by electronic mail.

The draft agreement arrived later that day, and Edward sat down that evening with Greta to complete it. They were pleased to find that the sections were already partially completed. Damien had correctly assumed that they would want their new baby boy brought up in the same way as their planned baby boy, and had filled in the majority of the fields accordingly.

'Let's decide the name, honey,' said Edward.

'I never thought we would need another name. How about Max, or Jonathan?'

'I like them both but I prefer Jonathan,' replied Edward.

'I like it too – we'll name him Jonathan then.'

'All of the remaining options will be the same as for Alex,' said Edward.

'What about their sporting activities and their extramural studies?'

'I think they should be the same too, don't you?' asked Edward.

'Yes, I suppose so,' Greta agreed.

After going through the whole agreement, Greta said, 'Well, imagine that: if I was bearing my own children I would be carrying twins. How terrible!' she exclaimed.

'What a relief that we chose to use surrogates then,' Edward agreed.

'Oh! What about Dolores? How does this affect her?'

'I don't know. I will ask Damien tomorrow.'

'Yes, please do. And don't forget the trust money, darling. How will you handle it? Will you reduce what you had in mind for just two children?'

'That wouldn't be fair.' Edward shook his head. 'I'll provide all three with £30 million. It won't be until next year, after they're born. We'll be okay. It won't leave us short.'

The following day, Edward telephoned Damien to tell him what was happening and that his lawyer would be sending on the completed agreement soon. He asked about Dolores' feelings with regard to carrying twins and was told that she was very pleased because she would be paid almost double for twelve years.

'That's great. I am glad she's happy,' said Edward.

'Once we've received the final agreement and payment I will be able to sign it and send you your copy.'

'Thank you, Damien. Goodbye.'

XI

From there on everything went smoothly. The payments were made, the agreements became effective and nine months later, almost to the day, three babies were born by caesarean section. The delightful news was immediately communicated electronically to Greta and Edward, who were ecstatic to be the proud parents of two identical twin baby boys, Alex and Jonathan, and a baby girl, Emily.

'How shall we celebrate their arrival?' Greta wondered.

'It's a huge event, darling, we must have a party. Who shall we invite?'

'It's a family thing, so I think it should be just close family and friends – everyone who was here when we first told them of our plans. I'll organise it for this Saturday if that suits everyone,' Greta said.

The guests arrived at 7.30pm and, as expected, they were all very pleased about Greta and Edward's news. Naturally they wanted to know everything about the babies. Greta told them that the babies were due to be christened and confirmed in the following few days. The sooner they were brought into the Roman Catholic faith the better, she felt. All three were to be christened on the same day.

There had only been four hours separating the birth of the twins and Emily, just as planned with the caesarean section. The boys had been born around 10pm local time – Alex first and Jonathan a few minutes later – and Emily at 2am; effectively the next day.

A few days after the party, Damien called to say that all the formalities with the birth registration, the christening and the confirmation of American nationality had been completed. All the documents, blood tests, DNA tests and profiles had been completed satisfactorily, and it was time to set up the Child Trust Funds. Damien was going to email copies of the documents to Edward, and to the bank in Geneva. Once the bank accounts had been opened and the funds transferred, the bank would confirm this to both Parenting4U and to the parents, which would then complete all the financial obligations of the parents.

After much procrastination, Greta plucked up the courage and told her parents. Initially they were delighted, but the more they learned about the arrangement, the more concerned they became. They told her that they simply could not understand how she, as a Catholic, could believe that she was going the right way about having and bringing up children.

Greta knew that they would never understand how she felt, and her decision. She tried telling them that times had changed and things had moved on since they'd had children: people from all over the world were doing the same as her; she was not the first. But as she had expected, nothing in the world could change their minds. Still, she was adamant in her own opinion and resigned herself to the fact that the rift between her and her parents was both unavoidable and unbridgeable.

After the initial wave of excitement, things quietened down, and Edward and Greta carried on with their busy lives. There was nothing to worry about: no diapers to change, no screaming babies wanting to be fed or changed in the middle of the night. It suited them perfectly. The surromums were well looked after and there were no complications after birth.

All three babies were healthy and were being cared for in a "heavenly" place. They were protected and cherished. Everything was perfect…until they had that call from Damien with the dreadful news that their Jonathan had been abducted by Al-Qaeda and Taliban terrorists.

Part Three

I

After a flight that seemed like it would never end, Edward finally arrived in Manila and made his way to the hotel. He was tired and felt miserable at having no more news about the abduction. Fred Nicholls had already checked in at the hotel, and Edward told him that he would meet him at the entrance of the hotel restaurant shortly.

Fred was a stocky, six foot two man with blond hair; maybe forty or so years old. He wore jeans, a check shirt and a short, lightweight, black leather jacket. After brief introductions Fred enquired about the current situation.

'I have had no other news from Parenting4U,' Edward told him. 'Besides my son, a baby girl was also taken. The abductors spoke to Damien – the CEO – after taking the babies and told him to wait for further instructions.'

'No other phone calls since then?'

'None; on Matthew's advice I gave Damien permission to get the security forces involved and to let the abductors know, when they phone again, that we are willing to discuss their demands.'

'I understand,' said Fred. 'Though it's very unusual for such organisations not to state their demands outright...' He scratched his head, frowning. 'I find it strange bearing in mind it's now more than twenty-four hours since the abduction took place; it doesn't add up.'

'When they do contact us again, I want you to be the sole contact with the kidnappers, to negotiate the safe return of our baby. I am putting my trust in you. Whatever the size of the ransom, we'll pay it; we want our baby back at any cost,' said Edward.

'I've dealt with similar situations before and I will use all my experience to get the best outcome,' Fred reassured him. 'The safe return of your son will be my absolute priority. I must point out to you that officially, we cannot pay ransom to terrorists. That's considered by the US as funding terrorism. The money will be for information leading to the recovery of your son.'

'I understand.' Edward said.

They finished dinner, and Edward reluctantly agreed that there was nothing more that could be done until the abductors contacted Parenting4U with their demands. A meeting was scheduled at Parenting4U for 9.30am the next day so they said goodnight and went to their rooms, agreeing to meet the next day at 8am.

II

On their arrival at the offices of Parenting4U, Edward and Fred were taken to the boardroom, where Damien Jones was waiting with two other men: Leon Mendez, Police Chief Inspector, and Ramon Vargas, Senior Police Officer. After brief introductions they all sat down around the big oval table.

'There has been no further contact by the kidnappers,' Damien informed them.

'What do you make of that?' Fred asked Leon.

'I guess they are assessing their position and deciding on the ransom, or they may be waiting for instructions from someone further up their chain of command. They may be waiting for instructions, they may be amateurs who have panicked, or they may actually want the babies, and the telephone call was to keep us guessing so that they could cover their tracks and reach a safe place,' Leon replied.

'Have you conducted any surveillance yet on potential suspects, such as known Taliban and Al-Qaeda members and sympathisers, in order to try and discover where they are hiding the babies?' enquired Fred.

'We have set up a dedicated unit at our head office and have sent a coded message for extra awareness to all our contacts and undercover agents. So far nothing has been reported. Mr Jones was kind enough to allocate a dedicated room for us here at Parenting4U, which we are using as our command centre for today. We have a number of officers working there now; they are questioning some people here at Parenting4U. We also have a few officers at the private hospital where the babies were taken from; they are conducting inquiries and questioning staff. We have been looking at the CCTV footage of the abductors; the pictures show two women sitting in the back of the car holding the babies, and a man was sitting in the front passenger seat. Obviously there was a fourth person: the driver. Unfortunately, the pictures do not show either the face of the driver or the car registration number. Images of the babies and the three visible abductors have been circulated to the police force as well as the security units at the airports,' replied Leon.

'What is happening with the parents of the baby girl? Are they coming to Manila, and do you know what their position is if a ransom is demanded? Have you appointed anyone to act on their behalf with negotiations?' Fred asked Damien.

'The baby belongs to two women. One of them, Tracey King, is due to arrive later today; like Mr and Mrs Everest she is willing to negotiate with the abductors and pay whatever ransom is demanded, within reason.'

'Let me state the position of the Philippine government and its security forces,' Leon interrupted. 'We will not negotiate with terrorists; they cannot be trusted.'

'I have led a number of successful negotiations in the past,' said Fred, 'and Edward has instructed me to act in that capacity for him in this situation. If I am to also act on behalf of the other baby's parents I will need their authorisation to do so. I would ask that under no circumstances should anyone try to rescue the babies by force.'

'With respect, Fred, you cannot tell us how to do our job,' Ramon warned.

'The babies are both US citizens and I am responsible for facilitating their safe return,' Fred explained. 'It is *my* job to emphasise the danger that police action, or threat or use of force against the abductors, *will* endanger the lives that we all want to save.'

Leon squirmed in his seat and interrupted with a firm voice, 'Gentlemen, we have nothing to go on yet; you are both getting ahead of yourselves. The delay in hearing from the abductors is worrying me. We must reassess our options.'

'What do you mean? Explain,' demanded Edward.

'As I said earlier, there could be a number of reasons the abductors have not contacted Parenting4U again; we just don't know why.' Leon shrugged. 'If we can get a positive identification of the people from the CCTV we will have something to go on. So far we know that the two women were dressed as Parenting4U nurses, and the man was dressed as a security guard. They must have had this planned for days, weeks or months. They probably had the Parenting4U compound under surveillance for some time,' Leon said.

'Or they had inside information,' Fred added.

'Possibly,' Ramon said. 'That's the first possibility we considered. As Leon said, we are interrogating all staff connected with those babies right now, both here and at the hospital.'

'What exactly will you do with the CCTV images?' Edward asked.

'We'll study them and circulate them – along with photographs of the babies – throughout the police force and to our undercover agents, as well as to the media. Telephone numbers will also be published for the public to contact us with any information. We'll be looking for anything unusual that might have happened straight after the abduction, when the culprits hit the road – that's when they were likely to panic and make mistakes,' Ramon replied.

They carried on discussing the situation but, after a time, their deliberations came to an end. They sat there scratching their heads, waiting; there were moments of intense silence. At one point someone outside the room sneezed and made them all jump. Edward then stared at the phone; he was *willing* it to ring – but it remained stubbornly silent.

'Have you checked your phone? Is it definitely working?' he demanded.

'Yes it is,' Damien confirmed. 'We just have to sit tight and wait.'

They all stayed there discussing the situation; going over and over the same things, trying to interpret and make sense of the cryptic ransom call. They were intrigued and felt they did not have the whole story. Suddenly the phone rang and shook them from their deliberations. They all stared at the phone anxiously. Leon picked it up; it was Damien's secretary wanting to speak to him on an urgent business matter.

Hours later, Edward and Fred decided that the abductors were not going to call and, since they had to go to the US Embassy to seek the assistance of some of the officials there, they would leave the waiting to the others.

'I have already informed the US Embassy of the abduction. There is no need to get any officials actively involved,' Leon said. 'It will only complicate matters. However, since you are going there to discuss the matter, I trust they will be able to share resources and information with us. Would you kindly give them my card and ask your contact to get in touch?'

III

The two men left. Edward told Fred that he was feeling increasingly worried about the lack of communication from the abductors. While they sat around waiting for contact to be made, valuable time was being lost, time in which the babies could be moved further away – even out of the country. Fred tried to allay Edward's fears. He told him that it was not unusual for kidnappers to take their time, that maybe they were on the move and trying to find a new, more secure hideout.

At the embassy they met David Strickland, the agent Matthew had queried about terrorist cells in the area. Edward gave him Leon's card and told him what had been said. Strickland was a well-groomed man; tall and thin, with black hair. They discussed the case, and David expressed his surprise at such a thing happening in Manila, as he was not aware of any active Taliban or Al-Qaeda cells there. He was of the opinion that the abductors were from outside the area and were amateurs – hence the delay in contacting them again. He felt that if that was the case, it might be easier to capture them.

Edward was heartened by this but stressed that his only objective was to get his baby back. 'I simply want my baby back and I'm prepared to pay whatever ransom they demand. Any other action by security forces will put his life in jeopardy and must be avoided at all costs.'

'I sympathise with you, Edward,' said David. 'But this is a criminal matter and the law enforcement agencies will want to carry out their duties. I would like you to hear what Jake Mercer, our Chief of Security, has to say.'

Mercer came in. He was a broad-shouldered man with strong arms and had a grip like an iron vice when he shook hands. After he was introduced he sat down. He told them that he had been informed about the abduction by the Philippine Police, and that he was anxious to find out more. Due to the lack of any further evidence or leads, he had little to contribute. He told them that there was a large Muslim population in the Philippines, and some Taliban and Al-Qaeda sympathiser groups did exist. 'I'll contact my assets and see what they have to say. I can't be optimistic since they would have reported something to me before it happened, and they didn't. In any event I'll do my best to find some answers. My advice right now is to go public and release the CCTV images alongside the photos of the babies.'

David agreed and said he would relay the information to Leon and assure him that, if and when new information came to light, it would be shared between them.

With nothing further to discuss, Edward and Fred left; despite all the talking, there was still nothing they could do but wait. They had lunch together and made their way back to Parenting4U for further talks with Damien.

IV

When they arrived, Tracey King was there with him. She had just arrived in the country; she was sitting down and looked distraught. Damien introduced her but Edward, having recognised her, said, 'We've met before: about a year ago on a flight here we sat next to each other.'

'Yes, I remember; especially the turbulence,' Tracey acknowledged with a smile. She was elegant and smartly dressed. Being a famous TV chat show host, that was expected. 'I feel so guilty – I blame myself for this. If I had carried her like a normal mother and given birth to her in the US she would be fine. Now only God knows where she is and what has happened to her.

Also, because Masha has darker skin it makes her more recognisable – the kidnappers will feel vulnerable.'

'You mustn't blame yourself,' said Damien. 'There are terrible people in this world and bad things can happen wherever you are. I'm sure the kidnappers will hide both the babies' faces anyway, so the colour of their skin will be irrelevant.' He went on to say that the CCTV footage of the three abductors, the photos of the babies, and some other facts would be aired on the evening news and in the press.

'So where do we go from here?' Edward enquired.

'We wait. Information will hopefully start coming in once the images are released, and we hope to get some leads to follow up. It should also prompt the kidnappers to contact us again,' Damien replied.

'As soon as they make contact I'll take over – no offence, Damien. I am an experienced negotiator and I want to deal with all the discussions with them, not just the ransom. I want to assess their state of mind and establish a level of trust with them. Since I am a negotiator, a third-party, they will be more willing to deal with me,' said Fred.

By then it was late in the afternoon and Tracey King left to go back to her hotel. Fred stayed behind, while Edward went to see his other two babies, who were with their surrogate mothers in the complex. As it was the first time that he had seen them in the flesh, and because of the abduction of Jonathan, the visit was very emotional. Both Dolores and Marissa – their surrogate mothers – were pleased to see him, but were very upset themselves after what had happened, especially Dolores, who had carried Jonathan. As the two babies were asleep, Edward simply sat by them and watched over them, tears dripping down his cheeks. After about half an hour he kissed them gently and left for his hotel. By the time he got there the news had broken. The images were on TV and in the evening newspapers. The pictures of the suspects, taken from the CCTV images, were grainy, but anyone who knew them would be able to recognise their faces.

V

The story spread like wildfire around the world, and the next day every news station and paper had it as their headline story. In the West there was outrage and condemnation of the levels the Taliban and Al-Qaeda terrorists would sink to. People prayed for the safe return of the innocent babies. In contrast, in certain Muslim countries some factions rejoiced at the ability of the Taliban and Al-Qaeda to strike anywhere they wished with impunity, carrying out the will of Allah – as they saw it.

Edward, watching the news, gradually got more and more despondent. He worried that now that the news was out, the abductors would be more reluctant than before to get in touch. He kept in constant touch with his wife, who was also getting progressively more anxious, but she was convinced that now the story had been made public, developments would follow.

'There is bound to be some good news soon,' she told her husband. 'I haven't given up hoping that this nightmare will end well – and soon.'

'We won't give up,' Edward told her. 'We'll never give up. We have to get him back at all costs. If only they would make contact again, I would tell them outright that we will pay the ransom straightaway. The way I feel about it, I won't even let Fred negotiate.'

'We must be patient – we have no choice,' said Greta. 'Keep me updated of any developments, darling.'

Edward then told her that he had gone over and seen Alex and Emily in the afternoon, and he thought that they were really lovely. They had been asleep and peaceful, he told her, and he was going to go there again the following day when he hoped that they would be awake. He also told her about Dolores and Marissa being very upset and shaken by what had happened.

'I wish I was there with you to see Alex and Emily and give them a hug, and share the burden and ordeal you are going through. My heart aches for you; for us all. It's worse that we are apart at a time like this,' Greta said unhappily.

'We will get through this nightmare, darling – never lose faith! I love you. Bye for now. I'll speak to you soon,' he said to her.

The news remained in a state of frenzy the following day. With the lack of anything concrete to go on, the press began to speculate and conjure up all sorts of theories. The public, eager to help, started phoning in to police stations with "sightings": the women with the babies; two women pushing two prams; two women wearing yashmaks in a taxi, each holding a baby; and so on. Others phoned in with claims that they knew where the suspects lived. For all the information that was coming in, the police had to sift through it and try to establish what was credible.

Among all the calls that came in, one was from an informant who operated in the red light district. He had recognised the man and the two women: the man was a small-time drugs pusher and pimp, and the two women were prostitutes. They had their own place in a side street where they took their "Johns"; the man would hang around outside until the Johns left, then he would rush in and take the money from "his" girls.

It was the breakthrough Leon had been waiting for. He assembled his team and made plans to cordon off a big area around the place, so they could pounce in the early hours of the following morning. The plan was simple: in the early hours they would be asleep and would be caught unprepared. There would be no loss of life and the babies would be rescued. At last, he thought, he had a lucky break. He smiled and imagined his moment of glory, the headlines that would say it all: "Police Chief Inspector rescues babies in a flash; culprits caught napping."

VI

Maalik was at home, watching the news on the TV and getting anxious. His phone rang; at the other end was Hanif, the man who had dressed up as a guard from Parenting4U. As soon as he picked up the phone it became clear that Hanif was indignant and very angry. 'What's the matter?' Maalik asked, pretending to be clueless.

'You lied to us! Allena and Lola are here with me and are hopping mad. You deceived and implicated us! They are terrified to go out because they'll be recognised. We all need money – a lot of money – to get away from here. We need $5,000 each by tonight. If we had known what you were up to we would never have agreed to get involved! $200 each to do that job was an insult. You told me that the parents of the babies had fallen out with Parenting4U and that we were just helping them get them back; what a pack of lies! If you don't get us the money, we'll go straight to the police and tell them everything.'

'Calm down, Hanif, and don't be so stupid. Do you think the police will believe you and your two whores? It was you who was seen taking the babies, not me, remember? Anyway, give me till midnight – I will have some money for you, as much as I can lay my hands on in such a short time. Make sure Allena and Lola are with you too because I'm not leaving their money with you.'

'Good, I will. But make sure you've got the money for us; we want to get as far away from here as quickly as we possibly can.'

Maalik assured him he would go there with the money and help them out. But he knew that their predicament was grim. They would need to stay in hiding for a long time and, even then, sooner or later they would get caught. They would then tell the police who had paid them to abduct the babies. They posed a problem that would not go away. He knew he had to deal with it quickly, once and for all.

Abdul Hassan had said that everybody was dispensable, but he was not. After fighting the Russians with Abdul and kicking them out of Afghanistan, his jihad had come to an end. This mission, he thought, was a call to re-join the jihad against the infidels – the time had come. In the name of Allah, he would fight them wherever he could.

But first he had to tie up his loose ends: Hanif and his whores were waiting.

VII

The publication of the CCTV images had jogged people's memories and leads were coming in thick and fast. A CIA asset recognised the images from the CCTV and reported the names as being Hanif, Lola, and Allena. He knew where to find them and even gave directions. Jake Mercer from the embassy was keen to pass the information on to Edward but Leon, the Police Chief Inspector, advised against revealing too much as Edward, in his emotional state, might take matters into his own hands, jeopardising the police operation.

Jake went against Leon's advice and told Edward and Fred, impressing upon both of them that they were not to do anything without letting Leon know.

Edward and Fred, worried by the lack of further communications from the abductors, were desperate to move the investigation on. 'I cannot negotiate with the abductors until they make contact, and meanwhile valuable time is being lost. If you agree I would like to do some investigative work,' Fred said to Edward.

'I do. What do you have in mind?'

'I want to go to the red light district and see what I can find out; do some surveillance.'

'Yes, let's do it,' Edward agreed. They decided to go there in the small hours and see if they could see anything. They would take no action, but if they saw anything pertinent to the abduction they would contact Leon.

When they arrived in the area there was still plenty of activity. They walked around trying to look as if they had no set purpose, but taking in every detail of what was going on around them. They arrived at the narrow lane where Hanif reportedly operated from; it was deserted. Fred wanted to find the apartment and Edward reluctantly agreed. His many years in the boardroom had not prepared him for this kind of activity or situation, and he was uneasy. They ventured to the end of the lane and located the door; it was ajar.

'This is the place,' whispered Fred. 'Let's go in.'

They put gloves on and went in; Fred led the way and started going slowly up the stairs, which led directly from the front door. The floorboards creaked as they inched upwards; in the still of the night the noise carried and seemed much louder. They kept moving, eyes wide open, and holding their breath. Above the top of the stairs a single un-shaded light bulb hung from the ceiling; it had been left on. The place made Edward feel a strange sense of foreboding, as if he was crossing over to another world. When Fred's head reached the top of the stairs he stopped and listened as his eyes scanned the area, taking it all in. The place was eerily quiet. In front of him there was a short corridor and at the end of it was an open door leading into a kitchen. There were two other, closed doors, one on either side of the corridor. The only sound they could hear was their breathing, which was becoming more noticeable from the tension of the situation. They reached the top of the stairs, stopped and looked at each other, puzzled. Fred whispered, 'Something doesn't seem quite right.'

'We'll have to be quick and get out of here fast,' said Edward, just as softly.

They crept into the small and dingy kitchen. They looked around for any clues, taking care not to handle anything, and found a box of powdered baby milk and a dummy. It could have been a sign that the babies had been there, or they might not have been there at all; the milk and dummy might have been brought back after the babies had been abducted. Edward was anxious to find out what was in the other rooms, and moved out of the kitchen. There was still no noise coming from the other two rooms. He gently opened the door on the left, pushed it in slowly, and flicked on the light. He froze, his expression turning to one of horror. There on the floor was the body of a man. Behind him on the bed were two more bodies, both women. All had been shot; there was blood on the floor, the bed and some on the wall.

Fred came out of the kitchen and stood by the door behind Edward. He guessed they were the bodies of the three abductors who had been identified: Hanif, Allena and Lola. There was no sign of a struggle; they had been taken by surprise – or by someone they knew. 'Someone needed them dead, to stop them from talking,' whispered Fred.

There was no sign of the babies in there and Fred thought there was a chance that they might be asleep in the next room. They crossed over to the other room and opened the door with equal vigilance. Inside there was a bed and one chair. The babies were not there either, and there were no traces that they ever had been. 'The babies must be alive somewhere,' whispered Edward.

'Yes, I think so too,' affirmed Fred.

They descended the stairs and got out, disappearing into the dead of night.

On their way back to the hotel they saw numerous police cars, with flashing lights but no sirens, heading for the red light district.

'Leon is too late,' said Fred. 'Perhaps just as well, because if the babies were there earlier, and the culprits were cornered, they could have used them as human shields. They could have got them killed in a failed negotiating attempt, or while trying to escape under fire.'

'Should we reveal that we have been there?' asked Edward.

'I think we should keep it to ourselves. We'll only be accused of interfering, or worse, be implicated in the murders.'

They continued to walk to the hotel, both deep in their own thoughts about what they had just seen. Several moments later Edward said, 'It would seem that the babies were never there – there was no baby equipment, and bearing in mind what the women did there, two crying babies would have been noticed.'

'I agree – the babies were never taken there. We need to find out two things: first, who killed those three, and second, the whereabouts of the fourth person – the driver. Most likely he or she is the murderer. He hadn't been identified from the CCTV images but the other three had been,' said Fred. 'They were a threat to the driver's anonymity.'

'Will this complicate matters further? Whoever it was that killed them is desperate and dangerous,' commented Edward. 'On the other hand, the abductors' chain of command may have been shortened, which may speed things up. In that case we should hear something about the ransom soon.'

'We'll find out what unfolds tomorrow. Leon will let us know if he has achieved anything further,' said Fred, as they walked into their hotel.

VIII

The following day Edward went to Parenting4U to see his other two babies. While he was with them, Damien Jones called to say that Leon wanted a meeting with him and Fred at 11am, at police headquarters.

Tracey King and Ramon were also there with Fred, Edward, Leon and Damien. Leon informed them that they had carried out a raid at the suspects' place of business and had found three of the abductors dead.

'The good news is that the babies weren't there, so they must be being kept elsewhere. We believe that they are alive.'

Edward asked if they had any suspects in mind, and Leon told him that they didn't yet and were still waiting for the abductors to make contact. Also, they had not received any other useful information from the public or their informants.

'Was there any evidence that the babies had been at the place you raided?' asked Tracey.

'There was evidence that they may have been there for a short while, but nothing to suggest that they were there for any length of time. Even the evidence we found did not conclusively point to them having been kept there. As for the murders, it's very likely that the fourth, unidentified person killed them, to protect themselves from identification. Hopefully they will now act on their own to try to gain the ransom for themselves. I'll be surprised if we don't hear from that person by the end of the day.'

IX

The next day they all met again at Leon's office. Again there was nothing positive to report. The fourth person hadn't phoned: Leon's prediction had been wrong. The police had carried out further raids on known Taliban and Al-Qaeda sympathisers, both in Manila and elsewhere in the country. They had also questioned the friends and relatives of the three murdered abductors.

All parties expressed their extreme frustration. None of the investigations so far had proven positive. No link could be found between staff at the hospital and Parenting4U, and the three abductors. The operation seemed likely to have been masterminded by a group from outside the country, making it difficult to get any leads. That was Leon's conclusion.

'This is totally ineffectual,' said Tracey angrily. 'All this time and you still have no idea who is behind it, let alone where my child is. You should have closed the net tight, widened the investigation by contacting Interpol, and alerted all neighbouring countries – the abductors have probably escaped the country by now. Isn't there some sort of missing-person alert system – like AMBER – that you could have activated?'

'We have already done what we can in that regard,' explained Leon.

'Regrettably we have no positive information from anywhere.'

'Well, what are you going to do next?' asked Edward, with irritation in his voice.

'We are in constant communication with our agents, and we are investigating all leads. We will continue with this search until we have found your children,' Leon assured them.

'It seems that if you don't receive any further leads – or the abductors don't contact you – this investigation grinds to a halt. With all due respect, I don't think you are doing enough,' Fred said to him.

'Let me assure you, we are doing everything we can. Our resources are stretched to breaking point. Please bear in mind that other police work has to continue as well,' said Leon calmly.

'Nothing has been achieved – something else has to be done. We are in limbo. We can't just sit here waiting for information to land in our laps. We have to be more proactive. I feel so frustrated; so helpless,' said Edward.

Leon again expressed his regret at the lack of progress and reassured them that they were doing everything they possibly could, and hoped to have better news for them when they met the following day.

X

Edward spoke to his wife later that day and told her what little progress had been made. 'We are assuming they did this for a ransom but what if that one and only phone call was a hoax or a red herring to throw us off the scent?' he said.

'Darling, don't think the worst. You must be positive. There is no reason to suspect anything other than the ransom motive. We'll see this through and our darkest time will soon be over. We won't give up searching, hoping and praying that it will be all right in the end.'

'Yes, I do hope so, darling. This morning I spent some time with Alex and Emily. They are both lovely, really lovely. They look around with their clear blue eyes as though they are studying you. When I was looking at Alex I was thinking of Jonathan looking just like him. He is probably also staring and smiling at God knows who, totally unaware of the danger he is in. It was heartbreaking to think of it. As for Emily, she is so pretty – like a little angel. I must go now but I'll call you again later today or sooner if something comes up.'

'All right, my darling. I love you so much. Goodbye for now,' said Greta.

Edward then called Tracey King and invited her to join him and Fred for dinner at his hotel. He then phoned Fred to let him know she would be joining them.

When they all met and sat down, nobody talked for a while. The mood around the table was quite subdued and conversation was not forthcoming. They were all wrapped up in their own thoughts; the events of the past four days taking their toll.

Tracey spoke first. 'I was right,' she said quietly, sounding downcast.

Edward wondered if her emotions had been made worse by remorse, and asked, 'What about, Tracey?'

'It was a bad omen: the turbulence we encountered on the way to Manila. Don't you remember?' she replied.

'I do remember, Tracey, but I am sorry to say that I still don't think so. Let's not go into that; we've a more pressing matter right now,' Edward said in a friendly voice.

'The waiting is awful. I can't bear it – I feel like I'm on ice. They said to ask "mum" or "their mums", well I am here and I will tell them that we are prepared to pay whatever they demand. Why don't they phone?'

Edward felt the same and agreed. 'It's like a bad dream. I still can't understand why they haven't been back in touch with us. I wonder if something has happened to whoever did this.'

'The fact that they phoned and talked about a ransom proves that that was their intention. Nothing else has transpired to suggest the contrary. We must be patient,' said Fred.

'Unless something has happened since the phone call; maybe they have fallen out with each other. We know that three people have been murdered – could it be that the murderer was mortally wounded but managed to leave the scene before dying?' suggested Tracey.

'I don't think that happened because there would have been blood leading down the stairs,' Edward said.

'How do you know there wasn't?' Tracey asked.

'Leon would have told us if there was any,' Fred butted in.

'And he didn't,' Edward added quickly, having realised that he had nearly let the cat out of the bag.

The mood around the table was changing as they started to talk more.

'There was a serious lapse of security – I blame Parenting4U. I will be demanding a full review of what happened,' remarked Tracey.

'Well, the police have questioned everyone and it would seem that the lapse of security did not originate from within Parenting4U. In fact, the security there is excellent. Even at the private clinic where the babies were taken from, they had an armed guard twenty-four hours a day. They must have been watching cars going in and out for some time, and waiting for the right occasion to strike,' said Edward.

'I don't know about you, but as soon as I get Masha back I'm taking her home with me,' said Tracey.

'With respect, Tracey, isn't that a bit rash?' asked Edward.

'No, I don't think so. I've discussed it with Stella, my partner, and we both agreed. When I first visited Parenting4U, Damien Jones emphasised the importance they place on security; he told me the place was impenetrable. He obviously didn't consider external risks enough.'

'No security system is one hundred per cent foolproof. There is always the possibility that the system is vulnerable, and those who are intent on finding a weakness will find it and strike,' said Fred.

'You have a valid point, Tracey, but I'm not sure Parenting4U is totally responsible for what happened. I've been so wrapped up in finding our child I haven't even considered this aspect of this woeful situation. I'll have to discuss it with my wife but I wouldn't go as far as taking our children away from here.'

'It's day five tomorrow. Five whole days since the abduction and the longer the delay in finding them, the worse my fears are. Do you know what a wise man once said to me on my talk show?' said Tracey.

'What?' both men asked inquisitively.

'He said, "What you fear most in life will happen to you." I thought then how pessimistic that was. At the time, Stella and I were in the process of arranging to have a baby. I remember very clearly saying to her, "What if something was to happen to our baby while at Parenting4U?" That possibility terrified us and we have never ceased worrying about it since. Now it has happened.'

'Everything you do has a risk. You could go to a supermarket and get shot by a maniac; get run over by a car; or die in an avalanche while skiing. You can't just live your life worrying about what may or may not happen. You have to get on with it,' said Fred.

'But this is different, this was not an accident — it could have been avoided, if only Parenting4U had not sent them to an external hospital,' retorted Tracey.

'What's done is done. We have to focus our energies on getting our babies back,' Edward said.

'But how long is it going to take? I'll have to go back to the States. In fact, I may have to go back tomorrow, after we've seen Leon. The people at my TV channel are becoming impatient — although they are sympathetic, they want me back. I have arranged for Stella to come here instead, but nothing is happening here and it's killing me. I don't know what to do,' said Tracey, clearly in distress.

'What if we hear from them and they make demands, and you aren't here?' asked Edward.

'I've thought about that and I was going to ask you if I can engage Fred to negotiate on our behalf as well?'

'Of course you can,' Edward assured her.

'I will be glad to be of any assistance,' Fred said to her.

'That's settled then; thank you both. I'll fly back tomorrow, depending on the outcome of the meeting with Leon.'

XI

They met the next day at Leon's office. Once more, Leon had to report the disappointing news that there were no new leads. Edward and Tracey were beginning to lose faith in the police investigation. They were exasperated and disappointed, yet again. The investigation was in the hands of the police and there was nothing they could do themselves except wait. Leon was doing his best to assure them that the police were doing everything in their power to find their babies.

'I have to go back to the US, so I've engaged Fred's services and asked him to do whatever is necessary. My partner, Stella, will arrive in the next day or so and she will attend all future briefing sessions. Please don't give up on this case; you *must* find our daughter,' begged Tracey.

'I agree with Tracey. I've been thinking about how we can entice more leads. I suggest we offer a reward for any information leading to the safe return of our babies. Will you deal with the responses that come in?' Edward asked Leon.

'It is a police investigation, so of course we will handle this. All information received will be followed up. When you have decided on the amount I will release it to the media.'

'I suggest $250,000 from each of us,' Tracey said to Edward. 'It needs to be enough that even friends or relatives who know something are enticed to come forward.'

Edward concurred and, once they had agreed their strategy, they left. Edward headed back to Parenting4U to spend time with his other children, while Tracey and Fred went back to their respective hotels. Before they parted, Fred told Tracey that he considered it an honour to work for her and her partner, and hoped that by the time Stella arrived there would be better news for them.

The next meeting with Leon was the following afternoon. They all hoped that by that time the announcement of the reward would have prompted some further leads.

As predicted there had been many responses to the reward. Leon assured them that all calls were being recorded, and would be analysed and assessed. His preliminary impression was that there were some promising, some dubious, and some outright false. In particular, he told them that they had received a call from a man who, four days previously, had been slowing down at some crossroads when another car overtook, cut in front of him and didn't stop, though it scraped the corner of his car. It had turned right and sped away, but not before he saw four people in the car – two of them women, sitting at the back. The man hadn't been able to see their faces but had managed to get the car registration. 'We are now trying to trace it and the owner,' Leon said.

'Another call also aroused our interest,' Leon continued. 'It came from a woman who claimed that two days ago she saw two women in yashmaks pushing prams in a hurry by the Golden Mosque; officers have been sent to make enquiries. Another positive call came from a man who was at Manila airport taking a flight to Karachi four days ago. He reported seeing a couple with a small baby at the airport. The woman was trying to feed the baby with a bottle but was having great difficulty because the baby was intermittently crying and choking. The man's wife, who is a doctor, asked what the matter was but the woman turned her back to her without responding and her husband seemed jumpy; the passenger lists for the flights at that time are being obtained and will be scrutinised. Finally, another caller saw a woman, who was wearing a yashmak and holding a baby, get out of a car and into a taxi, and overheard her asking the driver to take her to the port – or it could have been the airport; details of passengers leaving on ships that evening are also being obtained.'

'If the last two are reliable and relevant, it may mean that the babies were abducted in order to be taken out of the country, and not for a ransom,' Edward commented.

'That puts a different slant on the intentions of the abductors. On that basis, and the long silence, I am convinced that there will be no claim for ransom. They just pretended to hold them for a ransom in order to confuse everybody and gain time to get them out of the country,' explained Fred.

'They must have changed their original plan,' said Leon.

'Why would they do that? Say that they are going to telephone later with their demands for a ransom and then give up without finding out whether we'd pay or not? It doesn't make sense,' remarked Edward.

'No, it doesn't. We are asking all taxi companies who might have picked up passengers, with babies and acting suspiciously, to contact us. We're also looking at CCTV from airports and checking passenger lists,' Leon told them.

By then Edward was sore. His tone hardened and with narrowed eyes he said to Leon, 'You should have done that immediately after the abduction – we've lost valuable time. Whoever took the babies has had plenty of time to escape, leaving us with no clues as to who they are or where they have gone!'

'Mr Everest, we have been working on this case twenty-four hours a day since it began,' Leon reminded him. 'We have dozens of officers conducting enquiries all over the country. We are doing everything we can. We have not been idle and we will continue until we find your child.'

'I'm sure you are doing your best but so far you have had no results; nothing positive has been achieved. All I can think about is my son. How can he survive such an ordeal? He was sick in hospital when it happened. I want to carry out my own investigations – it will not interfere with your work,' Edward said.

'I would strongly advise against it. You have no experience of police work or investigation. You could jeopardise finding the babies, with amateur detective work. However, if you choose to go ahead I cannot stop you. In any event, please ensure that you keep me informed of everything you are doing and any information you receive.'

'Of course we will,' Edward said, and then he left with Fred.

XII

Edward instructed Fred to carry out the private investigation, and Fred agreed. He gave Fred a freehand to set up an office and employ as many people as he thought necessary, and then left for the US. The police efforts had revealed nothing; Fred was hopeful he would be more successful.

He set about getting a team of almost thirty assistants, including a number of local private investigators and half a dozen office assistants who had good spoken English. They were to start with taxi firms, airports, ports and car hire firms, canvassing for any and all information that might be relevant. They were to carry out their enquiries during the day and meet regularly to discuss and analyse the information, then decide on follow-up procedures.

Any information they felt was important they would share with Leon.

Fred reported back to Edward in the US each day with information. Every lead was followed up. Fred and his team travelled the length and breadth of the country but all the leads came to nothing. Days became weeks, and the weeks became months.

Fred and Leon joined forces on numerous occasions and travelled together far and wide. They shared a common mission, which strengthened their resolve. They went to Jakarta in Indonesia, Kabul in Afghanistan, and Karachi in Pakistan. They spent days investigating every lead that led them there but always came to a dead end.

Soon a year had passed and another began. Millions of dollars had been spent but nothing positive had been achieved.

More time passed and Fred remained in Manila doing what he could with a smaller team; working and cooperating with Leon. After almost four years the leads had dried up, and Mr and Mrs Everest decided to call Fred back to the US. The thorough investigations were stopped. The majority of the police resources were pulled from the case. Although Leon assured Edward that the case was not closed, they both knew it was highly unlikely anything would be discovered from then on.

Part Four

I

In fact, the transporters had taken the babies to Kabul. Once there they had planned to stay a night in different locations, meeting up the next day to begin their journey north. There they would meet up with Hamid and hand over the babies. But the flight from Jakarta had been delayed, so Farouk and Leila hadn't arrived until late on Sunday. By the time they met Alima with the baby boy, stole a car and hit the road, it was midnight. They were tired, but thought that it was best to drive through the night to avoid attracting attention.

As they drove out of town, Alima asked if either of the others had noticed that the baby girl was not white but almost black, like a child with one black parent. Leila's response was that she had noticed but didn't think it was important or relevant.

'Don't you realise what this means? I mean the colour of the baby,' Alima asked, sounding alarmed. 'Oh Allah, didn't you realise? By now the whole world knows what we have done, and the police and the army – especially the Americans – will have been alerted. If they see us with the two babies – one white, one mixed race – they will figure it out in seconds!'

'But what are you worried about? We are out of town now, and before long we will be handing them over,' said Leila.

She had hardly finished talking when they turned a corner and noticed a makeshift US checkpoint ahead. Alima, now in a state of panic, said 'I am afraid we've had it. We are going to be caught. All the planning, the travelling to Manila and back, taking the babies; it all went without a hitch. We are now trapped; there is no escape. We cannot bluff our way out, with the evidence right here on our laps. What are we going to do?'

'What do you think I should do?' the driver shouted.

Leila said, 'Slow down, Farouk, pretend you are going to stop, then accelerate like mad. Go through the checkpoint – run them over if you have to. By the time the soldiers realise what happened we'll have disappeared into the distance.'

'That's exactly what I was going to do,' Farouk said. He slowed down as he was nearing the checkpoint, then he slammed the throttle down so hard the engine roared and the car sped through the checkpoint, knocking down one of the soldiers who was signalling them to stop.

The soldier who was standing to the side rushed to his comrade's assistance. He could see that the other man was hurt badly, but he managed to say, 'Leave me. Go, get them and do what you've been trained to do: shoot to kill.'

The soldier raised his MP5 submachine-gun, aimed and fired fifteen rounds towards the distant car, riddling its body. Quickly he ejected the empty mag, reloaded and fired again, but by then the speeding car was out of range.

Both windscreens disintegrated. Shards of glass were blown in by the wind from the front windscreen and scattered everywhere. Farouk continued racing away. Some moments after the sound of gunfire faded, he sensed that his crotch was wet and a warm liquid was spreading through his pants. He had been hit in the stomach. He didn't feel much pain and he concluded that it probably wasn't that bad.

'I have been hit – are you two all right?' he asked. There was no reply. 'Eh! Are you all right?' he shouted, shaking Leila who was in the seat next to him. Her body was limp and her head lolled forward onto the dashboard. There was no reply; the only sound was the crying of one of the babies. He realised that the situation was bad. He couldn't stop, he had to keep going as fast as he could, but from time to time he called out to Alima, asking if she was okay. Each time there was no reply.

It seemed to Farouk that he had been driving for hours. His stomach felt as though it was on fire and he was feeling tired and sleepy. He came off the main road onto a small side road and drove straight ahead, towards what, in the moonlight, looked like a wooded area. He stopped the car at the edge of the trees, on the right-hand side of the road, and surveyed the area. A few hundred yards from the road he could see a derelict mud building, mostly collapsed except for one wall, and manoeuvred the car so that it was parked behind the wall. He felt weak; he sat there for a few moments, gasping for breath, trying hard to think of what to do. As he struggled to get out, the throbbing in his stomach erupted, leaving him in agony. His guts felt like they were on fire, and he was still losing blood. He hobbled around to the door and had to summon all his strength in order to open it. Alima was slumped forward in her seat, lifeless.

'Oh no! They are dead! Abdul will kill me!' Farouk moaned. He had to phone; explain what happened, and get help.

II

After Maalik killed the three collaborators who helped him abduct the two babies in Manila in 2001, he flew to Jakarta, Indonesia, with the money that remained from the abduction. He had decided to dedicate the rest of his life to the jihad. There he met up with some Muslim extremist and militant contacts, and started to put the money into the jihadist cause. He orchestrated a number of suicide bomb attacks in the nightclubs where westerners revelled. As soon as the authorities started rounding up Muslim suspects and their contacts, he fled to Sydney, Australia.

There too he lost no time in perpetrating a number of atrocities against the infidels. His last attempt involved the recruitment of a Muslim boy of fifteen who had fallen by the wayside. He was a drug addict and had resorted to prostitution to finance his habit. Maalik promised him salvation through martyrdom, and everlasting life in paradise with an abundance of whatever his soul desired.

When the boy was under the influence he would agree to anything; one night Maalik dressed him up with a large suicide bomb and drove him as near as possible to the Sydney Opera House, where a grand gala was being performed. The plan was for the boy to get out of the car, walk inside the Opera House, and mingle with the crowd that was waiting to get in. Then he was to blow himself and dozens of others up. Although Maalik had allowed plenty of time to drive him there, on the evening in question they encountered a traffic jam and were delayed for considerably longer than anticipated.

By the time they arrived at the drop point, the influence of the drugs was wearing off and the boy didn't want to go through with the plan. Maalik tried to convince him that that was a normal reaction to the situation, and that he was only minutes away from entering paradise. Eventually, he persuaded the boy to get out of the car and start walking towards the Opera House. However, as soon as Maalik drove off, the boy panicked, went straight to a policeman who was patrolling the area, and told him all about it. He said that he did not want to die and kill innocent people, and that Maalik had forced him into it.

The terrified boy cooperated with the police fully and gave them a good description of Maalik, which enabled an artist to create an image of him. It was circulated to all the Australian and friendly security forces around the world. However, Maalik, having not heard the blast, had done a runner and escaped on a plane to Karachi, Pakistan, before the alert went out. Once in Pakistan he headed north to where Al-Qaeda was operating and joined one of Bin Laden's guerrilla training camps for Muslim militants.

III

Maalik was an expert bomb-maker and an experienced guerrilla fighter. When he joined the Bin Laden camp his expertise was welcomed. He became a training instructor; training volunteers and mercenaries in techniques to fight the infidels in Afghanistan. They were Taliban and Al-Qaeda Muslim activists who rushed to join the jihad – to die fighting and become martyrs. Some saw it as their last or only chance to achieve martyrdom and everlasting life in paradise, as they feared that there might not be another jihad in their lifetime. They arrived in their hundreds from all over Pakistan, and from other Muslim and non-Muslim countries from around the world.

They all had to be trained and that was where Maalik's experience from the old days – fighting the Russians with the mujahedin in the 1980s – stood him in good stead. Under his guidance, "his" fighters had many successes, with ambushes, sniping and suicide bomb attacks. He orchestrated multiple, coordinated, suicide vehicle attacks using high explosives; targeting government and allied compounds, armoured vehicles and other infidel trucks that carried military supplies and soldiers. The more deaths and destruction he inflicted on the invaders the more his esteem rose in the organisation.

As time went by, Maalik's achievements brought him in closer contact with the upper echelons of Al-Qaeda. He attended secret meetings both in Pakistan and Afghanistan. At one such meeting in Pakistan, Bin Laden was present and he congratulated Maalik on his successes and heroic exploits, and thanked him for his great contribution to the cause. He also revealed to him that the abduction of the two babies from Parenting4U, which had been a failure, had been sanctioned by him.

'The huge ransom money was to finance another project,' Bin Laden confided. 'Besides the moral blow it would have inflicted on the Americans. After the death of Abdul Hassan, the transporters and the babies, that project came to a dead end,' Bin Laden continued. 'Sayed Afridi, who was one of my lieutenants, was with Abdul Hassan the day that he was killed by an American drone attack. Farouk Ibrahim, the transporter of the babies, was another of my men who worked for Sayed. Farouk normally kept in touch with him but the last person he spoke to was me. He told me that he couldn't get an answer from Sayed, so he had to speak to me. He sounded in a terrible state – he must have been dying. He said that they had been hit by the Americans outside Kabul and that all the others were dead.

'Soon afterwards, I despatched three men to investigate and search for the money that Abdul had kept for the struggle. It was in vain – they found nothing. They concluded that the money had been destroyed in the drone attack. They also interrogated Hamid Ali, the schoolteacher – you know, the go-between, who brought the money over to you in Manila. He confirmed that they had all died, including the babies, and that he had buried them himself.'

'What a fiasco,' Maalik gasped.

'As you know, the abduction drew condemnation from America – the Great Satan – and from some other infidel countries, but for every condemnation there were twice as many jubilations from the Muslim world.' Bin Laden went on to tell Maalik that he was putting the pieces together for another project, codenamed "Midnight Sun", and Maalik asked him what it was about.

Bin Laden told him that the ransom money from the abduction had been earmarked for the purchase of a tactical nuclear bomb from the Russian mafia. He said that the Soviet Union once had a huge arsenal and assortment of nuclear bombs. A large number of them had been positioned in poor, satellite countries on the periphery of Russia, and after the disorderly breakup of the Soviet Union some of the bombs had gone "missing"; Al-Qaeda had agreed a price for one, through intermediaries.

He then added, 'The Americans would have actually paid for the bomb that obliterated Washington DC.' He paused and gloated for a moment, then laughed and said, 'It would have been a most befitting and ironic punishment.'

Maalik was delighted that the great leader was taking him into his confidence. He gaped as he listened to his holy warrior explain how he was going to deliver the final blow to the Great Satan. 'The failure of the ransom project was a major setback to Midnight Sun but it was not the end of it. I will fill you in at our next meeting; I want you to play a part in it,' Bin Laden assured Maalik.

Meanwhile, the fighting continued and Maalik became a lieutenant, obtaining more and more resources from Bin Laden: money, manpower and munitions. The exploits of Maalik and his men spread as far as the Ukraine and Chechnya. On his last, personal expedition to Chechnya he caused a huge amount of destruction and death. Under his command the insurgents continued with their strikes in Afghanistan, inflicting serious casualties and destruction on the allied and Afghan forces. They were fearless; death to them was their salvation and guarantee to martyrdom. They attacked indiscriminately: civilian establishments, places of worship, markets where large numbers of people gathered, and the coalition and local armies. The Afghan government and the coalition forces knew that Maalik was one of Bin Laden's most dangerous lieutenants. He had become notorious; a legend.

IV

A few months later, Maalik was summoned by Bin Laden for a briefing. He brought him up to speed, in particular about the Midnight Sun project. Unfortunately, Bin Laden explained, by not having been able to pay the Russian mafia at the agreed time, others had entered the market and the price had gone up. But Al-Qaeda had managed to raise the money by other means, and had recently outbid the Iranians. They had the bomb, encased in a big statue of Buddha, and were in the process of finding a friendly institution in the US to buy it, or accept it as a gift, which would enable them to import it to the US.

Once there, the statue would disappear, and one night soon after that the sun would rise in Washington DC. America would become a headless chicken. It would be the most catastrophic Al-Qaeda strike ever: the deathblow of the struggle. 'Our feats must be as great as our cause,' Bin Laden told Maalik. 'We have to maintain and surpass the momentum after our great and spectacular success on the 11th of September 2001. Allah awaits the fulfilment of our great cause.'

Maalik was mesmerised. He was inspired and elated as he listened to the man he admired and envied; the one Allah had chosen and blessed to accomplish the cause. When Bin Laden stopped talking, Maalik told him that he would be honoured to play a part, especially in the transportation and detonation of the nuclear bomb. He felt it was his destiny to become a martyr for the cause in that way.

The American and allied forces continued fighting the insurgents and Al-Qaeda in Afghanistan. In spite of their military might and strenuous efforts they could not bring the war to a victorious end. They attacked many locations with drones, with pinpoint accuracy, but they never managed to kill or capture their two deadliest enemies: Bin Laden and Maalik. They were repeatedly humiliated and demoralised by their failures and ineffectiveness.

Capturing, killing or assassinating Bin Laden in particular had been a top priority for the US security services long before things had escalated in Afghanistan. But an old Executive Order prohibited assassination by anybody employed by, or acting on behalf of, the United States, so a blatant attack on Bin Laden, if and when they discovered where he was hiding, was out of the question.

After Bin Laden issued his *fatwa* in February 1998, calling for all Muslims, in any country, to kill the Americans and their allies – both military and civilian – his capture or death had become an even more urgent priority.

In order to circumvent the old prohibitive Executive Order, different and secret Executive Orders were issued, legitimising certain kill-or-capture missions by the CIA and the Special Forces.

Success came on Sunday the 2nd of May 2011, when the Navy Seals ventured into Pakistan, without the permission or knowledge of the Pakistani authorities, and killed Bin Laden in his secret hideout in Abbottabad.

At the time, Maalik had been on his way there. He had been summoned to discuss the progress of the Midnight Sun project. He had not yet arrived because the vehicle he was travelling in had broken down and been stranded in the mountains.

The news of Bin Laden's death hit Maalik like a sledgehammer: he was overcome by grief, becoming distraught and despondent. He had worshipped Bin Laden, the inspiration to all believers and the personification of the cause. Maalik fell into despair; he felt that the struggle had been lost.

Though the war in Afghanistan had not ended with the death of Bin Laden, Maalik's enthusiasm for the cause had begun to dissipate. Bin Laden was no longer there to fire his enthusiasm. Depression set in and drained his energy. His standing in the Al-Qaeda hierarchy diminished fast. The Midnight Sun project had either died with Bin Laden or he had been taken out of the loop. His active involvement in planning and carrying out attacks declined and he became disgruntled with the new command structure.

Although he was occasionally still taking part in attacks on the invaders, Maalik's heart was not in it. The last mission that he commanded was a total failure. For once the allied forces had the upper hand and inflicted many fatalities on his fighters. The battleground was gruesome; body parts were scattered around a large area. Only a few made it back to the camp – Maalik was not one of them.

Part Five

I

Mr and Mrs Hussein, who were very poor, were in their forties when they were blessed with Sami. Apart from the few goats, and some land around their house, they had nothing else. They had been desperate for a child and when they had Sami late in life they were forever thanking Allah for him. He grew on goat's milk into a lovely, bonny little boy, with bright inquisitive blue eyes and a permanent smile. Although his parents had no experience in bringing up children, they found it easy with him; he was happy and contented with his life. He was healthy, ate well, was loved to bits and he hardly ever cried. The first few years went by very quickly.

By the age of four, little Sami would accompany his father with the goats to the scrubland, a few miles from home, where they would stay from dawn to dusk. It was a simple, carefree way of life. There was nothing to do on the scrubland, except to watch the goats graze. Sometimes the goats were spooked by a snake, and Sami would watch his father chase the snake and kill it with his goatherd's stick.

'Snakes are bad and dangerous; they can kill a goat or a person with just one bite. If you ever see one, don't go near it, Sami,' his father warned.

'All right, Daddy, I am not going to go near it if I see one. I'll just call you to come and kill it.'

'Also, if you ever see any birds fluttering over the ground, you must not go and try to find out what's happening because there will always be a snake there trying to eat their eggs or their chicks.'

'Where do snakes come from, Daddy?'

'I don't know, son. I suppose Allah made them. He made everything else so he must have made the snakes too.'

'Why did Allah make snakes bad, Daddy?'

'Allah did not make them bad. They became bad by themselves after he made them because of the environment that they lived in,' Sami's dad tried to explain.

The little boy, not quite understanding his father's explanation, just said, 'I don't like snakes, Daddy; they are horrible.'

Sami's father had been a goatherd all his life; goat-herding is a relentlessly monotonous job. For him, all the days of the week were the same, except Thursdays. Every Thursday, roughly by noon, his wife would come out of their house, which was situated on the slope of a hill, and would rush in a westerly direction towards the dirt road that crossed the valley in a northerly direction. It was a gentle valley and stretched down from their house and up towards the ridge on the other side, about two miles ahead.

As she arrived by the road, an open-air Mercedes sports car coming from the south was passing by. There was only one person in the car, Dr Omar Hassan, the driver. He was a clean-shaven young man in his late twenties and was wearing Western-style clothes. He was heading for his big mansion on the top of the hill a couple of miles further north. He raised his hand in the air and waved to her. She nodded her head in acknowledgement and then crossed the road and headed towards the other side of the valley.

In one hand she was carrying a glazed pottery ewer full of water, and in the other a basket. In the basket she had an enamelled metal cup and brunch for three: her husband, their four-year-old son and herself. Her husband and son had left the house at first light; they had taken their goats to graze on the scrublands on the other side of the valley. The brunch consisted of half a loaf of hot freshly baked, homemade bread wrapped in a tea towel, and three pieces of homemade hard goat's cheese that were wrapped in another tea towel. She always made bread on Thursday morning; just enough to last them for one week. Once the bread was baked it was covered and stored away. As there was no electricity in their village, they had neither a fridge nor a freezer. Consequently, by the time all the bread was consumed it was dry and hard.

The reason why her husband looked forward to Thursdays was because he liked to eat the warm freshly baked bread; he considered it a real treat. After Mrs Hussein walked for about an hour she could see the silhouette of a man, her husband, and that of a goat perched on a large boulder near him. He was wearing traditional Afghan clothes and a white turban. From that distance she could not see his long beard and neither could she see the shape of their son. As she approached, the distant silhouette became clearer and she could see her husband waving his hands in the air. By then she could see their son standing by his father. When Sami saw his mother coming he started running towards her shouting, 'Mammy! Mammy!' As soon as he reached her she gave him a big smile, and put the two things that she was carrying on the ground. She bent down, kissed and hugged him and then picked him up. He threw his hands around her neck and said to her, 'I love you, Mammy.'

'I love you too, my little darling; you make me and daddy so happy. Allah had been so good to us; we are so lucky to have each other.' After a few moments she put him down; she picked up the ewer and basket, and said to him, 'Come. Let's go to daddy.'

Her husband greeted her and said, 'You must be out of breath walking all that distance in the heat. Come and sit down, my love.' The three sat down on the ground by the big boulder, ate their brunch, and drank the water in the ewer by using the enamelled metal cup.

When they finished she poured out on the ground the rest of the water, got up and milked the milk-bearing goats, one by one, straight into the ewer. When she had finished, she half-filled the cup and gave it to their son to drink. He drank all of it and then wiped his mouth with his hand and said, 'Thank you, Mammy, it was nice and warm. That's how I like it.' She then filled the cup to the top and gave it to her husband; he drank half of it and offered the rest to her and she drank it.

After a while she gave a big hug and a kiss to their Sami and said goodbye to her husband. She then picked up the basket, and the ewer still half-filled with milk, and started walking back home. As she walked away the little boy stood still, his eyes fixed on his mother, as she gradually moved further and further, until her silhouette diminished into a small blob and vanished in the distance. He then walked up to his dad and grabbed his hand.

During the summer months when the moon was full, Sami and his dad would stay in the fields with their goats long after sunset. Sami would stare at the stars in the clear sky and, having an inquisitive mind, would ask questions like, 'Are the stars in the sky like lanterns, Daddy? I just saw one moving very fast across the sky. I think whoever was holding it must have been running very fast and then he must have put it out because it just disappeared.'

One afternoon, his father said to him, 'Do you see the skylark that is perched on the large stone by the dry tufts over there? It must have a nest there because I saw it fly there a few times. Let's go quietly and see if there is one.' The two of them started walking over to the stone, and as soon as they approached the skylark flew away. There on the ground, hidden between the stone and the tufts, was a complete and beautiful nest with four tiny eggs in it. Sami had never seen such small eggs before, let alone a nest, and was shrieking with excitement.

From then on he could not wait to see the tiny chicks, and every day he insisted that they go to that patch of the scrubland to see if the eggs had hatched. And one day they had; four tiny, naked, little chicks were there in the nest, huddled together.

'It's like a miracle,' his father said to him, 'how the eggs turn into chicks.'

After that, visiting the chicks became a daily necessity. They both watched them grow, bit by bit, and develop little feathers on their bodies and wings. Gradually, their feathers got bigger and one day they were gone; they had flown the nest.

Sami, like his father, loved the simple life on the scrubland.

II

When Sami was six years old, he stopped going with his father and the goats to the fields every day because he had to go to school. He only went with his father during the weekends. He was very keen and excited about starting to go to school, and learning how to read and write. He felt sorry for his parents because they were illiterate, and he promised to teach them when he learned himself.

He was a bright boy; he found learning easy and fun, and from the start he was the top boy of his class. His teacher, Hamid, used to say to his parents that they should be very proud of their son, as he was very clever and a pleasure to teach. As soon as he was able to read, he would ask his teacher to lend him books to take home to read to his parents. He tried and tried to teach them how to read and write but they found it hard, so he and they gave up, but he continued to read to them, especially from the Koran. His ability and interest in learning went beyond his school needs, and he was always taking books home about history, geography, mathematics and physics. At the age of ten he started learning English in school and soon he was borrowing books about English grammar, and later on children's stories in English.

One year, when Hamid was responsible for the distribution of charity clothes from the West, he gave Sami a pair of short trousers and a pair of black shoes, which were almost new. He was thrilled; he took them straight home and told his mum that he was going to keep them for best.

'I do not have to wear shoes in the summer, Mum, so they will last me longer,' he said.

'That's a very sensible thing to do, my darling,' she said, knowing that if he didn't, come next autumn he would have to wear his old, worn out shoes, which were already a bit too small for him. 'We cannot buy you new shoes this year, Sami, because our goats haven't been producing much milk, and we haven't any spare milk or cheese to sell.'

'Don't worry, Mummy. I'll look after my shoes and clothes, and they will last me longer,' he replied.

Life was hard for them. His father was struggling with his goats, trying to graze them on Dr Omar's scrubland, which was not the best way to fatten them up. Sami's mother was also finding it hard toiling on the land around their house, trying to grow some crops for them to live on. Worst of all was the watering, as she had to raise it in buckets from the well and carry it around the field.

Knowing that his parents were poor, Sami never asked for things, as he knew he would never get them. By the age of eight, he was doing odd jobs for a little bit of money. It was a pittance really but to him it was something; he used to go to Dr Omar's house, which was quite a way from his own house, to feed and give water to the animals when Dr Omar was away during the summer.

Because he was very bright and kind, he didn't mind helping his schoolmates with their maths, reading and homework, and later on with their English. Nearly all the parents in the village were illiterate so Sami's help was very much appreciated, not only by the children that he helped but also by their parents. Gradually, some of the children ended up going to his house for help during the week and over the weekends.

Although his mother was very pleased that her son was very popular and had lots of friends, she realised that they were not coming just to play but to get help with their schoolwork. 'What you do is like giving them private lessons,' she said to Sami one day.

'They are my friends, Mum. I don't mind helping them.'

'Yes, I know, son, you are very helpful and kind to them but there are so many who need your help. I think their parents are taking advantage of your kindness. I honestly think that they should pay.'

'But their parents are illiterate, Mum. Besides, they are poor like us and have no money.'

'I know they are; I'll ask your father and see what he thinks.'

When she told her husband of the conversation she had had with Sami, he agreed with her. He said, 'I know all their parents. They are all goatherds but some of them have bigger herds than us.'

'The thing is that they have no money,' she said.

'In that case they must pay in kind or stop taking advantage of Sami.'

'What do you mean in kind, dear? I mean, how?'

'Well, they could give us an egg, some goat's cheese, a slice of bread or whatever they have. Even an egg a week is something.'

'That's a good idea, dear. I'll tell Sami to tell them. I don't think he will like the idea but they must either pay or they must stop bothering him,' she said.

When they were told, some of them stopped going for help altogether, while some went only occasionally, but a few started paying in some way or other. In fact, some parents were glad about the arrangement and said that they had not known it was happening; they thought that they went there to play. So Sami continued helping some of the kids.

One afternoon, when Sami was about seven, Mustafa, his friend, came running into his house, shouting 'Mrs Hussein! Mrs Hussein!' When she heard him calling her, she was taken aback because he should have been in school at that time. And not seeing her son with him, she immediately realised that something had happened to him.

'What? What happened to Sami?' she asked anxiously.

'He is not well: he has tummy pains and can't walk, and Mr Hamid sent me to tell you to go and ask Dr Omar to come in his car and take him to the hospital quickly.'

'In the name of Allah, what happened to him?' she asked.

'I don't know but you must hurry and get Dr Omar; that's what Mr Hamid said.'

Dr Omar's house was about an hour's walk from her own house so she started walking fast, almost running, and wondering at the same time if Dr Omar was going to be at home and if he would be willing to help, and why Hamid hadn't telephoned for an ambulance instead. Only the school had a landline telephone and nobody had a mobile phone. The only person who had a car was Dr Omar; he was her only hope. On her way she prayed to Allah for Dr Omar to be home and willing to help. I am sure he will, she thought, after all, it's an emergency. If he doesn't, I'll plead with him, and promise to give him an extra goat for rent this year.

When she arrived there, she was not only upset but also exhausted and out of breath; she could hardly speak properly. Dr Omar, having seen her in such a state, told her to calm down, to take a deep breath and then tell him slowly what the problem was. After repeating what Mustafa had told her, she begged him to take her to the school and pick up Sami, and then take them to the hospital. There was only one hospital in the province and it was some fifty miles from the village. Dr Omar told her that he was only too pleased to help and did not want to be paid.

When they reached the school, they found Sami lying there on the floor of the hall with his knees bent up almost up to his chin, in agony. Apparently, Hamid had telephoned for an ambulance but had been told that it wouldn't start, and that was why he had thought of Dr Omar. They put Sami in the back seat, and his mother sat next to him, holding his hand and telling him that he would be all right. To him the journey seemed to take forever and the pain was not subsiding. Eventually they arrived and he was taken in.

The doctor who examined him told his mother that he had acute appendicitis and he had to have an operation as soon as they could fit him in. In the meantime, they would get him ready for the operating theatre as soon as possible. After waiting for a couple of hours, they came and took him away, while his mother was waving and whispering to him that he was in good hands and that she would pray to Allah to make him well.

In the meantime, Dr Omar had left, promising to stop by her house and tell her husband what had happened and not to worry. The waiting was agonising for her. She just sat there, with her eyes shut, praying quietly to Allah to make her son well. After a few hours one of the doctors came and said to her, 'The operation went very well. Sami was very lucky as his appendix was caught just in time. Another hour and it would have burst and caused serious internal damage to him. I am afraid you will have to wait a bit longer to see him, Mrs Hussein, as he has not come out of the anaesthetic yet.'

'Thank you, doctor, thank you! I am so grateful to you,' she said, almost in tears.

In due course Sami came out of the recovery room and his mum went in to be by his side. She stayed there with him right through the night and when he woke up in the morning he was feeling better already.

As Sami was otherwise a healthy boy, he came out of hospital after three days and made a quick recovery. By the following week he was back in school and had forgotten all about it.

III

Besides being clever, Sami was very energetic and good with his hands. When he was nine, during the summer holidays, he spent a lot of time constructing a large windmill, which he connected with a conveyor belt, made of goat skin, to a large revolving drum, which he positioned directly over their well. Around the drum he put a rope ladder, which acted like a conveyor belt, dangling all the way down and into the water. On the rope ladder he attached some small tins; facing down when descending and up when ascending. It took him some time to perfect his contraption but when it was finished and tested it worked. He was thrilled with the result and he shouted to his mum, 'I've done it! I have done it, Mum! It works! Come and see!'

His mother stood there and watched. As the windmill turned so did the drum, and the filled tins came up and started pouring the water slowly but steadily into the reservoir that he had built by the well. She was thrilled too and said, 'Now we'll always have water ready to use; for the house, the goats, my few crops and for anything else we needed it for, Sami.'

The windmill was always turning, sometimes slowly, sometimes fast. Their little house was on the top of a gently rising hill and the air funnelled up from the valley below, so it was perfect.

'In the spring I am going to plant some tomatoes, aubergines, peppers, cucumbers and watermelons,' Sami declared one evening.

'You need seeds, Sami, and they are expensive,' his father said. 'But you may be able to find seeds for tomatoes and watermelons by the market. Sometimes they throw away the bad or broken ones and you can collect the seeds from them. Go with your mother next week, when she takes the goat skins to sell, and look out for them. I am sure you will find some. You will have to buy the other seeds but don't worry, you will have plenty of time to save the money because you won't need them until next spring.'

When the spring came round Sami planted his seeds and watched them grow. There was plenty of water in the well in the spring and early summer, and his tomato, cucumber and other plants did well. When the produce was ready to pick, he took it with his mother to the market and sold it. His mother kept most of the money in order to buy other things that they needed.

On the way back from the market, Sami said, 'When another watermelon is ripe, can we keep it and eat it ourselves, Mum? Then I can save the seeds from it for next year.'

'Yes, I think we can, but first I must ask your father.' She knew he wouldn't say no but she thought it should be his decision. By the end of the first year of using Sami's water system they were all very pleased, both with the practical results and with the money they had been able to make.

The following summer Sami turned his attention to generating electricity. He built his own turbine to generate electricity. He used a dynamo, a car battery, a car battery-charger, electric wire and some switches. The wiring from the dynamo to the charger in the house ran overhead and was supported by a couple of posts. It all looked very makeshift but Sami was only interested in the result: lighting up the house, the goat's shed and the yard. He found the new project much easier than the first; as soon as the wind started turning the turbine, the small bulbs at the end of the wiring lit up. It was exhilarating; like magic.

'Even when there is no wind at night, we'll still have light because the battery will be charged during the day,' he said to his parents.

'Actually, there is always some wind up here. You are so clever, son. We are very proud of you,' his dad said.

The people in the village got to hear about Sami's innovations and some used to walk past the house just to get a glimpse of them working, especially at night when his house was lit up: nobody else had electricity in the village. They were also amazed by the greenery around the house and the crops his mother was able to grow when everywhere else there was nothing growing.

IV

Meanwhile, Sami was growing up, but when the time came for his circumcision, which was a big event in a Muslim boy's life, he didn't want it done. He said to his mum, 'It is painful and unnecessary.'

But he got no sympathy from her.

'Can't I just let my beard grow when I am older?' he insisted.

'Stop arguing,' she said to him firmly. 'You will have to do that anyway.'

Sami, being strong willed and used to having his own way, persisted with his arguments, but his parents were adamant: they were not going to give in on this one. It was soon after these regular arguments that Sami started having a recurring nightmare.

A menacing, ghost-like figure wearing a yashmak, with bright light coming from the eye-slit, waving a huge pair of scissors about and snipping the air, would start chasing him and shouting, 'Let me cut it! Let me cut it!' Terrified, Sami would start running as fast as he could but eventually the thing would catch up with him and grab him by the scruff of the neck. Sami would start screaming, 'Let me go! Let me go!' and then wake up, sweating and trembling like jelly.

At first his parents thought he was making it up but the nightmares continued for some time, waking both him and them up a few times every night, until they were convinced that they were genuine. After that they were afraid to bring up the subject of circumcision but later, being under pressure from the Imam, they agreed to talk to him again.

Another big argument followed.

Sami insisted that there was no need for it. He said, 'Centuries ago they had to do it for health reasons because they had no soap, they never washed and had no medicines for any related diseases.'

'It's not just that,' his father stated. 'It's our religion; that's why you have to have it done.'

'You are wrong, Dad – it was practised before the Muslim faith existed. We just inherited it from Judaism. It's not even in the Koran. So, even if I don't have it done, I'll still be a faithful Muslim.'

'You are making that up so that you don't have it done,' his mother said.

'No, I am not, Mum, honest. Why don't you ask the Imam? If it *is* in the Koran, I'll have it done, because I believe in our Koran. If it is not, will you both agree, now, that I don't have to be circumcised?'

His parents thought that he would stop at nothing in order to get out of it and that he must be bluffing. They were certain that such an important thing must be in the Koran in black and white. So, in the belief that they were going to win the argument once and for all, they agreed.

Thus, on the next occasion when the Imam reminded them, yet again, that Sami's circumcision was overdue, they asked him if it was in the Koran or not. To their shock and disbelief he said, 'No, it is not, but it is an introduction to the faith of Islam; the evidence of belonging.' They were astounded, but Sami had won the argument and they had to abide by their agreement.

V

Sami's parents had always been poor and had to try hard to make ends meet. He was growing up and could better understand their plight. One summer night his father was moaning about the other goatherds who had larger herds and kept squeezing him out of his grazing area. 'That's why the goats are thin and not producing much milk,' his father said to him and his mother. So, the next day, Sami went and told Dr Omar what was happening.

Although Dr Omar was sympathetic, he told Sami that the other goatherds gave him ten per cent of their herd every year as payment for grazing on his scrublands, whereas his father only gave him five per cent because he was poorer and had only a small herd.

'However,' Dr Omar said, 'if you are interested, I will sell you a piece of the scrubland; say, from the dirt road, which is about a mile west of your house and stretches two miles further. That will be more than enough for your dad's few goats. The other goatherds will be stopped for good from encroaching on your patch.'

Sami was intrigued by Dr Omar's understanding and kindness, and wondered how many goats he would expect every year afterwards, so he said, 'I can't see how we can pay for it; my father can't afford to give you more goats.'

'What I had in mind was for you to buy it. You can then come and work on my estate during holidays and in the summer; I'll keep ninety per cent of your pay and deduct it from the price of the scrubland. Within a few years you will pay it all. It won't be expensive because it's not good for anything apart from goat grazing – it's almost worthless.'

Sami liked the idea of being a landowner, albeit of a piece of useless scrubland, and said to Dr Omar, 'As long as you are prepared to wait, I promise you I'll pay for it, even if I have to work for five years, twenty hours a day during school breaks.'

'Well, I'm glad you agree. I will arrange for the title deeds and other documents to be prepared in your name. I like to do things properly, legally, so that everybody is happy,' stated Dr Omar.

And so Sami became the owner of a piece of scrubland by the age of fifteen. His father was very pleased but was also worried about the money aspect. 'It will take you years to pay it back, son,' he said.

'Don't worry, Dad, I will pay it all back no matter how long it takes me,' Sami assured him.

From then on, during the school breaks and especially the long summer vacations, Sami would go and work on Dr Omar's estate. Dr Omar's mansion was at the top of the hill, a few miles north-west of Sami's house, and Sami worked either on the building or on the farmland. Dr Omar also owned a very large area of arable and non-arable land, which he had inherited from his father, Abdul Hassan.

The arrangement suited Sami very well because it provided him with steady work during the school vacations and he was able to stay with his parents. His father was very pleased with the new grazing area and gradually managed to increase his number of goats.

'You bought a big but worthless piece of scrubland, son,' he would say to Sami. 'But that's all a goatherd needs. You should be able to earn your living from it too, and one day you will pass it on to your own children, and so on. The livelihood of our descendants has been secured, thanks to your foresight, hard work and determination.'

VI

Sami was a glutton for knowledge; at school he continued to excel and by the time he finished the elementary school he had read nearly all the books in the library of the province. Although he did not have much to do with Hamid Ali, his elementary schoolteacher, once he started high school, he occasionally met him in the village. On one such occasion Hamid told him about an opportunity to go to Turkey, to an interfaith conference, to represent his country, with all expenses paid. He told Sami that if he was interested, he would recommend him to the officials that he knew from his connections with the government, and religious dignitaries. Sami was interested but he wanted to know what it was all about and what he would have to do.

Hamid went into great detail, explaining to him why the conference had been organised. Because so many religious atrocities had been committed in the previous few decades, some religious dignitaries, thinkers and scholars around the world had come up with the following idea: let young people from across the world and across the religious faiths discuss the issues among themselves. Give them a free hand to be as outspoken as they wanted to be, not only in praising their religions but also in criticising them. As they would be young, under seventeen, they would be excused from the sin of blasphemy. In other words, they could say what their elders might want to say if their positions had not stopped them from doing so.

The organisers hoped that some common ground between religions would be found and a new order of respect for other religions would emerge. As the young people grew older, they would carry on with the new ideas in the future, thereby compelling all religions to accept a unified code of conduct towards each others' followers, and also to remedy any aspects of their own religion that no longer made sense.

The representatives would speak for a few minutes each, based around the concept of stating a reason why they *were* proud of their religion, and conversely a reason why they were *not* proud of their religion.

Having listened to this, Sami told Hamid that he was definitely interested, although in his opinion it sounded idealistic.

'I agree with you,' Hamid said. 'I think they have all gone mad, but that's what the committee wants.'

A couple of months later Sami received a letter from the committee, which stated that he had been selected to go to the conference. He was over the moon; to travel abroad, representing his country and his faith. It was beyond his wildest dreams. It also would not cost his parents a penny as it was all subsidised and paid for by the committee's funds.

When he told his parents they were equally pleased but worried that he would miss them or be sad and upset at having to stay away from them for the first time. Sami knew that although Turkey was a Muslim country, it was secular, more liberal and westernised. So he decided to use some of the money he had for the trip to buy jeans and other Western clothes. He had at last outgrown his charity clothes.

When his mother saw him she said to him, 'Now that I have seen you in those clothes, I realise that you have grown up without me noticing, and you have become a very handsome young man. I'm so proud of you, son.'

Part Six

I

Meanwhile, as time went by without success in the hunt for their baby, Edward and Greta's feelings were those of despair, sadness and emptiness. In order to alleviate their misery, they sought solace in their two other babies, Alex and Emily, who were healthy and lively children. Alex was a jovial and chatty little boy but his parents often wondered how much happier he and his brother would have been if they were together. In the belief that Jonathan was still alive somewhere in the world, Edward contacted Fred and asked him to start another search.

Edward realised that since Jonathan was Alex's identical twin, a photograph of him could be mistaken for Jonathan by those who knew him or had seen him. Fred's assignment was to publish Alex's photograph in the national newspaper for about ten days, first in the Philippines and then the other countries where the leads had taken them in their search after the abduction. The caption for the image was specific and simple: "Have you seen this five-year-old boy? Reward offered for information leading to the discovery of his whereabouts."

Fred was happy to help again. He was to visit the Philippines, Indonesia, Pakistan and Afghanistan – in that order. He would contact the police in each country in advance of his arrival and work with them on any leads during his stay.

First, he returned to the Philippines and paid a visit to Leon, who had in the meantime been promoted to Police Superintendent. They discussed the case details again. Fred explained that by releasing the photos of Jonathan's identical twin, it might jog someone's memory. The advertisement was placed for ten consecutive days, with the agreed caption, both in English and Filipino.

A couple of days went by without a single telephone call. Then there was a flurry of calls, most of which were inquisitive rather than informative. Several were followed up, but sadly they led nowhere. Fred conveyed the disappointing news to Edward and Greta which, although upsetting, did at least offer some psychological comfort that they were still making an effort to find their son.

Jakarta in Indonesia proved the same and so did Karachi in Pakistan, but Edward was still insistent that Fred complete the investigation in full. So he travelled to Kabul in Afghanistan. At the time of the abduction there had been a report of a couple flying into Kabul with a baby. This had already been investigated without success by Fred and Leon. They had received hardly any help from the local officials, as at the time the police had been dealing with more serious – relatively speaking – problems.

Yet again, nothing constructive emerged. Naturally, Edward and Greta were extremely disappointed, though it had been a long shot. Nevertheless, it had also been a brilliant idea. The fact that there had been no positive responses could have been due to a number of reasons, only the worst being that the boy was dead. Most other people with knowledge of the case, including Fred, believed the boy had probably been killed. Edward and Greta could have drawn the same conclusion but they did not. Against all odds they continued to hope and believe, deep down in their hearts, that their Jonathan was alive somewhere in the world. To believe anything else was to give up all hope. They were not going to give up, no matter how long, how much or how many times they had to try and find him. They vowed to continue the search and they were determined to never lose faith.

Five years later, they asked Fred to repeat the same investigation. Fred accepted but felt a sense of guilt in doing so. He wished his work would produce at least some sort of conclusive result but he knew it most likely wouldn't. He revisited the countries with a new photograph, and again nothing positive came from it. He did the same five years later when Jonathan would have been fifteen; yet again he came back with nothing.

Edward and Greta still did not give up. They continued with investigations from time to time, using the police and Parenting4U. On occasions, Greta would get a hunch or an idea and she would use her position, colleagues and friends at the CIA to investigate, but without any success.

So the years went by, while Edward and Greta continued their visits to Manila to spend time with their other two children and took them on exotic holidays. And during all that time, the trust fund that had been set up for Jonathan was growing with compound interest. It remained there, in the bank, undisturbed and unclaimed.

II

When Hamid was returning from Kabul one day, he passed by an open-air café where a man was sitting reading a newspaper. In the top right-hand corner of the page was a photograph of a young boy, of about five years old, who was the spitting image of Sami. When Hamid saw it he stopped dead in his tracks and immediately wondered if something bad had happened to Sami.

He quickly read the large heading, which asked, "Have you seen this five-year-old boy?" And below the photo it said, "You can receive a large reward if you help us trace this boy" and gave a telephone number to contact.

The man who was reading the paper looked up and said to Hamid, 'Are you all right, Sir?'

'Oh, yes, I am sorry,' said Hamid. 'I was just looking at your paper.'

'Here, you can have it; I've finished with it anyway,' the man said and handed the paper to Hamid.

Hamid, although somewhat embarrassed by this, took the paper and thanked the stranger for being so kind.

On the way back to his village, Hamid couldn't stop thinking about this development. If anybody knew Sami, they would recognise him instantly from the photograph. How could they, whoever produced it, have come up with such a perfect likeness? Hamid wondered, until he remembered that Sami had a twin brother. Sami had been chosen because he was in a private hospital at the time and it was easier to abduct him.

They must be identical twins, Hamid concluded. That's the only way there can be such a resemblance. However, I am not going to worry about it; nobody in the village gets a newspaper. He put the paper in his briefcase and forgot all about it until the following day when he went to his office on the second floor of the school. Then he took the paper out of his briefcase and looked at the photograph again. Leaving it on his desk, Hamid went about his day, knowing that when his office door was closed nobody could go in without a key. And he had the only key except for the cleaner, who was not due to arrive until late that afternoon after the school closed.

Unfortunately the cleaner, Mr Halabi, who was an old retired teacher, came a little earlier than usual and started cleaning Hamid's office. He picked up the newspaper and began to read it and, as he turned the pages over, he noticed the photograph of the boy, who he also recognised as Sami. It was a small, remote village and everybody knew everybody. He read the caption at the top and the bottom of the photograph and tried to figure out why there should be a reward for Sami. Unless, he thought, there was something suspicious about his adoption. Convinced, he turned around, newspaper still in hand, and picked up the phone that was by the opened balcony door.

Hamid walked in just before Halabi began to dial. 'What are you doing?' he demanded.

'What do you think I'm doing?' Mr Halabi retorted. 'I am going to tell them who this boy is. Both you and I know he is Sami, who was adopted. Obviously, his real parents want to trace him, which means that he was taken from them illegally. In fact, it was you who brought him here. Where did you take him from?'

'Put the phone down, Halabi. You don't want to meddle in matters that do not concern you.'

'No, I won't. Besides, there is a handsome reward; I'll get rich.'

'Look, Halabi, you always taught me, in this very school, to live for Allah and do whatever it took – even kill – to glorify Allah in the name of Islam! Sami is my salvation.'

'You were always a militant and a radical fundamentalist; I thought that you would've mellowed with age. Sami is clearly not an Afghan boy and he must be returned to his real parents. You must undo the wrong you've done. If you are not going to, I will. Either way, Sami must be given back,' Halabi said, forcefully.

By then Hamid was fuming, his eyes popping out with anger, and he shouted, 'I told you to stop interfering! I am warning you, Halabi, put the phone *down*.'

'No. I won't,' Halabi refused.

Hamid lurched forward and snatched the phone, pushing the old man away. The cleaner resisted and a struggle ensued. Hamid, being the younger and stronger of the two, pushed Halabi backwards. The old man staggered and hit the railing of the balcony so hard that he lost his balance and nearly fell.

Hamid, seeing the other man's vulnerability, ran up and tumbled him the rest of the way over the railings. Seconds later there was a deafening thud. Hamid leaned over the railings and looked down at the body of Halabi, sprawled motionless on the floor. He waited to see if there were any signs of life from him but there were none, so he concluded that the old man was either already dead or dying.

He went back to his desk and picked up the dust cloth that Halabi had been carrying, and took it down to the ground where the cleaner's body was. He leaned down and felt for a pulse but there was none. Then he lifted Halabi's hand up and put the dust cloth underneath it, in the blood that was oozing out of his head.

Hamid then went back to his office and phoned the police. He told them that he had just found Halabi, the school cleaner, dead on the ground with severe head wounds. 'He must have fallen from the balcony of the second floor,' he said.

By the time the police arrived it was almost dark. They concluded that Halabi must have leaned over the rail to reach something or other and lost his balance, falling to his death still clutching his duster in his hand – a tragic accident.

III

After the incident with Halabi, Hamid went through a period of extreme anxiety. He was worried that the advertisement might reappear suddenly. If somebody from his village, who might be travelling to another town, saw the picture they would recognise Sami, just like Halabi had, and want to claim the reward. There was no way Hamid could stop it happening. Unless, he thought, Sami was dead. Then they wouldn't bother. That is the only way to put an end to it for good. He cursed his decision to have Sami adopted in his own village.

The problem was finding somebody to kill the boy, as he did not want to do it himself. Getting a contract out on a child was not going to be quick, easy or cheap. But within a few months he found a penniless vagrant from Kabul who said he would do anything for money. Hamid did not tell him at the time that the target was a child, and later, when he revealed the fact, the man demanded more money than they had previously agreed.

The plan was to carry out a hit-and-run. By September, Sami was in school, and it was to be done as he returned home. Part of his journey took him along the dirt road through the area. Hamid had watched Sami make the journey a few times; he walked part of the way with Mustafa, a boy of the same age, and then carried on by himself for another mile or so before turning right and heading towards his house.

One Thursday afternoon, a black car appeared on the dirt road, moving slowly a few hundred yards behind the two boys who were walking home and unaware of its presence. When Mustafa turned off, Sami started running towards his house as he always did. The car accelerated, racing towards Sami. Mustafa heard the car and turned; he saw how close it was getting to Sami and shouted, 'Sami! Get off the road! There is a car behind you!'

Sami heard him and jumped for the side of the road but he was not quite fast enough. The side of the car clipped him while he was airborne, which softened its impact but threw him roughly to the ground.

Mustafa ran back to his friend as the car sped away. He was shocked to find Sami unconscious, with scrapes and cuts on his face, hands and knees. Not knowing how to help him, Mustafa ran to his own house and told his mother what had happened.

By the time Mustafa and his mother returned, Sami had regained consciousness and was sitting up, but he was still dazed. They asked him if he was all right.

'What happened?' Sami replied. When Mustafa explained to him what had happened, he still did not remember a thing; Mustafa's mother thought that he had concussion. After about half an hour he managed to get up, with their assistance, and they took him home. His mother put him to bed, tended his cuts and bruises, and by the end of the weekend he was up and about and ready to go to school as usual.

When Hamid saw Sami in school, he could only stare at him for a moment; he was taken aback because he had expected him to be either already dead or dying from the hit-and-run he had arranged and paid for. He pretended that he was troubled by the incident and decided to pay his assassin a visit in the very near future, as he had botched it up.

The man tried to extort more money from him to keep silent, after Hamid caught up with him. So Hamid followed him down a lonely road one dark night and stabbed him through the heart.

After that Hamid decided to take his chances with the advertisements if they appeared again.

…and they did. Five years later, almost to the day, another photograph appeared in the newspaper. This time the boy in the picture looked ten, and once again he was the spitting image of Sami. The advert had the same headline and promise of a reward as before, only the size of the reward had increased.

At the time, the only newspapers in the village were the two that were delivered once a month to the school; one for Hamid and one for Dr Omar. Nobody else had one. When Hamid saw the photograph, he decided that Dr Omar should not be allowed to see it, just in case he decided to spill the beans and claim the reward. He didn't really think that Dr Omar would do that, as he was indirectly implicated in the wrongful adoption of Sami. However, he didn't want to take any chances so he hid both newspapers and told Dr Omar's messenger that the paper hadn't come.

Hamid realised that there was a gap of five years between the two photographs and concluded the next one would appear when Sami was fifteen – *if* they decided to try again; having been unsuccessful twice they might not try a third time. However, Hamid decided he would be looking out for it, when the time came, just in case.

So he was not surprised when, five years later, while going through the newspaper, he came across a photo of the same boy yet again, this time aged fifteen. But Hamid only laughed because the boy in the photo was clean-shaven, with his hair combed backwards neatly. In contrast, Sami had grown a bushy little beard and had long hair dangling over his forehead, neck and ears. Hamid was delighted; Sami now looked nothing like his twin.

IV

Hamid, being also a vizier, made many acquaintances and friends, and had strong connections with the government in Kabul. Some visited him in his village and stayed with his family. Hamid's family comprised his wife, Sheeva, his daughter Hasti, aged fifteen, and his unmarried sister Samira, aged 45, who lived with them. Like so many other men in the village he had only one wife; hardly any of them could afford more than one.

One of Hamid's guests was Jacob Khan. Jacob was in his forties, had grey hair and sported a goatee beard. He wore European-style clothes and was smartly dressed. He was well travelled and, like Hamid, was educated and spoke very good English. A couple of times he went to the village school with Hamid on a voluntary basis and stood in for Hamid's English classes.

Sami was one of the children learning English, and Jacob was very impressed by his grasp of the English language. To Jacob, Sami's looks appeared different to all the other kids; he had light skin and blue eyes. Because all the village people had seen Sami grow up from a baby, they took his attributes for granted, but to an outsider like Jacob they were more apparent and somewhat inexplicable. He wondered if Sami was of Greek descent, from the days of Alexander the Great who had conquered Iran, Afghanistan and many other neighbouring countries, or from some other neighbouring tribe, and whether he had been adopted. One day he queried Sami's different looks and, since everybody in the village knew that he was adopted, Hamid told him that he was.

While staying there, Jacob would also go and pray at the village mosque and meet other worshippers. He projected a likeable character; pleasant, obliging and agreeable. He did his best to fit in and succeeded, as the villagers liked him.

At the time, the government was trying to modernise and revitalise its farming industry with the help of massive foreign aid. It brought in agricultural machinery, fertilisers, chemicals and crop sprays, and started to also grow new types of produce, including genetically modified crops. They were aiming to replace the widespread, illegal opium poppy farming. The transformation was being organised by Regional Agricultural Cooperative Societies which had direct contact with the local farming communities.

Jacob told Hamid that he would like to move into the area and that he had applied for the manager's position of the Agricultural Cooperative Society for their region, and wondered if Hamid could help. The contacts that Hamid had in Kabul proved very useful and Jacob got the job; it was in a town not too far from Hamid's village. This brought Jacob and Hamid closer, and Jacob became an even more regular visitor to Hamid's house. Within a year Jacob had married Hamid's sister, Samira, and they moved to the town where he worked, some fifty miles away, but they remained close with Hamid and his family, and used to go back and stay with them often.

Part Seven

I

What happened to Jonathan was irredeemable. After his abduction and disappearance, Edward and Greta Everest's plans for their two remaining babies changed. They had not planned to visit their children at Parenting4U regularly – in fact, quite the opposite; no visits had been planned at all, from the day they were born to the day they were to be taken away at the age of eleven. But now they decided to visit them often, throughout the year, sometimes together, sometimes separately.

When they were very small they didn't take the babies outside the complex. They stayed with them in the house that had been allocated to their surrogate mothers for bringing them up. But as Greta and Edward's stays became more frequent and for longer periods, a bigger house was allocated. After what had happened to Jonathan, the company bent over backwards to be as accommodating as possible.

As the babies became toddlers, Edward and Greta took them, together with their surrogate mums, on short holidays in the Philippines. As they grew older they took them further afield, to places such as Australia, Bali and China. Alex was learning to speak Mandarin, as planned in the education section of the agreement between his parents and Parenting4U, so their holidays were educational as well as recreational. They went to Peking and to the Great Wall. Emily was learning French, so on another occasion they went to Paris to see the sights, as well as spend a few days in Disneyland, which both children really loved. Another trip saw them visit India. The Everests wished their children to experience different countries, races, cultures and languages from an early age. They wanted them to broaden their views and know the world they lived in.

Each time their parents left, the children felt very unsettled and would play up, but after a few days they would forget and slip back into their usual routines. They went to school and they had extra tuition classes: Alex learned Chinese, Emily French and ballet, and they both had piano and swimming classes. They were spoiled for toys and later on, like all children, they moved on to IT: gadgets and computers. As they both had their own they never squabbled over them.

Within Parenting4U there were children's parties, which were greatly encouraged so that the children could develop their social skills and accept all the different nationalities at the complex without thinking about it.

When they were confirmed into the Catholic faith their parents went to the service. They were five years old then, and dressed in their special white clothes they looked like little angels. Both parents were proud and happy to see them both confirmed into the Christian faith. But at the same time they were saddened by the thought that Jonathan should also have been with them. That was the moment when Edward thought about publishing photographs of Alex in the press, and asking for anyone who had seen him to come forward. Greta thought it was a brilliant idea because they were identical twins.

II

When Alex and Emily were thought old enough to understand, their unusual situation was explained to them. They were told that they were lucky to have, in effect, two mothers – their surrogate mothers, who they referred to as their surromums, and their other, biological, "real" mother. This inevitably caused problems for the surromums, who had to contend with comments such as, 'Anyway, you're not my *real* mum, so I won't do as you tell me.' Emily, in particular, often used this as a retort, as she was by far the naughtier of the two children.

Alex, on the other hand, was quite the opposite of his sister. He rarely got upset or angry and, even on the rare occasions that he did, he always apologised later and tried to discuss the problem in a rational way to resolve it. He had a very keen sense of logic, even at such an early age. On one occasion, Dolores, his surromum, said to him, 'Your reasoning and deductive ability is very good, Alex. You should become a detective when you grow up.'

'I just like to think things through,' he said, 'and find an answer – like you do with a maths problem. Maybe I will become a banker or an accountant one day, but certainly not a detective; that's dangerous. You have to deal with criminals.'

On another occasion his reasoning, or rather excuses, did not make sense to Dolores. He was continuously kicking a small football in the sitting room, trying to keep it from falling on the floor. Dolores told him to stop before he broke something, to which he replied, 'The chance of that happening, statistically speaking, is about a million to one. And since I only do this for half an hour a day, at the rate that I am kicking it, which is about 3,000 times per hour, it would take me two years before anything got broken. As I am not going to stand here for two years, I won't break anything: QED.'

'Don't try to confuse me with your maths and logic,' Dolores replied. 'That's not what one in a million means: it can happen at any time from the moment you start kicking the ball, not necessarily at the end.'

And soon it did. Emily walked into the room, startled him, and he kicked the ball at an angle, causing it to fall on the table and knock down a vase, breaking it.

'QED,' remarked Dolores. 'You are grounded, and no i-gismos and computers for a week.'

III

Their parents continued with regular visits, each time taking new toys, clothes and books for their children. There were so many that some of them remained unopened until the children had grown out of them. But what Emily and Alex really liked was spending time with their parents and, most of all, the wonderful holidays they went on.

The older the children became the more interesting and far flung the holiday destinations were; always with an educational slant and with the aim of broadening their horizons given the otherwise closeted upbringing they were having. Sometimes the children got bored after a while but their parents insisted that it would benefit them and that they would always remember going to interesting and famous places. Emily wouldn't have any of it though and said to her father, 'I'm fed up of seeing ruins, churches and museums. I would rather go to the seaside and spend all the time swimming and sunbathing instead.'

'In that case,' said her father, 'our next holiday will be in the Maldives, which has white sandy beaches and clear blue sea. You can swim and snorkel to your heart's content. I'm sure you won't be bored there.'

So some months later, during the half-term at their school, they went to the Maldives for a week. They all loved it. 'This is like paradise,' said Alex on the first day. But by the third day, Emily had had enough of sand and swimming, and started moaning.

'I'm fed up,' she said. 'There's nothing to do here; it's so boring.'

'Nothing pleases you, Emily,' said her mother. 'You didn't like our last holiday and you don't like this one either. It was your idea to have a beach holiday. I don't understand you.'

'It's not my fault this place is so quiet. There is nothing else to do. We should have gone to Phuket again. I preferred it there.'

'Why don't you read a book to keep your mind occupied?' her father suggested.

'I didn't bring any.'

'Well, read one of mine then,' said Alex. 'You can have: Climbing the Matterhorn, Mathematical Logic, Born Free, or this Harry Potter.'

'I can't believe you've actually brought a maths book on holiday,' Emily said in disgust.

'For your information, it's not a maths book,' Alex responded.

'Anyway, I read that Harry Potter ages ago and I don't want to read about mountain climbing, thank you very much. I'll give Born Free a go. That will keep me busy for a few hours, that's all,' she said, still sounding grumpy.

Because money was no object to the family, they had everything they could wish for. They always travelled first class and stayed at the best hotels. They had several holidays every year as a family, and Edward and Greta also had a number of breaks by themselves.

The children never encountered less well-off people. Where they were being brought up there was everything they could need, and all of the very highest standards, whether it was clothes, food or education. Within the Parenting4U complex lived some of the most privileged children in the world.

Both Edward and Greta had had early financial and career successes in their lives. Before they were forty they had both reached high levels in their work and had started a family. They had two healthy children being brought up in a wonderful place. They were well aware of their privileged lives and were very happy to be in that position.

One day, Emily asked her parents, 'Why do we live here and not with you in America?'

'That's because we want you to have the best care and education in the world,' Greta replied. 'Your surromums spend all their time looking after you and nobody else. If you lived at home with us, we wouldn't be able to do all the things they do for you, as we work hard and for very long hours. It's like being in boarding school, except here it is better. This place is like paradise, and we come and visit you many times a year. We have lots of holidays together and you can see us on your computers and talk to us through satellite systems whenever you wish – it's as easy as talking to us from next door. As soon as you're eleven you will both come to America and we will live together. You can then decide if you want to go to a boarding school or a day school.'

'I don't want to go to another boarding school,' said Alex.

'Neither do I,' said Emily. 'And anyway, you said they weren't as good as here.'

'Fine, that's settled then. You can stay at home and go to a day school,' said Greta. 'Daddy's chauffeur will take you there and bring you home.'

'Why can't you take us?' asked Alex.

'We have to be at work early, so we can't. Most of the other children at the school will be taken by their parents' chauffeurs too, so you won't be alone. Both mummy and daddy have very responsible jobs, which are very demanding. It's because we do these jobs that we have the money to pay for all the things you and we need,' explained Greta.

'But, if you are already rich, you don't have to work then, do you?' asked Emily.

'Of course you have to work. Otherwise what else would you do to fill your time? You would just lie about all day, eating and drinking, and getting fat and unhealthy. It would be an empty and useless life, not to achieve anything and not to fulfil your potential. No, children, work is a blessing, I can assure you.'

'Yes, Alex and Emily, listen to your mum's profound advice; those are words of wisdom,' added their father.

IV

When the time came for Alex and Emily to go and live in America, Edward and Greta decided it would make the transition easier for the children if Dolores and Marissa came too. They stayed for the whole of the summer. During that summer the children were able to see some of their new country and meet their previously unknown relatives, before starting school in the autumn. By then they had got used to their new lives and environment. When they started school they were fully occupied, and surprisingly didn't miss their surromums when they went back to the Philippines.

Soon after bringing their children home to the US, Edward and Greta threw a huge party. They invited all their relatives and friends, and took great pleasure in "introducing" their children. All the guests were very impressed by the two children; they were so well-rounded, considering they had been brought up away from their parents. They were both impeccably behaved and were very at ease mingling with guests and chatting to all the unfamiliar faces. Many guests remarked that they looked like their parents: Alex like his father, and Emily like her mother. Both showed a confidence well beyond their years, and Edward and Greta felt very proud.

'You have two lovely children, Greta,' remarked her father.

'I had hoped you would come round to agreeing with us about the way we did it.'

'Let's forget all about that. What matters is to raise them yourselves from now on.'

'We will, Dad,' Greta assured him.

'They will get to know and be friends with their cousins, Bernard's kids Peter and Nancy. It's important that they have their relatives around them now; they will feel more secure in life.'

'It's such a shame Martha hasn't found anyone since she split up with Timothy,' Greta commented.

'Yes, it is. Her real problem is that she is finding it difficult financially. She can't make ends meet. She told me how kind you were with helping out with Gemma's school fees. I've decided to change my will so I can hand over her inheritance now. I will amend it accordingly, so that you and Bernard won't lose out.'

'Dad, don't worry about me. We have more than enough money.'

'That may be true, but it's not the amount of the inheritance that the appreciation lies in but in who the giver is. I just wanted you to know what I am going to do.'

'Thank you, Dad; please excuse me, I'm going to talk to mum for a while,' said Greta.

Over to the other side of the room was Ellie, Bernard's wife, with their two children: Peter aged ten, and Nancy who was eight. They were chatting to Emily and Alex. They got on very well; it was as if they had known each other for years. Alex was telling Peter about the new school that he was about to start, and wanted to know all about schools in the US. Emily was talking to Nancy about sports. She was lamenting that she hadn't been able to do much horse-riding at Parenting4U. The stables had been such a long way from the complex that they had only gone infrequently.

'I'll take you horse-riding when you come to stay with us,' Nancy said. 'I've been riding since I was four and I take part in competitions. I don't really do it to win; I just love it. I did come second once, though.'

There was a lovely atmosphere at the party and everybody appeared genuinely pleased to be there. However, every now and then Greta and Edward would look at Alex – or rather, gaze beyond him – at his double,

Jonathan, his missing twin. It had been eleven years since he had been taken and, while it was true that time healed, the pain of his loss was still there, etched into their souls, which was far worse than a physical wound could ever have been.

Part Eight

Istanbul

I

Sami looked forward to travelling to Istanbul to the Interfaith Symposium. He was very pleased to have been selected and thought it was an honour to represent his country and talk about his faith as an extended speaker. It was also going to be an important occasion from the point of view of meeting people from other countries, and seeing other places; a chance and an experience which might never happen again.

He had never been near an aeroplane before, let alone flown in one – it was all exciting stuff – but when he found himself in the air, flying to Istanbul, he was apprehensive. He had never stayed away from home, except for the time when he was taken to the district hospital to have his appendix out. He thought that the next couple of days would be awful, sleeping in a hotel, miles away from home and his parents.

After checking in at reception, he went to get the lift to his room, which was on the fourth floor. He entered the lift but, as he was about to press the button for his floor, a girl got in with an older woman, who looked like her mother. Since he was standing by the buttons he asked them which floor they were going to, to which the mother replied, 'Fourth please.'

When they got out of the lift, they all turned left as they started looking for their rooms. The mother spoke to Sami again. 'Pardon me, but are you here for the Interfaith Symposium?'

'Yes, I am.'

'I am Mrs Durrani, and this is my daughter Zafeera; we call her Zaf for short.'

'I am Sami. Pleased to meet you both.'

'Perhaps we can share a taxi to the venue tomorrow morning, if you wish,' she said.

'Yes, we could then share the cost,' Sami replied.

They all walked down the corridor looking for their rooms. The two women found theirs first and stopped. Sami said, 'Mine is the next but one. At what time shall I book the taxi for?'

'Shall we say 9am? That should give you plenty of time to travel to the venue and register,' Mrs Durrani said.

'Right, I'll book it for nine then, and I'll look out for you in the foyer.'

Sami found his room, unpacked, had a shower and got ready to go out for dinner. He stopped at reception on his way out and booked a taxi for the next morning.

On his way to the nearby café, where the receptionist had advised him that he could get 'a quick bite at a reasonable price,' he thought about Zaf, the girl in the lift. She hadn't said a word but had kept looking at him and smiling. He had found her very attractive; she was of medium height with a small, round face, sparkling brown eyes, and straight black hair tumbling down to her shoulders. She also had a fair size bust and small waist. They were most likely from Pakistan, originally, he thought.

At sixteen, a healthy young man could feel attracted to a pretty young girl and fall in love at the drop of a hat. Sami knew many young girls of his age from the village and from high school, but had never had a girlfriend as such. At the time, friendships between boys and girls were frowned upon, especially in villages. For Sami to see a pretty girl smile at him like that was quite something. Back home people would misconstrue such a smile as being alluring or even provocative. He knew though that European people were visually more expressive, unlike his country's folk.

The café was busy. As Sami was in no hurry he sat down and waited to be served. When his turn came, he ordered kebabs with a side salad and a drink.

II

By the time Sami walked back to his room at the hotel it was 8.30pm. He got his speech out but, not long after he started rehearsing his presentation, there was a knock on the door. When he opened the door he was pleasantly surprised; Zaf was standing there. She apologised for troubling him and explained that her mother had gone out for the evening to see a Turkish belly-dancing show, and as she wanted to practise her speech she had stayed behind. Then she asked him if he would like to hear it.

'Yes, I would love to,' he said. 'Do come in.'

'I have to go and get it,' she said, 'I won't be a minute.' Zaf rushed back to her room and soon reappeared carrying her handbag and speech.

'What time is your presentation?' Sami asked.

'It's on the first day, after lunch.'

'Mine is on the second day, roughly at noon. I'm an extended speaker,' he said.

'We are staying right through the symposium. I have to attend the plenary session as I am the rapporteur for my group.'

'Are you?' he asked, sounding rather impressed.

'Yes, I am. I'll have to summarise the outcome of my group's views and conclusions, and speak about them for a few minutes,' she explained.

'Do you mind doing that? I mean, will you be nervous?' he asked.

'No, I hope not; I am doing drama in school, and I have had a lot of practice. What about you?'

'Well, the only experience I have comes from school. We have to stand up in front of the class and talk about a subject and answer questions. I feel comfortable talking in front of the other students because, in general, I know the subject and all the facts, which gives me confidence.'

'You must be a clever guy then; that's why you've been chosen to come here, of course.'

'What's your speech about?' he asked.

'It's about the inequality of the sexes. As you know, Islam allows men to have more than one wife but does not allow women to have more than one husband. That's prima facie inequality, don't you think?'

He was so amazed to hear it that he burst out laughing and asked, 'But why would women *want* to have more than one husband?'

'If men can have more than one spouse, so should women; end of story,' she stated.

'Obviously you feel very strongly about it. Tell me then, would you?'

'Personally, I wouldn't. I would rather have the total and absolute love and devotion of one man, whom I would call my own love. Some women may want more than one, to spoil them with love and gifts, and fight over who will have her for the night. That would give women great esteem and power. Don't you think so?'

'Yes, maybe it would.'

'Anyway, I am dying of thirst; may I have something from your minibar?' she asked.

'Yes, of course. What would you like?'

'A gin and tonic would be nice,' she said.

'Are you serious?' Sami asked, sounding very surprised.

'Yes, I am, and here is another example of religious suppression. There is no scientific reason why I, we, as Muslims, shouldn't have an alcoholic drink.'

Sami got the small bottles of gin and tonic out and handed them to her. Without any hesitation, she opened the two bottles and poured them into the glass by the side of the bed, where she was sitting. After a sip or two, she said, 'Aren't you having one?'

'I haven't drunk alcohol before,' he said.

'Try some of mine and tell me what you think,' she said, offering her glass to him.

He tried a small sip and to his surprise he didn't find it offensive. 'It's nice,' he said.

'Of course it's nice. What did you expect? Poison or being struck down by Allah for your sin? Millions of people drink alcohol and there is nothing wrong with it in moderation. Why shouldn't you have one?'

There is some logic in her argument, Sami thought, and went and got himself the same as she had. He enjoyed every sip of it. By the time they finished their first drink they felt a little tipsy but they went on drinking whatever they found in the mini fridge. Sami had a couple of whiskies with ginger ale; Zaf had another gin and tonic, and then a vodka and tonic. Soon they were drunk; both lying there on the bed, laughing and giggling like little kids who had done something naughty and got away with it. They forgot all about their speeches.

'Do you know what,' she said giggling. 'Tomorrow, at breakfast, I'll have bacon and egg. This is an international hotel, they have guests from all over the world and they must have all sorts of food.'

'Aren't you forgetting something? Your mother will be there.'

'I'll do it and see her reaction. If she is too upset I won't eat it. That's fair, isn't it?' she said, giggling.

Neither of them were used to much alcohol. They both became relaxed and merry and content for having broken away from the norm. 'Rules are made to be broken,' Zaf said, laughing.

'Especially if they are over a thousand years out of date! Some are just inappropriate in today's society, as we have demonstrated tonight. However, my parents would kill me if they knew,' Sami added.

'If you don't tell them, they will never know.'

'What about your mother? Won't she realise that you have been drinking when she returns?'

'She often accuses me of drinking when I come back after going out with my friends. Some of them drink because they are not Muslim. They just do it to get a bit merry, that's all. That's how I started; I only have one at the beginning of the evening when I am out. Anyway, my mother won't come back for another two hours. By then I will have had a shower, a cup of tea, and brushed my teeth. She won't smell a thing.'

'You have it all worked out then.'

'I wasn't born yesterday; I am nearly seventeen. I should be able to do what I like, within reason. I had a boyfriend when I was fifteen. What about you? Have you got a girlfriend?'

'I haven't got one, not as such,' he replied.

'Don't tell me you are still a virgin?' she asked mockingly.

'Oh come on, surely you don't think…?' he mumbled, taken by surprise.

'Well, this will be fun!' she said.

'What do you mean?'

'I'll tell you what. Let's play a game. I'll take one of your hands and place it somewhere on my body. You then do the same: take one of my hands and place it anywhere you like on your body. Then I'll do the same to your other hand and so on, all right?'

'I get it. But does the game end after two moves each?' Sami asked anxiously.

'Of course not! That wouldn't be much fun. We carry on moving each other's hands to another part of our body.'

'Right,' he said. 'You go first.'

She did; her move was decisive. Sami hesitated and she urged him on.

He picked up her left hand and placed it clumsily on his head. His heart was pounding like mad and he felt a thrill of excitement; he had never been so close to a girl's body before.

After that, a flurry of hand activity followed, and the game took on a different dimension. Turns went from moving hands to removing items of clothing and back to moving hands. Soon touching turned to petting, and Zaf quickly guided Sami towards a mutually exhilarating climax.

Afterwards Zaf asked, 'Weren't you worried about getting me pregnant?'

'To be quite honest, I was so carried away it didn't occur to me. I hope—'

'Don't worry; I am on the pill,' she butted in, as Sami's tone of voice was becoming anxious.

'That was phenomenal!'

Her eyes turned mirthful as she looked at him and said, 'It was your first time, wasn't it? You will never forget your first lovemaking for as long as you live! Did you know that?'

'No, I didn't, but I can see why.'

'I have to go back to my room now before my mother comes back,' she said. She got out of bed and started dressing while he was looking at and admiring her shapely body. She was uninhibited; not at all shy about her nude body in full view of Sami's gaze. She put her lace panties on first, then her bra. After that she walked over to the mirror, combed her hair and then continued dressing.

Sami relished his first view of the naked body of a woman. He noticed how her full breasts, round hips and small waist were the foundation of a shapely female body. What a beautiful body Allah created for women. It is heavenly; the epitome of my desires, he thought.

'Will you come tomorrow night?' he asked wistfully, as she was getting ready to walk out of the room.

'I don't know. It depends on what my mother is doing. Look out for me at the conference. I'll tell you then.'

'Goodnight,' she said, and closed the door behind her.

III

By the morning both the excitement and the alcohol had worn off and Sami started reassessing the wisdom of what he had done. He remembered reading about the diseases that people could catch from unprotected sex and started to worry. He didn't regret what he had done but was concerned about any unwanted consequences. So he decided to get some protection from a pharmacy after breakfast, before going to the conference, in case she came to him again in the night.

When he went downstairs for breakfast Zaf was already there, sitting down with her mother. When she saw him, she signalled to him to come over to their table. 'Why don't you join us?' she said.

'Good morning, and thank you, I will.'

'We've just ordered tea,' Zaf said. 'I am going to get a cooked breakfast now; it's self-service. Are you coming, Mum?'

'No, you two go, and I'll order you tea – or do you want coffee?' she asked Sami.

'I'll have tea as well,' he replied, and got up and walked to the food counter with Zaf.

'About last night,' she said. 'I don't want you to think that I am some kind of floozy who sleeps around. I've only done that with my boyfriend. It all happened because I was drunk.'

'No, I didn't think that at all. In fact, I wanted to apologise for taking advantage of the situation.'

'You don't have to; we were both drunk,' she said.

'If I'd known you have a boyfriend I wouldn't—'

'Don't worry; my parents are doing their best to stop me seeing him because he is English. They broke us up before, and again last week, because he is also Christian. They want me to marry my first cousin.'

'I'm sorry,' Sami said.

'I don't know yet what my mother is doing tonight. Whatever it is, I'll tell her that I cannot go with her because I have to summarise my group's discussions and conclusions, ready to present them tomorrow at the plenary session. I hope I'll be able to tell you what's happening later, at the seminar.'

'I'll look out for you,' he said.

'Oh look, here is some lovely bacon. I'll have some with my scrambled eggs and fried tomatoes.'

'I'll have the same, but what's your mother going to say?'

'We'll find out soon enough. Anyway, there is nothing else, apart from those pork-free sausages, and they don't look too good!'

When they got back to the table her mother said, 'I have ordered your tea. I'll now go and get something for myself.'

'She didn't notice,' Sami said after Zaf's mother had left.

'When she gets back she will. Just leave it to me.'

As soon as her mother got back, she noticed. 'What are you eating? Don't tell me it is bacon!' she rebuked Zaf.

'Mum, there is nothing else there. The sausages didn't look nice at all; I'm surprised you chose them.'

'I am profoundly disappointed in you, Zaf. If your father knew...'

'He won't. Anyway, it's not as though I'm making a habit of it.'

'Do you eat bacon at home, Sami?' her mother asked.

'No, we don't. I thought I might as well try it, since I didn't fancy the sausages. Under different circumstances, I wouldn't dream of eating bacon,' he explained.

'Anyway, Mum, this is partly what the symposium is about. There are things that we do, or are required not to do, for which there is no scientific or logical explanation.'

'I am sure some delegate will talk about this very thing. After all, that's what we are here for: to thrash out not only the strengths of our faiths but also any perceived weaknesses,' Sami added.

'You can talk about things until you are blue in the face; in the end nothing will happen. It's all a waste of time,' Mrs Durrani said categorically; her mind already made up about the symposium.

'Mum, you've been going on about it being a waste of time ever since I was chosen to represent the Muslim community of Coventry. Now that we're here, I think we should all liven up and get into the spirit of it. Who knows, we may be witnessing the new dawn of an even more enlightened but modern version of Islam – one that will take us through the next millennium. It has to move with the times. I don't want women to remain the slaves of men forever.'

'Just because you don't want to be answerable to anyone, it doesn't mean it's your faith's fault. That's the problem with your generation: they want the freedom to do anything they want, forgetting family values and faith.' Turning to Sami, she said, 'I am sorry, but you can see where I am coming from. I can never agree with Zaf's liberal views.'

Sami didn't want to get caught up in their disagreement, so he decided to err on the side of caution. 'Not all young Muslims have liberal views. But freedom per se is a basic human right; people must be able to choose from a range of options without coercion. It's right that we should all be able to express our opinions freely. This is exactly why we are here; some will agree to changes, while others will object to them.'

'Sorry to cut you short,' Zaf chimed in, 'but we have to go and get ready. The taxi will be here in five minutes.'

IV

On the way to the venue of the symposium, Mrs Durrani asked the driver to drop her off near the city centre. She was going to do some shopping, go and see the Blue Mosque, and if time allowed see the Süleymaniye Mosque as well. She bid them goodbye and wished them a nice day at the conference. After she had left, Zaf told Sami that her mother was coming back to the hotel about 6pm so that they could all go out to dinner, if he would like to join them. He told her that he would love to.

When they arrived at the conference, they registered, picked up their badges and split up to join different discussion groups. 'I'll try and find you during the lunch break,' Zaf said.

'I'll look out for you; better still, we can meet by the reception at, say, ten past one.'

'I'll be there,' she affirmed.

Zaf found her group, which to her surprise was very large; more than fifty were present. The group leader was also the chairperson and rapporteur for the group and was to sit behind a table in front of all the delegates. She sat there and introduced herself and her faith, and reminded the delegates how proceedings at the meeting would be conducted. The mood of the delegates was subdued during the first few presentations and debates. Later, after about an hour, the debates became livelier and there were some heated arguments. Gradually they got worse, and some delegates became unruly. By the end of the morning session Zaf was very harassed and was relieved it was over. She rushed out and went to look for Sami, who was waiting for her with a big smile.

They walked together to one of the restaurants of the symposium while talking about their morning sessions. He told her that he had not contributed to his groups' debates yet, but he had found all the presentations and discussions interesting.

She told him that she had had a terrible morning; the mood of the delegates had been very subdued at the beginning, but later they had become very unruly and started fighting.

'Great Allah!' Sami exclaimed. 'I thought my group was bad enough.'

'We started off with a speech from a boy from Lahore, India. He said that Hinduism emphasised the need to live in a way that would result in each subsequent life being better than the previous one, explaining that Hindus believed that all forms of life had a soul that lived through eternal reincarnations; the acts of each life impacting on the next. Then he said that although cows in Hinduism are sacred, they are neglected and left to roam the streets. A Buddhist spoke next, and he was followed by a Sikh. The discussions that followed those presentations were flat but orderly.'

'Good,' Sami said.

'The next delegate to speak was a young girl of fifteen from Niger who, after praising Islam, spoke about her elder sister; apparently she was sold as a child bride to a wealthy man from Nigeria at the age of eleven. Then she said that her parents told her that the reason they did not sell her yet was because they still had some money from the sale of her sister. She concluded that she did not know how long it would be before they sell her as well. Most delegates were outraged by that practice. Later, when it was quiet, a Christian delegate said that that could never happen in Christian countries. Of course that provoked more unrest. But to my shock and disbelief some Muslim delegates, from Sudan and Nigeria, said that they saw nothing wrong with it. They argued that it was better than getting nothing! Can you believe it, Sami? And that was not all: a boy from Niger then chipped in with "Besides, there would be one less mouth to feed." That provoked even more anger and criticism.'

'That doesn't surprise me, but when did the fights start?' Sami enquired.

'It was when a Christian boy from Jerusalem spoke. He emphasised how modern Christianity had evolved, enabling explorations and sciences to flourish by allowing both sexes freedom to participate, contribute and benefit equally. Then he stressed that in Christianity both sexes were treated as *equal*, unlike in some faiths. The debate that followed was heated and unruly. The Muslim camp was convinced that it was an indirect attack on Islam because it is perceived by the West as outdated, especially by its treatment of women. I reminded the delegates to stick to the rules of the debate, and I managed to bring the proceedings back under control.'

'Good for you. Well done!'

'Thank you; but they only calmed down for a while. FGM (female genital mutilation) was then brought up and debated. All the delegates agreed that there was no room for such a barbaric practice in the 21st century, with a number of Muslim delegates stating that it was not grounded on the teachings of the Koran, although in general it is practised only in some Muslim countries.

Then there was a speech from a Christian girl who also stressed the equality of sexes, but she aired her doubts about virgin births, the divinity of Jesus, and whether he actually walked on water. Then she said that they must be metaphorical stories that over centuries have become part and parcel of the faith. A Muslim boy's response was that, one way or another, Christianity was based on a fairy tale. Many Christian delegates took offence at his remarks and started heckling, calling Islam names and shouting that it was breeding death-wishing fanatics who sought martyrdom through suicide attacks that slaughtered innocent men, women and children, not to mention the blessing of child brides. At the same time, some Muslims countered with reminders about the pillaging crusaders, the witch-hunts and, more recently, the boy-molesting priests. In no time the atmosphere became charged with hatred and hostility. They started stamping their feet on the floor, and then the fights started. Before I knew it, it escalated into pandemonium. I was shouting and telling them to stop but they wouldn't. The Christians started crying "Bias" and a girl threw her shoe at me.'

'Were you hurt?' Sami asked anxiously.

'No. Fortunately, it just missed my head. I left the room then and called security. They came in force and escorted the worst offenders out. Order was restored and we carried on. More delegates made their presentations and by the end of the session a range of religions had been represented. To nearly everybody's surprise the motions for change and abolition were always carried, almost unanimously. I was pleased with the progress made and of the clear outcomes. It will send a clear message to all concerned that certain changes are desirable and long overdue.'

'We had problems too,' Sami said

'What happened?'

'Two guys came to blows. There was a moment when I thought things could get really nasty and out of control. One of the delegates said that

Christianity was a peaceful religion, unlike a certain other religion, which encouraged the killing of innocent people in the name of martyrdom. The man who was sitting next to him was a Muslim; he took offence and asked the speaker to take it back, but the speaker said, 'It's the truth – I will do nothing of the sort.' That's when the first punch was thrown. Fortunately the security men came in quickly, stopped them and escorted them both out of the room. We were told later that they wouldn't be allowed to come back to the conference.'

'That was equally shocking,' Zaf said.

'Disgraceful,' Sami agreed.

'Yes, absolutely.'

They had their lunch while talking. Then they discussed the organisation of the conference, the venue and the food. In general, they thought it was very good. By then it was time to return to their groups and carry on with the business at hand. They agreed to meet at the end and share a taxi back to the hotel.

V

In the afternoon Sami's group got out of control again. The trouble started when a Muslim boy said, 'The supremacy of Islam stems from the fact that it was created by God through his messenger, Mohamed, which is prima facie evidence that God is in fact a Muslim.' There was uproar from those representing other monotheistic faiths.

When some control was re-established, a Christian girl said, 'If the previous speaker was a little more enlightened, he would know that Jesus was the *son* of God, and therefore God cannot be anything else but Christian, because anything else would make him the Antichrist, which is a contradiction.'

As further uproar followed her statement, Sami stood up and said, 'We have to accept the fact that neither premise can be verified scientifically, or disproven to the satisfaction of the two sides. These are strong beliefs, handed down through the ages. On the face of it, both cannot be right. However, we have to accept their status quo, for if we don't we must pursue the demolition of one of the two faiths because the foundations for both rest on the position that God has.' The discussion then got back on track and the topic's vote was passed with a large majority.

By the end of the day all twenty groups had thrashed out dozens of religious and theological issues, trying to iron out the differences from opposing camps. It was the quintessential purpose of the symposium to find common ground, creating respect for each other's faiths, and searching for dogma that was universally agreed to be outdated and trying to eliminate or update it. How successful their efforts would be, especially in the wider context of their religions, remained to be seen.

Sami and Zaf met afterwards as arranged and shared a taxi to the hotel. On the way back they talked about the afternoon sessions. Despite Zaf's enthusiasm and optimism at the start, they had come to the same conclusion: the issues that were raised by Hindus and Buddhists paled into insignificance compared with those raised by Christians and Muslims. The symposium was a slogging match between Christians and Muslims; the same old hatreds were resurfacing. The differences between them and other faiths were deep-rooted and it was difficult to find common ground.

Sami said, 'The only common ground that was highlighted in my group was that the monotheistic religions worship one and the same God, and that all religions strive to improve the lives and spirits of their believers. I think there should be another symposium that should be dedicated to discovering just common ground. The scope of this one is so wide.'

'You are right: I think the most we can expect from this one is to instil respect and tolerance, and a greater understanding of each other's beliefs now that the world is "shrinking" and people of all faiths intermingle.'

In regards to their personal relationship, Zaf told Sami that she still did not know what her mother was doing in the evening and that she would find out after they got back to the hotel.

VI

When they arrived, Zaf's mother was waiting for them in the foyer. She enquired how the conference had gone, and both said very well.

'Except for the fights that broke out,' Zaf qualified.

'You must tell me all about it later, over dinner,' Zaf's mother said.

They both then asked Zaf's mother about her day, and she said that she had enjoyed it but was very tired and was looking forward to sitting down in a nice restaurant and having a nice evening meal. They all agreed to go and get ready and meet downstairs again at 7pm.

The restaurant, which was recommended by the lady at reception, was within walking distance from the hotel. It had been, in some respects, a hectic and tiring day for all of them. They ordered their meals and, while waiting for them, they explained to Zaf's mother the opinions, discussions and fights that had taken place. The last topic was about a serious incident in Sami's group. It was about a Muslim boy, who said he was from the Islamic State of Iraq and the Levant (Isil).

Sami said, 'He was very uncompromising and belligerent and was saying, "The infidels should be thankful for being given the chance to convert to Islam before—" when an American Christian girl suddenly butted in with, "Are you going to kill us *all*, like you did to James Foley?"'

'Who was James Foley?' Mrs Durrani asked.

'He was the first American journalist who was beheaded by Isil in 2014. A video of the execution was posted on the internet for the world to see.' Sami explained.

'Well, what did he expect from a jihadist war zone?' Mrs Durrani commented.

'Mother! He was a civilian war correspondent. Sometimes I don't know where you're coming from.' Zaf said, questioning her mother's mentality.

Sami was taken aback, so he chose to drop the subject and did not tell them how the incident ended. For the record, the Isil boy's response was horrific, he shouted at the girl, 'How dare you question our ways?' Then he suddenly pulled out a knife and stormed towards her, screaming, 'In the name of Allah, I'll kill you, you pious American!' Sami stuck his foot out as he rushed by him, tripping him up, and was about to tackle him when two boys who were sitting next to Sami, jumped on the boy quickly, and managed to disarm and restrain him. The guards then came and escorted him off the premises whilst he was shouting 'Long live Jihad, Allah is great', and handed him to the Turkish authorities.

Mrs Durrani brushed off her daughter's criticism, and said, 'I am not surprised that there has been so much animosity between the different faiths,' and then added, 'I told you so!'

'That's why we are here, Mum: to air our differences, get some under-standing and respect for each other's faiths, and hopefully find some common ground.'

'You won't,' Zaf's mother said, 'because there isn't any.' She was adamant: it was all a waste of time!

Sami, on the other hand, was optimistic and had an open mind. 'Even if we don't find any common ground, at least we'll learn to respect each other's religions. Killing people just because they do not agree with our beliefs is inexcusable. And a dialogue between opposing sides to instil tolerance, and pave the way for mutual coexistence, is surely a good thing.'

'In other words, we should all agree to disagree,' Mrs Durrani stated stubbornly.

Zaf, changing the subject, said, 'Tell us about your day shopping and sightseeing in the city.'

'I was only looking for clothes, though I didn't find any dresses that I liked. But I did find some beautiful silk scarves – I bought one for myself and one for you, Zaf.'

'Thank you, Mum. I'd love to see it.'

'You'll probably find an excuse not to wear it but I bought it for you anyway,' her mother said in a grumpy manner.

'Oh, Mum,' Zaf protested.

'Did you manage to go and see any important places or monuments afterwards?' asked Sami.

'Yes, in fact I did,' Mrs Durrani said. 'I took a taxi to the Hagia Sophia. Do you know that it is nearly 1,500 years old and was the centre of Orthodox Christianity until 1453, when Constantinople – Istanbul as it's known now – was conquered by the Ottomans? It then became the grand mosque and was the jewel of the Muslim world until 1931, when it was secularised. Four years later it was opened as a museum. It is really grand; you ought to see it. I am looking forward to seeing the Süleymaniye Mosque tomorrow as well; it's a pity you two can't come.'

'Sorry, Mum, but I'm sure you'll enjoy going there.'

'Yes, you'll love it,' Sami added. 'From what I've read about it, it's equally magnificent, but it's not as old as the Hagia Sophia.'

After they finished their meal, Mrs Durrani asked if Sami and Zaf wanted to go with her on a city trip called "Istanbul by Night", which started at 10pm and ended at 1.30am. They both said that it could be very interesting but neither could afford the time.

Zaf said, 'I couldn't possibly spare any time because I have to summarise my group's discussions and conclusions for the plenary session tomorrow. I'll be up all night writing it and preparing my presentation of it. Sorry, Mum – I wish I could go but I can't.'

'I also have to prepare for my speech for tomorrow,' Sami said.

'That's all right; it sounds like you both have much work to do and you'll need some peace and quiet to do it, so I'll go on my own.'

There was a silent sigh of relief from Sami, as he was hoping to be alone with Zaf again. He had been thinking amorously about her all day. He just couldn't get her off his mind: she was his first love. He wanted to be with her again and again before the conference was over. That would be the end between them forever; despite the fact that he was falling head over heels in love and it was killing him!

Zaf was also relieved that her mother was going out. On the one hand, she wanted to spend time with Sami, but on the other she was genuinely concerned about the work she had to do, and getting ready for the plenary session. 'I'll try and do both,' she decided, 'even if it means working through the night.'

VII

When they got back to the hotel, Zaf's mother walked into the lift first, followed by Zaf and then Sami. Zaf was dying to send a signal to him about the night ahead, so she put her hand behind her, showing a thumbs-up sign.

Sami got the message and gave her a large smile when her mother wasn't looking.

As soon as her mother left for her tour, Zaf went to Sami's room.

He was delighted to see her and said, 'I haven't stopped thinking about you all day.'

'Listen, Sami,' she said. 'I don't want you to go potty over me, because tomorrow it will all be over. We'll both go home and...we may never see each other again.'

'I must admit, I have never felt this way for someone. I don't know what it will be like after tomorrow. Would you like a drink?'

'No thanks,' she said. 'I don't need one...' She moved close to Sami, looked into his eyes and then drew him into a passionate kiss.

Soon they were naked in bed; making love like there was no tomorrow. After they both collapsed, spent, they felt as if they were in heaven. Neither spoke for a while for fear of spoiling the moment.

'It was my first time, you know,' Sami said at last. 'You were right yesterday. Now I feel I want to be with you all the time, forever. I have fallen in love with you, so suddenly, so quickly, so madly.'

'Oh, Sami, I'm flattered, but you'll get over me soon enough – didn't I say you'd always remember your first? Now, I really have to go back to my room and do some work,' she said. Zaf got out of bed and started getting dressed.

'No, please don't go yet,' Sami begged.

'If I go now and get on with it, with a bit of luck I'll finish in plenty of time. Then I can come back and see you again before my mother returns.'

'Promise? I'll be waiting,' he said, looking lovingly at her.

'Yes, I promise,' she said. Then kissed him and left.

VIII

Sami had a shower and afterwards sat down and read his speech. He already knew it by heart and decided to recite it as he would at the conference. After trying it aloud a few times, he was satisfied with his delivery.

Not having anything else to do, he turned the television on and started watching the film that was on – "Casablanca". It was in English so he could follow it very well, and he found himself liking it very much, though he found the ending rather upsetting, to the point that tears started forming in his eyes.

It was when Rick tried to persuade Ilsa to get on a plane and leave without him, and said to her, 'We'll always have Paris.' Sami compared his situation with Zaf, and he imagined himself saying to her, 'We must go our own ways now but we'll always have Istanbul.'

There was a knock on the door. Without thinking, Sami rushed and opened it with his still-watering eyes. It was Zaf: she had come back as promised.

She noticed his eyes. 'Were you crying because you thought I was not coming?' she teased him.

'Sorry, no,' he said. 'I was watching a film that had a sad ending and my eyes started watering.'

'Which film was that?' she asked.

'Casablanca.'

'Yes, parts of it are very emotional,' she said. 'You need a drink now to cheer you up. May I also have one?'

'Yes, why not? It's a good job the minibar contents are included in the room price.'

They sat down on the bed side by side, drinking their gin and tonics. 'It will be sad tomorrow when we leave here and go our own ways, probably to never see each other again,' Sami said.

'Don't think about tomorrow; think about now,' Zaf said. She turned her head towards him and leaned over and kissed him.

It was urgent and passionate; their drinks were forgotten as they leaned back on the bed and made love again.

They knew how very little time they had left together, and when they finished Sami pleaded with Zaf to visit him in the morning before going down for breakfast.

'How can I? What shall I tell my mother?'

'I don't know. Just think of something, please.'

'I'll try, but I can't promise anything. It's best if you don't expect me, so if I do come it will be a nice surprise.' She got out of bed and started to dress. 'I have to leave now before my mother comes back.'

'I'll be thinking about you all night,' he said.

'And I'll be thinking of you,' she said as she left.

When she had gone, Sami started reflecting on the situation. Before that week, he had never experienced emotions like these. It was not just lust – he was sure he had fallen in love with her. He had believed that falling in love was a gradual process but he had been wrong: that was not what had happened with Zaf. It had been so quick. It might have been because they had made love or perhaps because he was away from home alone for the first time – it was normal for feelings and emotions to run high in those circumstances, he reasoned. The need for friendship and love was felt more then, to counter feelings of loneliness.

Sami was confused. I must learn to control my feelings and emotions, he decided. Saying goodbye to her tomorrow won't be nice; it will be heartbreaking. After being so intimate, it's inevitable. If falling in love means so much heartache then I will make sure I'm more prepared for it in future.

The last two days had been the most wonderful and exciting days of his life, without doubt, and he had no regrets. If Zaf came to him in the morning then Sami decided it would be proof that she felt the same as him. We'll see, he thought, as he drifted into a sound sleep.

IX

The alarm woke Sami up early as he had allowed enough time both for packing his few things and for Zaf, if she came to him. He showered and, as he was getting out of the shower, he heard a gentle knock on the door. He opened the door with his dressing gown over his shoulders and there she was, holding some papers and beaming.

'I told my mum that I wanted you to read my notes before I hand them in,' Zaf said as she entered, closing the door behind her.

Sami took the papers from her and put them on the table by the bed. He knew that they didn't have much time but he wanted her and sensed that she wanted him just as much.

He turned around, wrapped his right arm around her waist and pulled her towards him, threading the fingers of his left hand through her hair. Her familiar perfume alone filled his nostrils with ecstasy. She put her hands inside his dressing gown and hugged his body, her grip tight and urgent. As he looked down she turned her head up to face him, their mouths met and they kissed passionately. He let his dressing gown drop on the floor as he undressed her quickly, urgently, and both tumbled into bed. His hands, lips and tongue were all over her breasts, while she groaned with ecstasy, spontaneously overwhelmed by what was happening within her. What a quick learner, she thought fleetingly. Moments later he was on top of her. Slowly the rhythm escalated and culminated in a simultaneous, mighty climax.

Afterwards, Zaf whispered in his ear, 'I want you so much, it hurts. I find you so attractive, I can't help it. When you stood opposite me in the lift when we arrived, I felt weak at the knees. I couldn't stop looking and smiling at you, hoping that you would speak to us.'

'Actually, I did notice you looking at me and smiling, but I didn't know what to make of it.'

'I was flirting with you. I was so glad when my mother spoke to you. But now I have to go back, my Adonis. I'll see you at breakfast.'

During breakfast, Sami told Zaf that he had read her notes and thought that they were very well written. And that he liked her firm conclusions for the changes needed in order to bring some faiths, in particular Islam, into the current millennium.

'Specifically, which one do you think is best?' she asked.

'That suicide bombing in order to kill people should be declared a crime.'

'Personally, I think that was long overdue,' Zaf agreed.

'Surely that would outlaw jihad?' her mother said.

'Yes, Mother, it would, because the infidels are also human, and homicide is a heinous crime, no matter how you dress it up.' She turned back to Sami. 'Was there anything else that stood out?'

'Well, the abolition of polygamy for men,' Sami said.

'Even I agree with that. That's long overdue for sure,' Mrs Durrani said.

'I don't agree with the alternative though: polygamy for both sexes. How will that help women and society?' Sami asked Zaf.

'That's absurd!' Zaf's mother exclaimed before Zaf had a chance to reply.

'It's all a question of equal rights, Mum. Anyway, we have to get going. If there is anything else, you can tell me about it in the taxi, Sami.'

On the way, Mrs Durrani asked them what they thought about the symposium so far. Sami said that he had been surprised by the huge miscellany of issues and the strength of delegates' beliefs, even over aspects that appeared, to a great number of others, to be nonsensical.

'Exactly – I could have told you that. How can you achieve harmony with, and respect for, such religions? Islam may not be perfect but it is far superior to any other religion.'

'Those are isolated and extreme instances, Mother. I think the symposium will succeed in the promotion of better understanding of different faiths, and in highlighting the need for change. In fact, for a great number of the issues we discussed in my group, there was unanimous agreement among delegates for change.'

'As I said before, I think that nothing real will come of it. The ideological shift required for any meaningful changes in our faith is insurmountable.' With those parting words, Zaf's mother got out of the taxi to go and spend the day sightseeing.

When she had gone, Zaf took Sami's hand and said, 'I am going to miss you after today. It's terrible knowing that most likely I'll never see you again.'

'I feel exactly the same: as I already confessed, you are my first real love and I will never get over or forget you. Will you at least write to me?'

'Of course I will,' she said. 'You must give me your address. I'll give you mine now.'

The two young lovers exchanged addresses, by which time they had arrived at the conference. Both went to the plenary session; Zaf sat at the top table with the other group leaders and the Senior Committee who were there as observers, and Sami sat in the front row with the other speakers for the day.

X

A young man stood up after everybody was seated. He introduced himself and explained that he was the assigned leader for the plenary session. He would call upon the speakers of the day to make their presentations and then invite delegates to comment. He said that it was very likely that the speakers would cover topics that had already been discussed but that it should not prevent new discussions and voting on the issues if necessary. 'In a way, today's debates are more important than all the others, both because of the size of the audience and because the delegates are now more informed,' he concluded.

The first delegate to speak was a Hindu boy from Deshnok. He explained that in Hinduism the soul moved on after death to another living being, which could be anything – animal, bird, fish, etc. – towards its eventual oneness with the universe. 'This cycle of moving on is known as *samsara*,' he said. He then went on to say that he was pleased with this aspect of his faith. It did not depict a paradise or hell for the soul and it taught people to improve their present life so that the next one would be better. Conversely, it taught that if people did bad things in their present life, then their next life would be made worse.

He continued, 'An important theological point is that our Gods and Goddesses can take any form, even that of a rat, which brings me to the problem I have. In my village we have the Karni Mata Temple, which is dedicated to rats and treats them like royalty. I regret having to admit that there is a grain of truth in the opinion that the rat is in reality a dirty rodent – certainly it is known more for the diseases that it causes or helps to spread than its holiness. Because they are cared for they are multiplying at an alarming rate; sooner or later they will spread outside the temple and we'll cause an epidemic.'

The debate that followed was not at all constructive. Some of the delegates tried to ridicule the issue as not dissimilar to attributing holiness to scatology. A delegate from the UK stated that the world would have been better off without the rat. The best way to exterminate the thousands and thousands that lived in the temple was by poisonous gas, he suggested.

The chairman put an end to the debate, reminding the non-constructive respondents that their behaviour showed a deep-rooted and old-fashioned hatred and prejudice towards other religions, which was against the spirit of the symposium.

XI

A number of other delegates delivered their speeches before it was Sami's turn as the first extended speaker. By then his theme had been covered many times but he delivered it with clarity, enthusiasm and conviction, and it was well received. During the discussion that followed one of the delegates said,

'How can the speaker on the one hand praise his faith for its strength and resilience to change, and on the other propose a change. Surely the second point negates the first?'

To which Sami responded, 'Yes, your comment is valid. I gave my speech as it was originally written, and at that time I thought one request for change would not nullify my argument. But now, listening to endless requests for change, I see that it is never just "one request for change", and the point about resilience is a past strength that should not be marginalised, but at the same time should not be allowed to become a weakness. It is clear that in the 21st century there is no room for archaic dogmas, and there are so many things in our modern lives that were beyond the imagination of those alive when Islam was new – are we supposed to shun these or *must* Islam embrace change before it becomes irrelevant to a new generation?'

Another delegate then asked Sami to elaborate on why, exactly, he believed that women were not treated equally by Islam.

Sami said that he would be glad to, and started by saying that the reasons had already been alluded to by a number of speakers on both days. 'To begin with,' he said, 'free-thinking women are unacceptable, so they are deprived of the right to be educated, or vote – in some countries around the world women have been allowed to vote for centuries. They do not have the right to drive a car, work, travel or open a bank account without permission from a male relative or guardian. In some Muslim countries rape victims are treated as criminals and little girls are forced into marriage before they stop playing with dolls. Finally, multiple women should not be enslaved by marriage to the same man, like a herd of sheep provided for a ram.'

Sami sighed and admitted, 'People around the world, especially in the West, are ranting and raving about the treatment of women by Islam. The Arab Spring had set things in motion for women's rights but it has since stalled. However, let me remind you that no religion is perfect. Horrendous crimes have been carried out through the ages by the leaders of many different religions, or by fanatics who obeyed their teachings blindly. Many atrocities have been carried out, not only against people of other faiths but against people of the *same* faith. There are numerous instances throughout history that demonstrate this.'

Sami paused and turned towards the chairman, asking if he could carry on, since by then he had exceeded his allotted time. The chairman nodded and Sami continued.

'We hear a lot about religious violence but very little about religious suppression, which is just as bad and harder to detect. Not only atrocities but also suppression is wrong because, among other things, it curtails people's freedom. Article 18 of the Universal Declaration of Human Rights United Nations 1948 states that everyone has the right to freedom of thought, conscience and religion; this right includes freedom to change his religion or belief.

'Freedom is a *basic* human right and people should be free to believe and practise their faith as they wish – so long as doing so does not harm others. They must be just as free to hold opinions which may be considered offensive by their own or other faiths. It's a natural human instinct to strive for freedom; without freedom there can be no enlightenment.

'All the representatives here, myself included, have praised their faith but also condemned aspects of it. Some religious beliefs and practices appear to rely on hearsay, handed down from generation to generation, which has been taken as gospel, irrespective of how implausible our knowledge of the world around us makes it. I am sure I am not the only one here today who thinks that many religious beliefs and practices are illogical and inhumane. And while their followers continue to blindly comply, things will not change.

'We are pressured to carry on in the status quo by those in spiritual authority and, if we do, we thereby lose our freedom. We value and protect our freedom, whether spiritual or physical. In doing so, we demonstrate our understanding and moral obligation to bestow freedom on others and defend their right to it. That is why, at this symposium, we must recognise our respect and understanding of the right of people to acquire and enjoy their freedom. The corollary of this is that our rights to freedom are *equal* – my freedom does not supersede that of someone else; I may not blow up an infidel, for they have a right to the freedom to worship as they will.'

There were murmurs from the listening delegates. 'In my opinion,' Sami pressed on, 'freedom is the most common ground among faiths. And if people ask for explanations and reasoned answers as to why some things are practised, they should be entitled to do so. One should be able to debate such issues without fear of condemnation or punishment by zealots of their faith who, by doing so, demonstrate their fear of losing their stranglehold on enlightenment. We have reached an enlightened era; an age where scientific proof and information is at our fingertips. Religions should no longer expect the faithful to be contented entirely by "blind faith".'

An angry delegate stood up and interjected, 'You do not need proof to have faith in Allah; that's *why* it is called "faith" – or do you not even know the meaning of the word you throw around so casually? Why are you representing your faith if you are so sceptical of it?'

Sami turned towards the standing delegate and said, 'Firstly, I know what the word "faith" means. But that's how it was in the Middle Ages, when people in general were not educated and the sciences were not advanced. Now, in the 21st century, people expect more to base their conviction on. Secondly, I am not sceptical about my faith but neither am I blind to its flaws – the things that it would have us do out of habit that are no longer relevant.'

Looking at the wider audience again, Sami concluded, 'We are all here to air our convictions and doubts about our faiths and the cultures surrounding those faiths. Doing so is the only way to highlight the need for change, and that is the quintessence of the symposium.' He turned towards the chairman and said, 'Thank you for allowing me this time to speak.'

When Sami sat down he received a standing ovation for his frank and daring talk.

The voting that followed was almost unanimous in declaring that respect should be given to both spiritual and physical freedom – the common ground between all human beings. In addition, a resolution was passed declaring that women must be treated as equal to men. The proposal that condemned and abolished malpractices and outdated dogma was also passed, though by a very narrow margin.

A number of other extended speakers followed with their presentations and then there was a brief break for lunch.

XII

After lunch the group leaders presented their summaries and conclusions from the group sessions of the previous day. The same message came up time and again: freedom, tolerance and better understanding of other faiths. There were also numerous requests for changes to outdated dogma and an end to malpractices, from almost all faiths.

In conclusion, the delegates were thanked by the organisers for their attendance and contributions. It was also announced that all the speeches, and conclusions reached by the symposium, would be published in the form of a book, which would be available in due course. The organisers asked for those interested in a copy to register their names with them and that the price would be decided by the level of interest.

Sami and Zaf met again by the entrance of the venue and got a taxi back to the hotel together to collect their luggage and meet Zaf's mother who was waiting for her. They sat in the taxi thinking about the results of the symposium, and about their relationship, which was doomed to end then and there. They held hands throughout the taxi ride and made promises to keep in touch by letter, as Sami did not have a phone or Internet access.

They arrived at the hotel and collected their luggage. Sami was leaving first as his flight was earlier than theirs. When Zaf and Sami said goodbye, the two young lovers were almost in tears. Mrs Durrani noticed that they embraced and were whispering to each other for a long while and she wondered why.

Later, when they were on their plane, Zaf thought of the fact that she was flying west and he was flying east, destined never to meet again, and wished the symposium had been longer.

Her mother asked her why she was upset.

Not lying, she said, 'Mum, I enjoyed the conference and our stay in Istanbul so much, I wished it would never end.'

'Well, I was very pleased you got on well with Sami,' her mother said. 'You cheered up and forgot our altercation from last week; I hope you've got over splitting up with John now.'

'What?' Zaf exclaimed. 'You're forgetting that it was you and dad that split us up!'

'We won't go into it again but you must realise that we did it because we love you; it's for your own good.'

XIII

Sami was also thinking of his love affair with Zaf as he flew in the opposite direction; he felt a sharp pang as he realised he was missing her already. He had known it would end as quickly as it had started but he had never thought it would upset him so much. He hoped she would at least write to him and keep their memories alive.

His parents were very pleased to see him when he returned home, just as much as he was to see them. They of course wanted to know all about the conference and its outcome, though they were negative about its purpose, just like his teacher, Hamid, and Mrs Durrani had been. Not wishing to upset them, he did not dwell much on the proposed changes.

A few days later the first letter from Zaf arrived. He was so pleased he couldn't wait to open it. It was very intimate, or so it felt to him, full of how she was missing his company and that every night she prayed to Allah that they would somehow meet again. She also told him that her mother was very pleased that the two of them had got on so well, and was hoping that she had forgotten John Murphy – the English boyfriend they had forced her to break up with – but that her parents were wrong; she had not forgotten him.

Her letters continued to arrive twice a week and he would write back to her each time. This continued for a few months and then he started to receive letters less and less frequently, until the day he received what he knew would be her last letter to him. It was all about John Murphy; how they had managed to meet again and resume their relationship. She wrote that if her parents and brothers threatened her again, she would run away with John and they would seek asylum in the US. She said she still thought about him and the wonderful time they had had in Istanbul but her heart had always truly belonged to John. Under the circumstances, she said, she was not going to write to him anymore and hoped that he would understand.

Sami had known that it would come to this sooner or later, but he was still not ready for it. He had looked forward to reading her letters; it had pleased him that she still thought of him and, he had believed, wished like he did that they could be reunited – even married. However, he took what he could from it: it was a lesson to be learned and now that it had ended he had to move on.

He wrote her a short letter, just to wish her happiness and a good life with John. But she never replied, and for years he often wondered if they had made it to America, or if something had happened to her. Honour killings were all too common.

XIV

When Sami was nearly seventeen and had just one more year to finish high school, Hamid asked him what he was going to do after. Sami knew that his chances of going to university were zero. His parents couldn't afford it. So he was planning to find a job as a clerk or something, preferably in some government department.

Hamid was not very impressed with that and said, 'You won't get very far without a university degree, Sami.'

'What's the alternative?' Sami queried. 'I suppose I could stay here with my parents and carry on working occasionally for Dr Omar, or become a goatherd and take over from my father one day.'

'A brilliant boy like you should be thinking about going to university, and a good one at that, not staying in this remote, hick village and ending up as a goatherd.'

Sami shrugged and said, 'The way things are, I cannot see me going to university, so I am not going to upset my parents by talking to them about it. They know, and I know, that they can't afford to send me to university.'

'Right you are, Sami. I am sorry for bringing the subject up; I was not trying to upset you.'

During the summer vacation of that year, Sami stayed in the village as usual with his parents and carried on working for Dr Omar. Living in a small village, it was inevitable that Sami and Hamid would bump into each other occasionally. Hamid always made a point of talking to him about something or other. On one such occasion, he told him that there was a scholarship to study at Harvard University in the US in a year's time. 'If you are interested you should apply. In my opinion, you are the ideal candidate. Why don't you?' Hamid suggested.

'What's the scholarship for?' enquired Sami.

'It's for studying Mathematics and English,' Hamid answered.

Sami told him that he liked the idea but that he would have to discuss it with his parents first.

He did, they advised him to apply, and in due course he was awarded the scholarship. It was a four-year degree scholarship and, as it was specifically for Harvard, he would have to leave the village and his parents and go to America.

Although his parents were delighted for him, they were also sad, as he would be going away for very long periods. He was their only child and they knew they would miss him immensely. He would also miss them, as he loved them very dearly; they were the people he most cared about in the world.

'I'll be coming home during the summer vacations,' Sami promised his parents.

'I am worried about you, living in some faraway place, all alone, with no one to look after you,' his mother said.

'Mum, I am a grown man now, I can look after myself. And although I will miss you, I will have my books for company. I will be busy studying so I won't have time to be lonely. Anyway, it isn't for another year yet,' he said, trying to allay her fears.

*

During the following year Sami was very busy with his high school studies and with some pre-admission work he had to do for Harvard.

That year went by very quickly and Sami graduated from his high school with flying colours. In the summer he worked for Dr Omar as usual and spent the evenings with his parents. By the middle of August he was ready to go to America to start studying for a BA at one of the most prestigious universities in the world.

On the day he was to leave, the whole village came to say goodbye and wish him good luck. He was the first person from the whole province to go to a foreign university. He was sad to say goodbye to them all, especially to his teacher, Hamid, to whom he said, 'I owe it all to you and I would like to thank you from the bottom of my heart. It's befitting at this moment to recite what Alexander the Great said: "To my father I owe my life, but to my teacher I owe my *good* life."'

'I was just doing my job, Sami. May Allah be with you.'

Sami then turned to Dr Omar and said to him, 'I promise you, Dr Omar, I will be back, definitely in the summer – every summer until I graduate – to work for you until I finish paying for the scrubland you sold to me. Both my parents and I are very grateful for it.'

'Don't mention it, Sami. Just do your best at Harvard – thousands of students would give their eye-teeth for a chance to go there. Good luck.'

He left his parents until last to say goodbye to. They put on brave faces, trying hard to hold back their tears. He was their only child and he had never stayed away from home for long, and now he was leaving for such a long time. They knew that they were really going to miss him.

'Don't be sad, Mum and Dad,' Sami said. 'I'll be thinking of you all the time, and don't worry about me; I can look after myself.'

'We know you can,' his mum said. 'But you must read the Koran and pray to Allah every day, to help you and keep you from harm.'

'I will, Mum. I will.'

'And we will pray to Allah for you too, son,' his father added as Sami headed for the bus. 'Goodbye – may Allah be with you always.'

Part Nine

I

By the age of eighteen, Sami was a handsome looking man: six feet tall, with blue eyes, longish black hair and a short beard. He had promised his parents as an eleven-year-old that he would grow a beard in return for their agreement not to have him circumcised, but kept it trimmed and neat rather than letting it grow wild. He looked and dressed just like any other young man and felt comfortable in his new environment. He allowed himself ten days to settle in and familiarise himself with his new surroundings before the start of the fall term at Harvard.

Both at college and everywhere he went, he was impressed by how polite everyone was. People were generally very civil and helpful – not at all what he had imagined. It was a different world; many other things proved a welcome surprise to him. It was a luxurious world, replete with opulence, amazing architecture and wide, well-kept roads full of expensive-looking cars. The people were smart and looked happy; and to his mind the women were beautiful and sexy. He was very attracted to them but he was determined not to let it distract him. When he had been growing up in his tiny, peasant village, he had dreamed and fantasised that some day he would go and see, or even live, in one of the glamorous cities in the West that he used to read about. He was now living the dream and secretly wished he would never wake up. However, he was there for one thing only – education; he would have to subdue his dream wish. Besides, the women were mostly infidels; it wouldn't be right for him.

But as a young man his physical emotions were running rampant; it was normal and his thoughts flitted from guilt to pleasure and back. He realised that the problem wouldn't go away; the only way to ignore it was to become engrossed in his studies – his sole reason for coming thousands of miles from his home.

Quickly, he was absorbed in his work – so much so that sometimes he even forgot to pray. There were so many lectures and tutorials to attend, research to undertake, and projects to complete. It was a question of prioritising. He could not afford to fall behind and, above all, he was not going to let his parents down. They would be missing him too; he had to do well in America and go back to them a better man.

To keep physically fit, Sami joined two college sports societies: swimming and basketball. He was sure that both would keep him mentally and physically fit.

That was how he spent his first year. The time flew by. Sami found it a tough year, but due to the amount of sheer hard work he got through his exams. In the summer he went back home to his parents, who were delighted to see him, as was Dr Omar, who was also grateful to have another pair of hands to work on his estate.

II

Once a year, a school inspector called Rastin used to visit and inspect Hamid's school. Over the years Hamid got to know him well and, when he was inspecting the schools of the province, he used to stay with Hamid's family and travel from there. Although he had been married for a number of years he had no children. But he wanted children, and since his wife could not have any he decided to take a second wife, hoping that she would produce children. Hamid's daughter, Hasti, was an eligible young woman by then, of marrying age. Her parents, since Rastin had a good government position and Hasti liked him, agreed to the marriage. That had been three years ago but she too had not succeeded in having children.

By then Rastin was in his late thirties. Desperate for children, he wanted to take a third wife, in the hope that she could bear them. Hasti was averse to the idea and towards the end of the summer she came back from Kabul, where she lived with her husband, to her parents for a couple of weeks. She wanted to discuss the problem with them and her aunt Samira who was also staying there with Jacob, her husband. Hasti's father, Hamid, had already decided to take up the matter with Rastin; he was going to tell him that the ball was in his court but he should not use it as an excuse to get yet another wife.

The Friday before Sami was due to fly back to the US, he went to the mosque for the special Jumu'ah prayer as usual. After prayers, he was chatting with Dr Omar, Hamid and Jacob, and before they all parted and headed home Hamid said to Sami and Dr Omar, 'Why don't you both come to lunch with my family tomorrow? We'll have a nice lunch and you can tell us about America and your studies at Harvard, Sami.'

'I'd be delighted,' Dr Omar said.

'Well, that's very kind of you, Hamid, I would love to,' Sami responded.

'Come about 12.30pm,' Hamid told them.

*

The following day, Dr Omar gave Sami a lift to Hamid's house. When they arrived they were welcomed by the whole family; they all knew each other well. There was Hamid, his wife Sheeva, his daughter Hasti, Jacob and his wife Samira.

The food was plentiful, and beautifully laid out; a floor spread, known as the dastarkhan, was ready. It was and still is an important expression of culture in Afghanistan, and a plentiful dastarkhan is necessary when having guests.

It included a variety of traditional Afghan foods like kebabs, tandoori chicken, nan, extra long rice, and Qabili Palao – the national dish made with meat, stock and topped with fried raisins, slivered carrots and pistachios. There was also a number of side dishes including a salad.

For drinks they had Shomleh, or Shlombeh, a cold drink made of water, yoghurt and fresh or dried mint; a common drink used in Afghanistan at lunchtime during the summer.

Sami was very surprised by the abundance of so much nice food; his family's lunches and dinners were very frugal in comparison. He thought that Hamid must have a good income as a teacher and vizier.

Hamid had always been fascinated by and admired Sami's intellectual ability when he had been his teacher at the elementary school. Sami had always been the star pupil. On many occasions he had said to Sami, "Your ability to learn, and thirst for knowledge, is like a dry sponge: when it's immersed in water it absorbs a lot instantly." At one stage during the lunch Hamid asked Sami to tell them how he coped with his studies and everything else in a strange and non-Muslim country.

'I found it hard to start with, as my standard was well below that of the other students, and I struggled at first. I had to put in the hours in order to catch up; it was work, work and more work for a long time.'

'Don't tell me you didn't have time to pray five times a day?' Jacob asked.

'I did pray a few times a day at first, but then my studies took all my time and energy, and I am ashamed to admit that sometimes I used to forget to pray.'

Hamid's wife looked at her daughter; they both frowned. She then said, 'I think Western education is bad for Islam and should be avoided by all Muslims. Anyway, how did you like the people, Sami? I mean living among all those infidels – it must have been awful.'

'Well, actually, I found them very civil; I didn't encounter any hostility. Ordinarily, faith is never broached. I have formed the opinion that religion is not important to Americans – most of them are Christians in name only.

They are weary of their faith and it doesn't feature in their daily lives. But when Islam is mentioned they feel threatened.'

'Sooner or later, Islam will prevail all over the world; this century Islam is galloping west, next century it will gallop eastwards to India, China and Japan,' Hamid declared.

'Yes, it will; it's only a question of time,' Jacob added in support.

'However, people of different faiths need to get on with each other. I know that we are taught to deny tolerance to other faiths but the world has shrunk and inevitably we do encounter and mix with people of other faiths. That's happening all over the world,' Dr Omar chipped in.

'I suppose,' Sami said, 'the importance of religion must first be reduced to the level of indifference; similar to, say, different diets among people. For example, I do not care if someone I know is a vegetarian or prefers beef to goat's meat. When that happens, warring faiths will stop fighting each other. Only then will lasting peace—'

'That will never happen,' Hamid interjected. 'Surely you don't think that our passion for our faith will ever diminish?'

'In theory it could; because of globalisation, international travel and immigration. Many countries, especially in the West, have become multi-ethnic and multi-faith societies. By living together, people's prejudices and strength of feeling towards ethnicity and faith will change; in time faith will lose its importance in people's daily lives. It's inevitable and necessary, otherwise religious conflict in the world will continue, ad infinitum.'

By the time he stopped talking some of the people around the dastarkhan were gobsmacked. Sami noticed their expression and realised that they had not taken it in the spirit it was intended, so he repeated with emphasis, 'In theory, that is.'

Dr Omar, changing the subject, asked Sami when he was going back to the States, and Sami replied, 'Next week.'

'Reading between the lines, I guess you are looking forward to going back,' Hamid's wife said.

'Well, I need to get back and start studying again, as I haven't done any during the whole of the summer.'

'I hope it wasn't because you've been working on my estate every day,' Dr Omar said.

Sami laughed and said, 'Well, as a matter of fact it was – but I'm not complaining. I'm lucky to have had a job during the whole of the summer.'

After that, the conversation centred on education, poverty and the economy in Afghanistan. Sometime after they had finished lunch, Dr Omar invited them all to his house for dinner the following Saturday. They were all delighted and accepted his invitation, except for Sami, who regretted he would not be able to as he would have gone back to the US by then. Sami and Dr Omar then thanked their hosts and left.

III

The second year at Harvard passed pretty much the same as the first, and in the summer Sami returned home. One Friday, when he was coming out of the mosque, he waved to Hamid and Jacob as they turned and headed for home, but they did not respond; they probably did not see him, he thought.

At the time, Hamid was telling Jacob that it was Dr Omar who had set up the scholarship for Sami at Harvard because his parents were very poor and he was extremely bright and deserved it.

'Does Sami know that?' Jacob asked.

'No, he doesn't.'

'I don't understand,' commented Jacob.

Hamid then confided in Jacob: he recalled the events as they had unfolded when the transporters were bringing the babies to him after the abduction.

'I was woken by the sound of the phone ringing. When I answered, the man on the other end was distressed; his voice sounded weak and his breathing was laboured, as if he was in great pain. It was Farouk, and he said, "There has been a horrific turn of events tonight, Hamid; it's all gone wrong. We were hit by American soldiers at a checkpoint outside Kabul. I drove through it and they shot at us. They are all dead except me and one of the babies, and I have been hit in the stomach. Bring bandages, a pick and shovel. We must bury them. Come quickly, hurry, please."

'"That's terrible, and not what I wanted to hear," I said. "After all the care and planning!" Then, to be sympathetic, I said, "Forgive me, Farouk, this is not the time for recriminations. You sound awful. Tell me where you are and I will be there as soon as I can." He told me where to find him, and I picked up what medical stuff I could find, along with a garden shovel and a pick. I set off as fast as I could but despite Farouk's directions it took me some time to locate the car. By then the night was giving way to first light. I approached the car and saw to my horror that Farouk was slumped against the steering wheel where he had bled to death. They were all dead, except for the baby boy who slept soundly in the back of the car, completely unaware of the horror around him.

'I knew then that the mission had failed,' Hamid continued, 'so I had to deal with the incriminating evidence. I pulled out Farouk's body and drove the car a few feet away and began digging next to the remains of the dirt wall. I carried on until I was satisfied that it was large enough to take all the bodies. Tired, groaning with effort, I dragged the corpses out of the car, one by one, and pushed them into the pit. Then I turned my attention to the sleeping baby. It was true that Abdul had wanted two babies, but there was nothing anyone could do about the fact that only one had survived. That's at least some degree of success, I thought.'

Jacob's mouth gaped as he listened in silence.

'I filled the makeshift grave and then loosened the earth around the wall until it became unstable. With a big shove I managed to topple it over on top of the grave, neatly covering the freshly dug ground beneath. I was pleased with that; it was impossible to tell that a grave was hidden beneath the rubble, and the fallen wall crumbling further would arouse no suspicion.

'I still had to get rid of the car; it was stolen and it was full of evidence of the abduction. I had a vague knowledge of the area so I decided to drive the car to the top of the ridge, set it on fire and push it down the ravine, hoping that it would look like an unfortunate accident. I transferred the baby and its belongings to my own car and locked it. Then I drove the stolen car to the top of the ravine – a few feet from the edge of the precipice. Pushing a strip of cloth into the petrol tank I waited a minute for it to absorb some liquid, then removed it and tore it into smaller pieces that I scattered around inside the car. With the engine running and the handbrake off, I lit a match and threw it into the car. The petrol-soaked cloth burst into flames as I pushed the car over the edge. It tumbled over and over until it struck the bottom of the ravine, where it exploded into a ball of flames and smoke, and I left the scene.'

'And the baby?' Jacob asked.

'I returned to my own car and was relieved to find the baby still inside, peacefully sucking his thumb. I fed it some of the milk I had been able to rescue from the transporters' car and set off for my village. But while I was driving back home, the horror of what had happened started to haunt me and I began to think what the consequences might be. Abdul Hassan had had an accord with "mum", his contact. That accord had been broken with the death of the baby girl. Likewise the transporters were also dead. Abdul Hassan would be furious – and there was only me remaining to take the blame…

'When I arrived at Abdul's mansion, I couldn't believe what had happened to it. Omar told me about the drone attack and the death of his parents. He had started his PhD course as a mature student at the university in Kabul, and fortunately for him he was away from home at the time.

'He was inquiring about the baby that I was holding and I told him that I had organised its abduction in accordance with his father's instructions. I told him that all the documents relating to the baby were in the envelope, which I gave him. After a short discussion about what to do with the baby, we decided to have it adopted by Mr and Mrs Hussein. I left with the baby and took it to them; they were over the moon and they have been thanking Allah ever since.'

'Well, they are still happy, and so is Sami; perfect,' said Jacob.

'Except that I have regretted it ever since – having him adopted in my village, I mean.'

'Why? What's wrong with that?' Jacob asked.

Hamid confided in him further about the trouble he had had, over the publication of the first photograph of his twin brother, and how he had resorted to killing Halabi in order to save himself. He also told Jacob about the botched attempt to have Sami run over by a car and that he wished he did not have to be reminded of all those things every time he saw Sami.

'It was all in the name of Allah, Hamid; no need to feel guilty about it.'

'I wish there had been a better closure to that saga.'

'Perhaps I could do something about it for you, once and for all. I do travel to the US sometimes on business; I could pay my respects to the son of the infidels. As long as he is alive, there will always be a possibility that the whole messy business will erupt.'

'Perhaps you are right but I still can't see a neat end to it. I don't want things to get worse. I like the guy and admire his intellectual ability – that's why I have helped him on more than one occasion. Over the years I have been torn between my duty as a teacher and my guilt for not pursuing the cause.'

'Okay, I understand,' Jacob replied, and the subject was closed.

The next time Jacob saw Sami in the village he greeted him with a big smile and told him how lucky he was to be returning to one of the top universities of the world. Sami told him that he was getting ready to go back and was looking forward to it. Jacob also inquired about the weather in the US and then he asked Sami how he travelled to the university every day. Sami told him that he walked there and back because it was not too far and he liked the exercise. After that Sami excused himself, as he was on his way to work on Dr Omar's estate and had to go.

IV

By his third year at Harvard, Sami had become more confident and relaxed about his studies. He found his course subjects quite easy, which left him with more time to socialise and engage in his favourite sport – swimming. Whereas in the previous two years he had had little time for friends, he now started mixing more and going out with his fellow students to restaurants, the cinema, or parties, especially at weekends.

It was during one of these parties that he was introduced to Alisha, an Arab princess who was also studying at Harvard, doing a PhD. Sami was instantly mesmerised and smitten by her looks. The first time he saw her she was wearing a colourful silk scarf and a snug-fitting dress that accented her tall, slender and shapely body. She had an oval, demure face, large chestnut-coloured eyes and full lips. Furthermore, she possessed great poise and had a charming and lively personality.

Back home Sami had had lots of girlfriends but nothing intimate. He had met his first love when he was sixteen, in Istanbul, when he went there for The Young People's Interfaith Symposium. But since arriving in the US to study, he had not had any relationships.

As the evening progressed, Sami and Alisha became more absorbed in each other's conversation, so that anyone watching them and their body language would easily have concluded that they were very attracted to each other. Alisha was fascinated by Sami's tales of the way of life back home in his remote village and how he had ended up being a student at Harvard. She was captivated by him; each time she asked him a question, she would lean over and touch his arm or hand. Sami would look straight into her beautiful eyes as he told her how his family scraped a living from herding goats and raising a few meagre crops.

'Life was, and still is, very hard in my village,' he said. 'I am so lucky to be here, living this kind of life. In fact, I often have misgivings about my being so fortunate.'

'I'm so impressed, considering where and how you grew up. You've done well and you deserve it, Sami. You have worked hard to get here. You have to take what's coming your way if you want to get ahead in life,' Alisha said. 'Look at me: I have had everything I could ever have wanted in my life. Do I feel guilty about it? No, I don't.'

As it was getting late, Alisha told him that she had to go home. Sami tried to persuade her to stay longer but she explained to him that she never stayed long after other people had started to leave – she was never the first to arrive or the last to leave.

Sami wished he could see her again but felt that, being a princess, he couldn't just ask her out. Instead he said to her, 'It's been a pleasure meeting you, and a wonderful evening. I hope that we'll meet again.'

'For me too,' she said. 'My parents are coming here next week for a few days, so give me a call the week after. Here is my number.'

Sami didn't know what to make of it. He was pleased that she had given him her number, but by the time he was meant to call her she might well have forgotten about him. He therefore decided to keep her number and call, but did not realistically expect anything to come of it.

Ten days later, Sami phoned Alisha. To his surprise she seemed genuinely pleased to hear from him.

'I've been waiting for you to call,' she said. 'I started to think you weren't going to.'

'Well, you told me that your parents were coming so I didn't call before. Anyway, did they come, and did you all have a nice time?'

'Yes, they did, and we had a lovely time. Listen, do you want to meet for coffee, or perhaps dinner sometime?' she asked.

'Yes, I'd like that very much. How about tonight at Sidoli's? It's near the university – about 7.30pm?'

'Yes, I know it. I'll see you there then,' she said and hung up.

Sidoli's was a local Italian restaurant that was very popular with students. Sami and Alisha were both excited about seeing each other again and, once at the restaurant, they were soon engrossed in conversation. They talked so freely and easily to each other that it was as if they'd been friends for years. They had a wonderful time, enjoying each other's company, and they were also attracted physically to each other. The evening passed very quickly and ended with them agreeing to meet again the following Saturday.

After a few weeks of seeing each other, Alisha invited Sami back to her apartment. Sami did not know how to take their relationship to the next level because of the difference in their status, so he was relieved when she took the initiative. Alisha lived in an upmarket place in town. On arrival, Sami was met by a middle-aged man who came out of the elevator. 'I am Cairo,' he introduced himself, 'her Highness's attendant; she is waiting for you.'

Cairo took Sami up to Alisha's apartment. She was with a middle-aged woman who was introduced as Mrs Cairo, the cook and housekeeper. The apartment was very large and beautifully decorated with stylish furniture, Persian rugs and fine art paintings.

After offering them drinks, Mrs Cairo went off to the kitchen to prepare dinner. They ate in the dining room, which was as impressive as the sitting room. The large dining table was set for two and, once dinner had been served, Mrs Cairo left them alone. After eating they retired to the sitting room and sat together on an expensive sofa with a beautiful rug in front of it.

'How does it work with Mr and Mrs Cairo? I mean, what do they do?' enquired Sami.

'Well, Cairo is my chauffeur and bodyguard, and his wife is my maid: she looks after the apartment and cooks. She does everything for me. They live on the ground floor and they also look after my parents when they come and stay here.'

'I guessed that that was what they did. I hope you didn't mind me asking.'

'No, I didn't.'

'Do you have any brothers and sisters?'

'Yes, of course, many,' she said. She got up and went to her study and quickly reappeared with an album in her hands. 'Here, let me show you.' She opened it up and showed him the first photograph; it was large, with a lot of people in it. It looked as though it had been taken by a professional photographer. Sami recognised her immediately; she was in the front row, standing between a young-looking woman and a middle-aged man.

'There you are; I can see even at that age you were gorgeous,' he said, laughing.

'Yes, that's me. I was fourteen. And that's my mother and father.' She went on, pointing at each person and explaining who they were. Then she said, 'My mother only had me but as I explained, my father has four other wives and from them I have twelve half-brothers and nine half-sisters. Although I know them all well, I am not very close with any of them; my mother is the youngest and my father spends most of his time with us. There is quite a lot of jealousy between the wives and my siblings, as you can imagine, but I don't care.' With that, she closed the album, looked at him, and said jokingly, 'Is there anything else you want to know?'

'All right then, tell me, what do Mr and Mrs Cairo think about leaving us here alone, together?'

'Look, Sami, I don't know where you've been hiding for the past few decades but since the Arab Spring, things have changed for Arab women where I come from.'

He was glad to hear that and said so. He put his arm around her shoulders and pulled her towards him, thrilled as she leaned over and her head touched his. He turned his head and looked into her eyes, then kissed her slowly, gently and then passionately. She responded in the same way and with enthusiasm. After a few moments, Sami whispered in her ear, 'Shall we move into the bedroom?' He was sure she would say yes.

'No, Sami, not so fast,' she said. 'Actually, I think it's time for you to leave.' She stood and moved away from him. 'It's late. I'll call for Cairo to give you a lift.'

Disappointed, Sami said, 'There's no need, I'll find my way back. Don't worry.'

'No, I insist. Let him take you,' Alisha said. She dialled Cairo's number and told him that Sami would be downstairs in five minutes, and he was to take him home. Unable to refuse, Sami thanked her and promised to call her the next day.

Sami persevered, despite the rocky start, and their relationship slowly went from strength to strength as Alisha thawed towards the physical aspect of it. They became lovers and saw each other almost daily.

But it was always Sami who ended up in *her* apartment and *her* bed – never his. Alisha was shy and modest about her nudity and never let herself be seen naked. Nor did she want to see Sami undressed – it had to be done in the dark or in the bathroom, and pyjamas had to be worn. It didn't bother Sami but he couldn't help comparing her with his first love, Zaf, who hadn't minded being seen with nothing on.

His memories of Zaf, in his hotel room in Istanbul, remained as fresh as ever. She had had no inhibitions about undressing in his presence. She had been totally unselfconscious about her naked body; her ways provocatively sexy. On one occasion, when she got up to leave after making love, she had put on her lacy panties and bra, and then walked around the room doing little things like putting lipstick and deodorant on, combing her hair in front of the mirror, and bending down to look at her toenails; all to the delight of Sami's eyes. Her nearly naked body had acted like a magnet on his gaze; he had followed her every movement with affection and desire.

Zaf had created an atmosphere charged with sensuality; she had been mesmerizingly desirable. She had known what power her physique and movements had over him. From time to time she had turned her head and looked at him, her face radiating with happiness. He could never forget such moments.

Alisha came from a different background. Sami attributed her extreme modesty to her status and upbringing. She must have thought it was unseemly to parade herself in the nude. After all, she was a princess, and she knew she was loved and desirable. He was too much in love to question her about her fetish – or her fears – and possibly upset her. He felt he was in heaven: he was in love with a beautiful princess and she was in love with him too. It was gratifying to be there with her, in her bed. One Sunday morning when he stayed there the night, he woke up before her. She was still asleep; he could not take his eyes off her beautiful face. Her full lips were relaxed and desirable, and her dishevelled hair was scattered on the pillow. She woke up gradually, opened her big brown eyes and gave him a dreamy smile and moved closer; the sign of things to come.

It was all beyond his wildest dreams. He had fallen in love with a beautiful princess – and it terrified him. After all, he was painfully aware that he was only a poor goatherd's son and was there as a result of a scholarship. He had no money of his own. He was moving and mixing with the elite, and now with royalty. Sooner or later someone would realise that he had no right to be there. His milieu was neither bourgeoisie nor royalty, but peasant. He had never felt devalued before, but since meeting Alisha it had become a recurring sensation. He felt inferior: she was out of his league. He did not deserve her and when she realised it, it would be the end. Sooner or later it would happen and when it did he would be devastated. Be prepared, he kept telling himself. Be prepared.

One evening, Sami revealed to Alisha that since he had arrived in the US he had encountered a number of strange incidents. Several times he had seen a European-looking, heavy-set man standing on the sidewalk looking at a newspaper and then following him after he had passed by. At the beginning he had ignored it, thinking it might be a coincidence or that he was becoming paranoid. When it persisted he had started taking evasive action, like entering a shop through the front and exiting through the back. After that he became wary. One day, when he was on his way to the university, walking along the sidewalk, a motorcycle had suddenly swerved, mounted the sidewalk and passed so close to him that, if he had not jumped, he would have been knocked down.

Alisha, listening to this, was very concerned. 'Oh no!' she exclaimed. 'You could have been killed. You should have a bodyguard – like me.'

'I don't need a bodyguard, I can look after myself,' Sami said with confidence.

Then he told her that he did not think that the two types of incident were connected; they had been months apart. But he had encountered another incident only yesterday, which had really scared him. A man who was walking nearby had been shot dead – by a sniper, the police had told him. Then he said in earnest, 'Maybe it was me they wanted to kill.'

'Don't make me laugh,' Alisha said. 'Who on earth would want to kill a goatherd's son?'

Sami was hurt by her comment; it was insensitive and unsympathetic. He knew very well who he was. Since he had met her he had felt socially inferior. He didn't give himself any airs and graces but she didn't have to rub it in. 'One way or another, I was nearly killed, Alisha – the victim was very close to me,' he said in a grumpy voice. 'Is that all you can say?'

'No, of course not.' She shook her head. 'I'm sorry – I was just being silly. Please forgive me. But seriously, I don't think there is much gun crime here. Places like Chicago and New York are a different story; they are violent cities! Just ask yourself though, darling, why should anybody want to kill you? You have no enemies, you are not involved in drugs, you are not a spy and you are not old enough to be a veteran Al-Qaeda terrorist in hiding.' She paused and looked at Sami with a wicked smile. 'On the other hand, coming from Afghanistan, what do you expect?'

Sami wasn't in the mood to respond to her new dig, so he just grinned and let her carry on.

'Anyway, you know that Americans are gun crazy: they have no gun controls – anybody can have a gun. Some have a whole arsenal in their houses. There have been many cases where somebody, out of the blue, goes on a shooting rampage, killing people indiscriminately.'

'Thank you, Alisha, that's very comforting,' Sami said sarcastically.

'Oh! Feeling sensitive tonight, are we?' she asked. She leaned over and kissed him on the cheek and the subject was dropped.

Their passionate romance continued for many months, until one evening Alisha went into the bathroom when Sami had just started showering. As soon as she saw him she cringed, as she realised that he was not circumcised. 'Oh no!' she screamed.

Sami thought that it was because she had seen him in the nude. He got dressed quickly and followed her into the bedroom. There the questions began and a big row erupted because he was not circumcised.

'You are not a true Muslim: you haven't had the *tahara*, the purification. To put it bluntly, you are not circumcised. You deceived me so that you could get into bed with me!' Alisha yelled at him.

'Of course I am Muslim,' Sami countered.

'Not according to the evidence before me,' Alisha said. 'You are probably an infidel and you have contaminated me. Sami, do you understand me? I thought you were one of us and you are not. I am sorry, but we are finished,' she declared.

Sami quickly realised the seriousness of the situation and took his time to explain to her why he was not circumcised, hoping that she would understand.

Having listened to him, Alisha said, 'What kind of respect do you now expect from me? I find your reasoning in order to avoid complying with your faith simply pathetic. We can only move on from this if you have it done, otherwise it's over between us.'

'Don't make me laugh, Alisha. Come on,' Sami joked.

'It's no joking matter, Sami; can't you get it through your head?' Alisha shrieked.

'You are putting me in a very difficult position, Alisha. If you think you have some sort of power over me, let me tell you that I don't do anything under duress. Even the power of religion didn't succeed in forcing me to do what I don't agree with. I value the integrity of my body and I will not have it mutilated to please you. I was made by Allah in the "most perfect form" and I will remain intact for as long as I live,' Sami stated.

'If that's your decision, you can no longer have me. My advice to you is to go and find some other woman who doesn't care. I'm sorry but my faith is too important to me.'

Softly, after a moment, Sami said, 'You can't be serious. Come on, we're both flared up and upset. Why don't we talk about it in the morning?'

'I have never been more serious in my life. It's a question of faith and it is not negotiable. End of story. What can't you understand? There is nothing left to talk about,' Alisha said, in a steely voice.

Sami shook his head; he had lost her! His face filled with dismay. He remained there for a moment, riveted, looking at her, and with every moment that passed his heart sank further. Having realised that they had reached an impasse, he calmly said, 'In that case, we'll have to part company. But I do hope we'll remain friends.' He gathered up the few items of his that were lying around.

'Goodbye,' Alisha said bitterly, and with a grim face showed him to the door.

Sami left holding his head up high, trying to hide the fact that he had been spurned. He knew she had meant every word and would never change her mind, but neither would he. It was the end; although he had thought it would happen sooner or later he felt worse than he had anticipated. Now he had to find the strength to get over her. It wasn't going to be easy but there was no going back, of that he was certain.

The first few days were unbearable. Sami was heartbroken and could not stop thinking about Alisha. If only she would change her mind, phone to apologise for showing him the door, and accept him as he was. He would rush back to her. But, being realistic, Sami knew that she was never going to do that. Gradually he accepted the inevitable and eventually stopped thinking about her.

One day when he was walking in town, where he had previously been followed by a heavy-set man on a number of occasions, he got a glimpse of the same man talking to Cairo, Alisha's bodyguard. He thought of walking up to them and confronting them, and wondered whether it was Alisha or her father who had asked Cairo to have him shadowed. On balance, he concluded that it must have been her father and, since they were no longer an item, he decided not to pursue the matter.

A couple of months later a news channel asked Harvard University for the name of a knowledgeable person from Afghanistan who could talk about the tragic consequences of the severe earthquake there. Sami had in fact just returned from Afghanistan, as the earthquake had claimed the lives of his parents, and he agreed to appear on the news programme.

When Alisha switched on the television to watch the news as usual, her heart jumped when she saw Sami on the panel, talking. He was saying, 'What are still urgent and necessary are search teams and sniffer dogs to look for survivors who may still be alive under the rubble. The earthquake covered a vast area in the north of the country, where I come from, and almost all of the buildings have been flattened. Those that have not are in danger of collapsing, and are uninhabitable. The wounded and those who survived are being looked after by the government and voluntary agencies from the US and many other countries. Medical supplies, food, clothing and tents have been flown in, and the people of Afghanistan, including myself, are extremely grateful for that.' Alisha was in tears, listening to Sami and watching the tragic scenes and devastation shown on the screen.

*

The following day she looked for Sami at the university during a lunch break, and she appeared out of the blue. The moment Sami saw her, his heart leapt. She came over and talked to him; not about them, but about the earthquake. She told him that she had seen him on television talking about it and was concerned about any casualties in his village – friends and relatives. Her appearance opened up two deep wounds: the loss of his parents, and her. When he had learned his parents had died he had been devastated. He had lost them and felt alone in the world; he had no other relatives. To alleviate his suffering he had immersed himself in his studies with new vigour, like he had when Alisha finished with him.

He told her about the tragic death of his parents and she said she was very sorry to hear it. After chatting for a short while about the effect of the earthquake on the country, she told him that she was midway through writing her thesis for her PhD and that afterwards she would be returning home. They wished each other good luck and said goodbye. Sami realised that he still had strong feelings for her and getting her out of his system would take longer than he had thought.

V

Sami graduated with a first class degree from Harvard and went back to Afghanistan. Having paid off his debt to Dr Omar, in the summer he found a job in Kabul and stayed there. During the weekends he would go back to his village, and one day he bumped into Dr Omar.

They spoke about his job and prospects, and Dr Omar told him to aim higher and expect more from life. He advised him to go abroad again and get a higher degree qualification. Sami liked the idea but could not see it happening because of the financial cost, so the subject was dropped and, for a while, forgotten.

A few weeks later he received a call from Hamid, who had always taken an interest in his academic achievements. After exchanging pleasantries, Hamid mentioned that he had learned of another scholarship at Harvard, for a post-graduate degree, and had immediately thought of him.

'If you are interested you must apply. I can send you the form to complete; when you have filled it in send it back to me and I'll forward it to the right channels for you.'

'What a coincidence,' said Sami. 'Only a few weeks ago I was talking to

Dr Omar and he suggested I should go abroad to study again.'

'Oh, did he?' said Hamid. 'Dr Omar is a good man, unlike his father. Do you know that he is still very bitter about his father and still blames him for what happened?'

'What do you mean? What happened to Dr Omar?'

'Well, when he was in his early teens, his father took him with him on his skirmishes against the Russians. He wanted to make his son like himself – a warrior. Unfortunately for Dr Omar, a grenade exploded near him. The shrapnel destroyed his manhood and large parts of his thighs. It's a miracle he survived. Ever since he has blamed and hated his father, the Taliban, and Al-Qaeda for all the suffering they caused.'

'I had no idea – poor Dr Omar!' Sami said in a sympathetic voice.

'It's an old story, Sami, and he doesn't like to talk about it anymore.'

Sami thanked him for telling him, and for all the help he had given him in the past. He then promised to think about the scholarship and let him know soon.

Of course, Sami knew that such an opportunity was too good to miss but he didn't want to appear too keen.

A few days later the forms arrived; Sami promptly completed them and returned them to Hamid. This was not the first time that Hamid had helped him and pointed him in the right direction and he wondered if he could manage it again. Some weeks later the answer came: he had been awarded the scholarship.

Sami was ecstatic. He had never believed in his wildest dreams that he would be going back to Harvard, and he contacted Hamid immediately. Hamid congratulated him, and Sami thanked Allah for being so magnanimous.

So Sami went back to his alma mater. During his previous time there he had got to know and admire, and even become fond of, the country. As before, he devoted himself to his studies and was rewarded with a first class Master's Degree at the end of the year.

VI

After Sami graduated for the second time, he returned home to Afghanistan and started looking for a job in Kabul. As the little money he had was running out, he contacted his old friend and schoolmate, Mustafa, who had been working in the Ministry of Agriculture since leaving high school. Mustafa told him about a temporary job in the ministry; Sami applied and got it – with a little help from his friend.

At the time Sami was interested in whether the government had any plans to irrigate his province, his village in particular, which would have enabled him to convert his scrubland into agricultural land. In the event, there was no such plan, and Sami's hopes of growing agricultural products on his land were thwarted.

While working at the ministry, however, he had met Mikhail, who worked in the Afghan Resources Department. Over lunch one day he told Sami that he was recording, in great detail, area by area, the country's potential and identified resources.

Sami asked him if there were any underground water reserves in and around his village.

To Sami's surprise, instead of replying yes or no, he laughed and gushed, 'Who cares about water? It's oil *you* ought to be thinking about.'

'Ah,' said Sami. 'Are you telling me that there's oil by my village?'

'I'm not telling you anything,' countered Mikhail, looking worried.

'Do you know or don't you?'

'Of course I know but I'm not going to tell you – it's confidential.'

'Listen, I won't tell anyone that you told me. Surely you can trust me.'

'You're wasting your time. I'm not going to tell you – I'll get into serious trouble.'

'All right, I'll log in and find out for myself.'

'You'll need my password and I'm not giving it to you, so forget it,' said Mikhail. Unfortunately for Sami, Mikhail couldn't be talked into giving him more information.

Of course, Sami couldn't stop thinking about it. He had to find a way to log in and find the answer. As Mikhail's friend he was in a position to gradually find out all his personal details. Of all the bits of information he gathered, the most promising one was Mikhail's fiancée's name, which was Mastana.

Sami had it all planned out in his mind. He knew that his friend always went to a meeting after lunch every Monday, leaving his office door unlocked. So, one Monday afternoon, Sami watched Mikhail leave to go to his meeting. Once he was gone, Sami went into his office and sat down. He switched on the computer and punched in "Mastana" as the password. To his relief it was accepted.

It took him a while to navigate through the various sections but eventually Sami found the details he wanted. There was a map of his village and the surrounding land – he recognised his portion of scrubland, which had a shaded area right in the centre, where the government had carried out seismic explosions some years earlier under compulsory powers. He quickly printed the map and logged off. There were some symbols on the shaded area that were explained at the bottom of the map as "Oil reserves: high probability". There were no references to any other type of resource, just oil.

That was it, Sami thought. Mikhail was right. Forget about water; think about oil – liquid gold. Sami realised that he might cause trouble for his friend and was going to be cautious about his discovery. What surprised him though was that he didn't feel guilty about hacking into the government's secret resource database. His conscience was clear; he already owned the land, so he would not be misusing the information. Besides, the country needed oil, and now that he knew it was there he would do his best to develop the oilfield and generate wealth – some for himself and some for his country. He was certain that he was doing a good deed and nobody would suffer.

Armed with his knowledge and documents, Sami considered the possibilities of exploring the wealth all on his own. But he was penniless and had no access to any venture capital.

He suffered many sleepless nights, sometimes frustrated and worried, others overexcited, thinking about the immense wealth that lay beneath his scrubland – but out of his reach. Eventually, he found the answer: go to Dr Omar.

Dr Omar was very wealthy and Sami knew him very well. Ironically, Dr Omar had sold him the scrubland about ten years ago, thinking it was worthless, so it was only right he be a part of Sami's scheme. I'll tell him about it and then ask him to either be a partner or a shareholder, Sami thought. I'll get all the paperwork and go to him with my proposal. First, I'll form a company and obtain any required licenses. I'll find out if there are any government grants available for drilling for oil, and go to Dr Omar prepared.

As soon as he got paid at the end of the month he went to a specialised organisation and enquired about having a private company incorporated, called "Samoil". As he couldn't pay the entire fee at once, they agreed on one-third on completion and submission of the relevant legal documents, and one-third at the end of each of the two months after that. In order to make ends meet, Sami had to sell the car he had recently bought and economise on food and going out – but his company was no longer just a dream.

In the meantime, he found out the procedures for applying for a drilling licence and the costs involved. He made contact with the relevant officials and they helped him to fill out the necessary forms and applications. By now the country was stable; the government had managed to stamp out the endemic corruption and it was keen to get the economy going. Oil and mining were at the forefront of its efforts, so Sami found everything was completed and processed with relative ease. The only problem was a lack of any financial assistance.

By the end of the third month everything had been completed; it was just a question of waiting for the licences and approvals to be issued. Eventually, Sami had everything he needed and was ready to approach Dr Omar and ask about the possibility of his financial backing.

Sami called Dr Omar and told him that he would like to see him the following weekend. Fortunately, Dr Omar was free all that weekend and was pleased to see him. After a few polite exchanges Dr Omar asked, 'Well, what did you want to talk to me about?'

'It's about a business proposition. Do you remember that you once told me to think big and expect more from life? Well, now I am. Since I started working for the government, I have become privy to information that indicates there are oil deposits under the scrubland you sold me some years ago.'

'That's very good news, Sami. Congratulations,' said Dr Omar, sounding genuinely pleased.

'Don't congratulate me yet because I cannot take it any further. So far I have managed to deal with all the requirements of the Central Registry. I have formed a company, which I have called "Samoil Inc.", complied with all legal formalities, and obtained all the necessary government permits. As you can see from these documents, the project is now ready for the next phase.'

Dr Omar examined everything and then said, 'Well done, Sami, I am very impressed. You have done well, especially in light of all the bureaucracy and corruption in government circles.'

'It was actually not that bad; things have changed quite a lot. The problem I have is that I cannot take the project to the next level without financial assistance. I was wondering if you would like to be my partner in the venture.'

'Of course I would. I wouldn't miss such an opportunity. What sort of deal do you have in mind?'

'If you can finance the cost of the drilling, then you can have a percentage of the company that I have formed. I have transferred to it the rights to whatever lies beneath the land. All the government licences and permits have been granted, and issued in the name of the company. The oil reserves can be calculated after the oil well has been drilled, then we can value them and calculate your percentage of the equity of the company,' explained Sami.

Dr Omar was listening, taking it all in and asked, 'All right, but how will the money I put in for the drilling be reflected in the accounts before then? Will it be in shares or as a loan?'

'I had in mind a secured loan on all the assets of the company, with the option to convert it into the appropriate percentage of equity when the oil reserves are determined and valued,' explained Sami.

'That's doing it the proper way,' said Dr Omar, jokingly. 'The way I see it right now, I'll be taking a big risk and I may end up with nothing if the well turns out to be dry. On the other hand, if the oil reserves are there, both of us will benefit enormously. If I join you, I want my share of the company from the beginning. So I'll put in whatever money is needed to drill the well in return for a percentage of your company – a minority holding of twenty-five per cent. That still leaves you with a substantial majority holding. Effectively, the company will still be yours, but I must be a director as well. Does my proposal appeal to you?'

'I do want to work with you; it will be good for the company to have you on board. That's why I came here, and without the initial injection of money I won't ever be able to proceed any further. So, on that basis, I'm delighted to accept your offer. Let's shake hands to signify our agreement, and go ahead.'

They shook hands and then Dr Omar said, 'Let's hope the two of us make a lot of money and neither will have any regrets!'

'With you on board, the world is our oyster. Let's start straightaway by getting quotes for the drilling. I'll get the bids in and we can have a meeting to discuss them and choose one,' said Sami with enthusiasm.

'Not so fast. Formulating the requirements for such quotations is a specialist job. We need to employ a consultant with prospecting experience. The same people will then be retained to oversee the drilling and report to us on progress and compliance with the quotation. The drilling and all sorts of other things will have to be monitored,' explained Dr Omar.

That was how the business of Samoil Inc. commenced. The two men worked together and watched the progress of the drilling with anxiety, until late one afternoon, almost two years later, the well came to life. There was a loud roar, which was followed by the ferocious spewing of black oil, like a beautiful black fountain. The oil reserves were there, as predicted! The two men were jubilant. They had discovered a huge oilfield; beneath their feet lay riches beyond their wildest dreams.

With phase one completed, phase two began. The financing of phase one and the cost of drilling the oil well had been manageable, but even a man as wealthy as Dr Omar could not provide the funds now required for the next phase. The costs of extracting, transporting and selling were beyond Dr Omar's means; outside finance had to be raised. Since the banks in Kabul did not invest in long-term projects, they were advised to seek venture capital from overseas. Sami, being the majority shareholder, went to Britain, trying to raise money through venture capital and to join London's Stock Exchange AIM-listed market. Unfortunately, his company did not attract any investors and AIM was deemed unsuited to his company's needs, so Sami returned empty-handed.

Some time afterwards, Sami and Dr Omar were having a meeting, discussing the company's finances at Dr Omar's mansion, when Jacob Khan paid them a visit. Since Jacob had married Hamid's sister he had integrated well in the village community. Both Sami and Dr Omar were well acquainted with him and would talk to him freely about their business, so Jacob knew that they were having difficulties trying to raise the money for their company. He told them that, when he had been in New York recently, he had enquired at a merchant bank called Stanley Goodman about possible funding opportunities for small companies in Afghanistan. Then he gave them the wallet of papers that he had picked up from there. Naturally, both Dr Omar and Sami were very pleased and thanked Jacob for being so kind and thoughtful.

'Why don't you have a look at them?' Jacob said. 'You never know, they may be interested in providing finance for your company. It's another channel to explore at least – have a go and see what happens,' Jacob said as he was leaving.

Sami and Dr Omar found the brochures from Stanley Goodman relevant: the bank had a specialist investment unit for their part of the world. Sami promptly got in touch with them and was pleased that they were prepared to discuss his proposal. So he went to New York to negotiate the terms of the investment.

Part Ten

New York

I

Sami was in the lift on his way up to a meeting on the twenty-third floor. At one level the lift stopped; a beautiful young woman got in and smiled at him but he did not notice. He was totally absorbed in his thoughts about what he was hoping to achieve at the meeting. Later, when he was alone in the lift, he looked in the mirror, adjusted his tie and slicked his dark and rather long hair by pushing it away from his face and ears with his fingers, then turned around and waited for the door to open.

He had been in New York for nearly two weeks and had spent every day in meetings at Stanley Goodman's offices with a team of bank officials. He was trying to raise a capital injection of $30 million for his company. Today he was feeling optimistic as he was getting closer to securing the much-needed capital. He had already discussed the developments on the telephone with his business partner, Dr Omar, and they had agreed that they were on the right track to securing a good deal.

Dr Omar paid for the drilling of the oil well, which had cost nearly $10 million US, and in exchange he received a quarter of the company's equity. The company's prospects were excellent because the oil reserves amounted to many millions of barrels of oil. In spite of that, the company had so far been unable to raise the required finance for the development of the oilfield.

They had run out of money, and in desperation Sami had come to New York to try to raise the money from Stanley Goodman. The bank was a large multi-national, providing corporate lending, venture capital and financial advisory services across the globe. Alex, who was leading the negotiations, was a Harvard graduate and Certified Public Accountant. He had been headhunted by Stanley Goodman and quickly fast-tracked to higher positions. He had recently been made manager of the bank's department for the Asian region.

During the break for lunch Sami contemplated the outcome of the morning's meeting. He was very pleased that they had reached an agreement on a number of points but he was not happy with the valuation of the company, which meant that on securing the $30 million investment he would lose control. He felt frustrated and decided to discuss it with Dr Omar.

He used his mobile to call Dr Omar in Afghanistan. The phone rang for ages before Dr Omar picked up; he had been clearing out some old rubbish from the basement of his mansion. Sami told Dr Omar about Stanley Goodman's latest offer. Neither liked the valuation, but both men knew that there was no other option; all other fundraising channels had been exhausted. Both of them were in agreement. They would be giving too much away but there was no other option. Sami would press on with the negotiations but would have to eventually "bite the bullet" and sign on the dotted line.

After his meeting in the afternoon, Sami returned to his hotel. He was disappointed to find that the usual receptionist was not there. A beautiful young Hispanic girl, Conchita reminded him of Princess Alisha, who had ditched him at the height of their passionate romance five years ago because they strongly disagreed over the question of circumcision. Whenever Conchita saw him she greeted him with a big smile, determined to attract his attention. Sami wore European-style clothes and was a good-looking man, six feet tall, with blue eyes, a warm smile and a short beard. On one occasion, when it had been quiet in the foyer, Conchita had said to him, only half-jokingly, 'If you need someone to show you New York's best night spots, you only have to ask.' Sami had thanked her and told her that under normal circumstances he would love to but unfortunately he had too much to do. There was too much at stake and he did not want to be distracted. However, that afternoon, if she had been there he would have made an exception.

He went to his room, had a shower and got dressed. He sat down for a moment but decided not to work on the company's fundraising proposal and wondered what to do instead. His face lit up as he visualised Eva's beautiful and smiling face. She was an old friend and fellow student from Harvard, for whom he had had secret feelings; there had never been anything but friendship between them. He was about to phone and invite her out for dinner when the phone rang; it was Alex from Stanley Goodman inviting him to dinner. Alex lived with his parents and sister in Manhattan and would sometimes invite clients for dinner. Sami hesitated and then asked for an assurance that they would not be discussing the deal all evening. Alex put his mind at rest – it would just be a social evening – so Sami accepted.

He went out, bought a bottle of "Faustino Gran Reserva" wine and some flowers before taking a taxi to Alex's house. When he arrived, a butler opened the door and escorted him to the lounge where the whole family was gathered: Alex, his sister Emily, and their father and mother: Edward and Greta. They rose, shook hands and welcomed him to their house.

It had not taken Sami long to realise that the family was extremely wealthy. He took in the location of their enormous house, the imposing iron gate at the entrance, the long driveway leading up to it, and the illuminated (probably for security), landscaped gardens that formed a large part of the grounds. The interior was equally impressive; aside from the various servants, the house was filled with expensive-looking furniture, magnificent rugs and original antique paintings. The hallway was extravagantly vast and lavish, topped with a huge dome from which hung a large chandelier, dwarfing the large round table beneath it. Along the hallway there were discreetly-lit alcoves with white marble statues and framed pictures hanging on the walls. He knew there were a lot of wealthy people in New York who lived in palatial houses but he never thought he would be invited to one of them.

His hosts were immaculately dressed and impeccably mannered. Sami thought that Greta was in her late fifties; she had beautiful but strained blue eyes, which gave her an air of melancholy. She had black, wavy, shoulder-length hair and wore a smart blue two-piece suit, which looked like it had cost a bundle. Under the jacket she wore a cream-coloured silk blouse and had a silk scarf around her neck. Emily also had black hair, cut shorter than her mother's, with a neat fringe above her eyebrows that drew attention to her clear blue eyes. Her face had no wrinkles and her gleaming skin shimmered with youth. She wore a grey silk blouse and a short blue skirt, which also looked expensive. Edward, their father, looked a little older than his wife; he had black hair but it was turning grey above his ears, which made him look very distinguished. He wore a silk shirt and a tailor-made blue, faintly-striped suit with a matching tie. Alex also wore a suit and was equally smart.

As Edward and Greta usually offered alcoholic drinks to their dinner guests, and knew from Alex that Sami was a Muslim, they were concerned that he would be offended. However, in the event, he admitted, with a little embarrassment, that he partook now and then and wouldn't be averse to joining them in a glass of wine.

A variety of drinks were then offered by an appropriately-dressed serving lady. After a while, Greta asked the lady to serve the dinner, and they moved into the dining room. The dining room was large and equally impressive; a crystal chandelier hung from the ceiling above the dining table. There was a floral arrangement in the centre of the table and the finest linen, china, silver and crystal stemmed glasses graced each place.

As there were only five people around the table, there was generally only one topic of conversation. Unfortunately for Sami, it was him. They all seemed keen to learn more about their guest. The questions ranged from, "How did you end up studying at Harvard?" and "How did you get into the oil industry?" to "Are you married?" and "How many wives do you have?" It was all done in a casual manner, making sure that Sami was not in any way offended.

'Do men still have more than one wife in your country, considering the economic pressures of the modern way of life?' asked Emily.

'Yes, some still do, and besides the economic pressures it causes other problems too, like jealousy and stress for all concerned. Muslim men are not required to have more than one wife but they can if they wish. However, it's my opinion that in today's society one wife should be the norm for all men.'

'One is more than enough, as long as she is the right one,' Edward promptly added.

'That sounds like a compliment, dear,' his wife chipped in.

'It *is* important that one should find the right partner. That's why I'm taking my time,' agreed Alex.

'At home, women still don't have much of a choice. In the West both sexes enjoy so much freedom – they abuse it. That's obvious by the number of marriage break-ups. Mind you, divorce gives Western men the chance to have more wives. The only difference is that they can't have them at the same time,' Sami said.

'If you put it that way, I suppose you're right,' Edward commented.

Sami felt sufficiently relaxed to open up a bit about his life. He explained that he had realised at a very young age that his parents were poor. So he had decided to try to earn some money himself. From the age of eight he had worked on Dr Omar's farm during the summer holidays, looking after the animals, while Dr Omar had spent the summer abroad.

He went on to explain that he had received his education by winning two scholarships: one when he was eighteen, to study at Harvard for a degree in Maths and English, and another when he was twenty-two for an MBA, also at Harvard.

'You must have been very bright to win those scholarships,' commented Edward.

'Well, perhaps I was; I am an avid reader and I found learning easy. At school I read as many books as I could lay my hands on. I taught myself things which we were never taught in school—'

'Such as?' interjected Emily.

'We had no radio, television or access to Internet, so I read instead. I was particularly fond of maths, physics, philosophy and literature. I had read about the Big Bang and Einstein's theories of relativity by the age of ten, and later on about the Higgs boson. I remember very clearly when they announced at the Large Hadron Collider in Geneva in March 2013 that they had found it: the Allah particle—'

'The God particle,' Emily butted in.

Her mother frowned but did not say anything.

'The same thing,' Sami said, ignoring Emily's gentle dig about religion, and went on. 'I read Homer, Plato, Aristotle and some of the classics. I was particularly interested in the history of the Western civilizations: from Alexander the Great to World War Two, and of course the American Civil War. I love historical fiction as well, especially "Gone with The Wind" – I mean the book. I read it in English when I was about fifteen—'

'Did you like the film?' Emily cut him off again.

Greta was annoyed by her daughter's repeated discourtesy. 'Emily, dear, let Sami finish.'

Emily rolled her eyes slightly and mumbled, 'Sorry; I always speak out of turn.'

'That's all right,' Sami said. 'Actually, I have never seen the film.'

'You must see it; it's a fantastic film. As a matter of fact it's showing at the Cinema Village,' said Alex.

'Perhaps I will, one night. To go back to my education: I was lucky in having an inspirational teacher who helped me and pointed me in the right direction. The odd thing about it was that when he was dying – well, he thought he was dying – he told me that it wasn't him who had helped me; it was Dr Omar. He had set up the scholarships, knowing full well that I would win them. Then he told me that Dr Omar had saved my life and that he was a good man. I asked him what he meant by this but he didn't answer.'

'How strange!' Greta was fascinated by Sami's account.

'Did you say he thought he was dying?' asked Edward.

'Yes, he did. He was badly hurt in the same earthquake in which I lost my parents, about five years ago.'

His statement produced a quiet chorus of commiserations from the whole family.

'I was in my third year at Harvard but I went home as soon as I heard.'

By then they had finished their dinner. They moved to a spacious and attractively adorned drawing room, where coffee and a variety of liqueurs were offered. Sami opted for coffee.

'Have you travelled much, apart from America?' asked Greta.

'No, not much; I have only been to one other country and that was Turkey. I represented my country in "The Young People's Interfaith Symposium" when I was sixteen.'

'What a coincidence! Alex was also due to attend, as a representative of his school, but he broke his leg the day before the trip while we were skiing in Denver,' said Edward, glancing at his wife.

'I was so upset: not only was I in agony but I also missed the conference,' recalled Alex.

'Not to mention the girlfriend that went without you and found true love,' added Emily with a mischievous grin.

Alex said nothing.

'Do you remember what you were going to say, Alex? It would have been something about what made you proud of your religion and what didn't,' said Sami.

'It was something along the lines of being proud of my religion because it respected other people's faiths, but not proud of its association with slavery, which was practised by Christians for eighteen centuries or more.'

'What did you say, Sami?' asked Emily.

'I said that I was proud because of Islam's strength and resilience over the centuries, and that I was not proud of the way it tells us to treat women. At the conference it didn't take me long to realise that in a changing world, change was necessary. There were people from all over the world at the conference. The idea was to find common ground and create a dialogue promoting understanding and respect for each other's faith,' said Sami.

'I wonder if it had a lasting effect on the people who attended,' commented Edward.

'How did you enjoy your time at Harvard? Do you keep in touch with anyone from those days?' Emily changed the subject.

'The first couple of years were tough but it became easier when I made some friends. In fact, I was just about to call a girl I met there when Alex called.'

'Oh, Alex – you spoiled it for Sami,' teased Emily. 'What's she like?'

'Emily!' exclaimed her mother, while her father frowned. Turning to face Sami, she said 'I apologise for my daughter's impertinence. Please don't feel obliged to answer anything you don't want to.'

'Not at all,' said Sami. 'I don't mind telling you that she's a very sweet and clever lady.'

'Please indulge me, Sami. Let me put a theory to the test. If a guy describes a female friend as "sweet and clever" it usually means she's not exactly blessed in the looks department. Am I right?' asked Emily.

'Well I'm afraid, on this occasion, your theory is wrong. Eva Nowak is not only very clever, she is also very beautiful, and wealthy I might add. She is one of those lucky people who have everything from birth.' Sami smiled.

'You must excuse my daughter's opinions!' Greta studied his face closely, trying to decipher Sami's thoughts.

'I don't mind them at all. I like frank and honest people – you know where you stand. However, now is the time for me to thank you all for your kind hospitality and to call it a night. It's been a lovely evening. I'll see you at the meeting tomorrow, Alex.'

'It was a pleasure to meet you,' said Greta, still gazing at his face.

'I hope my questions didn't offend you in any way,' added Emily.

'Not at all,' replied Sami, and he followed Alex to the door.

The next morning Greta went to her office in the house, still thinking about their dinner guest from the previous evening. Sami was certainly charming, she thought, but there was something about him that unsettled her. She picked up the phone and called Matthew, an old friend and a senior agent at the CIA. He was not surprised to hear from her. Although Greta had recently stopped working for the Agency, having retired on reaching fifty-five years of age, they had kept in touch. Greta told Matthew what she knew about Sami, the business friend of Alex, and asked him to see if he could find out anything about him.

'Is this another one of your hunches, Greta?' Matthew asked.

'Sort of, but this time it's different. He came to dinner last night. He seemed well-educated, and charming but there was something about him that unnerved me.'

'The invitation to dinner originated from Alex and was business-related, wasn't it? There's nothing strange about that,' stated Matthew.

'If you could do this for me, Matthew, I'd be ever so grateful.'

'Sure, no problem; I'll see what I can do and get back to you,' replied Matthew. Greta thanked him and went out to meet one of her friends.

II

After a few more meetings, Sami's negotiations were coming to a close, but he was still faced with the low valuation of his company; it was a major stumbling block. He was far from happy with what Stanley Goodman wanted in return for the $30 million venture capital. He would have to give up a large proportion of his shares in the business. Under the existing ownership, Sami owned three-quarters of the equity of the company and Dr Omar the remaining quarter. Under the proposed deal, Sami would lose overall control because Stanley Goodman wanted a fifty-one per cent stake, leaving him with thirty-nine per cent and Dr Omar with ten per cent. However, he would still remain as managing director and Dr Omar would be kept on as a director. He knew he had no other options as he had already exhausted all other fundraising possibilities. The possibility of raising finance in Afghanistan was non-existent and he had already tried London's AIM-listed financial market and failed. Only a miracle could save him from losing control of his company and he did not believe in miracles. As there was nothing further to discuss, Sami thanked Alex and his team, and told them that he wanted to sleep on it and discuss the terms with Dr Omar before returning the following day with a final decision.

That evening, Sami had an early dinner in a nearby restaurant. He ate alone and then went to the cinema. He had wanted to see "Gone with the Wind" ever since he had read the book but somehow he had never managed it. So when Alex had told him that it was showing at the Cinema Village, he had made up his mind to go and see it at last.

When he returned to the hotel there was an urgent message to call Dr Omar – no matter how late it was. Sami had switched his mobile off when he was in the cinema, so Dr Omar had been unable to reach him. Sami phoned him immediately. Dr Omar seemed very excited about something. 'What's so urgent, Dr Omar? I thought we had discussed everything earlier and we agreed that I should sign tomorrow.'

'No Sami – you mustn't sign yet. You must postpone the meeting for a week or two and get a flight to Geneva tomorrow. Book in at the Zavvi Hotel. I'll meet you there, either tomorrow evening or the following morning.'

'You're kidding me, right? Or have you gone mad? We'll lose the money for the development of the oilfield that we've worked so hard for, and we'll have to start all over again.'

'Sami, you know me better. I'm serious, very serious. I found it all in an envelope in an old chest in the basement. I nearly burnt it without reading it. It's too complicated to explain over the phone but I'm certain that I have the answer. It's unbelievable! This is big, really big. Now do as I say: postpone your meeting any way you can and get on a plane.'

Because Sami felt indebted to Dr Omar and had always respected him, he reluctantly said, 'All right, but on your head be it. Stanley Goodman won't give us another chance.' Sami went to bed tired and confused.

III

Early the next morning Sami booked a flight to Geneva with a stopover in London for refuelling. He expected to get to the hotel by the early hours of the following day.

After checking out of his hotel he took a taxi to Stanley Goodman's offices, just in time for his 11am meeting.

Once everyone was seated, Sami said, 'I don't know how to put this but, having discussed your proposal with Dr Omar, we have decided that we are unable to sign the agreement, at the moment.'

'I thought everything was agreed yesterday?' said Alex. 'We've arranged for the money to be transferred over to your company today.'

'Could I ask that we postpone finalising the deal for a week – maybe two?' requested Sami.

'It's too late for that, Sami. You either sign now or the offer is withdrawn. The financial markets are so volatile; we cannot possibly keep the offer open beyond this meeting.'

'I see,' replied Sami. 'In that case, as I cannot sign today, I'll have to withdraw.'

Alex, trying hard not to show his anger, said in a controlled tone of voice, 'The deal is off then, and should you decide to come back to us in the future, we'll have to start the process again with a new business plan and new valuations. You may find our terms less favourable though.'

A member of Alex's team chipped in, 'Absolutely.'

'I realise all of that and I'm sorry it came to this. I apologise for all the trouble and inconvenience that I've put you to,' said Sami.

The meeting was then closed, and Alex followed Sami on his way out. Alex had regained his composure; he said how sorry he was that things hadn't worked out and asked Sami to get in touch next time he was in New York.

It was nearly noon. Sami decided to have an early lunch before heading out to the airport. He found a nearby restaurant and sat down at a table. He ordered lunch and opted for water rather than wine, as he needed a clear head to think things through.

He wasn't really interested in his food. He mulled over what he had just done – turned down an offer to finance his company. Not many people would have done that. He had worked so hard over the years, jumping through numerous hoops to get the deal on the table, and now he had turned it down at the last minute – it was ludicrous! I'll kill Dr Omar if he doesn't have a very good reason for it, Sami thought. We'll get a bad name; nobody will take us seriously, and it will be harder to get finance in the future.

IV

Geneva

Sami arrived in Geneva late that night and checked in at the Zavvi Hotel specified by Dr Omar. In the morning he woke up late, had breakfast in his room, and enquired at the reception if Dr Omar had checked in. They told him no, but that they were expecting him around lunchtime. Since he had nothing else to do, he picked up a Geneva tourist guide to see if there was anything that might interest him. He was not interested in shopping or sightseeing on his own, so he flicked through the book until he came across a page on the Farmers' Market, which took his fancy. He asked at the hotel reception how to get there and chose to go by bus rather than by the recommended taxi.

Ever since he had been a young boy, Sami had been interested in growing things, and was curious about the local produce. When he arrived at the market he strolled around the stalls, admiring the beautiful displays of fresh fruit, vegetables and wheels of Savoy cheese. By the time he had finished looking around, he was feeling hungry. He decided to walk back to an olive stall that he had passed a few minutes earlier.

A middle-aged woman was standing behind the stall; she looked Italian and had her hair tied back with a colourful scarf. 'Can I help you, sir?' she asked.

'I was just admiring your olives. I never knew that there were so many different types,' he said.

'Why don't you treat yourself to some? You can enjoy them with some handmade bread.'

'Okay, I think I will, but which ones?'

'Well, my favourite are the green, cracked ones with coriander, garlic and lemon. I am sure you will like them.'

'In that case I'll have some of those then. Do you eat them as a snack? Or in salad, or what?' he enquired.

The lady picked up a small plastic container and said to him, 'Shall I fill this up for you?'

'Yes, that will be enough, thank you.'

'You can have them at any time of the day: breakfast, lunch, *merenda*, whenever.'

'What's *merenda*?' he asked.

'Sorry, I thought you were Italian. It means "afternoon snack".'

Sami paid the lady, took his olives, and thanked her. He walked away in the direction of the bread stalls. When he arrived there, he was astounded by the different varieties of handmade bread on display. As he was only interested in a small amount to eat his olives with, he bought a small crusty loaf.

On his way back to the bus stop, he came across a vacant bench. Since he was in no hurry, he sat down and started wondering again about what Dr Omar had to tell him. While sitting there in deep thought, he began eating his bread and olives straight from the bag. The lady had been right to recommend them; they were delicious with the bread.

When he saw the bus coming Sami stopped eating and hurried to the bus stop. He climbed aboard and returned to the hotel just in time to hear the clocks striking one o'clock.

V

There were a number of people moving around in the foyer; among them was Dr Omar. He was waiting for Sami and holding a large bottle of whisky. Dr Omar was nearly six feet tall, medium weight, had short grey hair and was clean-shaven. Although he was in his early fifties, he still had a youthful face. He was wearing Western-style clothes and looked smart. They greeted each other and enquired about their journeys.

Sami couldn't wait any longer; he was desperate to find out what was going on. He started asking questions and demanding answers all at once: 'Why are we in Geneva, Dr Omar? Where is the money going to come from? And why are you holding that bottle of whisky?'

'The whisky is for you, or both of us.'

'Now you are pulling my leg,' said Sami.

'And what's that for?' asked Dr Omar, pointing at the bag that Sami was holding.

'For my *merenda*,' said Sami laconically.

'Who is she?' Dr Omar asked.

'It's not a she; it means "afternoon snack" in Italian. I had nothing to do so I went to the Farmers' Market and bought some olives and bread,' explained Sami.

'How interesting!' said Dr Omar, sarcastically.

'Anyway, we digress. What's the whisky for? Really, that's not like you, Dr Omar.'

'You're right, it's not like me, but this is to celebrate – or drown our sorrows. One way or another, after today, things will be different – very different.'

'Now you are being melodramatic, Dr Omar. I do not know what on earth you are going on about. I am mystified. The suspense is killing me.'

'Patience, Sami,' said Dr Omar. 'I'll tell you everything, all in good time. We'll have lunch somewhere nearby or in the hotel if you like.'

'The hotel is fine.'

'After lunch I'll tell you everything. I have some very important documents to show you. They are the reason why we're here. All will then become clear.'

'What are these documents you are talking about?' Sami asked impatiently.

'Like I said, you'll have to wait a bit longer.'

After lunch, which seemed to Sami to take forever, Dr Omar suggested a walk. But Sami's patience had run out. 'Why on earth would I want to go for a walk? I can't wait any longer. I need to know what's going on.'

With that they went up to Dr Omar's hotel room. Dr Omar brought the evidence that he had found with him. It was in a large envelope which he locked up in the safe in his hotel bedroom. Sami was agitated, angry and confused; he could not wait any longer to find out why Dr Omar had suddenly made him stop the negotiations in New York and come to Geneva.

Part Eleven

I

'Take a seat,' he said to Sami. 'You'll need one when I tell you…' He hesitated, then went and took out the large, bulky envelope from the safe. With his gaze fixed upon Sami's face, he said, 'You will find what I am about to tell you earth-shattering; it will put you on a path from which there can be no return. Everything in your life will change after…' He left the sentence hanging for a moment, and then added quickly, 'The documents in this envelope confirm that your real name is not Sami and you are not an Afghan.'

Sami's eyebrows furrowed and he threw his hands in the air and bellowed, 'Bullshit! I'm not sitting here to listen to any more of this rubbish. You've gone mad, or you are playing some sick joke.' He got up to leave, visibly unsettled.

Dr Omar shook his head and said, 'No, no, Sami, don't go. Sit down, please, I am serious. I warned you that this was really big. Just be patient. Let me tell you about when I first set eyes on you. You were only a few weeks old. Hamid Ali, your teacher, had you in his arms when I opened the door. He was in a terrible state and you were crying non-stop. Hamid asked where my father was. He mumbled something about you being one of two babies and that the other had died. He said he'd buried it along with the bodies of the transporters – the three people who were bringing you over. He pushed past me, talking and looking around for my father.

I told him both my parents were dead, killed by a US drone strike that had also destroyed a large part of our house. I would have been killed too, if I had been there, but at the time I was doing my PhD at the university in Kabul. Three of my father's Taliban and Al-Qaeda associates were killed with him. "You must have heard about it," I said. He hadn't. He had been hiding somewhere north of Kabul, waiting for the babies to be brought to him. Confused, I asked him who the babies were and what he wanted to do with the one in his arms. He stared at me and explained that they were American babies that my father had arranged to be abducted from Manila. Hamid had been the go-between and he wanted to know what to do with the baby, as my father was dead. Without thinking, I suggested he take it back.'

Dr Omar gave a mirthless laugh. 'Of course he shouted at me not to be so stupid and that the only thing left to do was to kill the little infidel and bury its body in the fields. I asked how committing infanticide would appease Allah, and he cursed my father and blamed him. He said that if he had refused to go along with the plan he would have been killed; that he hadn't wanted to do it but that he had had no choice. I told him to calm down; that we should both try to think of a solution.

I thought of your parents, who desperately wanted a child, but couldn't have one,' Dr Omar continued. 'I told Hamid to make up a story about the baby: that it was an orphan whose parents had been mistakenly killed by the British, and that he had been asked by the government to place it for adoption. He, being a teacher and a high official, was able to arrange the necessary papers. Realising that it was the lesser of the two evils, he took the baby – you – to your parents.

As you can imagine, they were thrilled to have a child at last. They thanked Hamid and Allah until the day they died. They told him that they had always wanted a boy and if they had had one of their own, all those years that they were waiting for one, they had been planning to call him Sami. So, they called you Sami. Hamid queried it because it was rather unusual, but that was what they wanted. He told them that it was Iranian and meant elevated – we have inherited a lot of Iranian names from the days of the Persian Empire, as you know.

'Hamid arranged for the adoption papers to be issued in the name of Sami Hussein, and told them not to publicise your arrival before the adoption papers were issued. As a semi-official of the government, he entrusted you to them. And so, unknowingly, they accepted you, an American Roman Catholic baby, as their own, and were committed to love and care for you and bring you up into their own faith, the faith of Islam. The rest is history.'

Sami listened in stunned silence. It was too much to comprehend. He started shaking his head in disbelief. 'I don't know what to say. If all this is true, I am not who I am! Who am I then?' he said, in a state of bewilderment.

'The answer is in these papers that I found,' said Dr Omar. 'Before Hamid left with you in his hands, he gave me this envelope and said, "That's why this baby was chosen. We first obtained inside information and documents about a number of babies, and then I selected who to abduct. It's all in there." The evil plans of my father and his associates had died with them. I chucked the envelope in an old chest in the basement and forgot about it until I came across it two days ago when I was clearing out the basement – I nearly burnt it along with the other rubbish. You can see it yourself. Your birth certificate, DNA profile and christening certificate are all here.

'You are American and you are called Jonathan. You were born a Christian, Sami – an infidel! One of the documents is a financial arrangement made for you by your parents. It's a Child Trust Fund for $30 million US, signed by the three parties involved – the bank, your parents, and Parenting4U.' He went on to explain to Sami what Parenting4U was, the type of people who used it, how the children were raised by surromums and eventually handed to their parents when they reached the age of eleven or eighteen. Then he added, 'If you don't believe me, why don't you read it yourself?'

Sami's jaw fell. He was dumbstruck and felt that the earth had just opened and swallowed him up. He stood there, paralysed by the revelation, and wondered if it was just a bizarre dream from which he would soon wake up. When he recovered from the shock, he said in anger, 'How can you expect me to think about money at a time like this? I do not want to read the papers that have just destroyed my life! I was happy to be who I was: Sami, an Afghan and Muslim. I have never wanted to be anyone else. I thought I was doing all right in my life. Do you understand?' Sami shouted. 'I don't want to know or read these papers. You demolish my life at a stroke by telling me that I'm an infidel, and then start talking about surromums and money. I cannot accept any of it. Burn the papers as you should have done twenty-six years ago. And forget about the money,' Sami snapped.

Dr Omar began to feel remorseful and wanted to sound upbeat for Sami, but couldn't think of what might cheer him up. 'I am sorry you feel that way. You'll just have to start again and build another life, a better one at that. You must accept what you can't change. That's the only way forward.'

Both men fell silent. Dr Omar opened the bottle of whisky and poured two glasses. He kept one and offered the other to Sami.

'Let's drown our sorrows. May Allah forgive us for drinking alcohol. Let's drink to the future,' said Dr Omar.

'To the future!' muttered Sami, almost in tears. After a few drinks, Sami said, 'Do you know, Dr Omar, all my life I have had this feeling, this sense, that all was not what it seemed. Strange, don't you think?'

'Yes, but everybody has that feeling at times; it's just normal paranoia. On the other hand, in your case...' Dr Omar paused, and then added, 'I don't know what to say.'

They carried on drinking until the bottle was empty.

II

Sami woke up in his own room the following morning with a fierce hangover. He called Dr Omar and told him he was going for breakfast. Dr Omar said he'd meet him in twenty minutes. During breakfast Dr Omar said, 'In your absence I took the liberty of making an appointment with the bank at 11.30am. We have to decide on a plan by then.'

'Just a minute, Dr Omar, I haven't agreed to anything. Even if everything is true, I don't want that money anyway.'

'Listen, Sami, we have to in order to keep the company. We've run out of options. You told me yourself, you don't want to lose control of the company.'

'Of course I don't but it seems so wrong to go after the money before trying to find my genetic parents.'

'I know how you must feel. On the face of it, it seems awful. But your parents will understand that you had to start from somewhere. I do believe that this is the best place to start. It must have been the will of Allah to let this happen this way.'

'If that is Allah's will, then he is cruel beyond belief to allow so much hurt and suffering to innocent people,' Sami snarled.

'Let's not go into the rights and wrongs. Can we just accept what happened and move on? I was thinking that I have to protect myself – although I was not involved in the abduction I became aware of it and I did not report it to the authorities. You must appreciate that I would have been a dead man if I had. I hope you can find it in your heart to forgive me. Things have changed over the past twenty-six years. People hated the British, the Americans and all the other invaders,' explained Dr Omar.

'You needn't worry, Dr Omar, I'll never reveal your secret to anyone. I owe you too much. I would never have had the education I had if you had not set up those scholarships. You once said to me, "You are so intelligent and ambitious, you don't belong to this village," and then you added, "I wish I could have had a son like you." I was so touched,' Sami said almost in tears. 'Also, Hamid told me that both scholarships were your idea and you put up the money, knowing full well that I would win them. And, he told me that you had saved my life.'

'I had no idea that you knew,' said Dr Omar. 'I might as well tell you where the money for the scholarships came from. A few days after my parents died and a large part of our house was destroyed by the drone strike, some Taliban and Al-Qaeda men came to search what was left of the house for the stash of money that my father had collected and maintained in order to finance their joint operations. They found nothing, and left. A few years later I was in the basement of the outhouse when the slab I was standing on moved. I lifted it up and found the money in a box. It was all in used notes: dollars, sterling, euros and various other currencies. I took it and deposited it in stages in a special bank account in Kabul. I also put some of it, years later, to good use by having the village school and the village hall rebuilt after the earthquake.'

'I wasn't aware that you had done that but why didn't you rebuild the mosque?' asked Sami.

'I thought about it but decided the school and village hall should come first. I left the mosque for the mullahs to do. I have never told anybody about this. As you know, my father was very rich anyway, so nobody questioned where the money came from. Now you know everything.'

'Thank you for telling me – you didn't have to. Anyway, we have to go to the meeting without the documents, otherwise you will be incriminated,' said Sami.

'And then how do we explain our knowledge of the facts?' asked Dr Omar.

'What if we say Hamid sent them to you just before he died and you gave them to me?' suggested Sami.

'That would still implicate me. Why not do it the other way around? He sent them to you and you asked my advice. I was merely acting on your behalf when I arranged the meeting,' said Dr Omar.

'That sounds more plausible; I agree, that's a better approach, and what's more it puts you in the clear. We'll go to the meeting and start the process. I expect it will take some time to sort everything out. We can decide later whether to accept the money or not.'

'It's your money, Sami. It's up to you.' Dr Omar looked pensive.

'Then we are in agreement. I received those documents. You are my adviser. I'll tell them who I am and then I'll claim the trust money.' Sami paused. A deep sense of unease came over him. 'Wait a minute, this is awful, I can't believe I am doing this. Here I am, an abducted baby who discovers years later that he is not who he thought he was. His parents are not his real parents and all he thinks about is how to get hold of the money set up for him by his genetic parents. I don't think I can go through with this. First and foremost I have to find them.'

'All right, I agree. I got carried away because of the company's need for money,' said Dr Omar. 'However, in my opinion, this is the most expedient course of action. If we try to find your parents in some other way, it may take a long time, and we may stumble at the first hurdle.'

'Why?' asked Sami.

'Who would believe this story without any evidence, Sami?'

'But we have the papers.'

'The papers by themselves are worthless. They are photocopies for a start, and they could have been forged. They refer to a baby who would be by now a fully-grown man, like you but not necessarily you. Without the DNA match you could be anybody.'

'Well, I am still not entirely convinced that this is the right way to proceed...' After hesitating, Sami added, 'However, under the circumstances, I am compelled to go ahead – but only with a view of finding my genetic parents.'

III

At the bank, Sami and Dr Omar were greeted with courtesy and were taken to an interview room on the second floor. Two bank personnel were already waiting for them. They introduced themselves as Gaston Brandenberg, Departmental Director, and Lukas Bingelli from the Legal and Administration department. Gaston was in his fifties, of medium height, rather obese with greyish hair, and was wearing a white shirt, a tie and blue striped suit; every inch the stereotypical banker. Lukas was slightly taller, slim and much younger, with black hair. He too was dressed like a stereotypical banker.

'Gentlemen,' Gaston said after everyone had been introduced, 'I understand you are here to discuss an extremely delicate matter.'

'I'll come straight to the point,' said Dr Omar. 'You have a trust fund in the name of Jonathan Everest, who was abducted as a baby. My friend and business associate here, Sami, is – I mean, *was* – that child, and we have come here today to prove it.'

Gaston and Lukas shifted, and looked at each other in disbelief. They both knew the history surrounding the account in question. For years people in the bank had been anticipating the arrival of imposters, or fortune hunters, claiming the money for themselves. Nothing had been heard about the whereabouts of the two babies since their abduction twenty-six years earlier. All hope of finding them alive had been abandoned a long time ago, except by their parents.

'You can imagine what our first thoughts are, when someone comes to us claiming to be the long-lost child in line to claim a huge trust fund. Naturally this claim will have to be investigated, not only by the bank but the authorities, both here and the US. To begin with, what proof do you have to support your claim?'

'We are not criminals and we have not committed a crime,' Sami said. 'The crime was committed twenty-six years ago; I have here all the evidence you need. Please take us seriously. In your vaults you should have the originals of these documents, and among them you will find my DNA profile. I am willing to have a DNA test done, the results of which will prove that I am Jonathan Everest. I understand that the bank is obliged to do this, in accordance with the procedure laid down in the original agreement between yourselves, Parenting4U and the Everests, my genetic parents.'

'I see you've come prepared,' Lukas responded, while looking straight into Sami's eyes. 'Your DNA will have to be verified by two independent specialists. This is a common procedure for the bank when beneficiaries become entitled to their settlements.'

'Do you agree to proceed with the checking of my DNA?'

'Yes,' confirmed Lukas, 'but we must keep this confidential until the results are known. I must point out to you that if the results are negative this case will be passed on to the Serious Fraud Office. If the results are positive we will notify Mr and Mrs Everest, and Parenting4U. All parties must agree that you are the genuine beneficiary before this is taken to the next stage.'

'Which is?' asked Sami.

'The finalisation of the bank procedures for payment of the money.'

'I'm not interested in claiming the money just yet. First I want to find my real parents, meet them, and find out who I really am,' said Sami emphatically.

'Tell me what happens next, and how long will it take before you pay over the money?' Dr Omar enquired.

'Once everything has been established beyond doubt, it will take two to three days at most,' said Lukas. 'We have to make appointments with the hospital for DNA and blood testing, and arrange to see the representative from Parenting4U. We will then have to wait for the test results, which will take a day or two. I will make the appointments now, if you'll excuse me.'

When he left the room, Dr Omar gave Sami a look full of contentment. A few minutes later Lukas came back and said, 'I've arranged for you to have the tests done at the hospital at 11am tomorrow, and after that we will meet with you and the Parenting4U representative here at our offices.'

'Excellent,' Sami said. 'We will not speak about this to anyone but let me assure you that within a week the whole world will know.'

'There's no denying that there will be a lot of publicity if you are indeed who you say you are,' remarked Gaston.

'I am,' said Sami. With that he and Dr Omar left.

Gaston and Lukas remained in the room discussing the extraordinary meeting.

'It's clear that Sami has been brought up very well. He was very polite and charming, and clearly well-educated. It doesn't seem that he has suffered as a result of the abduction, but then he was probably totally unaware of it,' said Gaston.

'You seem to have made up your mind already that he is, in fact, Jonathan Everest. If it is him, he will have a lot of issues to deal with – not least the conflict in religions: Islam versus Christianity,' said Lukas.

The bank was duty-bound to inform Mr and Mrs Everest and Parenting4U about the development forthwith. Lukas decided to be cautious and gave only a few details away at that point, and wrote that he would keep them informed of any progress in the case.

Meanwhile, Sami and Dr Omar had gone to find somewhere to have lunch. They found a restaurant and sat down in the corner for privacy.

'How do you think the meeting went?' asked Sami.

'I would like to think it was a complete success, but I wonder what they thought. You can understand their disbelief – it has been twenty-six years after all. Most people will have concluded that you died soon after the abduction.'

'Don't say that; it sends shivers down my spine. I think the meeting went as well as can be expected, under the circumstances. For obvious reasons they have to be on their guard; it's a lot of money and they have a standard to maintain, and responsibilities to their clients. I'll have a more informed opinion of them after tomorrow.'

'Tomorrow is crucial. Everything will become clear once the results are in, in a couple of days,' commented Dr Omar.

'They could of course get the police involved, even at this stage. They are duty-bound to investigate us; they wouldn't be doing their jobs if they didn't. There are probably thousands of attempts every year to gain money fraudulently by stealing other people's identities. It's one of the most common scams. Maybe we should get a lawyer to help us through this?'

'That's a brilliant idea, Sami! Why didn't I think of it?'

'Good, I'm glad we agree. We must engage one as soon as possible. He will guide us legally and speak on our behalf if necessary.'

'I agree; we'll do it straight after lunch. We need to approach an international company with considerable clout. The other thing you could do, Sami, is change your appearance – shave off your beard and try to look more European – or American. After all, that's what you are.'

'I don't know whether you are being insensitive or just realistic, Dr

Omar. You must try to understand, I still haven't come to terms with all this.' Sami sighed. 'However, I will shave off my beard; even at home not many young men have beards now.'

IV

After lunch, Sami and Dr Omar went back to their hotel and started searching the Internet for international lawyers. There were many but only a few were represented in Geneva. Sami telephoned a couple but no one could give them an appointment for that afternoon. Eventually, they found one by the name of Caspari, Fehrmann and Schelling, who had had a cancellation and had someone who could see them at 4pm, if they could be there in time. Very pleased to have found one, Sami said that they would definitely be there.

Sami and Dr Omar both now felt safeguarded against any unexpected twist in events that might occur the following day. They went to the meeting and met Mr Marcus Caspari. He was a tall, middle-aged man with thinning dark hair, and was wearing a blue striped suit. They introduced themselves as businessmen from Afghanistan, and they told him everything, showing him the documents they had.

He inspected the documents carefully and then leaned back in his chair. 'Well, what can I say? First of all let me congratulate you, Sami, for wanting to find your roots – your genetic parents. In an ideal world I wouldn't advise you to do it this way but be that as it may, you have to make a start from somewhere, and right now going to the bank first is as good a start as any, under the circumstances. These papers may prove what you are saying but they won't be accepted in a court of law because they were obtained illegally. Here in Geneva we are familiar with such documents. They are usually issued in triplicate: one for the company, one for the parents, and one for the bank. Yours are duplicates of one of those copies. Normally all three sets of original documents must be produced at the bank, which, together with a new and matching DNA profile, stands as conclusive evidence of a rightful claim. So, possession of photocopies means nothing. Quite frankly, I am rather surprised they agreed to carry out a DNA test on you, Sami.'

'What do we do if tomorrow they refuse? What are our options?' enquired Sami.

'Well, we could ask the court to issue an order to comply with the clause in the document relating to DNA matching, but that will take some time. Our best hope is to convince them to be more cooperative by offering to pay for any costs, if the results are negative. However, if the results *are* negative, you will also inevitably be accused of being an imposter.'

'That's not going to happen; I'd stake my life on it!' said Dr Omar. 'What we need from you is your presence and advice at tomorrow's meeting at the bank, to deal with any legal formalities or whatever else they may spring on us.'

'I'll gladly come to the meeting and afterwards I will represent you throughout any legal proceedings that may follow. You are aware of the retention fees that will apply?'

'We are,' confirmed Dr Omar.

Sami then thanked the lawyer and said that they would see him tomorrow at the bank at 10am, and left.

After their meeting and successful retention of a lawyer, Sami and Dr Omar went back to the hotel, feeling confident that they had done everything they could to ensure it would all go smoothly from then on.

The following day Sami, Dr Omar and Marcus met at the bank as agreed, and were taken to an interview room on the second floor. There, beside Gaston Brandenberg and Lukas Bingelli, were two other men who were introduced as being there for security reasons. Sami and Dr Omar looked at each other, remembering what Marcus had said the bank could spring on them. However, after they introduced Marcus Caspari as their lawyer and said that they wanted him to be with them at all times, the two security men excused themselves and left.

Soon after, the five men left the bank and went to the hospital to get the DNA and blood tests done. The removal of a tissue sample and blood from Sami was carried out in the presence of the other four men, and it was all done in a matter of minutes.

The following day Sami had a phone call from Marcus, who said that he wanted to see them to discuss the agreement between Parenting4U and his parents, because there might be a problem with some aspects of it. 'I'll discuss them with you when you get here,' he said. 'Can you be here at 12.30pm?'

'Yes, we can,' replied Sami.

Both Sami and Dr Omar were wondering what the problem might be. 'Surely all the bank requires is proof that the person in question is alive, and the claimant. What's the agreement between Parenting4U and the parents got to do with the bank?' Dr Omar wondered.

When they arrived at Marcus' office, he apologised for dragging them back so soon and explained that he considered it necessary for them to be made aware of what could be a problem. Dr Omar and Sami looked at each other, frowning.

'What could be a problem?' Sami asked impatiently.

Marcus leaned back on his chair, looked at Sami and said, 'It's the question of your religion.'

'But that's irrelevant,' Dr Omar said before Sami had a chance to reply. 'Sami is the lost son of Mr and Mrs Everest, for whom this settlement was set up. Now that he has been found, he is, *ipso facto*, the rightful owner of that trust fund.'

'Yes, absolutely,' added Sami.

'I hope that you are right but we still have to consider the implications of some of the requirements for the upbringing of the child. It is all laid down in great detail as to, for example, faith, education, upbringing and so on, which the child must have. None of this was complied with as far as you are concerned. It's right here, in black and white. You should have been brought up as a Roman Catholic, gone to Sunday school, learned the bible, gone to Mass, etcetera, etcetera. I appreciate that Christianity is no longer practised per se by most Christians, but that's irrelevant. None of these requirements have been complied with,' explained Marcus.

'I can't see what that has to do with my existence and right to the fund that was set up for me,' said Sami.

'You have to be prepared. The final paragraph of this agreement is what worries me. It says here, and I quote, "On the basis of the aforementioned undertakings by Parenting4U, we, the undersigned parents, agree to pay the required fees and charges to the company, and to set up a Child Trust Fund in Geneva, Switzerland. Signed by the Company Director, and Mr and Mrs Everest of Washington, DC" You see, it's very clear to me that there is a serious conflict here. Being a Muslim may negate your right to the trust fund if any one of the parties involved argues that Parenting4U is in breach of contract, and was long before you became eligible to claim the fund.'

Both Sami and Dr Omar felt dispirited. They were both happy and proud of their faith. To make such a condition an issue was an abuse of his human rights, Sami thought.

'What does this mean? What can we do if this becomes a stumbling block?' asked Dr Omar.

'We'll have to wait and see. It's possible that they may overlook it, which is unlikely, or they may waive the clause due to the circumstances. Unfortunately, it's not up to you and me. If one of the parties does make an issue of it, we could apply to the court for an order to nullify the relevant clause, but going down that route will take time and the costs may escalate if the case is contested and drags on.'

'It doesn't look good then!' Sami said, sounding discouraged.

'We just have to play it by ear and we won't know for certain until the other two parties are summoned by the bank. I imagine the company will go along with your parents' decision, since they have nothing to gain by contesting your right to the money, so, eventually, it will be up to your parents.'

'I understand,' said Sami. 'As you say, we now have to wait. Thank you for alerting us to these issues.' They then said goodbye to Marcus and left.

On the way back to the hotel Sami said, 'Dr Omar, do you know something, I just had a most absurd thought.'

'What is it?' enquired Dr Omar.

'When I was in New York I was invited by Alex Everest, the manager from Stanley Goodman with whom I was dealing, to his family house for dinner one evening. I went and met his mother and father, and his sister Emily. I had a nice dinner and evening with them, and thought that they were such a nice family. After a while I felt very comfortable being there with them—'

'Come to the point,' Dr Omar interrupted. 'What are you trying to say?'

'Wouldn't it be a bizarre coincidence if they were my genetic parents?'

'Don't be absurd,' Dr Omar said, narrowing his eyes. 'The probability of that happening is incomprehensible.'

'Yes, you are right – forget it. Anyway, my resolve is beginning to waver. Just think if you hadn't found that envelope when you did, we would have secured the investment from Stanley Goodman by now, whereas now we're up the creek. Perhaps I should telephone New York tomorrow and request to reconvene the meeting for signing the agreement. After all, we don't know how long it will take before we are summoned back by the bank.' Sami sounded disheartened.

'No, just be patient; a few more days delay won't hurt our company. Besides, you do not want to part with the majority holding of the company, do you? I tell you, this is the best way forward. In fact, the loss of the majority holding was the very point that I was not happy with,' Dr Omar stressed.

'But without that injection of money, the extraction and sale of the oil will be delayed, perhaps for years. We simply haven't any alternative and I do not want to wait any longer. In fact, I hoped to get married before reaching thirty, at the latest, and then have kids. I simply cannot do that until I achieve something. The company is my only hope.'

Dr Omar could see that Sami was down and wallowing in his pathetic outlook. Touching him on the shoulder and trying to sound upbeat, he said, 'Cheer up, Sami. It's only a matter of days before your identity is confirmed, then perhaps things will move faster. Go and shave that beard – you said you would. Look at me. I never grew a beard and I am as good a Muslim as anyone. Take your mind off things. Relax a little!' pleaded Dr Omar.

Sami was still sceptical. He was worrying about their chances of finding the money for their company, and also about the surname of his parents; he could still hear Marcus' voice resonating in his ear. He brushed aside the possibility that there could be a connection with the Everests that he met in New York. As Dr Omar had said, it would be highly implausible. Besides, his parents' address was in Washington DC, according to the documents, not in New York. On balance he concluded that the name had to be a coincidence: there was no connection. 'Dr Omar must be right,' he decided.

V

When they returned to the hotel, Sami, as advised by Dr Omar, got on with shaving his beard off. He washed his face and looked in the mirror; he didn't recognise himself. He hadn't seen his face without the beard since his early teens, when it had started to grow. True, he had kept it short, but now that he had shaved it off it was as though there was another person inside the mirror staring back at him – a familiar person at that. He kept looking at his reflection in the mirror, turning his face left and right and lifting his hair away from his ears and forehead. Sami was astonished; the resemblance was uncanny. It's inconceivable, yet true! He thought. Dr Omar was wrong – we were both wrong. I look just like Alex Everest!

Sami moved away from the mirror and went and lay down on the bed. He closed his eyes and tried to make sense of it all; it was earth-shattering. 'In the name of Allah, how can it be?' he shouted. 'Have I met my genetic parents, my brother and sister, and didn't know it? This mystifying, miraculous fate can only be due to the work of Allah.'

He got up, went back to the mirror, and stared at himself. He visualised Alex, whose hair was neater and shorter than his; they both had a slight dent on their chins. Their eyes were also the same colour. I am actually looking at Alex, he thought. He must be my twin brother; an identical twin for sure.

None of them had realised at dinner in the Everests' house in New York: they had been a united family, all together for the first time ever.

'But wait a minute,' Sami said to himself. 'The address of my genetic parents is Washington DC, not New York. They may be different people – maybe I am only related to them, which would explain the resemblance. On the other hand, they may be the same people and have moved to New York some time after the contract with Parenting4U was signed. That's the only missing piece of the jigsaw! How can I check that?' He immediately thought of Eva Nowak.

She had never been far from his mind, since he had thought about inviting her for dinner when he was in New York the previous week. Sami's first vision of Eva was still very vivid; it was in the swimming pool where he used to go swimming regularly. He was resting on the edge of the pool with his feet dangling in the water, after a few lengths in breaststroke, when he noticed her. She was walking in his direction and waved to a girl on the other side of him; she was wearing a swimsuit, had a swimming cap on and her swimming goggles on her forehead. He thought she looked vaguely familiar; he couldn't take his eyes off her shapely body. As soon as she passed behind him he turned his head mechanically, like a robot, as though he was hypnotised, and carried on staring at her. When she stopped a few metres away to talk to the girl that she waved to, she looked round and caught Sami staring at her. He felt very embarrassed and ashamed, and quickly turned his head away. I expect she is used to men staring at her, he thought.

Sami never knew that, in fact, Eva had already noticed him a few times and felt drawn to him as they both attended the same lectures on corporate law. Later, at one lecture, she had intentionally gone and sat next to him and asked him if she could borrow his notes for the previous lecture because she had missed it. He was delighted to help. They had gradually become good friends and sat next to each other on many occasions.

While they were having coffee one day, during a break between lectures, she had told him that her forefathers came from Poland and that they were Catholics. They had come to the US before the First World War, and her great grandfather had made his fortune from property.

He had thought Eva had everything: tall, blond, beautiful and also very smart. She looked younger than him and had a vibrant and lively face, which seemed to have a permanent smile built into it. When she actually smiled, her cheeks formed two captivating dimples. In other words, she was breathtakingly beautiful. Strangely enough he had an affinity for blond women but he had never had a blond girlfriend. He was very attracted to her but kept his desires a secret because of the difference in their religions. At times he had felt sorry for himself for being inhibited because of his faith. His emotions were in conflict with his faith and he had had to restrain and control them. He envied people who had broken away from the shackles of the Middle Ages, and acted like free people should.

He picked up the phone and dialled Eva's number. 'Hello, who is it?' She sounded annoyed.

'Eva, it's Sami. Have I got you at a bad time?'

'No, you haven't. Only you woke me up! Do you know what time it is?' she demanded.

'Oh, no! I forgot about the time difference. I am really sorry.'

'Never mind. Why did you phone? Don't tell me you're coming to New York and you want to buy me lunch tomorrow,' she said, jokingly.

'No, sorry. Listen, I want you to do me a big favour – I'll buy you lunch, but not tomorrow. Can you check if the Everest family, you know the people with the "EverSoft" computer software, ever lived in Washington DC? Phone me back at the hotel, room 307; if I am not in, leave a brief message.'

After he gave her the hotel telephone number she said, 'How am I going to find that out, and how soon do you want the answer?'

'Well, you are a lawyer and resourceful, I'm sure you will think of a way. I need the answer soon; the sooner the better. I am in Geneva, Switzerland, on business, and I need that information quickly. Please will you do this for me?'

'Sure, for you I'll do—'

'Thanks,' Sami interrupted before she could finish the sentence. 'I've got to go now. Bye.'

Sami was convinced that the answer would be that they were the same people and that they had moved to New York. I must tell Dr Omar and Marcus; I won't even wait for the answer from Eva, he decided. This changes things considerably. What will the Everests, my parents, think? Especially when they realise that it was me who, a few days earlier, entered their home and came into their lives as a business contact of Alex's. Will they think it is some ploy on my part to infiltrate to their world? Me, a Muslim as well. That's what may keep us apart; split us up all over again! I must run it by Dr Omar and see what he thinks. I'll tell him when we go to dinner, Sami thought.

Dr Omar did not think that there would be a problem and tried to convince Sami of the same. He said, 'Faith will not be an issue: it was imposed on you. If you were not Jonathan, it would have been someone else. Try and disassociate yourself from it. Suppose it was someone else who had been abducted under such terrible circumstances. Can you imagine the jubilation of his parents when they found him? So, let that person be you, and since you've turned out to be such a fine and personable young man, they'll be overwhelmed. Don't feel guilty for what happened to you: *you* didn't choose to be brought up as a Muslim, or to grow up in a tiny village in a remote part of Afghanistan. Besides, since the resemblance is so great, as you say, they will instantly know who you are.'

'They will be mesmerised at first, and then very emotional,' Sami said. 'I know I will be.'

'Yes, it will be an emotional moment,' Dr Omar agreed. 'I do not think it should take place in public, or at the bank. Perhaps it would be best if you, we, met them at Marcus' office, or at the hotel, sometime before the meeting with the bank?'

'Of course,' agreed Sami, who then became excited and cheerful. 'I'll run it by Marcus and take it from there. In the meantime, we don't know how the bank will react when they get confirmation of my DNA match. They will have to inform both my genetic parents and Parenting4U.'

'For all we know, they have already notified your parents. We must ask Marcus to contact the bank as soon as possible and try and pre-empt the meeting taking place in public by telling them how you want it handled,' Dr Omar suggested.

Sami promptly telephoned Marcus and told him what to do. A few minutes later, Marcus phoned back and said, 'The guys at the bank were very noncommittal. They said that whatever they decide to do after the DNA results, will have to be discussed with their clients, i.e., Mr and Mrs Everest and Parenting4U.'

'Well, I am their client as well,' Sami stressed.

'I did tell them that, and that they should consider your wishes too. They agreed to keep us informed of any developments. I think you ought to take a day or two off and go sightseeing, as there is nothing else that can be done by us until we hear from them,' Marcus advised him.

'Sure, maybe I will,' Sami agreed. 'Thank you for trying. Come back to me as soon as you hear from them. Goodbye.'

When he got back to the hotel, Sami had a message telling him to ring Eva. He rushed to his room and dialled her number. When she answered, he said 'Hello, Eva. It's me, Sami. What did you find?'

'I found the answer to your question. They did live in Washington DC, up until twenty years ago. They then moved to New York and have been there ever since. Does that help?'

'Yes, absolutely – it's just as I thought. Thank you. You are wonderful,' he said in a charming voice.

'I am glad it helped.'

VI

New York

When Lukas Bingelli went back to his office at the bank, after the DNA extraction, he sent an electronic mail to Mr and Mrs Everest informing them of recent developments. He stressed, however, that nothing positive had emerged yet.

When they read the letter, they were both very excited. They had never given up the hunt for their son and they had always prayed and hoped that somewhere in the world some caring couple was bringing him up. Their faith and patience had kept their hopes alive over the years.

'Maybe the time has come to tell Alex and Emily that their long-lost brother is alive,' Edward said to his wife.

'Well, I would rather not tell them just yet, darling. Let's wait and see what happens next.'

'All right,' Edward agreed.

Later on, in the afternoon, Greta phoned Matthew to see if he had anything to report to her, following her request to investigate Sami.

'Well, yes I do,' Matthew replied. 'As a matter of fact, I was about to phone you. Sami comes from a small and remote village in Northern Afghanistan. He is the adopted son of a peasant couple who died in an earthquake there a few years ago. He owes his education to some scholarships he won – obviously he is very bright. He is the major shareholder of an oil company, called Samoil Inc.; his business partner is called Dr Omar, and he is the only son of Abdul Hassan, an Afghan warlord who was killed by an American drone strike on their house some twenty-six years ago.'

'Did you say warlord?' Greta asked anxiously.

'Yes, he was. The strike killed both Dr Omar's parents and three other men who were there at the time. Dr Omar was away, so he survived. Does any of this help?'

'I don't know,' said Greta. After hesitating a little, she said, 'Maybe. Thank you for doing this for me. Goodbye now.'

Greta then rang Alex at work and asked him, among other things, how his business with Sami was going.

'I saw him three or four times after he came to our house for dinner,' Alex said. 'On the last occasion he just came to apologise for having to cancel the meeting, and then left. I haven't heard from him since.'

'He seemed such a nice guy. All right, darling, I'll see you tonight.' She put the phone down in a state of stupor, and wondered, 'Could it be that Sami approached Stanley Goodman in order to meet Alex, and plan or somehow engineer his visit to the house? Was he here to secretly meet us? It would seem that he had an edge over us.' Suddenly she recoiled in disbelief, and a deepening sadness came over her as if a terrible catastrophe had befallen her. 'Oh my God! Oh…my…God…How dare he, that Muslim, find us? Please, please, God don't let it be him.

But soon she realised that she was overreacting; her emotions were all twisted and a sense of shame came over her. 'Why am I not rejoicing? What kind of a mother am I? After all, religion can be changed. I will have plenty of time to work on it; I will help him see the light and convert to Catholicism without pressure, by himself,' she contemplated. She took a deep breath and composed herself. Not wishing to believe what she had discovered, she said to herself, 'Anyway, it's probably not him; it's too much of a coincidence.'

Part Twelve

I

Hamid had not been in the best of health since he was hurt in the severe earthquake some five years ago, and recently more so. His sister Samira and her husband Jacob were spending a few days with Hamid's family when his health took a turn for the worse. Hamid got on well with Jacob; he was not only his brother-in-law but also a friend, a devout Muslim, and a good husband to Samira. When they were alone Hamid used to reminisce and confide in Jacob.

The topic was again the time he turned up at Abdul Hassan's mansion, with the baby in his arms, only to find out from Abdul's son, Dr Omar, that Abdul had been killed by the drone attack. 'I remember telling Dr Omar that the documents in that envelope showed not only who that baby was, but also why it was abducted.'

'Hamid, I just had a frightening thought,' Jacob said in earnest. 'If those documents still exist and were found, they could be incriminating.'

Hamid realised Jacob was right and asked him, if he didn't mind, to go and see Dr Omar and try and get them back, as he was too ill to do it himself.

'Yes, sure, I can do that for you; don't worry,' Jacob replied in his usual obliging manner. 'I'll get them and make sure they are destroyed.'

The following day Jacob paid Dr Omar a visit. He told him that he wanted to take away the large envelope that Hamid had left behind when he first arrived at his house with a baby in his hands. 'It came up by chance when I was talking with Hamid, and we both agreed that a number of people would feel unsafe if they knew that those documents still existed...' He hesitated and then emphasised, 'Including you, Dr Omar.'

'I do not remember ever seeing a large envelope,' Dr Omar said. 'It's been twenty-six years; if it was anywhere in the house I would have come across it by now.'

'Think, Dr Omar. Think. Where else could it be?' Jacob insisted.

'The only other place it could be is in the basement of the outhouse. I'll look for it and let you know if I find it.'

'You don't understand, Dr Omar. Hamid is very worried and he is very ill. I want to be able to tell him the answer and put his mind at rest. Let's go and look for it now,' Jacob insisted.

They went to the basement and started turning everything upside down. The place was full of old furniture, kitchenware, boxes of clothes, books and other household goods. Eventually they came across a large old chest that was covered in dust.

'If it's anywhere, it will be in here,' said Dr Omar, rather excited.

Jacob couldn't wait. 'Open it, quick,' he said.

When they opened it they found it full of old bed linen. They threw them out, and at the bottom they found the envelope among all sorts of other documents and papers. Jacob grabbed it, opened it quickly, and inspected the documents inside. When he was satisfied that he had found what he was looking for, he said, 'What a relief! I'll take it. Some people will be better off now – safer, I mean.'

'Now I remember,' said Dr Omar. 'I brought this old chest down here when I had the part of the mansion that was destroyed rebuilt.'

Jacob took the envelope back to his house and examined every document carefully. He was particularly excited about Sami's Child Trust Fund money – $30 million. He thought it could still be there in the bank account in Geneva, waiting for the arrival of the rightful heir to claim it. In the event that the Everests had reclaimed the money, they would certainly give it all back to Sami when they were reunited. Jacob thought that if he could somehow engineer it, that would be tremendous.

Sami was a multimillionaire – and had no idea about it. In fact, he and Dr Omar were currently struggling to raise money for their company. Jacob knew that because Sami had only recently returned – empty-handed – from his trip to London, where he had gone to try and raise the investment they needed.

Poor guys, Jacob thought. They don't know that they could lay claim to more money than they need. The Child Trust Fund is waiting. He had to, somehow, get Sami to claim the money. And it would have to be done through a legitimate and normal process, which meant that he would first have to find Sami's genetic parents. They would need to warm up to him gradually, and take him into their hearts, and hopefully sign the money over to him pretty damn quick because according to the documents in the envelope, he had been entitled to it since he was twenty-one years old.

II

Soon after, Jacob left for Washington DC. He had to get on with it; there was a lot of research to be done. He began by searching for the Everests. He hoped that because they were extremely wealthy, many people would have heard of them – that would make it easy for him. He was right, and within a couple of days he found that the only very wealthy Everest family was that of the EverSoft Corporation, who had moved to New York many years earlier. From then on it was easy. Once in New York Jacob located their Head Office and the Everests' family home. He decided to find out what all the family members did, so that he could somehow plan for Sami to conveniently meet them.

On a number of occasions he walked up to the entrance of the Everests' house, stopped, took a good look through the bars of the large iron gate, and then got into a taxi and followed any car that came out of the house. One by one he found out where each member of the family worked, but to him the most interesting discovery was where the son worked: Stanley Goodman, the merchant bank.

The day after learning where the son worked, Jacob walked into the bank and introduced himself as a businessman who had been advised to see Mr Everest about a finance deal for his company. The lady behind the reception desk explained to him, politely, that Mr Alex Everest did not see people without a prior appointment.

'I appreciate that,' Jacob said. 'But before making an appointment, I would like to know if he is the right person to see.'

'That depends on where your company is located, Sir, because Mr Everest only deals with financial arrangements for Asia,' she replied.

'I have a gold mining company in Afghanistan and need to raise some capital for the next phase of development. Would he be the right person to see?' Jacob lied.

'Yes, Sir, he would be the right bank official to see because Mr Everest is in charge of that department.'

Jacob thanked her and said that he would discuss it with his fellow directors and then possibly be in touch to make an appointment.

'No problem,' she replied, and then gave him a wallet of their business leaflets.

Jacob took the documents, thanked her again, and left.

'Have a nice day,' she said to him as he was leaving.

Meanwhile the security men who monitored the movements of people in and around the grounds of the Everests' house had spotted the man with the goatee on a number of occasions. Coincidence was not a concept that they ascribed to, so they put a tail on him. They were alarmed to discover that his taxi journeys always ended up where the Everests worked, so they reported it to Edward Everest. He thought it was probably nothing but to be on the safe side he had told them to send the CCTV images to Matthew O'Malley at the CIA.

Jacob's mission was successful and when he returned, he lost no time in handing the documents from Stanley Goodman to Sami and Dr Omar.

III

Some time later, when Sami was in New York negotiating the funding for his company with Stanley Goodman, he used to speak to Dr Omar every day, and kept him informed about the progress he was making. Negotiating an equity investment in a company was neither easy nor something done overnight. There was due diligence work to be done, and valuations to be obtained and verified, which took time.

In the process, Alex Everest got to know Sami, his prospective client, and they got on well with each other. By the tenth session the negotiations were at an advanced stage – that was when Alex invited Sami to his house for an evening meal with his family.

At the time, Jacob was staying in Sami's village with Hamid, whose health was deteriorating fast. Jacob kept in touch with Dr Omar, and was always enquiring about Sami's negotiations and progress in New York. When he found out that a deal had nearly been reached, he went to Dr Omar's house with the large envelope and showed him the various documents. Dr Omar realised that Sami was the rightful owner of the Child Trust Fund, which, with compound interest, would amount to many millions of US dollars. 'Well over $50 million, I imagine,' Jacob commented.

Although Dr Omar was amazed by the size of the fund, and pleased to hear about it, he was more concerned about the impact the revelation about Sami's true identity would have on him. He said to Jacob, 'This will destroy him – he may even turn it down. The psychological implications are horrendous!'

Jacob was more interested in the financial benefit, and convinced Dr Omar that it was the best thing for their company as they would not have to give up any control. He told him that it would be better if he, Dr Omar, told Sami that he had come across the envelope by chance, and nearly burnt it with some other rubbish from the basement that he was clearing out.

Dr Omar, seeing only a selfless act of kindness, agreed that it was only right that such good news should come from him, and thanked Jacob for being so helpful.

IV

When Matthew was asked to look into the images taken by the CCTV camera from the Everest family home, showing a man with a goatee beard peering through the iron gate, he had assigned the investigation to a young agent called Denzel Bassi. Denzel was a bright young agent with a promising career in the CIA. It had not taken him long to find out that the man in question was staying in a cheap, run-down motel in New York, and was called Jacob Khan.

Matthew was suspicious about Jacob's interest in the Everest family. His suspicions were heightened when Greta Everest called him almost two weeks later and asked him to find out what he could about a young man from Afghanistan called Sami Hussein.

As a result, Matthew had Sami's telephone at his hotel in New York bugged, and Denzel had heard – and reported – the strange call from Dr Omar, asking him to abandon his negotiations with Stanley Goodman and go to Geneva because he had found something 'unbelievable' in an envelope.

Though Matthew had reported back to Greta, he had only conveyed just enough of his findings to her to keep her at bay.

Once Denzel Bassi got his teeth into something he wouldn't let go; he was like a dog with a bone. He carried on working on the case and found that Sami was in business with Dr Omar Hassan, the son of Abdul Hassan, who had been killed by an American drone twenty-six years earlier. Denzel then concluded that Jacob must know them, since his wife came from their village, and reported his findings to Matthew, his boss.

On the basis of Denzel's findings, Matthew deduced that there must be a connection between the three men and the two babies from Parenting4U. If Greta Everest's suspicions were right, and Sami was her abducted son, then he must have survived the abduction and been brought up by someone in that village. 'That's the most likely scenario,' Matthew decided. And on that basis he was convinced that the three of them must be up to something.

He needed somebody that he trusted to go to Geneva and do some surveillance. Evelyn Withers would be just the right person for the job, he thought. She was not an employee of the Agency but an independent operator, and she was used occasionally for some low-level activities, such as surveillance and information gathering. Her assignment would be to shadow Sami and Dr Omar; to try and make contact with Sami through some pretext, befriend him, and find out what she could about him.

Matthew trusted Evelyn implicitly as he knew her well – very well. After her husband had died, some ten years earlier, they had become an item. Their relationship had lasted for a number of years but they had gradually drifted away from each other, though they had remained good friends. Although she was a part-time lecturer at Maryland University, she had worked on assignments for Matthew on a number of occasions. He rang her up on a safe line and said, 'Hello, gorgeous. Do you want to relieve the monotony of your life and go on an exciting assignment for me?'

She laughed and said, 'Oh, Matthew, can't you think of something original for a change?'

'I'm serious,' Matthew replied, ignoring her gentle dig. 'I want you to go to Geneva and do some surveillance, and while you are there you can pop across the lake and see Lorraine. How do you like that?'

'That sounds wonderful, Matthew. When do I go?'

'The sooner the better; there are some guys from Afghanistan I want you to keep an eye on.'

'What's up?'

'It could be terrorist activity, a bank job, or it may be nothing at all. I'll send a brief to your home computer.'

'I'll go and get ready; I'm leaving now, Matthew.'

'Evelyn, we may have to join you or take over, depending on what you come up with. Good luck,' he said, and rang off.

Evelyn booked her flight and left the same day. On arrival she went and checked in at a hotel near the Zavvi Hotel, where the two subjects, Sami and Dr Omar, were staying. Once she tracked them down she didn't take her eyes off them. She followed them to the bank, to a lawyer's office, and to the bank again. She did this for a couple of days, reporting back to Matthew each night that nothing untoward had happened. Nevertheless, Matthew told her to be careful, not to be spotted by them unless she could befriend Sami alone, and to carry on.

V

After the last meeting Sami and Dr Omar had with Marcus, their lawyer in Geneva, a lull followed. A sense of uneasiness was growing in Sami, as his conscience was starting to trouble him even more. 'I'm having second thoughts about all this,' he said to Dr Omar one night.

'Why?'

'Lots of reasons.'

'Go on, tell me.'

'Well, that clause in the agreement about religion, and the money in the trust fund. Frankly, I agree with Marcus. I am *ipso facto* disqualified and, being a true Muslim, I should just waive my right to it and walk away from it all: the money, and my genetic parents.'

'Don't be absurd, Sami. It is not your parents' fault what happened to you. You can't reject them. Imagine the additional pain and suffering you would cause them. Accept the inevitable: you are no longer who you thought you were; you have just been reborn. You'll get used to the new you – given time.'

'It's all right for you to say that but it's not that easy for me in practice. I have to think about it tonight and decide what to do.'

The following morning they met for breakfast as usual. Dr Omar was anxious to find out if Sami was still a troubled man. 'Well, how do you feel this morning?' he enquired.

'I didn't get a wink of sleep last night. The more I thought about it, the more confused and baffled I became. Do you realise that I actually have three mums?'

'Lucky you!' Dr Omar said with a grin.

'I don't know if you are just insensitive or cruel, Omar.'

'Sorry, I didn't mean to upset you.'

'The beginning of my life is unbelievable; it was like a game of pass-the-parcel. It's a miracle I am here, and normal. I am normal, am I not, Omar?'

'Everybody's life is a miracle, Sami, and if I may borrow and modify a phrase from George Orwell, "all people are normal but some are more normal than others",' Dr Omar said jokingly.

'How droll!' said Sami laconically, and after a moment added, 'That's no help; you don't seem to identify with my predicament, do you?'

'Please forgive me; I was just trying to lighten the issue.'

'Well, anyway, today I am more confused than yesterday, and I want to spend the day alone somewhere, to see if I can get an answer to all the things that are troubling me. To begin with, I don't want to meet my genetic parents here. There will be no more meetings here in Geneva. I want to meet them in New York. Will you tell Marcus to tell the guys at the bank that that's what I want?'

'Sami, for all we know they are on their way, or may even be here already. The bank and their lawyers will have told them everything – they are professionals, you know.'

'I'm going to spend the day on the lake, on a boat, thinking over my life so far and considering my future. In the meantime, will you please tell Marcus what I've said?'

'All right, I hear what you're saying, and I won't interfere. You must work it out yourself.'

Soon after, Sami took a taxi to the lake and boarded a ferry that was just leaving. He didn't even inquire where it was going until the ticket collector asked him where he wanted to go.

'It's going to Ouchy, by Lausanne, Sir,' the man replied.

'Then that's where I'll go,' said Sami. He went up on deck and stayed there, gazing at the scenery, looking but not taking it in, as he was lost in his thoughts. After a couple of hours he felt hungry and thirsty, so he went to the restaurant. There he bought a cup of tea and a brioche, and sat by a small table near a window. The restaurant gradually filled up, and soon a smartly dressed, middle-aged but still attractive woman with intelligent eyes asked if the chair opposite him was free. Sami said that it was; she thanked him and sat down. She drank her tea and ate her cake while gazing out of the window.

Sami carried on thinking about the issues he was faced with, until he gave a ponderous sigh.

The woman opposite said to him in a friendly voice, 'Forgive the observation, young man, but you seem to have the weight of the world on your shoulders.'

The comment caught Sami by surprise, and he asked, 'I beg your pardon?'

'You seem troubled: something is bothering you.'

'I've got a lot on my mind at the moment.'

'I'm Dr Evelyn Withers,' she said, offering her hand.

'And I am Sa – Jonathan.'

'I don't mean to pry but is it that bad, Jonathan?'

'I am sorry, but I don't want to offload my worries onto a total stranger.'

She shrugged. 'I'm a good listener, and talking about things is therapeutic. Besides, there's nothing much else to do for the next hour or so.'

'Well, something is weighing heavily on my mind. I'm at a major crossroads in my life and there is a huge conflict between my past and what could be my future.'

'Have you been away?' the woman asked.

'Do you mean in gaol? No, no, of course not, but I suppose that's one way of looking at it.'

'I'm not an expert on such matters but talking it through can help. It's a form of catharsis, and as an independent observer I may have a different perspective on the issues you face that you haven't considered.' She then told him that she was from the US, a lecturer at Maryland University, and was on holiday on her way to meet her daughter in Ouchy.

Jonathan told her simply that he was there on business.

'Well, what is this problem that's causing you such distress?' she persisted.

'Let's suppose that you have adopted a child and brought it up your own way, with your own beliefs and religion. What if that child had never been abandoned – it could have been brought up in a different place, culture and faith. What would you say if that adopted child grew up and abandoned his upbringing in favour of what could have been? Would it be disloyal – a betrayal of all you had done for him or her?'

'It sounds like there is a deep-seated conflict between one upbringing and the other. You imply that they are diametrically opposed: what a dilemma! The issues are so personal that only you can answer your question. But ask yourself this: will *you* be happy afterwards? Who will be hurt the most – you, your adoptive parents, or your genetic parents?'

'My adoptive parents are dead.'

'I'm sorry to hear that. In a way, though, that should help solve your dilemma. It absolves you from abandoning them and their ideals, which they imposed on you as they brought you up – to put it bluntly.'

'But the problem is that I did, and still do, believe in their ideals. They were good people and I never want to criticise, betray or abandon them.'

'And you won't, because they are dead. You must let go and move on, even if it means moving in a different direction. You are free, and it's only when human beings are free that they can appreciate and choose freely from the full range of choices available to them. Considering how important the issues are here, you must embrace them wholeheartedly, or else you will spend the rest of your life wondering what your life would have been like if you had. You are fortunate to have been given such an opportunity. Find your roots and embrace them; a new life is on the horizon.'

Jonathan was taking it all in, encouraged, but still mentally tormented and said, 'If only it was that simple.'

'Let me tell you something personal, Jonathan. When my husband died eleven years ago, I used to feel guilty and miserable every time I looked at a man. One night I had a dream: my husband came into my bedroom, sat on the bed, and said, "Why are you so unhappy, Evie? It's not your fault I died, and I don't want you to live the rest of your life like this. You are still young and attractive – live your life to the full; forget about me. Promise me you'll do that?" "But…" I said. "No buts," he replied. "I promise," I said to him in tears.

After that, my outlook on life changed. I was happy again. Do the same – move on. Sometimes it takes an outsider to show you the wood from the trees. It will take time to get over this difficult phase but you'll do it. You have already started by talking to me about it.'

While Evelyn was talking, Sami's expression changed; he saw the light, as though a flash of enlightenment had struck him.

She eyed him, and noticed that he was no longer sceptical. She realised he must have been touched; she smiled, then glanced out of the window and exclaimed, 'Oh! Look! We're docking. We've arrived.'

'That didn't take long!' Jonathan said in amazement.

'It did, but it didn't seem to because we were deep in conversation. You are very welcome to join me and my daughter for lunch,' Evelyn invited.

'Yes, I think I will. Thank you so much for asking me, but you must let me treat you, and promise not to talk about what we have been discussing.'

'Sure,' she agreed.

They disembarked and found Evelyn's daughter, Lorraine, waiting. She was a rather tall, slender young woman with green eyes and blond straight hair. Her mother introduced them and told her that Jonathan would be joining them for lunch. They walked to a nearby restaurant where both Lorraine and Evelyn had eaten before. During lunch Jonathan asked Lorraine what she did.

'I'm doing a PhD at Maryland University, where mum is a part-time lecturer.'

'That's quite congenial for the two of you. What's your thesis about?'

'It's about the vandalising of the human body through the ages.'

'That's very interesting. Specifically, what are you covering?'

'Well, all aspects of deliberate actions to modify or transform the body by attaching, integrating, removing or adding something, that is done with the perception of "improving" the physical and/or mental health of the individual.'

'It sounds like you are defending these actions, whereas your title – vandalising – suggests the opposite,' remarked Jonathan.

'No, it doesn't mean that at all. Vandalising is the process from which one derives the perceived benefits, and I start my thesis with the hypothesis that the human body is perfect, since "God created man in his own image" according to Genesis 1:27.'

'He created man in the "most perfect form" Koran 95:4,' Jonathan said.

Lorraine gave him an incredulous look, while her mother observed, 'Am I right in saying you are a Muslim and not a Christian?'

220

'I never thought,' Lorraine mumbled.

'I suppose I am both,' Jonathan replied.

'How can you be both?' said Lorraine, laughing.

'Is it something to do with what we were discussing earlier on the ferry?' asked Evelyn.

'Partly,' he said. 'Lorraine, you were saying that you begin with the hypothesis that the human body is perfect, and then?'

'Then I examine its origins, meaning and practice by various tribes, and its evolution to the present day. Personally I do not agree with it: it defies logic. I see no reason why I should infuse a permanent picture or sign into my skin. Changing the appearance of your body is okay in exceptional circumstances.'

'Such as?' enquired Jonathan.

'For psychological reasons, for example, if it genuinely makes you happy or improves your mental wellbeing, then it's okay, and on medical grounds too such as the removal of a troublesome wart or mole, etc.'

'My own view is that the practice evolved from the "rites of passage" practised by some north-eastern African tribes, which was later incorporated into some religious and ceremonial practices, like circumcision, for example, which was adopted by Judaism and Islam,' stated Jonathan.

'Sure, I agree with that, but that was then − the practice has since taken on a new dimension, especially since the 1990s, with body art. You only have to walk down the road or go to a supermarket to see dozens of men and women with body art on their necks, arms and legs. Personally, I rarely see any which are appealing or have any artistic value; in fact a lot of them are unsightly and nonsensical. Anyway, enough about body art; tell us something about your studies, Jonathan. You seem to have an American accent. Did you study in the US?'

By this time Jonathan had temporarily forgotten his troubles and was enjoying their conversation. As he was well read and educated he could talk about most things and fit in easily in any social environment. So he talked about his studies at Harvard, and how he had enjoyed it so much that he fantasised about settling in America one day.

'That's what I like to hear − think about the future; forget the past,' Evelyn said to him.

'I am beginning to see the light at the end of the tunnel. I am inclined to agree, that's the way forward.'

By the time they had finished lunch some two hours had lapsed, and Jonathan felt it was time to go back to Geneva.

'It's been a pleasure meeting you, and thank you very much for lunch. If you ever come to Maryland, please be sure to get in touch with us, as I'd love to hear how you resolved your issues. I'm sure you'll go places in life. Who knows, one day I may read about you in the press and I'll be able to tell my friends that I met you! Here's my card; do keep in touch,' Evelyn said.

'Sure. I hope you will hear about me too!' Sami laughed and walked away, and he muttered to himself, 'Sooner than you realise.'

When he had gone, Lorraine asked her mother, 'What did he whisper as he walked away; did you hear?'

'It sounded like, "Sooner than you realise." He is a troubled young man and I hope he doesn't mess things up for himself.'

'I don't know what you mean, Mum. He seemed happy enough, and he made a big impression on me.'

When he got back to the hotel, late that afternoon, Sami had a message from Dr Omar asking him to get in touch.

Not wishing to appear as though he was prying, even though he was, Dr Omar just asked if he had had a good day. Sami told him that he did.

That evening they decided to have dinner out in the city. Over dinner Sami asked Dr Omar how he had spent his day and Dr Omar told him that he had bumped into Jacob, of all people, and they had spent the day together sightseeing.

'What on earth is he doing here? Is he spying on us?' asked Sami in a semi-jovial manner.

'He said he was here on business – and a bit for pleasure. He promised to come round to our hotel and see us one evening.'

'Do you know something, Dr Omar? I think I'm becoming paranoid. You remember I told you yesterday that I thought we were being followed? Well, today a woman came and sat by me. I thought she had planned it because she wanted to meet me. I just had that feeling.'

'What woman?'

'This morning I took the ferry to Ouchy by Lausanne, to try to clear my mind and collect my thoughts. I was up on deck when I noticed this nice looking, smart lady looking in my direction. Later on I went down and got myself a drink and a brioche and sat down. Soon after, that woman came and sat opposite me and started talking to me.'

'What of it? You are a very good-looking man. I don't know much about women, but that sounds normal to me – she was coming on to you.'

'I don't think so; she was old enough to be my mother. Anyway, I must be imagining things. Did you speak to Marcus, and what did he say?'

'Yes I did, and he in turn spoke to Lukas at the bank. Unfortunately it is too late to make changes, as your parents are already making arrangements to come over here soon.'

'I hope he made it absolutely clear that I do not want to meet them at the bank. It's just not right,' Sami stated.

'Rest assured, they have been made aware of your wishes,' Dr Omar confirmed.

Part Thirteen

I

Alex and Emily, having moved to the US when they were eleven, spent the summer meeting their relatives, going to interesting places and gradually getting accustomed to their new environment. For a while they kept in touch with some of their old friends and schoolmates from Parenting4U, some of whom had also gone back to their respective countries. However, it was inevitable that they would gradually lose touch with them.

In the fall they started school and integrated well. They made new friends, and would go and stay with them, and relatives. During the school breaks they went on holidays with their parents. One holiday that Alex and Emily had with them was when they were sixteen years old, and went skiing in Denver. That was when Alex broke his leg in an accident on the last day of the holiday and consequently could not go to Istanbul to attend the "Young People's Interfaith Symposium".

Alex preferred going with his friends on wilderness adventure holidays. He became keen on white-water rafting and kayaking, and often went to Ottawa in Canada. He also became keen on safaris and mountaineering. One year he, his then girlfriend, and several others, went mountain climbing and attempted to climb Mount Kilimanjaro. They did well, but ran out of time and didn't manage to reach the summit. Still, they thought it had been great fun, even without reaching their goal. The following year they all teamed up again and went on a safari in Kenya, which they all found very exhilarating and a lot less exhausting.

In the year when Alex and Emily were eighteen, their parents took them on some fantastic holidays. In February they all went to Rio de Janeiro to see the giant statue of Christ the Redeemer on top of the Corcovado Mountain, and then to the carnival. One evening they went to the legendary Magic Ball at Copacabana Palace Hotel, which many local and internationally famous personalities frequented. It was full of elegance and worldliness, and they were all captivated by its magic.

In the summer they all went on a world tour, staying here and there, wherever took their fancy, before returning home, having had six glorious weeks of travelling around the world. It had been the holiday of a lifetime and they had all enjoyed it very much, although Greta and Edward had found it rather strenuous, and they had all felt the jetlag effect.

When the summer had ended, it had been time for Alex and Emily to go to university. Alex had gone to Harvard, following in his father's footsteps, to study economics, and Emily had gone to Yale to do Psychology and Fine Arts. Their parents had been very sad to see them go; they had missed their presence, noisy music, and even the occasional rows the siblings had had between themselves.

Once the children had left for university none of them expected that they would come back to stay with their parents after they graduated; they were likely to get their own homes, move out, and move on. The children were as sad as their parents about this but they were also looking forward to it: to living on their own and standing on their own two feet, making new friends and facing new challenges.

During their university years, both Alex and Emily made lots of friends, through their courses and by joining some university athletic societies. Alex took up sailing and fencing, but he focused mostly on fencing, where he excelled. In his third year he represented his faculty in the intra-college championships. He made it to the semi-final but lost to a tight 15-12. Emily chose tennis as her main sporting activity.

After graduating from Harvard with a first class degree, Alex returned to New York and joined a large firm of accountants. In due course he qualified as a Certified Public Accountant and then moved to Stanley Goodman, the merchant bank, working in the investments and acquisitions department. He proved himself there and, thanks to his fluent Chinese, he was made manager of the Asian department within a short time.

Emily stayed on at Yale after she finished her degree, and did a doctorate on the "Psychology of Fashion". After that she too returned home and started her own e-magazine on fashion, which turned out to be a great success.

Alex and Emily were both doing well in their chosen careers; they were going to be successful in life. They were single-minded, focused, clever and well-educated, but they also had the means and good contacts. In addition, they were presentable, good-looking and had grown up in a very privileged, wealthy and elite society. However, they did not rest on their laurels. They worked hard: the work ethic had been embedded into their lives from an early age. It was one of their primary and quintessential purposes in life: work hard, do well and enjoy life. To them it was not an obligation or a duty but a desire to fulfil their potential through hard work and thrift.

When they were twenty-one, both Alex and Emily became entitled to their Child Trust Fund money, which their parents had set up for them when they were born. It had grown with compound interest to the tidy sum of almost $50 million each. The summer after they completed their degrees at university, their parents took them to Geneva to facilitate the transfer of control of the trust fund money to them. Although Alex and Emily were young, their parents knew that they were already mature and sensible people. They were also not new to extreme wealth, and thus were not likely to go over the top, spending the money in an irresponsible and extravagant manner.

Mind you, they did live well and enjoyed life. It wasn't just hard work; they were always going out with friends or relatives to parties and long weekend breaks, but most of all, loved their summer holidays. They always went on holidays that had a sense of excitement and adventure.

One summer, all the cousins, namely Alex, Emily, Peter, Nancy, Gemma, and girlfriends and boyfriends, flew to Athens and chartered a big sailing boat with skipper and crew, and sailed from Piraeus to a number of Greek islands including Mikonos, Kos, Rhodes, Santorini (Thira) and Crete and back to Piraeus after three weeks. They sailed, drifted, fished, ate, sunbathed, slept on the boat and swam in the sea. It was heavenly, they all thought, except for one late afternoon when they suddenly encountered a violent storm. The sails had to come down pretty fast, lifejackets put on, and for a couple of hours it was like a nightmare. A freak storm emerged out of nothing and then it was calm again; as quickly as it had started it faded away into nothing.

'You wanted excitement and adventure? Well, you sure got it!' said Emily to Alex.

'For a moment there I thought we had it. I really thought the boat was going to capsize,' said Peter.

'That was too close for comfort,' said Alex's girlfriend.

'Yes, I am afraid you are right; we were in trouble, darling, but fortunately we are all okay. In years to come, we will all be laughing about it,' said Alex, sounding quiet relieved.

'I for one will never forget it and I do not think I will be repeating this in a hurry!' added Emily.

With the holiday over, they returned home and got engrossed in their city lives of working and socialising.

II

Two days after the first message about the appearance of a young man claiming to be their Jonathan, from the bank in Geneva, the Everests received an electronic mail, which stated that, according to their investigations and the results of the blood and DNA tests, the bank was satisfied that the young man in question was their long-lost son. They were advised to make arrangements to go to Geneva for further discussions, and eventually to meet him. No details of the young man were given. They were to inform Lukas Bingelli of the day and time they would arrive, and it was stressed that the matter was still very much confidential.

To Greta this did not come as a complete surprise. From the moment she had met Sami she had had a gut feeling that he was their Jonathan. She now knew for sure who the young man was but she was not going to disclose it to anybody yet. She called her husband and told him about the email. He was, of course, delighted and wanted to come home straightaway to be together on such a momentous occasion, and to make the travel arrangements. Greta, on the other hand, thought that there was no need to rush. She thought their priority should be to tell Alex and Emily – once they knew that their long-lost brother was alive they might well want to accompany them.

They agreed to tell them that evening. She promptly called Emily and Alex and asked them to cancel any social arrangements they might have had for the evening and to make sure they came home for dinner. She then told them that there was something very important that they needed to be told.

Both children still lived at home but they regularly went out straight from work without telling their parents. The fact that their mother had specifically asked them to come home made them worry that it might be something unpleasant. She reassured them that this was not the case and that all would be revealed that evening.

During dinner, Emily was the first to broach the subject. 'What's this important thing that you need to discuss with us, Mum?'

'We'll tell you after dinner,' their father replied.

'I can't wait; can't you just tell us now? What's it about?' enquired Alex.

'You're not getting divorced, are you?' Emily asked impatiently.

'No, we are not,' both parents answered in unison.

'Well, what is it then?' demanded Emily.

'Obviously they don't want to tell us yet,' remarked Alex.

After dinner they moved into the drawing room. Alex and Emily looked at each other in anticipation of the "bombshell" that was about to be dropped.

Their mother spoke first. 'As you know, you were both brought up by Parenting4U until you were eleven. We...' she paused for a second and then said, 'As you know we also had another baby there.'

'I thought he died when he was a baby,' Emily interrupted.

'Yes, that's what I thought too,' Alex added.

'Well, let me tell you all about it. He was an identical twin to you, Alex. He was called Jonathan, and when he was two months old he was abducted by terrorists – the Taliban and Al-Qaeda.'

'Oh my God!' gasped Emily.

'What?' said Alex in distress.

'We offered to pay the ransom but no one came forward. We hired a private detective and a number of investigators who worked with him, and the police continued to search for him, but after years of enquiring and searching no trace was ever found,' their father explained.

'But we never gave up. We continued to search, and we hoped and prayed that he was alive and well somewhere in the world.' Tears welled up in their mother's eyes and her voice trembled as she spoke.

Their dad continued, 'It now looks as if our long wait is over and our prayers have been answered. Apparently, Jonathan is alive, and we have been asked by the bank in Geneva to go to Switzerland to meet him.'

'Why Geneva?' asked Emily promptly.

'Well, we had set up a trust fund for Jonathan on his birth, as we did for both of you, and it has been held in the bank all this time,' explained their father.

'It sounds like he's after the money then, rather than wanting to meet his long-lost family,' Emily muttered.

Her father, disappointed with Emily's comment said, 'How can you say that, Emily? The bank is the only way he could trace us. He doesn't have our address, so he had to use the bank to find us. Tests have been carried out to make sure he is indeed our biological son, and a positive identification has been made. You remember when you became entitled to your trust funds? You also had to have DNA tests to ensure you were the rightful recipients of the funds. The same process was applied to Jonathan, and that's why we can say for sure he is our son – your brother.'

'When are you planning to go to Geneva? I would like to come too but I will need to arrange time off work,' said Alex.

'Me too,' said Emily.

'It's up to us. We'll try to get flights the day after tomorrow. We'll have to travel on different flights, like royalty. It halves the risk; in case of accidents the whole family is not wiped out – God forbid. Emily can fly with me and Alex with your father.'

'Is there anything else you know about him?' asked Emily.

'No. Not for sure,' her mother said.

'You mean you know something? You've got an idea who he is?' asked Alex, rather surprised.

'No. Not really; forget I said anything.'

The next day, Greta arranged the flights and called Lukas Bingelli to say they would be in Geneva on Wednesday, and would be available for a meeting on Thursday morning. The first meeting was to take place at the office of Jonathan's lawyers: he considered it more appropriate for the first meeting.

She was pleased with the arrangements and told him that they would be staying at the Sabina Palace Hotel in Geneva.

Later that same evening, she received another call from Lukas, saying that Jonathan's lawyer had called to say that he no longer wanted to meet them in Geneva: he wanted to meet them in New York. Greta explained that all the travel arrangements had been made and it was too late to cancel them.

She spoke to her husband and they decided to go ahead with the trip because the trust fund would still need to be dealt with by them in person.

'I want Jonathan to know that we still care for and love him, and would travel anywhere in the world to find him,' Edward said.

'Of course we would, darling. Bye now.'

III

The time they had been waiting and praying for, for twenty-six years, was about to end. Edward and Greta were about to meet their son who had vanished without a trace all those years ago, and Emily and Alex were going to meet the brother who they thought had died when he was a little baby.

The reunion will be emotional and earth-shattering for mum and dad, Alex thought. I wonder what he'll look like – it will be so strange! But why am I thinking of my feelings? It's Jonathan's I should be thinking about. I wonder what sort of life he had.

Before going for breakfast, Greta and Edward took a call from Marcus Caspari, who told them that the meeting had been arranged for 11.30am, and would be followed by a quiet, in-house lunch and drinks. It had been arranged by Jonathan, who wanted it kept confidential, as he did not know when his parents would want it announced to the public at large.

Edward, who answered the phone, told Mr Caspari to tell Jonathan that they were more than delighted to accept and agree to whatever he wanted.

They were all silent during breakfast, but behind the quiet exteriors lay jubilation, anticipation and impatience.

'The suspense is killing me. Will it be too emotional and stressful for you two?' Emily asked.

'The agonising, waiting and wondering are over – that was the worst part; a nightmare that was never-ending. During all those years I prayed for this moment, and finally it has arrived. I must rejoice – we must all rejoice in this delightful news,' said Greta.

'It must have been hell for both of you: not knowing what had happened and imagining the worst – blaming yourselves. All I hope is, now that it's over, you won't be disappointed in some way,' said Alex.

'No, we won't be disappointed, regardless of what is going through your mind. I'm sure there will be difficulties to overcome but no child of ours will disappoint us. I have faith in all my children, no matter where and how they were raised,' stressed their father.

'I'm not thinking anything, Dad. I'm just concerned about you and mum. I'm sure you are right and I shouldn't worry,' said Alex.

'When are you going to announce it to the public?' asked Emily.

'We haven't thought about that yet. At the moment no one else knows – only those involved here. It's something we'll have to discuss with Jonathan – it will affect him more than us. I will suggest we hold a press conference tomorrow afternoon. What do you think, darling? Or shall we wait and see what unfolds? After all, it took twenty-six years to come to this; a little longer won't make any difference,' said their mother.

'I think we should go ahead with it, subject to Jonathan agreeing to it,' their father said.

IV

They took a taxi to the office of Jonathan's lawyers. When they arrived they were welcomed by the receptionist, who took them to a waiting room and told them that Mr Marcus Caspari would be with them shortly.

As they entered the waiting room, Emily caught a glimpse of someone's back as he was getting into the lift. Good God, that's Sami, she thought and uttered in astonishment, 'Do you know who I just saw getting into the lift? Sami, your client, Alex – I'm sure it was him! Isn't it a small world?'

'I wonder what he's doing here?' said Alex.

'I think we should prepare ourselves for the unexpected,' said Greta.

Marcus Caspari came in shortly after that and introduced himself. He told them that Jonathan was waiting in the boardroom, and asked if they all wanted to meet him together, or if the parents would like to meet him alone first.

Greta, who by this time was certain she knew exactly who Jonathan was, said, 'No, I think we'll all go in together.'

As they walked through the door they looked at the young man standing there, alone, in the middle of the room. Their faces were simultaneously transformed to triumphant joy as they all recognised him instantly – it was Sami with his beard shaved off. He was their Jonathan all right: he looked the mirror image of Alex. They were all stunned.

Jonathan opened his mouth, but before he could say anything they all rushed over and were hugging him with a mixture of excitement, jubilation and disbelief.

It took some time before they all calmed down and separated from one another. It was the bonding of a lifetime. They all sat down; Greta in tears on the one side of Jonathan, Edward on his other side, also in an emotional state, and Emily and Alex opposite. None of them could take their eyes off Jonathan. The likeness to Alex was eerie – he was like a carbon copy.

When they sat down, his mother, choking with emotion, said to him, 'Words cannot describe our happiness – neither can they describe what your father and I have gone through for twenty-six years. We've turned the world upside down looking for you, Jonathan; we've never given up.'

'Yes, Jonathan, our efforts have been relentless, but now we must rejoice – this is the greatest relief of our lives; our anguish is over,' his father said, in a voice filled with emotion.

Jonathan took a moment to find his words; he did not want to spoil the moment. 'I am so happy we've been reunited. I am overwhelmed with a sense of caring and belonging.'

'I feel like coming over and hugging you again and again,' said Emily, rather excitedly. 'Who would have thought I had another nice brother? There is so much I want to know about you.'

'There isn't much else to tell you, really. I think I told you everything when I came as a stranger to your house for dinner the other night. Incidentally, I want you to know that I did not engineer that invitation – I had no idea we were family at that point.'

'I'll take the credit for the invitation to dinner. Though it was purely out of kindness, and a little bit of business,' said Alex.

'It was a real pleasure having you for dinner, but Alex told me that a couple of days later you pulled out of the deal. What happened?' enquired their mother.

Jonathan explained to his newly found family what had happened when he went back to the hotel that night; his business partner, Dr Omar, had told him that he had found something really momentous and called him over to Geneva. Jonathan explained that he trusted Dr Omar more than any other man in the world. He had been like a guardian angel to him over the years, and that he felt more like his family, since his adoptive parents had died.

'Where is he now?' his mother asked.

Jonathan told her that he had taken the liberty of inviting him to the lunch that was arranged for after their meeting. 'I hope that's all right?' he added.

'Of course it is. We are all looking forward to meeting him,' his mother assured him.

'Jonathan, I hope you won't mind me asking this question. You know, I presume, that you were born and christened a Catholic Christian,' Emily said. 'What are you going to −?'

'Honey, Emily, darling, don't embarrass Jonathan. It's far too soon to ask such a question,' her mother interrupted.

'It's all right,' said Jonathan. 'I have already given it some thought.'

'Good. And anyway, it may come up tomorrow in the press conference; it's best to talk about it now, before Dr Omar arrives,' said Emily.

'I didn't know you had arranged a press conference − tomorrow?' said Jonathan, sounding rather surprised.

'Yes, we've already discussed it. We were planning on holding it at 3pm, if that's all right with you, Jonathan?' his mother asked.

'Of course it is. 3pm is fine. But going back to Emily's question − it's all right to ask. I have been raised a Muslim, and am proud to be one. You will appreciate that it was beyond my control, since I was kidnapped as a baby and taken to Afghanistan. I was brought up by Muslim parents in a Muslim country. It wasn't until I saw my actual birth certificate that I realised I had been christened in the Christian faith. Now that I am an adult I must choose what I will be, but unfortunately that is as far as I've got right now.'

'Well, we won't rush you into anything, Jonathan,' said his mother.

There was a knock at the door and Mr Caspari came in and announced that Dr Omar was there, enquiring whether he should be shown in then or if they needed some more time.

Greta and Edward looked at Jonathan and nodded their approval, and Jonathan asked for Dr Omar to be brought in.

They all greeted him with the utmost politeness, and after the usual pleasantries they sat down. Edward moved so that Dr Omar could sit next to Jonathan.

Greta said, 'I've only known my son for a few minutes and during that time I've learned that he holds you in very high esteem and considers you family – we would love to do the same. I want to thank you from the bottom of my heart for everything you have done for him over the years, Dr Omar.'

'Don't mention it, Mrs Everest. I've known your son all his life, and if I could have had children I would have wanted a son just like Sami – I mean, Jonathan. As I can't have children – I never married – I wanted to do some good in the world, unlike my own father, who was a member of the Taliban and carried out many atrocities in the name of Islam.'

'Dr Omar has been there for me for as long as I can remember,' said Jonathan. 'He was always kind to me and interested in what I was doing, but I didn't know the true extent of his kindness until recently.'

There was another knock at the door and Marcus came in to say the lunch was ready in the company's dining room next door.

V

They all moved to the dining room and Edward gestured to everyone to get a drink, as he wanted to propose a toast. Before doing so he turned to Jonathan and Dr Omar and said, 'Of course, you may not want to drink wine. If not, please have something else.'

'It's all right, I will drink wine. It won't be the first time, and the occasion demands it,' said Jonathan.

'You needn't worry about me, I'll definitely have some,' Dr Omar said. 'For a long time now I haven't considered myself to be a devout Muslim.'

Greta just stood there looking at everyone and taking it all in. She was happier than she could ever have imagined, and tears sprang to her eyes.

Edward raised his glass and asked them all to drink to the long awaited reunion of their family.

'To our reunion,' they all said.

Over lunch the conversation centred mainly on Jonathan's life. Greta listened intently as he spoke about his early years. She was saddened to hear that he had never had birthday parties, toys, holidays or all manner of other things that her other children had taken for granted.

Jonathan explained that he had not suffered because he had missed out on these material things. In fact, he told her, he had never felt sad, unloved, neglected, or that he had missed out on anything. He had been content; busy reading, making things and learning. He had been a happy child who could not have wished for better parents.

'I understand what you are saying but to me, coming from the West, growing up on goat's milk, yoghurt, cheese and scant vegetables doesn't seem like a good diet for a growing boy,' remarked his mother.

'Well, there is no doubt that the US diet and mine are two extremes. But Western diets in general are so rich and laden with additives, fat and artificial things, they are in fact far less healthy than mine.'

She agreed, and went on to say that she wished she could have met Jonathan's adoptive parents, to congratulate them for doing such a wonderful job in bringing him up.

Meanwhile, on the other side of the table, Dr Omar was talking to Edward. Dr Omar was not embarrassed to talk about his father's infamy; after all, it was public knowledge. He told Edward what fragments of a grenade had done to him, and that it was the only thing that had stopped his father taking him on more of his skirmishes against the Russian forces. He recounted to Edward the American drone strike on his home, the death and destruction it had caused, and how he had escaped certain death.

Edward told him that when they went back to the States they intended to hold a party for Jonathan and that they hoped that he would come too and stay with them, and Dr Omar thanked him for his kind invitation.

Greta, having overheard this conversation, turned around and said, 'Yes, you must come and stay with us any time you are in New York.' Then she turned towards Jonathan and asked, 'Did you hear that, Jonathan? We'll hold a party to introduce you to the rest of our family and friends. When shall we hold it? Have you thought about whether you will continue to live in Afghanistan, or join us in America?'

'Yes, of course. But as well as tidying things up here, I have to go back to Afghanistan to sort a few things out there too.'

'I hope that by the end of tomorrow everything, or nearly everything, will be resolved: the whole world will know you are alive and that your father and I are the happiest parents in the world,' Greta said. 'We will start the process of transferring your trust fund money to you, but we won't tell the press about that.'

'Thank you so much,' said Jonathan.

'I don't suppose you'll come back and renegotiate a new funding deal with Stanley Goodman now, Jonathan, will you?' asked Alex jokingly.

'On the basis of what I am hearing, I won't; at least not in the immediate future,' replied Jonathan with a smile.

VI

After lunch they decided to split up. Edward and Greta went to the bank, while the others wanted to go sightseeing. 'Where shall we go?' asked Emily.

'Well, Jonathan definitely doesn't want to go to the Farmers' Market as he has already been there,' Dr Omar said.

'How about going down to the Square du Mont Blanc to see the water fountain?' asked Alex.

'That sounds just the place to go to,' Dr Omar said.

'And, on the way back, we can take a look at St Peter's Cathedral,' Emily added. Then she quickly turned towards Jonathan and Dr Omar and said, 'On second thoughts that may not be appropriate or appealing to you guys. It's just that I want to see it so much now that we're here,' said Emily.

'I don't mind at all,' said Dr Omar.

'Neither do I,' added Jonathan.

They caught a taxi and Emily, being fluent in French, told the driver where to take them. When they arrived there, she asked the taxi driver to return in an hour to pick them up.

It was a bright and sunny afternoon, and the fountain, one of the largest in the world, was jetting water high up into the sky, where it formed rainbows that could be seen and admired from the Pont du Mont Blanc that they were strolling along.

'Isn't it magnificent?' exclaimed Emily.

'It's gigantic. Look at that lovely rainbow the spray has created,' observed Jonathan.

Alex, turning towards Dr Omar, said, 'Isn't it just splendid, Dr Omar?'

'It was definitely a good idea to come and see it,' Dr Omar replied.

They strolled up and down the bridge admiring the spectacle, and nearly forgot that they had to go back for the taxi. When they returned, the taxi was waiting for them and took them to the Left Bank, where the cathedral was. On arrival, Jonathan and Dr Omar opted to head straight for the North Tower, and climbed up to the terrace where they admired the panoramic but giddying view over the city's rooftops; the lake and the mountains looked very picturesque.

Alex and Emily went into the cathedral for a quick prayer first. In particular, Emily prayed that Jonathan would "see the light" and convert to his rightful faith as soon as possible. They then admired the cross-ribbed vaulting of the ceiling and the huge rose window, before joining Jonathan and Dr Omar on the terrace.

The four of them hung around for a while on the terrace, chatting and feasting their eyes on the views. It wasn't just the scenery that pleased them; it was also the newly found sense of togetherness that now bound them. They all shared an inner feeling of tranquillity and contentment. It was as though they had all found something they had never known they had lost, until they had found it again. Even Dr Omar, who was an outsider, felt he was part of the whole.

Once they had had enough they came back down and decided to walk around the medieval Old Town, make their way down to the lake, and then get taxis to their respective hotels from there.

VII

At the bank, Edward and Greta were met by Lukas Bingelli. He congratulated them on finding their son and said that he was happy for them. They told him that the time had come to transfer all the money that was sitting in Jonathan's trust fund over to him. Mr Bingelli was pleased that everything had worked out all right for them eventually, and said that he would do it gladly, once the usual formalities had been complied with.

He explained that he was still waiting for authorisation from Parenting4U, and would arrange a meeting for the next morning at 11.30am where, hopefully, they would be able to finalise the transfer.

'Will that give you enough time?' enquired Edward.

'Yes, by then I should be able to wrap things up,' Lukas replied.

As there was nothing else to do, Greta and Edward said goodbye and left. They went back to the hotel and made several calls back home to report their good news to relatives and friends; they wanted them to hear the wonderful news from them rather than through the media. Of course, none of them could quite believe it, after all those years. They had always hoped that this day would come, and now that it had they were all delighted and looking forward to meeting Jonathan.

When Alex and Emily returned from their sightseeing trip they wasted no time in telling their parents what a great time they had all had. Their mother, being anxious to also know how they got on together, listened carefully. 'We had such a wonderful time, Mum, down by the lake, watching the fountain, and at the cathedral,' said Emily.

'You would have both loved it. It was great to spend time with Jonathan and Dr Omar, and they seemed to enjoy being with us too,' Alex added.

'That's what I like to hear. He must enjoy being with us and feel that he is one of us; spending some time with us here in such a wonderful setting will create beautiful and lasting memories of our reunion,' their mother said.

'They are both really nice and amiable. They came to the cathedral too and climbed to the terrace,' Emily said.

'I'm really glad that you enjoyed your afternoon with them. We must arrange for us all to go and have dinner together,' their father chipped in.

'Yes, we must do that. In fact, I'll telephone them now and tell them what we are planning in case they go out. We can decide where to go later,' their mother said quickly.

Jonathan was delighted and said he and Dr Omar didn't mind where they went and were looking forward to being with them all.

In the meantime, Alex started looking up local restaurants on the Internet and came across La Perle du Lac, off the Rue de Lausanne, in Parc Mon Repos. It was on the expensive side but to them that was irrelevant and the occasion required the best. Besides, it had great reviews and delightful views of the lake.

On arrival at the restaurant later that evening, the maître d' led them to their table. The place was incredible. The food was excellent and they passed a wonderful evening, with them chatting and joking together. Everything was superb: the food, the scenery and above all their unity and harmony. They all had a wonderful time.

VIII

Emily, Alex and Dr Omar had agreed to meet the following day at the Horloge Fleurie, and afterwards do some shopping before having lunch.

When Alex and Emily arrived, Dr Omar was already there taking pictures of the beautiful floral clock. The wonderful display was formed by a great number of brightly coloured flowers and plants. 'You just can't resist taking pictures of this beautiful floral arrangement,' Dr Omar said to them.

'Isn't it wonderful?' exclaimed Emily.

'It's not just the floral clock that is lovely but also the whole Jardin Anglais we are standing in, with its fountains and statues,' Alex pointed out.

'Look, you can get a lovely view of the lake and the water fountain from here too,' said Dr Omar.

'It's very nice here but we can't stay long as we have to go shopping, then have lunch somewhere, and still get back to the press conference for 3pm,' said Emily.

'We don't have to walk around much because we can do any shopping we want in the Rue du Rhone, which is right here,' explained Alex.

After walking up and down the street, looking in the shop windows, they decided to go into a jewellery shop that caught their eye. 'They have some very nice, but expensive, things in this shop,' said Alex.

'Look at those gorgeous Cartier and Bulgari creations,' said Emily.

'Well, we don't have to buy anything, but let's go in and have a look anyway,' said Dr Omar.

Emily though had already decided what she was looking for and asked the shop assistant if they had any crucifixes for men: plain silver – or at least not too ornate.

'Are you thinking what I'm thinking?' Alex asked.

'Yes, I am,' said Emily.

'Isn't it a bit presumptuous, and premature?' queried Alex.

'I think I know what you guys are talking about and I'm inclined to agree with Emily,' interjected Dr Omar.

'I'm sorry, I didn't mean to exclude you. I didn't know how you felt,' Alex said, turning to Dr Omar.

'I'm a realist, Alex. I have sensed a change in Jonathan already,' explained Dr Omar.

The assistant brought them a selection of crucifixes and Emily chose a simple one that she felt was the most appropriate for Jonathan's re-christening and confirmation.

Dr Omar said, 'I'd like to buy it for him.'

Emily and Alex looked at each other in amazement, and Emily said, 'Thank you for your magnanimous offer, Dr Omar, but I insist that I buy it for him. If you still want to buy him something for the occasion, you could always get him some cufflinks.'

'And what shall I buy him?' queried Alex.

'I don't know. You'll have to ask mum, or think of something yourself.'

Having bought the cross and cufflinks, they carried on with their walk and window-shopping. They came to a large department store called Globus

241

and decided to explore it. As time was running out, they split up to go to the departments they each wanted to visit. They met again at the entrance, laden down with their purchases – Dr Omar had bought chocolates and tea, Emily a silk scarf, and Alex lingerie and perfume for his girlfriend and aftershave for himself.

By then they were all tired and thirsty, so they headed back towards the cathedral. They were pleased to come across the Taverne de la Madeleine which specialised in "local flavour", and stopped there for lunch. They sampled some of its great food and drink, and then took a taxi back to the lawyer's office for the press conference.

IX

Meanwhile, Edward, Greta and Jonathan went to the bank and met Lukas Bingelli, Gaston Brandenberg, the Assistant General Manager, and Oscar Hedinger, the General Manager. Mr Hedinger apologised for the way they had treated Jonathan at the beginning but reiterated that they had had no choice but to be cautious in such a situation.

'I am sure you will all appreciate the bank's position,' added Mr Bingelli.

'Sure, we couldn't imagine it any other way,' replied Edward.

Mr Bingelli then explained that all the necessary formalities could be dealt with forthwith, except for the agreement from Parenting4U, to transfer the trust fund money to Jonathan.

'Does that mean that we cannot complete the transfer of the money to Jonathan today?' asked Edward.

'I'm afraid it does. We'll need Jonathan and either you or your wife to come back another day. We'll need to open an account in your name, Jonathan, and also deal with the outstanding matters with regard to Parenting4U.'

'In that case, I'll stay, and you go back with Alex and Emily,' Greta said to her husband.

Edward explained to Mr Bingelli that it was important that he went back to New York for business reasons.

The three of them signed what they could, and then Jonathan's father said to him, 'It's only a matter of a couple of days, then it will all be yours, son – just as we planned it all those years ago.'

'The handing-over is long overdue. Have it with our blessing, Jonathan,' said his mother.

'I don't know what to say. I'm overwhelmed with emotion and gratitude.

I don't feel I've done anything to deserve your love and generosity. I feel unworthy,' said Jonathan humbly.

'You mustn't say that,' his mother said. 'You are our son and that's all that matters. You don't know how happy you have made us since you found us. The money is yours.'

Afterwards, Mr Hedinger invited them to lunch, which they gladly accepted as they had no prior engagements apart from the press conference in the afternoon.

X

By the time the Everests had all arrived at Marcus Caspari's office, some members of the press had also arrived and taken their seats in the conference room. Edward and Greta went in straightaway and sat at the long table at the far end of the room.

After a few minutes, when it had just turned 3pm, Edward cleared his throat and said, 'Ladies and gentlemen, I would like to welcome you to our press conference. My wife and I have some wonderful news about our long-lost son, Jonathan. He is alive and well, and he will be here shortly to answer any questions you may have. Before you meet him, my wife Greta would like to say a few words.'

'Our son was abducted by the Taliban and Al-Qaeda twenty-six years ago, as many of you here know. Those years have been an endless nightmare for us. We never gave up hoping and praying that he was alive somewhere in the world, that he was happy, and not suffering in any way. Our prayers, at long last, have been answered: Jonathan is alive and well, and has returned to us. We are circulating a handout that will give you the basic facts about his life, and how we found him again. Please read it, and we'll answer any questions you have before our three children join us.'

After a couple of minutes a reporter stood up, introduced himself and who he represented, and said, 'First of all, let me congratulate you on finding your son. Now, I see from the factsheet that his adoptive parents died in an earthquake in Afghanistan – I assume from this, and from their names, that they were Muslims – and Jonathan too?'

'Yes, that's right,' said Edward.

The next reporter said, 'I understand that you met here in Geneva. Did it have something to do with the trust fund that you would have set up for Jonathan when he was born – as part of the Parenting4U contractual requirements – and if so, how much has it accumulated to after twenty-six years?'

'Jonathan became aware of us through some documents that he acquired recently. The papers were twenty-six years old by the time they came to light, so some information was incorrect, such as our stated address. Therefore, his starting point for finding us was the bank. As soon as his identity had been confirmed we came over to meet him. I won't disclose the amount in the trust fund – that's a private and confidential matter, as I'm sure you understand,' Greta explained.

A lady from the back row stood up and asked, 'How does Jonathan feel about being brought up a Muslim, but now finding out he is Catholic by birth?'

'You can ask him that yourself; he's just about to join us,' Greta told her.

Emily, Alex and Jonathan entered the room and went and sat with their parents.

Another reporter stood up, 'Before I ask my question, which one of you is Jonathan? You are both so alike.'

'I was just going to introduce them,' Mr Everest said, and then introduced them one by one.

'Thank you for clarifying that. My question is for you, Jonathan. Can you tell me how you felt when you discovered who you really are?'

'I couldn't believe it. I thought somebody was playing a joke on me. I was, and still am, in a state of shock and disbelief,' Jonathan answered.

Another journalist asked, 'Emily and Alex, how do *you* feel – discovering a brother you never knew you had?'

Emily answered first. 'It was a real shock. Both of us believed that we had a brother who died as a baby. Neither of us knew that he was abducted, so we didn't share our parents' endless suffering.'

Alex then added, 'I was absolutely astounded, and quite upset, because he is my identical twin, and I wondered what his life must have been like.'

The next question was addressed to Jonathan. 'What are your plans now, Jonathan? Will you go to New York and live with your newly found family, or will you return to your life in Afghanistan?'

'I haven't had time to consider my future yet, so I can't say for sure. In the short term I'll divide my time between the two countries, as I have a business in Afghanistan. However, I want to get to know my family more and meet all my other relations, so I'll be travelling there often.'

Greta had not forgotten the journalist who had asked a question meant for Jonathan before he'd arrived, and she signalled to her to ask the question again.

'Jonathan, I wanted to know your thoughts on Islam, and how you now feel, knowing that you were born a Catholic Christian – will you change faith?'

'I was waiting for that question,' Jonathan smiled. 'Until a few days ago, I was a Muslim and proud to be one, and couldn't imagine that would ever change. I still believe that Islam is one of the great religions of the world. I was raised a Muslim by my adoptive parents, and everyone I knew was Muslim, so all my life I have known only one faith. When you are born, your parents choose your religion for you – you have no say in the matter. Now I am older I can make my own decisions. I want to learn more about Christianity and make an informed decision in due course.'

His father invited a final question.

A beautiful young woman from the front row said, 'I can see from the factsheet that you are well-educated and a businessman, and I can see that you are also a very good-looking man – are you married or spoken for?'

Everyone in the room burst into spontaneous laughter.

In reply, Jonathan said, 'Thank you for the compliment, and I'm not married or involved with anyone at the moment.'

That ended the question and answer part of the press conference, and the reporters were invited to stay for drinks and canapés in the adjoining room. The young female reporter who had asked the final question sought out Jonathan, who was with his family. After apologising for intruding she asked him what kind of business he was involved in. Jonathan told her that he was in the oil business, and they continued to talk while his family moved away to find Dr Omar.

The young woman stayed there talking to Jonathan for some time, and expressed her pleasure at meeting him. She told him that if he was staying around for a few days he should give her a call.

Jonathan explained that he had to fly back to Afghanistan soon to attend to business matters, but took her card and promised to call her in the future if possible.

He walked over to his parents, who were talking to a familiar man. His father said to him, 'Jonathan, let me introduce you to Fred Nicholls. He is the man who turned the world upside down looking for you for years after you were abducted. He is a private investigator, and the moment the bank informed us that someone was claiming to be our son, we asked him to come over and work with the bank. We wanted him to confirm your identity and, believe it or not, provide some protection for you. I hope you'll understand why we couldn't tell you this before.'

'Yes, of course. I understand perfectly. That explains why I've had so many glimpses of you in Geneva before today. I did wonder if you were actually spying on us,' Jonathan said in a jovial way.

'I'm sorry, Jonathan, there was no other way. I didn't know I was so conspicuous,' Fred apologised.

The following morning, most of the newspapers around the world carried Jonathan's picture on the front page. They reported that it was amazing to find him alive and well after all those years. He had been very fortunate to have been adopted and raised by a wonderful couple in Afghanistan, unaware that he had been abducted. The impression was that he was a bright, well-educated and normal young man. Many papers speculated that he was dashing, wealthy and would soon be one of the most eligible bachelors in New York.

XI

After the press conference, Edward, Alex and Emily returned to New York because of their work commitments. When they arrived home they found a letter from the Criminal Investigation Department in Kabul.

Accompanying the letter was a confession from Hamid Ali and newspaper cuttings of the advertisements that Edward had placed many years earlier.

'What about the letter, Dad? Is it in English?' Emily asked impatiently.

'Yes, it is. I'll read it out:

> 'Dear Mr and Mrs Everest,
> It is with great relief that we are now finally able to place the pieces together regarding the abduction of your son, Jonathan, twenty-six years ago. This has been made possible by a confession by the late Hamid Ali, which we received a few days ago.
>
> As you will see from the enclosed confession, Hamid played a major role in the abduction of the two babies from Parenting4U, and also in the ensuing adoption of your son by an Afghan couple in his village in Northern Afghanistan. At that time he was a teacher and high official, and was able to hide his crimes. Only on his deathbed did his conscience force him to a partial confession of his heinous crimes. He still did not reveal who his collaborators were, and who actually killed the two prostitutes and their pimp after the abduction of the babies in Manila.
>
> I have sent a similar letter to Parenting4U and to the parents of the other child who was abducted. We are currently trying to locate your

son to explain this matter to him in person.

On the basis of our investigation and the confession of Hamid Ali, we do not propose taking any legal action at the moment. This does not preclude any legal proceedings in the future, should we discover any collaborators who may still be alive.

If you wish to discuss any of these matters with me, I will be glad to do so.'

The expression on their faces was one of horror.

Their father said, 'This man was involved from the beginning and continued afterwards with his evil deeds: he actually recognised Jonathan from your photographs, Alex, and he kept them for all these years, knowing very well that we were looking for him.'

'What a monstrous man!' exclaimed Alex. 'What does the actual confession say, Dad?'

Edward began to read it out:

'I, Hamid Ali, confess that I organised the abduction of two babies from Parenting4U, twenty-six years ago. This was a Taliban and Al-Qaeda operation and was masterminded by Abdul Hassan, the Taliban commander. Although he coerced me into it, I was fully aware of the consequences of my actions. I take full responsibility for what I did, but I have no regrets. I leave this world with a clear conscience, as my mission was ordained by Allah, and I am glad to have been chosen to serve him in this way.'

The confession went on to give full details about the planning of the abduction, the rogue CIA agent referred to as "mom", how the babies had been chosen, abducted and transported, and how Sami had ended up being adopted by a childless couple. Hamid had taken pride in saving Sami from being brought up an infidel.

He also confessed to the killing of Halabi, who discovered who Sami was from the publication of Alex's photograph, as well as to the killing of the man that he hired to run over Sami. He had wanted to prevent anybody in the future from telephoning and claiming the reward.

He stated that he did not seek forgiveness from those wronged, but understanding, because he was Allah's messenger and had carried out his will to kill infidels, thereby cleansing the earth and bringing about the Islamisation of the West.

The confession concluded:

> *'Sooner or later, Islam's supremacy will prevail all over the world. The demise of Christianity is almost over, and Islam's encroachment into the Western world is now unstoppable. This is only the beginning as it is Allah's wish for a pan-Islamic world.'*

They were all gobsmacked.

'What an evil, murderous and fanatic man that Jonathan had the misfortune to encounter in his life. He abducted and then, in a way, imprisoned him. By having him adopted in a primitive community he stifled his freedom and personal development. It's like putting an animal in a zoo. You can keep it alive but it will never flourish and fulfil its potential. That's what he did to Jonathan: it's a miracle he grew up into such a fine man,' said Emily.

'It was his genes; that's what turned him into who he is now. Anyway, I must let your mother and Fred Nicholls know about his,' their father said.

Part Fourteen

I

At the CIA

At the beginning of the Afghan war in 2001, Matthew had been assigned to work behind the scenes in the field, as a specialised skills officer. His duties had been to put together operations from intelligence reports, and to look out for any possible threats to US National Security.

While gathering and analysing intelligence information, he had deduced that a Taliban commander, named Abdul Hassan, was considering selling information about the whereabouts of Osama Bin Laden. Matthew had decided that even the slightest possibility of his conclusion being correct should be investigated urgently. Bin Laden was public enemy number one of the US, and Abdul Hassan had had previous connections with the US intelligence services during the war in the 1980s between the Soviet Union and the Mujahedeen in Afghanistan. Matthew had promptly returned to the US to try and discover more about Abdul Hassan's previous dealings.

He had sieved through the archives of all the CIA databases for any dealings with Abdul Hassan or his known aliases. Matthew had quickly discovered that Abdul had featured in a number of secret deals with the CIA: for training Afghan insurgents, the supply of arms and, most importantly to Matthew, for the supply of intelligence information. All the communications to and from him had been with a senior agent called Ryan Webster, who had since retired. Having located Ryan, Matthew made an appointment to go and talk to him about an old matter of National Security.

When Matthew arrived at Ryan's house he was surprised to find a frail old man, who did however still have a clear mind and a good memory. He remembered Abdul Hassan well. 'I had a lot of dealings with him,' he said. 'I organised and sent to him teams of trainers, ammunition and lots of military intelligence information that they used against the Russians. He was brash and arrogant, but a shrewd young man, who would deal with the devil in order to get what he wanted.'

'No shit!' exclaimed Matthew.

'Mind you, I might have had a high regard for his daring and his valour, but I didn't trust him an inch.'

'Why?'

'I told you. He was a ruthless man who would cheat and double-cross anyone, friend and foe alike, if it suited him.'

'He is not an honourable man then,' Matthew muttered.

'My advice to you is: tread carefully,' Ryan told Matthew as he was leaving.

II

As soon as Matthew left, Ryan telephoned the CIA and spoke to George Mears, who was a senior officer in National Security. He told him that Matthew O'Malley had paid him a visit, wanting to know about Abdul Hassan, and somebody else in the CIA should be made aware of it. He told George that he'd had dealings with Abdul during the Russian conflict in Afghanistan, and had found him not entirely trustworthy. George thanked him and assured him that everything was under control.

Matthew realised that his chances of success were not very good, but everything in his line of business had an element of risk and uncertainty; he had to take the chance because the opportunity might never arise again, so he decided to press on, and quickly. He returned to Afghanistan and arranged to go with a convoy of armoured vehicles in the hills and woods around Abdul Hassan's mansion, under the pretext of searching for Taliban insurgents in the area. He gained access to Abdul Hassan and introduced himself. He told him that his former collaborator, Ryan Webster, sent his regards.

When Abdul heard the name of Ryan Webster, he livened up and invited Matthew in for a nice cup of tea. 'I came to like English tea,' he said, 'when I was a student at Harrow in England.'

Matthew gladly accepted the invitation.

Having exhausted all the simple pleasantries, Abdul asked, 'What are you really here for, Mr O'Malley?'

'Call me Matthew.'

'Very well, Matthew; call me Abdul, if you please. You are Irish, I presume?'

'Right; Irish descent,' replied Matthew. 'I've heard rumours that someone has information to exchange, for a large sum of money.'

'Let me tell you this, Matthew: I have no scruples with regard to what commodities I deal in as long as I get what I want.'

That did not surprise Matthew; it fitted in with what Ryan had told him, but he said, 'I am sorry, I don't understand.'

'I'll come straight to the point. The time has come to put an end to *his* meddling. He's lost the plot, you know; people don't realise that. I want $10 million US upfront for information leading to his whereabouts, and another $25 million on his apprehension. You *do* know who I am talking about?'

'I know by the $25 million. There is only one man with that price on his head, but there is no appropriation for an extra $10 million upfront payment. If you would accept an advance of $5 million and a further payment of $20 million on his capture, then we can do business. I'll proceed with the transfer of the money into your bank account.'

'There will be no bank accounts. All the money must be in large, unmarked bills in US dollars. As for the total amount, it's not negotiable. Take it or leave it,' said Abdul categorically.

'I understand. Your proposal will be passed on to the right channels. I hope we can accommodate you somehow,' Matthew assured him and left.

A few days later Matthew was back in the US, in conference with the echelons of power in the White House, discussing the matter. Their final decision was that the extra $10 million upfront payment was unacceptable. It was not authorised and there was no guarantee that the information that they would receive in exchange would be fruitful, so it was rejected. In any event, the amount was fixed at $25 million, and it would only be paid after the successful capture of Bin Laden.

Matthew, though, was hell-bent on seeing things through; he wasn't going to give up yet. It was the chance of a lifetime for him to be a hero, get quick promotion, and in the process serve his country and the President well.

III

Matthew returned to Afghanistan and paid Abdul Hassan another visit. He told him that the official offer could not be changed and asked him if he would reconsider the offer.

Having listened to him, Abdul said, 'You are wasting your time and mine. You don't realise what you will gain by accepting my proposal now, and what you will lose if you don't. Firstly, he will remain at large, inspiring home-grown and foreign Muslim fanatics to hold the Koran in the one hand and kill innocent people with the other in the name of Allah. Secondly, your government will continue to "spend billions of dollars", as your Mr Romney put it not long ago, trying to capture him – for years to come, perhaps. On the other hand, if you were to take up my offer, you could pick him up from his bed within a matter of days.'

'I hear what you are saying but we cannot accommodate all your demands. I was thinking though, if we could direct you to another source for collecting the extra $10 million, would you consider it acceptable?' asked Matthew.

'Yes, I would, but what or where is that other source?'

'Well, it would involve an element of risk and bad publicity, but at the end we would all get what we wanted: the ends justify the means, as they say.' Matthew noticed that Abdul was still listening to him intently. He told him that some extremely wealthy people from the US and around the world were known to go to Parenting4U, in Manila, to have their babies conceived, born and raised there. If, for the sake of argument, a couple of American babies were abducted and held for a $10 million ransom, then either the parents would pay up or, failing that, the US government would secretly step in and pay instead. 'The babies would then be returned and nobody would ever link it with our arrangement. You would get your extra $10 million, and we would get *him*,' Matthew concluded. 'But you must guarantee the safe return of the babies.'

Abdul listened in disbelief. He had known the Americans were desperate to get Bin Laden but even he considered what Matthew was proposing to be appalling. He had them over a barrel. They will stop at nothing, he thought. But in their position I would do the same. Aloud he said, 'You are determined to find a way, I can see that, but can it be done without any unnecessary casualties? The logistics will be difficult.'

'You will have time to organise the whole operation so that it can go smoothly, with the minimum collateral damage. In any event, both sides must be prepared to make sacrifices in order to get the desired result. I can guarantee that you will get the extra $10 million, one way or another. If the parents cannot get to that level, then we'll step in to save the babies and the deal,' Matthew assured him.

'That would make your government look good, and us bad.'

'You've always been the bad guys in the West anyway,' Matthew said. 'Anyway, you tell us where he is hiding and we pay: that's the deal. That concludes our business for now. From here on *you* will lead the way. We'll deny all knowledge of your deeds and will condemn them in the strongest possible terms, irrespective of the outcome. This must remain a secret between you and me. There can be no other way. If you agree, we'll shake hands on it now.'

'I understand perfectly: "mom" is the word,' said Abdul, while looking at Matthew and smiling wickedly.

The two men shook hands and parted.

When Matthew left he was jubilant; he was within a whisker of his ultimate goal, to catch the big one: public enemy number one. His cause was just, and had to be achieved by any means. When he got back to the base he told the Commanding Officer to be wary of Abdul Hassan but not to carry out any operations in and around his province, and that he was returning to the US to inform the President of a major breakthrough in the important initiative that he was working on.

IV

On his return to the US, Matthew did not disclose to the Agency and the President what exactly he had contrived, in order to protect them. He was also worried in case they put an end to his initiative. He just reported that his proposal had been accepted by the other party and that it would be only a matter of weeks before they could, at long last, seize their public enemy number one.

When the President heard that Agent O'Malley had made good progress he was very pleased, and asked to see him. 'I've been hearing some encouraging news about your work for the capture of Bin Laden, Agent O'Malley,' he said.

'On the basis of my progress so far, I am optimistic, Mr President, but it is still premature at this stage to assume its eventual success. I don't wish to burden you with the knowledge of what it entails but I can confirm that I had a breakthrough in my negotiations and expect to see further developments upon my return to Afghanistan.'

The lack of detail worried the President, and he said, 'I know you are dedicated to our nation's security and interests but I hope you have not exceeded your authority and promised more than we can deliver. Whatever it is, it must not tarnish the image of the President, or any of the White House staff, and our country as a whole.'

Matthew took the President's words as a sign that his initiative had been sanctioned by him, albeit subject to certain conditions. Before leaving he said, 'Mr President, I am confident that it won't. If it goes badly, we can scupper the deal and obliterate the other party. No one else is involved; I take full responsibility.'

The President was not happy that the negotiations for such an important operation had been left in the hands of one agent. When Matthew departed he telephoned George Mears at the CIA and told him that the Agency must, as a minimum, be aware of what agreements Matthew O'Malley was entering into.

George assured the President that, unknown to Matthew, they were listening to and keeping track of everything he did, but that at the same time they didn't want to spook the other party and felt it was best to continue as Matthew had begun.

Part Fifteen

New York

I

Twenty-six years later, while Evelyn Withers was carrying out her surveillance in Geneva, she was surprised to discover that she was not the only one who was shadowing Jonathan and Dr Omar. She casually got her mobile phone out, took a picture of the man in question and promptly sent it to Matthew in Washington DC. When he received it, he was dumfounded.

He immediately telephoned her and said, 'Be extremely vigilant because he is very dangerous. His presence means the time has come for me to make plans to come and join you.'

'Don't worry, I'll be careful. When do you think you'll be here?'

'Soon, I hope; depends on any new developments. Meantime, keep me informed. Bye now,' Matthew said and rang off.

Matthew's conviction that those Muslims were planning something was reaffirmed. He has concluded that whatever they were planning in Geneva must have something to do with the Child Trust Fund that had been set up by the Everests on the birth of their son, Jonathan. He must have survived the abduction and been brought up in Afghanistan as Sami Hussein, a Muslim.

Matthew had spent his career chasing terrorists; trying to think like them, to be one step ahead in order to catch them. Despite his many successes his career progression had stalled. He was very ambitious and had expected more; more money, power and esteem. He knew why it had not happened but still felt bitter about it. His failure to get the big one, Bin Laden, twenty-six years ago had left him with a personal vendetta against the Taliban and Al-Qaeda.

The following evening Evelyn reported back to Matthew. She told him that she had met Sami and he had actually had lunch with her and her daughter. She said that he was a nice young man; well-educated but very confused because he was at some crossroads in his life – something momentous was about to happen. 'Whatever is going on in his life will happen soon,' she concluded, 'because as he was leaving, he said that we may hear about it sooner than we realise.'

As soon as Matthew heard that, he said, 'A serious situation is developing fast; now is the time for me to come and take over. I'll speak to you when I get there. Goodbye.'

'See you then,' Evelyn said.

II

Meanwhile, Denzel Bassi, the young CIA agent, carried on digging into the story of the abduction of the Everests' baby twenty-six years earlier. While looking through the newspaper reports and commentaries about the abduction, he came across what the abductors had said during their only telephone call: 'Stand by for the ransom demand.'

When the CEO of Parenting4U had asked the caller, "What do you want?" It was reported that the caller had said, "Ask mum", or possibly "Their mums", and had hung up.

For a ransom call, Denzel thought, that didn't make any sense. It spelt disaster for both sides. Since he had found no reference to the last comment in the CIA archives, he became suspicious and wondered if it had been left out intentionally, or if it might have been erased deliberately afterwards – and if so, why, and by whom?

He knew that his boss had been involved in Afghanistan at the time, on some kind of initiative for catching Osama Bin Laden that had fizzled out. Though Matthew *could* have made the alteration, it seemed unlikely.

Soon after the ransom call, Matthew had ordered the drone attack that had killed Abdul Hassan and his associates. And now Dr Omar, who was Abdul Hassan's son, and a young man of twenty-six from the same village, who had very recently visited the Everests' house, had suddenly turned up in Geneva with Jacob. He found it all very intriguing, and continued digging. He was thunderstruck when he found a photofit match for Jacob; he wrote the name down on the notepad on his desk, and carried on deliberating on the cryptic phone call, scribbling his thoughts underneath the name.

"Ask mum", or "Ask their mums". Possibly a sneer at the two lesbian mothers, a collaborator, perhaps – but why betray him or her? And why delete such a reference from the CIA archives...unless it was to protect a *CIA* asset.

To protect a source – or an agent? Mum...mom...MOM...Matthew O'Malley.

'That's it. Eureka!' Denzel whispered. Realising the precarious predicament he was in, he left the office in a great hurry.

III

Denzel went and made a phone call straightaway, from a public booth, to CIA central. 'May I speak to the Section Head of National Security please? I don't remember his name.'

'Who wants to speak to him?' the lady at the other end asked.

'I am Agent Denzel Bassi, Miss.'

'Please hold.' There was silence for a moment, and then her voice returned. 'I'll put you through. His name is Tony Flannigan.'

'What do you want to talk to me about, Agent Bassi?' a man's voice asked.

'It's an old matter of National Security that has resurfaced and I am convinced that you would want to hear it, Sir.'

'Did you say National Security?' Tony Flannigan asked, sounding rather excited. Then he said, 'What's it about?'

'May I come up and talk to you in person, Sir? I can be there in five minutes.'

'Sure, come on up.'

When Denzel entered the office, Mr Flannigan was sitting down behind his large desk writing something down. He looked up, gave a piercing look at the young man, and signalled for him to sit down. He had an air of seriousness about him, Denzel thought, and must be in his mid-fifties, as he had thinning grey hair. He introduced himself, approached the desk, and thanked him for agreeing to see him.

'What's this shit that you want to talk to me about and why didn't you speak to your immediate superior?' Mr Flannigan asked.

'It's like this, Sir: I work for Matthew O'Malley, and I think I discovered something terrible that he was involved in twenty-six years ago. It's going to erupt soon. That's why I didn't think I should talk to him first.'

On hearing that, Tony Flannigan became all ears. He leaned over his desk towards Bassi and coaxed him on. 'You don't say! Go on, spit it out.'

When Denzel finished telling him what he had found, Mr Flannigan asked, 'Have you told anyone else about this? It's important that I know if you have.'

'No, Mr Flannigan. No, Sir, I haven't.'

'Good, you were right not to, and to come to me first. Keep it between us, Denzel – you've done well!'

'Thank you for listening to me, Sir. Goodbye.'

As soon as Denzel left, Tony telephoned George Mears, the Director of the CIA, on his direct line, and requested an urgent meeting.

When Tony arrived George greeted him and said, 'What's up, Tony?'

'Something has just resurfaced after a quarter of a century that could be very damaging if it became public. Denzel Bassi, a young agent carrying out some research for Matthew O'Malley, discovered something very disturbing.'

'You've got to stop it, nip it in the bud before the shit hits the fan, whatever it is, Tony.'

Tony went on to explain what Denzel had been working on, and what exactly had been discovered. 'They are now converging in Geneva, and Matthew hasn't been seen for some time. He might have already gone there himself,' Tony concluded.

'You had better go after him and put an end to this shit once and for all. Under no circumstances should this be allowed to go public. Take *whatever* measures you have to, to stop it,' emphasised George.

'Yes, George. I understand. Goodbye now.'

'Good luck,' said George.

IV

While Denzel was out, Matthew had gone back to the office just before it was shut, looking for him. He happened to look down on Denzel's desk and had seen his scribbles; he realised that his secret was out and pondered the implications of this unexpected development. His brow furrowed as he stormed out of the building. Before going to the airport to catch a plane for Geneva, he made a detour via Denzel's apartment. He broke in and waited there, with a silenced gun in one hand and Denzel's scribbles in the other, until the junior agent arrived.

'Hello, Denzel,' he said. 'I wanted to see you, so I let myself in.'

'What the hell are you doing in my apartment? You scared the shit out of me!' screamed Denzel.

'Good. You should have taken your notes with you, or destroyed them. Who have you been talking to about this, Denzel?'

'No one, Mr O'Malley. I swear, I told no one,' replied Denzel, sounding worried and unconvincing.

'You should have come to me straightaway. I am your superior officer

– your boss. You've violated protocol. I took you on board, trained you and trusted you – you were my prodigy. And this is how you repay me, you son of a bitch?'

I'm sorry, Mr O'Malley, I didn't know what to do. I got scared and panicked. It won't happen again, I promise. I...I only told Tony Flannigan.'

'You told *Tony Flannigan*? Oh, no! You fucking shithead! Do you know what you've done? You've put us both in a very precarious position. We are *both* as good as dead now,' bellowed Matthew in anger. 'If you'd only come to me first it might have been okay; I *might* have been able to cover it up. You've put us both in an untenable position – I can see no way out of this for you.' With that, he shot and killed Denzel. He then left the apartment and went straight to the airport without a backwards glance.

V

The following morning George received a letter from a senior officer from the Criminal Investigation Department in Kabul, which enclosed a confession letter from Hamid Ali. In the letter Hamid made allegations that a CIA agent, referred to as "mom" had instigated the abduction of the two babies twenty-six years earlier from Parenting4U.

George immediately called Tony and said, 'Tony, it's George, I need to see you.'

'When?'

'Now.'

'I'm on my way,' said Tony.

As soon as he arrived George gave him the letter with the enclosures from the CID in Kabul, and said, 'Read this, will you?'

'Holy shit!' Tony blurted out after reading it. 'These are serious allegations. Are we to believe them? We can always deny them. After all, he is a self-confessed murderer.'

'I'm afraid it's all true. I might as well tell you the whole story now. It was a special operation with both clandestine and covert elements. It was instigated and masterminded by none other than Matthew O'Malley – hence the reference to *MOM*. At the time, we and the President were desperate to get information that would lead to the capture of Osama Bin Laden. We knew all about Matthew's plan and didn't stop him. When the abductors mentioned *MOM* in their ransom demand, they were exposing not only Matthew but also the CIA connection.'

Tony nodded.

'You see, we'd had a tip-off about Matthew's plan from a CIA agent who'd had dealings with Abdul Hassan in the past – Ryan Webster, who by then had retired. The President was also getting edgy about Matthew's activities, but by then we had put a tap on Matthew and discovered what he was up to. When he was betrayed, we ordered the drone attack on Abdul's mansion – we had to terminate him before he revealed Matthew's plot. Matthew had ordered an attack as well and didn't realise that we did it just before he did. His plan had been scuppered by a single word. It was a ginormous intelligence screw-up. Everything possible was done to bury it. You can imagine the loss of faith in the President if it were to become public – the government back then would have fallen. So it was all hushed up, and all references to a CIA connection were erased from all internal documents, emails and databases. It was top secret. Only a handful of us knew about it. You can see why it must never get out.'

'Sure I can,' Tony agreed. 'I'll do my best to stop it, George.'

'Your best is not good enough, Tony. Do I make myself clear? You *must* do it; otherwise it will be a national scandal with grave consequences. Is that understood?' demanded George.

'Yes, George, perfectly. Should I get in touch with the Everests and warn them about Matthew and Jacob?'

'They've probably been alerted by the letter from the CID in Kabul. It says that a similar letter was being sent to all those who were affected by the abduction. Nevertheless, it is our duty to protect them; I don't want another screw-up. Make sure they are not harmed, Tony.'

'Absolutely; we owe it to them. I expect they are still celebrating in Geneva. I'll get in touch with them immediately,' said Tony.

'The media said that he grew up to be a fine young man. It's a miracle he came out unscathed. Quite frankly, I don't know which one is the most dangerous now, Jacob or Matthew. Off you go, and keep me informed.'

'Right you are, George. Goodbye now.'

VI

Tony Flannigan planned to leave for Geneva with two agents, Wayne Marshall and Denzel Bassi. They were going to put an end to this saga once and for all. He telephoned Denzel's office but was told that he hadn't checked in since he'd left the day before, and that he wasn't answering his mobile either. Suspicious, Tony and Wayne went to his apartment to look for him. When they arrived they found the door of his apartment ajar.

'Something is wrong,' Tony whispered to Wayne.

They walked inside with their guns drawn. On the floor by the telephone was Denzel's body. He had been shot through the forehead. There is only one person who could have done this, Tony thought, since Denzel had said that he hadn't talked to anybody else. Not being able to do anything, they reported the situation to HQ and left.

On the way to the airport Tony telephoned the Head Office of EverSoft Corporation and asked to speak to Edward Everest. 'Is that Mr Edward Everest?' Tony asked when he was put through; to make sure he was speaking to the right person.

'Yes, that's me. What can I do for you, Mr Flannigan?'

'First of all, let me congratulate you on being reunited with your son, Jonathan. I work for the Agency, and I believe by now you will have received the letter from the CID in Kabul. You may have guessed who *MOM* is.'

'Yes, I have the letter, and Hamid's confession, and I have been deliberating what our options are.'

'Mr Everest, I cannot comment on that, but let me assure you that our priority now is the protection of your family. You may also be aware that a man who calls himself Jacob, who had been watching your house, has also turned up in Geneva. We do not know what this means but under the circumstances we are going to Geneva to investigate the situation. I understand that your wife and Jonathan are still there, and although I don't think there is anything to worry about, I suggest that you advise them to be vigilant. We are on our way to the airport now and we'll get in touch with them as soon as we get there. Will you give me the name of the hotel that your wife is staying at, please?'

Mr Everest gave him the name of the hotel and said, 'Thank you for letting me know. Is there anything else?'

'No, nothing else, thanks. Goodbye.'

Because of the time difference, Edward did not telephone his wife until late in the evening. He was pleased to hear that she and Jonathan were all right, and that Fred was in close contact with them. He told her that Agent Flannigan and another agent, following a lead on Jacob, who might also have been connected with the abduction along with Matthew, were on their way to Geneva and would get in touch with her.

She said that she had heard of Tony Flannigan but never met him, and that he hadn't spoken to her yet. Having been a CIA agent herself, although not a field operative, she had an air of confidence and control about her. However, deep down she was beginning to feel edgy about what might unravel in the next day or two.

'Tell Fred what I said, and give my love to Jonathan, honey,' Edward finished. 'I wish I was there and not you; I'll be happier when you are both home.'

'I will, and don't worry. I love you. Bye, darling.'

VII

When Matthew had shot Denzel dead, he had felt no remorse. He had killed people before: it wasn't the first time. It had all been in the line of duty, of course. But the pulling of the trigger and the actual shooting didn't feel any different now. He was trained to weigh the risks, assess the situation, make a quick decision, if warranted, and carry it out. His primary objective was to protect his country and the President. He would do what he had to do, that was his job — it had always been his job. This and the trip to Geneva were part and parcel of the same thing. Any threat that was likely to harm either had to be eliminated. So he had walked away from Denzel's apartment feeling good.

On the way to the airport though, a sense of guilt came over him. He was wondering why he had felt that he had to justify what he had done earlier. He had been trying to convince himself that he had done the right thing, which meant that he had doubts. He had never questioned his actions before, so why now? Have I crossed the Rubicon by shooting Denzel? He wondered. Should I cut my losses now and make a run for it? No, of course not, he reassured himself, in denial.

VIII

Geneva

Matthew arrived in Geneva the following morning, checked in at the same hotel as Evelyn, and got in touch with her. They met for lunch and she filled him in on the situation. She told him that the three men, namely Sami, Dr Omar and Jacob, were in on it together, whatever was going on, but for some reason Jacob was staying in a different hotel. Matthew thanked her for the good work she had done and told her to return to the US, as she had fulfilled her assignment.

With her out of the way, Matthew felt relieved and free to do what he had to do.

Evelyn hadn't realised that there had been a shift in his behaviour. He obviously thought that a serious situation was developing, and yet repeatedly he had said it was time for *him*, not them, to take over. There should have been at least another agent with him. However, she did not query it; it was not her job to question CIA procedures.

That evening, Matthew went to Jacob's hotel bedroom after obtaining the key by devious means. He pulled his already silenced gun out, turned off the safety, and unlocked the door as quietly as he could. He gently pushed it open and slid inside. Although he had a small torch held in his teeth, diffused light from the corridor spilled into the bedroom and he could see the bed, which was on the right-hand side of the room. There was somebody in it, asleep – he could just make out Jacob's goatee beard. He gently pushed the door closed as slowly and carefully as he could. Matthew inched forward to the top of the bed from the left-hand side. He was only a couple of feet away when he saw Jacob turning his head and reaching towards a gun on the bedside table. Evidently, Jacob was prepared for trouble and because of that he must have been a light sleeper, or the faint noise and light from the torch disturbed his sleep. Matthew's reaction was fast; before Jacob could grab the gun, he swiftly pushed it off the side table and then jumped on top of him, pressing him down with all his sixteen stone weight. He pressed one hand hard over Jacob's mouth so he couldn't scream, and with the other pushed his own gun against Jacob's temple.

Jacob was struggling hard, trying to reach Matthew's throat with his hands, jerking his body and legs around and making smothered noises while trying to free himself from under Matthew's big and heavy body. However, it only took him a few seconds to realise his predicament. Pinned down, not having been able to free himself, and having a gun pressed against his head, Jacob realised that the only chance he had to stay alive was to capitulate; at least for the time being.

Matthew let the torch fall out of his mouth and said, 'Hello, *Maalik*. Mind telling me what the three of you are up to? I am going to release some of the pressure of my hand so that you can answer my question. If you scream, you die instantly.'

'My name is Jacob,' he protested strongly. 'You must be mistaken. Who are you and how did you get into my room?'

Matthew smacked his palm hard back over Maalik's mouth again and said, 'Don't you start playing games with me, Maalik. If you don't want me to roughen you up, listen good – I shot Denzel, my best agent, because of all this shit, so don't you dare play games with me. My patience is thin nowadays. To answer your question, getting into your room was easy. I pretended I was drunk and gave the pretty boy at the reception 100 Euros to give me your key. He refused and said it was rather unorthodox, at first, but when I told him that I was your boyfriend and had come all the way from New York to surprise you, he couldn't bear to refuse – he gladly gave me your room number and a key-card. Anyway, you can call yourself whatever you like but you are still the old terrorist scumbag, *Maalik*. Was it you who abducted the two babies from Parenting4U? Yes or no? You can nod or shake your head without making a noise.'

Matthew released the pressure of his hand enough for Maalik to move his head, and Maalik nodded once with a stifled, 'Yes.'

'I thought the problem you created for me twenty-six years ago, when you referred to *MOM* in the telephone call for the ransom, had been resolved once and for all with the drone attack. When the deal was compromised, I had to end it. You signed Abdul Hassan's death warrant, and scuppered the deal when you opened your big mouth. You shouldn't have done that, should you? *MOM* stands for Matthew O'Malley – that's me. I was certain you were all killed; dead and buried. What was I to think when you showed up, twenty-six years later, in New York, spying on the Everests? And now, you, Hassan's son, and a supposedly-dead boy turn up in Geneva. What shit are you up to? Before I move my hand from your mouth, let me remind you again; if you scream or try and do anything stupid, you won't live another second.'

'I still don't know what all this is about,' the man said, the moment his mouth was freed. 'Will you please explain? What do you want from me?' he demanded, sounding anxious and perplexed.

'You are still a wanted man, Maalik. I could kill you right now and be a hero, but thanks to you I'm done with all that, so I won't – on one condition: you cut me in on the deal. All I want is to get away from it all. Disappear and retire on a beautiful island in the Pacific. I get sixty per cent of the Child Trust Fund money and you get forty per cent for killing both Sami and Dr Omar afterwards. I want permanent closure to this shit so that I can live the rest of my life in safety and comfort. You can walk away and disappear, go wherever you want. You and I need to cooperate on this, but if you cross me a second time, I'll make mincemeat out of your miserable body. I've come prepared for any eventualities. I am warning you – don't try your *MOM* stunt again.' He pushed his gun harder against Jacob's temple and with a firm voice said, 'What's it going to be?'

'Yes – yes, I'll do it,' replied a stunned Jacob.

'When and how?'

'Tomorrow night. I will pretend that I have a business proposition and get them to go to Sami's bedroom to use his laptop. Once he logs in to the Internet, I'll pull my gun and threaten to kill both of them if he doesn't transfer the money to my account, sorry, *our* accounts. It will be a piece of cake – like taking candy from a baby!'

'Good. Remember, Maalik, you've got a lot to lose and nothing to gain by crossing me.' Matthew put his gun away and got off.

Jacob regained his confidence with his freedom, and said, 'Do you know something, *MOM*? Now that we are partners in crime, I realise that you and I are alike. You've betrayed the principles that you were sworn to uphold, and I betrayed the jihadist cause.'

'Listen to me, Maalik. Don't let this go to your head, if you don't want to lose it. You are still a wanted man and I'll be watching you. I'll be there tomorrow night with my bank account details.' After that Matthew left.

The next day Jacob stayed away from Dr Omar and Sami until the evening, which suited Matthew because he didn't want to be seen by anybody. Matthew was already rejoicing; the bounty was within his grasp. He visualised himself basking in the sun on a beautiful island, with white sandy beaches, green sea and beautiful half-clad Polynesian girls dancing nearby. He thought he had served his country well and deserved it. That was all he wanted now: to get away from it all and spend the rest of his days in paradise.

Part Sixteen

I

About a week earlier, when Edward and Greta had first been notified by the bank in Geneva that a young man was claiming to be their Jonathan, they had become very excited, wanting to drop everything and go there. However, the bank had told them that there was nothing definite yet, so they had decided to recall Fred Nicholls and have the young man followed and investigated. They had briefed Fred on recent developments, including the CCTV security alert at their home, and had sent him to work behind the scenes with the bank: he was to keep an eye on the subject and report back to them when something concrete came to light.

They had informed the officials at the bank of Fred's arrival, and got them to agree to work with him where necessary. He had to be involved with their own security measures but he would also carry out his own investigation and surveillance.

Before Fred had left for the airport he had spoken to Matthew on the telephone and asked him if anything had transpired from the security alert at the Everests' house, but he hadn't told him that he was going to Geneva.

Matthew's response had been that nothing had come of it, and that it must have been a false alarm, although he had known by then that the person in question was a wanted terrorist who had been on the run for twenty-six years. Although Fred and Matthew had known each other for over twenty-six years they were neither friends nor colleagues, and had never actually met. They were just business contacts dealing with matters over the telephone. Fred was a private investigator and hostage negotiator, and was used by the CIA in a professional capacity. However, he worked independently and never shared his clients' problems and instructions with the CIA.

After Edward had read the letter from the CID in Kabul, he, Alex and Emily had been shocked and horrified, but what had alarmed them most was the reference to *MOM*, the CIA agent who had allegedly instigated the abduction. When he telephoned Greta, Edward told her all about it.

Having learned that there was a CIA agent who was referred to as *MOM*, Greta realised immediately that that person could be Matthew O'Malley. She had thought she'd glimpsed him in Geneva the day before, and now the coincidence was worrying.

Following this turn of events, Greta telephoned Fred Nicholls at his hotel and appealed to him for help. They both cast their minds back to the day the babies had been abducted. She, on the one hand, remembered Matthew's reaction when she had turned to him for help. She distinctly remembered that he had been more surprised to learn that they had babies at Parenting4U than about the actual abduction of their baby. He'd said something like, "You never told me you had babies there," and had sounded more bewildered than upset.

Fred, on the other hand, remembered the endless discussions he'd had at the time in Manila with the Police Chief Inspector and the CEO of Parenting4U about the telephone call from the abductors. 'We all thought that *MOM* referred to the mothers of the babies,' he said. 'Especially of the other baby, whose parents were two famous lesbians. It is now obvious that they revealed too much and thus sealed the outcome of the affair.'

He also told Greta that he had seen a man following Jonathan and Dr Omar on two occasions, whom he recognised as the man in the CCTV images who had been seen watching their house. He had followed the man back to his hotel and managed to find out that he was called Jacob Khan, and that he had a room on the fourth floor by the fire escape.

'I don't like what I am hearing,' Greta said, sounding very worried.

'Let me think,' said Fred. After a few moments he added, 'I know what I'll do. I will try and book a hotel room as near to Jacob's as possible, and somehow plant a bug in his room to listen to whatever is going on in there.'

Greta was concerned about Fred's plan, as Jacob's behaviour worried her. Fred assured her that he would be careful, not to worry, and left.

He returned to his hotel, checked out, and then went and checked in at Jacob's hotel. He told the lady at reception that he was quite particular, and wanted a room by the fire escape on the fourth floor, overlooking the lake.

'Fortunately,' she said, 'one of those rooms is available.'

II

Fred went up to the room and unpacked his suitcase. He had wedged the door open a fraction and listened for any noise coming from Jacob's room, which was directly opposite his. Having heard nothing for a while he was convinced that Jacob was out, so he took his own "Please clean room" sign and hung it on Jacob's doorknob. He waited until the cleaner arrived to do Jacob's room, and then, while holding a small towel to his right cheek, he went and asked her if she would go and get him a plaster because he had cut himself while shaving. The moment she left, he planted a listening bug by the phone that was next to the bed.

Later he telephoned Greta and told her that he was well positioned for capturing any new developments. He promised to get in touch with her as soon as something came to light. He stayed in his hotel room for the rest of the day with the plaster on his cheek. He ordered sandwiches in his room for lunch, read the paper, and kept listening for anything coming from Jacob's room. He heard the door opening and closing, but there was no talking. By the evening Fred was frustrated and despondent. He had lost a day and achieved nothing. Nobody had come to see Jacob, and neither had he received or made any phone calls.

Fred ordered dinner in his room and stayed in all evening; still nothing.

He went to bed late, leaving the listening/taping device switched on by his pillow, and went to sleep. In the early hours he was awakened by voices coming from the device. He sat up and listened to it intently. He heard a man saying that when Jacob had used the word *MOM* he had sealed their fate because he was *MOM*, Matthew O'Malley, and had been exposed.

Fred recognised Matthew's voice − it was him all right. He heard them agree on a plan that horrified him, and it was all scheduled to take place the following night. He heard everything, and the beauty of it was that it had all been recorded.

III

The following morning, when Fred telephoned Greta, she had an uneasy feeling that whatever he was going to tell her was not going to be pleasing. He told her that it had been a successful night, gave her a brief account of his discovery, and told her to warn Jonathan immediately. He would see her straight after breakfast. Time was of the essence; they had to act quickly. In order to avoid bumping into Jacob, he ordered breakfast in his room, which had arrived by the time he'd shaved and dressed. He ordered a taxi and left the hotel by 9am.

Mrs Everest shuddered as she listened to Fred. As soon as he got off the phone she telephoned Jonathan and said to him, 'Jonathan, it's your mother,' and then added in a low, whispering voice, 'If you are with Dr Omar, Jacob, or both, just listen to me quietly. You will find what I tell you hard to believe, but trust me, my son. Do not tell Jacob, under any circumstances, that your trust fund money has been transferred to you; you will be in grave danger. Come to my hotel at lunchtime; we'll be waiting for you.'

Sami was thunderstruck; he understood the severity of the situation and although he was alarmed he managed to keep a calm expression, and said, 'Yes, Mother, I'll be glad to have lunch with you. See you later.'

When Fred arrived at Greta's hotel, he found her waiting in the foyer with two men, whom she introduced as Tony Flannigan and Wayne Marshall. After the introductions they found a quiet corner in the lounge and started talking.

Tony spoke first, saying to Greta, 'As you know, in the last few days there have been some very disturbing revelations about the alleged connection of a CIA agent, namely Matthew O'Malley, to the abduction of your son and another baby from Parenting4U twenty-six years ago.'

Fred butted in and said, 'It's no longer alleged, as I obtained definite confirmation last night about his involvement, and I have given the gist of it to Mrs Everest.'

'Let's hear it all, Fred,' said Greta eagerly.

'Forgive me, Mrs Everest,' Tony interrupted. 'But before we get on with anything, I must point out to Fred that in view of the CIA connection and National Security issues, this whole matter must be treated as classified. Both you and he must agree to abide by the Official Secrets legislation and not to divulge any information,' Tony said emphatically.

'Yes, I agree, but time is of the essence,' stressed Fred.

Greta fretted and said, 'I agree as well. Now let's listen to Fred's recording, shall we?'

Fred told them that after he had bugged Jacob's room, he had stayed in all day and night. He had gone to bed late and fallen asleep. He had been awoken by voices coming through his listening device. As there was nobody else in the lounge he decided to play it back for them. Everybody concentrated and listened. Their mouths dropped and their eyes opened wide in horror as they heard Matthew tell Jacob to rob Jonathan, and then kill him and Dr Omar. Matthew had been the villain all along, and now they had the evidence on tape.

When it was finished, Greta said that she was shocked and dismayed by the revelation. 'I thought he was a friend for all those years,' she said, 'and now I find that he conspired to have my baby abducted and held for ransom, to pay for information leading to the capture of Osama Bin Laden.' Her expression was a mix of anger, shock and disbelief. 'And he is now planning to rob and have my son killed. I've been so wrong; how could I have been so blind?' she asked, her voice anguished.

'Because he comes over as the kind of person who is honourable, helpful and could never commit such treachery,' said Mr Flannigan.

'He had me duped all right,' Greta agreed. 'How I wish I could be the one to pull the trigger that kills the bastard.'

'I am sorry you had to listen to this,' said Fred.

'Mrs Everest,' Tony said, 'I know how you feel, I am sure we all do, but we must handle it from here. This is a CIA operation now. You've done well, Fred, very well. Both of you please stay away from them. I don't want any of you hurt and I don't want them spooked.'

'You must not, under any circumstances, put my son's life at risk, whatever you are planning to do,' Greta insisted. 'And I want to be there when you pounce on them.'

'As I already told you, and your husband, we are here firstly to protect you and your son, and secondly to capture those two villains and bring them to justice. Having heard their scheming, I think the safest approach is to let them go ahead with it, lulling them into a false sense of security before we intervene. We'll seek the cooperation of the bank, and obviously Jonathan. They know you at the bank, and there is no reason why they won't cooperate,' said Tony.

'Yes, they know us very well,' Greta said.

'And they also know me,' said Fred. 'I worked with them for days, while Jonathan was trying to prove who he was.'

'That's to our advantage. We've got time to formulate a plan,' Tony added.

IV

Since Jacob had shown up in Dr Omar and Sami's village some fifteen years earlier, nobody had known who Jacob Khan really was, apart from Hamid, the schoolteacher. He had been introduced to them as Jacob by Hamid, and later on had married Hamid's sister. Nothing untoward had happened and they had had no reason to suspect him of anything.

When Jacob arranged to see them one evening in their hotel in Geneva, they treated it as a normal meeting between friends. So when Jonathan arrived at his mother's hotel, and was briefed about Jacob and Matthew's objective, he was absolutely flabbergasted, and gutted beyond belief. 'No wonder Jacob put us in touch with Stanley Goodman and turned up in Geneva. He had schemed the whole process in order to steal my trust fund money,' Jonathan exclaimed.

'What about Dr Omar? Do you think he's in on it too? Could he be conspiring with Maalik?' his mother asked.

Jonathan shook his head. 'He is my friend and my business partner – the trust fund money will go towards financing the business, so Dr Omar would only lose with this plan. There is no doubt in my mind that he is not involved in this. I have to tell him about it, I must.'

'I advise against it,' Tony said.

His mother looked dubious and asked, 'Are you sure, Jonathan? Is it necessary?'

'Yes, I am. I owe him so much.'

They all realised that he was determined to tell Dr Omar about the plan.

By then Tony had worked out his plan. 'Since we know that they will end up in Jonathan's hotel room for the transfer of the money, we'll plant a listening device there and book a room next to, or opposite, his so that we can hear what's going on. As soon as the money is supposedly transferred, Jonathan must remind them that it may take several minutes for the money to be available from their accounts, which they could check on his laptop. One of us will then telephone Jonathan to try and startle them, and at the same time we will charge in,' he explained.

'I'm sorry, but surely that will put Jonathan's life at risk. I can't allow that,' Greta said.

Jonathan jumped in, and said, 'Mother, don't worry; I can handle it.'

'I assure you, Mrs Everest, it won't. We'll be quick – they won't have time to react and Jonathan will be prepared to take evasive action,' reasoned Tony.

'Nothing will go wrong; we've done this sort of thing before. It works,' Wayne added.

Jonathan then suggested that they should seek the bank's assistance to set up dummy Internet bank accounts, to stop the money from disappearing into a black hole, like some international safe haven, and also to cooperate with the local police. The CIA agents agreed that it was a good idea to work with the bank, but they thought there was no need to get the local police involved. They would notify the police if necessary after they had apprehended Matthew and Jacob.

His mother continued to worry about Jonathan's life being at risk, and insisted that the CIA agents provide him and Dr Omar with a bulletproof vest each. When all the arrangements had been made, she asked Jonathan again if he was sure that he wanted to go through with it.

'Mother,' he said, 'after what has happened to me, because of Jacob and Matthew, I assure you I am determined to be there when they get what they deserve.'

After lunch, Jonathan went back to the hotel and told Dr Omar what was happening. He was shocked by Jacob's scheming and conniving. 'He deceived and manipulated us both – how could I have been so stupid?'

'Don't blame yourself, Dr Omar, how could you have known?' Jonathan reassured him. 'He is the most evil man I have had the misfortune to encounter. He hoodwinked us both. He has been so cunning. I'm confident that tomorrow night justice will prevail; he will get his comeuppance.'

V

The following evening, as expected, Jacob arrived and met Dr Omar and Jonathan in the foyer. After a quick chat, he told them that he wanted to sound out a business proposition with them, and asked if they could go to Jonathan's room, as they would have to use his laptop.

In the adjoining room were Tony, Wayne, Fred and Greta, poised for action.

When they went to Jonathan's bedroom and settled down, Jacob said, 'Are you pleased that you broke off the negotiations in New York for the funding for your company?'

'Yes, of course,' Jonathan replied. 'Everything is working out perfectly. I've discovered my genetic parents and everything is looking good.'

Jacob, wanting to make sure that the money had been transferred and was available before pulling his gun out, asked, 'Well, have you got the Child Trust Fund money to fund your business yet, or not?'

'Yes, I have, why? What do you have in mind?' asked Jonathan. 'Is it something to do with the business proposition that you mentioned?'

It was all Jacob needed to hear. He drew his gun, pointed it at Jonathan, and said, 'Listen to me, you two. If you want to stay alive, you must do exactly as I tell you. Switch your laptop on, now, and log on to your bank account, Sami. Do it now!' Jacob demanded, waving the gun in Sami's face.

Both Jonathan and Dr Omar exchanged quizzical glances. Jonathan asked, 'Is this a joke or have you gone mad?'

Jacob scowled, but before he had a chance to say anything, Dr Omar sputtered out, 'I don't know what you are up to but whatever it is, you won't get away with it. You two-faced, snake in the grass, double-crossing bastard.'

Jacob's scowl deepened and his eyes filled with anger. He clenched his fist, swung his arm and knocked Dr Omar to the ground. Jonathan was astounded; he rushed to help Dr Omar get up but he was forced back to his seat by Jacob, who had his gun pressed hard against Jonathan's ribs and shouted in a rasping voice, 'Get back to your laptop! My patience is running out with you two.'

Jonathan felt helpless as he watched Dr Omar, who was dazed and struggling to stand up. His heartbeat jumped and his expression turned to one of fear and horror as he realised that a grave situation was developing. He switched his laptop on and played along.

There was a knock on the door. Jacob walked backwards slowly towards it while aiming the gun at Jonathan and asked, 'Who is it?'

'It's Matthew – let me in.'

When Matthew entered the room he too pulled his gun, and asked, 'Is everything under control, Maalik?'

'Yes, absolutely,' he replied.

'I've got my bank account details. I assume you've got yours. When it's done, you know what to do.'

'Have you logged in yet?' Jacob asked Jonathan.

'Not yet,' Jonathan said.

'You are procrastinating – do it!' Jacob screamed at him.

Jonathan started pressing the keys and after a few seconds said, 'It's ready. I'm in.'

Matthew handed Jacob a piece of paper with his bank account details on it and said, 'Get it done. Sixty per cent and forty per cent, as agreed.'

'Copy that,' said Jacob. 'Soon you'll make me, and *MOM* here very rich; you won't miss it, as you never knew you had it. Lucky for us I didn't take a second shot in Cambridge, Massachusetts, five years ago, Sami boy,' Jacob said mockingly, and then added, 'Mind you; if I had I wouldn't have had time to get away.'

The horrific sight of a man being shot dead, inches away from him on the sidewalk, not far from the Harvard University, flashed before Sami's eyes instantly. He remembered telling Alisha that he might have been the target and how she had found it incredulous.

VI

Meanwhile, everybody next door was listening intently. They heard Matthew telling Jacob how to share the money, and a few moments later Jonathan telling them that it would take a couple of minutes for the money to appear in their accounts. At that moment, Greta telephoned; the phone rang and simultaneously Tony and Wayne burst in with their guns drawn and ready to fire, followed closely by Fred, and then Greta further back.

'Put your weapons down! It's over!' Tony was shouting.

Jacob had his gun pointed at Jonathan, and warned, 'I'll kill him if you come any closer! Put your guns down!'

'Thank God, you've arrived just in time, Tony!' Matthew exclaimed. 'Shoot that man – he is the one who abducted Jonathan from Parenting4U!'

Greta tried to get closer to her son but was stopped at the doorway by Fred.

For the first time in his life Jacob was sweating and felt a wave of terror; his plan for quick riches had been ingenious and would have worked had Matthew not interfered. The money was no longer the issue but his life, as he could never get away, so he changed his tune. He shouted, 'Please don't shoot! Don't shoot! It was Matthew who forced me to do this: he orchestrated the abduction of the babies – he is the one I referred to as *MOM* in my telephone call for the ransom!'

Matthew, still pretending to be innocent, demanded, 'Are you going to listen to him? He is *Maalik*, alias Jacob Khan, a notorious terrorist who has been on the run, and on the wanted list of half a dozen countries, for over twenty-six years!'

Again Tony shouted, 'Both of you release your weapons! Do it now!'

Jonathan and Dr Omar, not having been exposed to such situations, were horrified at the charged atmosphere and terrible scene that was unfolding around them.

Matthew frowned and then with a firm voice said, 'For Pete's sake, shoot that fucking piece of shit.' Neither Tony nor Wayne did, so he continued, 'Well, if you won't, I will.' And with a sudden move, Matthew raised his hand, swiftly took dead aim and fired, while Tony was yelling at them to put their weapons down.

The bullet went through Jacob's temple and came out the other side, splattering blood and brains on the white wall behind him as he dropped dead on the floor. The sound of the shot reverberated in the room like thunder. Everybody was stunned and remained still for a moment, except for Greta, who had by then moved into the room; she did not flinch, her eyes bulging with hatred and riveted on Matthew.

He lowered his gun, turned towards her, and said, 'I've just saved your son. That Muslim terrorist had been cornered, and would have killed Jonathan if I hadn't shot him first.'

Greta scowled. 'It's over, Matthew,' she yelled. 'Hamid, the go-between, confessed in a letter that he sent to the Criminal Investigation Department in Kabul, and they sent copies to us and to George Mears at the CIA. *You* are the person referred to as *MOM* in the ransom telephone call. I trusted you and looked up to you for all these years. You deceived me – you shamed the Agency, our country and the President. You lousy bastard, you orchestrated my son's abduction and then tried to rob him of his Child Trust Fund money and have him killed. We've got it all on tape.' By then Greta's eyes were filled with rage, and her voice rose by a number of decibels. 'What kind of man are you? I'll kill you, you evil…' She turned towards Wayne and reached for his gun but he managed to keep the weapon from her, only for her to go ballistic afterwards. She screamed at Matthew; calling him everything under the sun, and vowed to never rest until she gunned him down herself. Fred and Jonathan escorted her out of the room and stayed outside, trying to calm her down. She was seething with rage, pacing up and down in the corridor, and attempting to get back in.

'I'm afraid that's it, Matthew,' Tony said harshly. 'We also found Denzel's body. You shot him after he discovered that you were *MOM*. You killed him for nothing because a few people in the Agency knew about your deal with Abdul Hassan all along.'

'How could they? You are lying. You are both lying,' insisted Matthew.

'No, we're not – but you lied during your debriefing twenty-six years ago, after your plan ended in disaster. They knew then and they hushed it all up. You see, Ryan Webster warned George after you'd been to see him. He said that you were planning something with an untrustworthy warlord called Abdul Hassan. He predicted that it would end up in disaster, and told George to keep an eye on you. So they did: they had taps put on you, Matthew. They knew everything.'

'If they knew, why didn't they stop me?' enquired Matthew, still confident and composed.

'You should know the answer to that. They too were desperate to have Bin Laden caught and they thought you could pull it off.'

'For twenty-six years I thought nobody knew. Why didn't they tell me?' demanded Matthew, now with an expression of bewilderment and disbelief on his face.

'Because everybody operates strictly on the need-to-know principle. And another thing, you ordered the drone attack but they had already ordered it just before you did. They had to act quickly to protect the Agency, the President,' he paused and then added, 'and you, Matthew.' He shook his head. 'Like I said, you killed Denzel for nothing. I have to take you in now. You are under arrest – hand me your gun.' Tony stretched his hand out in anticipation.

Matthew realised that the evidence against him was overwhelming. He was trapped and, seeing no way out from his predicament, with another quick movement he lifted his gun to his temple and fired. The roar of the second gunshot in minutes reverberated in the room. Matthew's knees buckled and his body crumpled to the floor. By the time his head hit the ground he was already dead.

At the sound of the second shot Greta rushed back in, followed by Jonathan and Fred, and after a brief silence, she murmured, 'It's a pity he shot himself. I would have rather shot him myself, in a way that would have killed him slowly; a quick death was too good a fate for him.' She moved over to Jonathan and said, 'I am sorry you had to witness all this, Jonathan. These people have caused us so much grief and suffering, they don't deserve any pity or magnanimity.' With a husky voice she added, 'Even when they are dead.'

The following day there was an official news release from the CIA. It read, 'Maalik Khalid, alias Jacob Khan, a notorious Muslim terrorist who had been on the run for twenty-six years, and was on the wanted list of half a dozen countries, was tracked down by CIA agents and shot dead in a Geneva hotel. Regrettably, Agent Matthew O'Malley was shot and killed during the incident.'

That was how the CIA buried one of its most shameful episodes in its long history.

VII

The following day, Greta and Sami went to the bank to see and thank the bank officials for their cooperation. Then, after dealing with some final paperwork at the bank, Greta left for New York, while Jonathan and Dr Omar returned to Afghanistan, as they had to deal with the finalising and signing of some contracts for the development of their oil well.

When Greta arrived in New York, she was met at JFK airport by Edward, Alex and Emily. By then they all knew in general what had happened in Geneva, and felt sorry for their mother and Jonathan for being put through such harrowing events.

They were all so overjoyed to see her and, notwithstanding the presence of others in the airport, they were all very emotional. On the way back from the airport they wanted to know more about events in Geneva; Greta gave them a detailed account.

Edward said that he was sorry for letting her stay behind, and he wished it had been him who had had to deal with everything.

They were also concerned about the impact it was all having on Jonathan.

Greta assured them that she thought he was coping with it very well and that she did not think he would be any the worse for it. 'It's all behind us now,' she said. 'We must look to the future.'

The day after Greta returned home, she and Edward were talking about Jonathan's religion. Greta asked, 'Do you think we've done the right thing by letting Jonathan have his trust money before converting?'

'Yes, I do,' Edward replied. 'We couldn't have stopped him from having it anyway, as there was no legal clause stating that he had to be of a certain religion. The trust stipulated that as long as the children had reached the age of twenty-one, and could prove they were the beneficiaries, once they claimed it, it became theirs. Our agreements to sign it over, and Parenting4U's approval, were just formalities that speeded the process up. The rest were the requirements Parenting4U had to meet in order to claim their contractual payments. In my opinion it's up to Jonathan – he has to make up his own mind, without any pressure. A person must be free from constraint and able to act according to his or her conscience, otherwise it becomes an imposition.'

'Well, perhaps you're right, but I think the sooner he converts, the better. Anyway, I won't say anything to him about it; he'll have enough on his plate coming to terms with what has happened to him, and with what happened in Geneva,' Greta said.

'Do you think I should send a copy of the letter from the Criminal Investigation Department in Kabul to Fred Nicholls? I imagine he'd be interested to know more about it,' Edward asked.

'Yes, of course. You must send him copies of everything, darling.'

That evening, after dinner, they all retired into the drawing room to mull things over.

Greta said, 'The letter from the CID in Kabul, and the confession, horrified me. That evil man, Hamid, abducted and indirectly imprisoned Jonathan, and then exercised the power and influence of a teacher over his life.'

'Does Jonathan know about his confession?' asked Alex.

'I haven't discussed it with him,' Edward said. 'I'm not sure whether we should. I assume that by the time he comes here, the Afghan police will have been in touch with him and told him.'

'I think we must. It's important that he knows everything. He was controlled by a man who, by his own admission, was a criminal, a religious fanatic and a murderer. Jonathan *has* to know. I want him to realise what they have done to him. I know it's not very Christian of me but after everything they've done to him, I can't help but hate them,' Emily said.

'He'll be arriving tomorrow. We'll tell him everything, but I suspect he will have either fathomed it out by himself or been informed by the police,' said Greta.

The phone rang, interrupting further conversation, and Emily answered it. The caller, who sounded like a young woman, asked if it was possible to speak to Jonathan Everest.

'May I ask how you know Jonathan?' enquired Emily.

'Well, I knew him as Sami Hussein, but I read in the papers that he's Jonathan Everest by birth.'

'Are you, by any chance, Eva Nowak?'

'Yes, how did you know? Who are you?' asked Eva.

'Relax, Eva. I'm Emily, Jonathan's sister. He mentioned your name in passing the other night. We aren't expecting him until the day after tomorrow but I'll tell him you called.'

Eva thanked her and hung up.

Emily smiled as she was putting the phone down. 'Can you believe it? Women are after him already. Isn't that nice? That was Eva, the woman he talked about the other evening – and did you see that reporter in Geneva? She was talking to him for ages.'

'It's wonderful. We want him to have friends here to make his transition into our society easier. Otherwise it will be very strange and awkward for him. He's a healthy, intelligent, well-balanced young man, so he should be able to cope, but it may take him some time to adjust – that's inevitable,' Greta said.

'By the way, we received a number of letters at the office for Jonathan. I brought them home for him,' said Edward.

'Gosh! That was quick. I wonder who they are from?' enquired Greta.

Edward picked up the first one, turned it over and said, 'This one says, "If undelivered return to: Princess Alisha Al-Haleem, The Ritz, Paris, France".'

'Well, fancy that!' said Greta.

'Never!' exclaimed Alex.

'Who is the next one from, Dad?' asked inquisitive Emily.

'This one is from a Doctor Evelyn Withers from Maryland, and the last one is from Lorraine Withers, also from Maryland.'

'What did I tell you?' asked Emily.

'Eva Nowak…isn't that a Polish name? And aren't Polish people Roman Catholic?' asked Greta.

'Yes, Mother. In fact it is a very common Polish surname, and yes, the Polish do tend to be Catholic, but what are you thinking? Isn't it a bit premature to try to play matchmaker?' said Alex.

'I was just indulging in some wishful thinking, Alex, that's all.'

'All I hope is that he is indignant about his past and looks to the future with delight and high expectations,' said Edward.

'By coming to the US and living here he can savour the freedom and opportunities that can't be found anywhere else in the world. A new dawn is rising for him, and with our love and solidarity he will prevail. We'll make sure of it, won't we?' asked Greta.

'Of course we will,' the others replied.

VIII

A few days later, after everyone else had left for work, Greta took the letters for Jonathan to his quarters and put them on his desk. She paused and sat down to contemplate Jonathan's life. By all accounts he had grown up in extreme poverty and had had a restricted upbringing, very much in contrast to what he would have had if he had not been abducted. Against all the odds, Greta thought he had done very well for himself. Still, she couldn't help wondering how much more he would have accomplished if he had been brought up like Alex and Emily. Edward must be right, she thought. It must have been his genes – our genes.

She got up, and then looked at the letter from Princess Alisha again. She found it most intriguing and wondered what her connection with Jonathan was. She picked it up, smelled it and then put it down again. It was not perfumed in any way; the story inside, if there was a story, was unfathomable. She is probably just an acquaintance, she thought, and left the room.

Later on that day, Greta returned to Jonathan's rooms with some flowers she had ordered to brighten things up. She saw Princess Alisha's letter again, lying on the top of the pile, picked it up again and looked at it a moment, lost in thought. She was still curious about it, to the point of opening and reading it. After the events in Geneva, all letters to the Everest household were screened by the CIA – in case something nasty was sent to them by radical Islamists. The letter had been resealed with a "security checked" tape but Greta carefully peeled it back and got inside.

The letter was handwritten in blue ink, and seemed personal; not something that had been scribed by a secretary or personal assistant. Greta felt ashamed of her behaviour but she was so mystified by the whole thing that she decided to read it anyway.

> *My dearest Sami,*
>
> *…or should I call you Jonathan? It was with great shock that I learned about your true identity. It all seems to make sense to me now. During the time we spent together I felt that you were different, not one of us, and when I accidentally discovered that you were not circumcised, that was conclusive evidence to me. Furthermore, you refused to have it done to save our love and conform to our faith. That refusal put me in an untenable position. I still think about that event a great deal: you must have wanted me to know, and that's why you hadn't locked the bathroom door. I still find it hard to believe that your adoptive parents didn't have it done when you were a child.*
>
> *When you failed to return, after I had told you to go, my world came to an end. I was so devastated I ended up on anti-depressants. How could you, a poor goatherd's son, have given me up just like that? Me, a beautiful princess, and at the height of our passionate romance! I tried to get over you by focusing on my studies. Through my hard work I finished my PhD at the end of the year, and then returned home.*
>
> *Some time after I went home, I was coerced into marriage. I am now officially the third wife of an important businessman. My father arranged it in order to strengthen their business relationship. The marriage is a sham. He takes me with him on all his business trips abroad; I am his beautiful young wife, always at his side. I play that part well but he tells me I am a disaster in all other respects. When he comes into my room at night, I close my eyes and think of you, my dearest. That is the only way I can get through the ordeal. He won't let me have any children, as he has thirteen from his two other wives. How did I, an enlightened Arab princess who had expected so much from life, end up being the third wife of a man I don't even love?*
>
> *On so many occasions I have wished I could find you and resume*

our passionate relationship. I want you so much, even though I am married and know that I could be stoned to death for adultery. I still want to be your paramour – if you still want me. I come to New York to meet up with old friends a few times a year, and we could meet up then. Please, please write to me, my darling, my love, and use the name Samantha. There is no need to write your address on the letter. If you write to me under any other name, I'll know you don't want me. Please do be honest with me. I am a big girl now and I can take rejection, although right now I don't know if I can live the rest of my life without at least some love from you. It will seem forever waiting to hear from you!

With all my undying love, Alisha x x x x

By the end Greta was shaking her head; she turned the last page over and found a couple of postscripts.

PS Please destroy this letter after reading it.
PPS You may think it is presumptuous on my part to write this letter to you, but once you said that you would always love me, and I never stopped loving you.

When Greta finished reading it, she sat down, staring at the letter in bewilderment. She was convinced the woman was deranged, and wondered what to do with the letter. She considered destroying it to protect her son but concluded that once he had read it, he would realise the truth for himself and walk away. I must let him make the decision himself she reasoned. She resealed the letter and put it back on his desk.

Since their return to the US all the family had kept in regular contact with Jonathan, who was still in Afghanistan, and had agreed to keep each other informed of any relevant goings-on. They had agreed to hold the party on a Saturday, three weeks after they had all left Geneva, giving them all plenty of time to organise it and allow relatives and friends to make arrangements to attend.

Greta asked Jonathan to let her know if there was anyone he would like to invite apart from Dr Omar.

He said he would think about it and let her know.

During a telephone conversation, Emily had told Jonathan that Eva had called the house asking for him.

'Oh dear, I meant to call her and forgot,' he said.

'You are excused,' Emily said. 'She'll understand, with everything that has happened. I told her you'd be arriving tomorrow.'

'Good, thanks. And how is everyone?'

'They're all fine and send you their love. I think Alex wanted to ask you if you would like to come on holiday with us later in the year, with some of our cousins and their boyfriends and girlfriends.'

'Actually, he asked me this morning, and I said I'd love to.'

'Good. We always have a great time. Can you find yourself a girlfriend by then?' she teased.

'You bet,' he said enthusiastically.

'See you tomorrow then. Goodbye for now,' she said.

'I'm looking forward to being with you all again. Goodbye now.'

Part Seventeen

I

After Princess Alisha ended her passionate romance with Sami at Harvard, her world had fallen apart. She had neither understood nor accepted that he had not been willing to do anything to keep her – after all, he was a common peasant. But he had just walked away! She had been used to having her own way and having everything she wanted, so she had been at a loss. She had still been madly in love with him but her faith was far more important to her, which was why she had kicked him out.

Torn between her heart and her beliefs, she had gradually lost control. She hadn't been able to sleep, hadn't been able to concentrate, had refused to leave the apartment, and stopped going to the university. She had lost interest in eating, going out, and even in her appearance.

Mr and Mrs Cairo had been worried about her and threatened to inform her parents. That had only made things worse.

Alisha had blown her top and started throwing things at them, telling them that they were just her servants and not her advisers or doctors. Then she had broken down and begun to cry uncontrollably.

Mrs Cairo had been left with no other option but to call the doctor, who had treated Alisha for a nervous breakdown.

Eventually Alisha had recovered to the point where she was able to return to university and concentrate on completing her thesis. When she had found out about the severe earthquake in Afghanistan, and thinking that she was over Sami, she had gone to the area where she knew he could be found at lunchtimes. Her heart had nearly jumped out of her chest when she had seen him, but she had managed to appear calm. It had been agonising to watch him, as he had been sitting with another girl.

Her love for him had been reignited. That night she could not sleep; she started crying, and carried on crying until she fell asleep from exhaustion. She thought he had been distant and that he hadn't seemed to care about her anymore.

Alisha realised that she had to focus on her work, finish her studies and go back home – to get as far away from him as possible.

…and so she had. At least, she had finished her thesis and been awarded her PhD, but she had never been able to forget him. Even after she had gone home, he had constantly been in her thoughts. On many occasions she would stare into the distance and dream of the times she had spent with him.

Her mother and father would ask, 'What are you thinking about, Alisha? You seem to be far away.'

To which she would say, 'It's nothing really. It's just that I don't understand why Allah made the lives of women so awful.'

Of course her parents would disagree and start talking about the wonderful life she had. She knew that they would never understand what it was for a woman to have the absolute love and commitment of one man, to the exclusion of all other women. They were old-fashioned and most likely had never experienced such love, so she never told them what she was really thinking about.

II

After a while her parents decided that she should either get married or find a suitable job and put her time to good use. Her father, who had a strong business relationship with Sheik Waleed Al-Haleem, asked him if Princess Alisha could be employed in some high-profile position in his business.

Waleed was much older than Alisha and had known her since she was a child. He had often attended parties at her parents' home with one or both of his wives. Alisha remembered them well; they had been smart and beautiful when they were young, but after giving birth to six or seven children each they were only smart now. To her they were fat and old, and Alisha felt sorry for their plight, and especially for their having to share the same man for all those years.

The Sheik was delighted to have a young, well-educated and beautiful princess working for him. All the important businesspeople he dealt with would feel honoured to have meetings and discussions with a beautiful princess. She could also attend business lunches and travel abroad with him. He knew she would be an asset to his business, so he engaged her as his personal assistant.

Alisha was pleased with her new job and liked the idea of accompanying him to functions and important meetings, as well as travelling abroad on business.

Soon after she started work, in order to impress her, the Sheik took her with him on a business trip to Frankfurt, Germany. He decided to throw in an element of mystery and told her she was to meet an emissary of a company and collect a package from him.

She met the emissary for lunch, during the course of which she said to him, rather anxiously, 'I am supposed to collect a package from you, but I don't see one.'

'On this occasion,' the emissary replied, 'the contents of the package are too big, so they are in a briefcase. It's under the table, out of sight, and I will push it over to your side. When you leave, take it with you and give it to Sheik Al-Haleem. Do not discuss it with anyone. Tell him that the code for unlocking the briefcase will be texted to him.'

'What's in it? Don't tell me it's a bribe,' she whispered.

'Certainly not,' he responded, looking affronted.

'What is it then?' she asked again.

'It's a small reward for his loyalty to our company.'

'How small?'

'Half a per cent of the contract value. It is a standard payment for a person who brings us business, that's all – a commission, if you like. The company pays it, not the buyer, so there is no problem,' he explained.

'Why is it hush–hush, then?' Alisha pressed. 'Presumably, if the person in question didn't get paid, then the buyer would benefit by way of a reduction in their price?'

'Forgive me, Your Highness, but that's how large contracts are won – we have to oil the wheels, as they say. You should talk to the Sheik about it,' he advised her.

'Yes, I will. I think it's unethical. Something is not quite right.'

They finished their lunch, said goodbye and went in different directions.

When Alisha returned to the hotel she gave the Sheik the briefcase and told him that the code to open it would be texted to him.

He said, 'The code is 987; they have already sent it to me. Go ahead and open it.'

When she opened the case she was shocked at the amount of money that was in it. The briefcase was full of US dollar bills of large denominations.

'There must be hundreds of thousands of dollars here!' she exclaimed.

'There should be $1.75 million. Will you count it, please?' he asked.

Alisha counted it all up and confirmed to the Sheik that it was indeed $1.75 million. She asked him how he had known it would be that much.

'It's half a per cent of the contract value,' he explained, giving the same answer that the emissary had given her. 'By the way, the emissary also told me that you tried to convince him that this is unethical.'

'Well, I think it is,' she said emphatically.

'I don't think your father would agree with that – half of it belongs to him. You see, my dear, this money relates to the contract for the government's programme to renew the medical equipment for our country's hospitals. Your father and I have been placing government contracts with friendly suppliers, who reward us generously for bringing work to them. If we didn't get the reward, someone else would.'

Although she was shocked to hear it, Alisha decided to remain quiet and mention it to her father when she saw him, to make sure the Sheik was telling the truth.

When she arrived back home she talked to her father about the matter. He didn't deny it; he simply confirmed that that was how big business was done all over the world. After that she carried on doing what was expected of her. She played her part perfectly: she fitted in well, the clients enjoyed her company, and many felt honoured to have dealings with royalty. But most importantly she enjoyed what she did as well.

III

Within a year the Sheik decided to make Alisha his third wife. There had never been anything between them apart from their business relationship but he broached the subject with her father and he agreed that it would be good for his daughter. 'It will bring stability to her life,' he agreed, 'and you both get on well. It will be good to have you as a son-in-law. I'll raise the subject with her gently.'

When he did, Alisha was flabbergasted. 'It's appalling! How could you possibly consider it? I don't love him for a start: he is about twenty years older than me and has two wives already!' she protested.

'This marriage will maintain your high status in society and you both work well together; it will cement your business relationship – you make a good team,' her father pointed out. 'You have been of marriageable age for some time now and yet no one has proposed to you. Think about it seriously. Don't turn him down, my dear. Your mother and I have your best interests at heart and we both agree it will be a good marriage, so please think about it.'

Alisha just walked away. She continued to work with the Sheik as though nothing had been said or was expected of her. Months went by and neither she nor her parents mentioned the subject. They were giving her all the time she needed to make up her mind and didn't want to press for an answer too soon. They mistakenly took her silence as a sign that she was considering it.

The Sheik, however, was getting impatient and wanted an answer. He was by then in love with her. Working with her every day, being so close to her, unable to put his arms around her slender body, and...it was killing him. She was so young, beautiful and desirable. To him there was no comparison between her and his wives. He had to have Alisha and he knew the only way was to marry her. So he asked her father again, and he agreed to do what he could.

Still believing that it would be a good marriage for his daughter, he decided to be firm with her and told her that she had had plenty of time to think about it. As she had not rejected him during all that time, there was clearly nothing left to do but give her consent to marry the Sheik.

Alisha cried, pleading with her father and mother not to push her into the marriage, but they wouldn't have it. They had known the Sheik for years; he was a good man, had a good position in society and was very wealthy.

'You will live in the style you've been accustomed to, for the rest of your life,' her father told her.

'Quite frankly, Dad, I haven't given it much thought,' she said. 'I never took it seriously because I consider it unthinkable. I don't love him and he is too old for me,' she insisted again.

'Love will come with intimacy, my dear,' her mother told her. 'You get on so well together in business. You will have a good and comfortable life with him. He will keep you in clover!'

'And his other two wives? And his *thirteen* children?' Alisha asked sarcastically.

'That's just how it is with us – it's our religion. Anyway, you are young and pretty. He won't have time for them once he has you,' said her mother.

'And that's supposed to make me feel better?' Alisha screeched.

'Listen to me, my dear,' her mother advised. 'If it becomes unbearable, find a way to bear it. All wives do that at times.'

'That's enough! I don't want to hear any more about it! I promise I'll think about it,' Alisha said miserably.

...and she did. A few days later, finding herself under continued pressure, and having no excuses, alternatives, or escape from her predicament, she reluctantly agreed. She enjoyed working and travelling on business, her professional life was excellent, but she had had no personal life worth speaking of ever since she had broken up with Sami. It wasn't as though he, Sami, the man she had once worshipped and still loved and longed for, would come on a white horse and whisk her away. Sami had gone. What a fool she had been.

After they got married, they flew to Rome for their honeymoon. They stayed in the same hotel that they had stayed in on business trips, but this time they were in the honeymoon suite as a married couple.

IV

When they retired to the bedroom at the end of the day, they started getting ready for bed. Alisha went and changed in the bathroom but when she returned her husband started getting undressed in the bedroom, in full view of her. Alisha, who had always felt uncomfortable with nudity, was taken aback by this and said to him, 'Please do not undress in front of me. Go and change in the bathroom, like I did.'

'We are married, my lovely,' he said. 'It's okay.'

'No, it isn't. Let's keep our modesty, please,' she begged him.

But the Sheik wouldn't have it. He carried on undressing and made sure she could see him when he was completely naked.

'Stop closing your eyes! Open them!' he shouted.

She did, livid, but her anger soon gave way to revulsion. What a horrible body, she thought instantly. He is hairy like an ape, and fat, with a big belly. But he has been circumcised; how ironic. That's a small consolation.

When he wore his traditional Arab attire, with his keffiyeh, agal and bisht, he cut a fine figure of a man. People would admire them during their business travels, as she also always looked smart and expensively dressed. Seeing him like this was devastating; the contrast was an eye-opener. Alisha started comparing him to Sami and wondered why on earth she had given him up just because he had not been circumcised. He had been physically perfect, like the Statue of David, whereas her husband looked like… She left her thoughts hanging for a moment. There were two naked bodies in the bedroom: one female, her body young, beautiful and in perfect shape; the other male, his body old, fat, flaccid and grotesque.

She had not married her husband, the Sheik, because she loved him: she had had no other options. What a pathetic fool I have been, she realised. How will I endure this? I know, I'll close my eyes and think of Sami, and relive the wonderful times I had with him. That's what my mother meant when she said, "find a way to bear it". That is the only solution to my problem, she decided, and she did. She closed her eyes and visualised Sami's face, his warmth and gentleness, his naked body in contact with hers, and his arms around her, slowly moving, caressing and exploring her contours. That's what making love was meant to be, with the man she was still head over heels in love with.

For Alisha it was a very bad start to married life, but it got worse as the days went by and her husband persistently demanded conjugal rights only from her, preferring her to his other two, older wives. She could see his leering smile as he insisted on her undressing in his presence, and she felt nauseous and mortified at the thought of his repulsive body lying on top of her. Within a year of her marriage she had become a mental wreck.

She had grown up believing that she would never be subjugated to her husband, that she was too important to be treated like a sex slave. Furthermore, she found everything about him off-putting. Even his skin was not right. It felt as though it was not firmly attached to his body, like hers and Sami's; he was old. But he was always pestering her for sex. A sense of revulsion would come over her every time she heard his footsteps coming to her bedroom.

His first two wives were so different from her; they had fought over who would have him for the night, before they had children, he told her one night.

'I want to have children of my own,' she told him.

'I already have thirteen and I don't want any more,' he said. 'Besides, I don't want your beautiful body ravaged by pregnancy, childbirth, stretch marks and breastfeeding.'

'You are the most selfish, callous and revolting man in the world, and I hate you! You are disgusting!' Alisha burst out.

That was an insult he would not tolerate; a loving and obedient Muslim wife would never say such terrible things to her husband. His temper got the better of him. He strode over to her, grabbed her by the shoulders and shook her violently, staring at her with menacing eyes. 'How dare you speak to me like that!' he shouted at her.

Alisha struggled to get free, and he swung his hand and slapped her so hard that she fell to the ground.

'Let that be a lesson to you!' he yelled at her, and walked away.

Soon after that incident she had a second nervous breakdown and became ill with depression. She was prescribed strong anti-depressants and had to stop accompanying him on his business trips. It took her a long time to get well enough to start travelling with him again, or even on her own to meet friends abroad, or to go shopping.

It was on one such trip to Paris, without her husband, that she heard the news about Sami and wrote to him. She was still mentally fragile, and when she received his rejection letter it tipped the balance of her mind. She couldn't believe that he meant it, and decided to go to New York herself, find him and confront him.

She gave her bodyguard the slip and left.

After a couple of days in New York, she managed to find the address of Sami's parents. She had made up her mind to go there in person and have it out with him. Their romance had ended so abruptly and on a sour note, and she had never understood why he had given her up so easily. Had he been looking for an excuse to end it? She wondered. Or is he the kind of person that falls at the first hurdle? If so, now that he has discovered his true parents, who are Christian, will he give up his faith, just like that? I must talk to him in person. She was convinced that when he saw her still looking beautiful and desirable, he would realise that he still loved her. I'll tell him how much I love him and forewarn him not to abandon Islam, his faith. She was certain that it was the right thing to do.

Without the protection of her bodyguard or her husband, and believing that New York was a violent city, Alisha acquired a very small revolver for protection by devious means, which cost her a packet. She had no intention of using it, and only had a basic idea of how to do so, but it made her feel more secure to carry it around in her handbag while she was there alone.

V

About three weeks after leaving Geneva, Jonathan flew from Afghanistan to New York. During the long flight he had plenty of time to consider his new life. His business interests were, and would remain, in Afghanistan for the foreseeable future, but his newly discovered, immediate family would be in New York. Both were equally important to him now. His adoptive parents had died nearly five years ago, and apart from Dr Omar there was nobody else that he was close to, consequently, at times he felt alone in the world. The recent extraordinary revelations and chain of events that had followed still appeared incredulous. But they had happened, and were destined to mould his new life.

As the aeroplane was descending towards the JFK airport, he caught a glimpse of New York's skyscrapers below, and was overwhelmed with joy and by an unexpected sense of homecoming. He recalled his first and only visit to the Everests' house; it was like yesterday, where he had sat down, as a total stranger, drunk, eaten and talked with them. It had been strange how quickly he had felt comfortable being there with them, and had opened up and told them his life story. Those brief memories conjured up an unexpected sense of euphoria and he felt wonderful. He had a family in New York and was on his way there. Evelyn Withers was right, he thought. My roots…my home…a new life.

When he arrived, all the family was there, waiting to greet him and welcome him. There was joy and laughter in the air. Later, after that loving welcome, he was taken to his new rooms. He unpacked the few things he had brought with him, had a shower and sat down by his desk. There he found a number of letters and started reading them, one by one. By then he had received many letters from well-wishers and sympathisers.

When he came across the letter from Alisha he read it a couple of times and thought about the good times they had had together, and how he had been heartbroken when she had ended it with him. He would have run back to her in an instant, had she changed her mind back then. But so much had happened since then, especially recently. Above all she was married, and an affair with a married woman was anathema to him, no matter how beautiful and desirable she might be. There was only one thing left for him to do: put an end to the hopes and fantasies that she had. It seemed harsh but he felt stringing her along would be deceitful and cruel. So he wrote a brief note expressing his thanks for getting in touch, and wished her well for the future. He signed it "Julia", and then shredded her original letter.

Over dinner that evening Emily said to him apologetically, 'We have been looking at the addresses of your fan mail – hope you don't mind. Alex was especially impressed by one of them in particular.'

Jonathan smiled and asked, 'Which one was it, Alex?'

'Actually, it was from a Princess Alisha. I didn't know you moved in such high circles,' Alex said to him.

'Tell us about her, Jonathan, why don't you?' his mother coaxed him.

'Well, she's a liberated Arab woman with whom I became very close when we were both studying at Harvard. She has since married an older man, who already had two wives and thirteen children, and now she's a very unhappy woman. I wrote back thanking her for getting in touch, and wished her well, that's all.'

'Poor thing,' said his mother. 'By the way, did you know that Eva wanted to speak with you, and should I invite her to the party?'

'Yes I know, Emily told me. I have already invited her; sorry, I should have told you.'

'Don't worry, that's fine. I'm glad you did. Have you thought of anyone else you'd like to invite?'

'Actually, yes, I'd like to invite Dr Evelyn Withers and her daughter Lorraine. One day when I was alone in Geneva I took a ferry to Ouchy, by Lausanne. I was feeling down and confused and I wanted to think things over. On the way there I met Evelyn, who was very perceptive and gave me some good advice. When we arrived there she invited me to have lunch with them. They both wrote to me expressing their shock at the revelations in the media and wishing me all the best.'

'Please, do invite them both,' said his mother.

'They're from Maryland. Dr Withers is a lecturer at the university, and her daughter is doing a PhD there. I'll invite them and hope they can come.'

'We've also invited Dolores,' Edward added, 'your surrogate mother; of course you won't remember her and her sister Marissa, Emily's surromum. And we invited Fred Nicholls, whom you met in Geneva. Incidentally, we were thinking of inviting some press people as well. They will most likely ask you for an interview, and possibly to appear on their TV shows. Are you all right with that?'

'Yes, of course – it has to be done. There must be a lot of people out there who want to know what happened to me.'

'I am sure there are,' his mother said, 'especially people who followed the case. The media people won't stop asking for interviews. They have been calling and knocking at the door every day since we came back from Geneva. Now that you're here they'll be even more persistent.'

'I'll do it, but at the end of the party. First I'd like to meet all my relatives and your friends,' said Jonathan.

'I spotted a letter from the Vatican – I couldn't miss the stamp and address on the back of the envelope. What did it say?' Greta enquired.

'That was the most unexpected letter of them all. I feel humbled to have received a letter from the Pope. He hopes that I will wish to become reconfirmed in the Roman Catholic faith soon, and has asked to bless me in person at that time.'

'Difficult! Does that letter push you into a corner? I mean, are you ready to deal with it? It's such a momentous decision,' Greta said.

'My mind is made up. I want to be what I was meant to be,' Jonathan said decisively.

'We hoped you would come to that decision in time, but I for one didn't think you would make up your mind so quickly. Is there anything in particular that has brought on this decision?' his mother asked.

'Yes, in fact two things. Evelyn was instrumental in igniting my interest in my roots and made me want us to be one family. "Take your place in the family tree", she said to me. The other thing was the confession of Hamid Ali, my schoolteacher. That monster was a pillar of the community! Can you believe it?'

'How did you learn about that?' Edward asked. 'The CID in Kabul sent us a copy that we found when we returned from Geneva,' his father explained.

'The police informed me when I returned to Afghanistan. I was dumbfounded. The things he did and his reasons for doing them. I can't believe it, or the irony that he did it all in the name of Allah,' said Jonathan.

'Diabolical!' Emily said.

'It's beyond my comprehension,' added Alex.

'I made up my mind instantly, then and there; I was sceptical before but I have seen the light. However, I don't want to upset all the people who know me as Sami Hussein. I am still an Afghan national with major business interests there. I must tread very carefully to minimise the repercussions. My reconfirmation into the Catholic faith must be a quiet, family affair. I'm afraid I must decline the Pope's request, though I will assure him that I intend to be reconfirmed.'

By the time he finished talking everyone was staring. They were all gobsmacked. Though they had hoped for it, his announcement was so unexpected that it had taken them all completely by surprise.

'Let me be the first to congratulate you on your decision. It's the right one, Jonathan,' his mother remarked.

'I am so pleased you made up your mind without any pressure from us,' said his father.

'I knew you would. I even bought you a crucifix in Geneva in anticipation!' Emily exclaimed. 'You can start wearing it as soon as you want to.'

'And I bought you a copy of the Bible yesterday. You can start reading it at your leisure,' Alex added.

'You were born to be a Christian, Jonathan, nothing else. You've made the right decision,' his mother repeated.

'Hear, hear!' said Edward.

'Thank you, Mother, and thank you, Father, for your steadfast love and dedication during my absence all these years. I am so happy that we are now all together; a united and caring family.'

VI

That night, when Edward and Greta went to bed, Edward said, 'I've been praying to God for twenty-six years to help us find our son. Now that my prayers have been answered I am the happiest person on earth.'

'Me too,' Greta said. 'Especially now that Jonathan has said he wants to be a Catholic. Shall I speak to Father Thomas tomorrow to see about reconfirming Jonathan after Mass next Sunday?'

'It's a bit soon, isn't it? I mean, you aren't giving him much notice. Wouldn't it be great though, if it was done before the party? Then we could tell our guests all the good news at the same time.'

The next day Greta spoke to Father Thomas on the telephone, and told him about Jonathan's wish for a reconfirmation.

He was delighted to hear the news and said that it would be an honour. Greta then confessed to him that when she had first realised her son was a Muslim she had been gutted. 'Me! A devout Catholic having a Muslim son; it's like your worst nightmare realised. I found it so repugnant.'

'He didn't choose it though, Mrs Everest. You and everybody around him must be more understanding,' said Father Thomas.

'I know it was imposed on him but I still find it very distressing.'

She then spoke to Jonathan about the arrangement, and he was happy to go ahead with the confirmation before the party.

Greta set about sending out the invitations for the party. As friends and relatives were coming from far and wide, some needed accommodation, which she was happy to organise. She booked caterers and additional security for the event, as there were many wealthy and influential guests attending. She kept the immediate family abreast of progress throughout.

On the Sunday, the whole family went to church and stayed on afterwards for Jonathan's reconfirmation. Once the other worshippers had left, Father Thomas performed the confirmation in front of the small family gathering. After, they all went out for lunch. Although it was a major event for everyone, they kept things low-key, as Jonathan wanted. They were all together and happy for the occasion, and that was a celebration in itself; no extras or frills were needed to make it memorable.

VII

During the following weeks, Jonathan kept himself busy. He spoke regularly to Dr Omar about their oil company, and wrote to friends and well-wishers. Among the letters he received there was one from a Mrs Zaf Murphy. He recalled with great detail the times they had spent together: she had been his first real love – he had never forgotten her. It read:

Dearest Jonathan,

I have been meaning to write to you for a few days now, since I learned about your true identity through the media. Needless to say, it came as a shock and I still can't quite believe it.

You have most likely forgotten who I am. Well, let me remind you – does Istanbul ring a bell? It's been ten years since then and so much has happened to both of us. I have learned a lot about you through the media, so let me tell you a bit about me.

I believe I told you in the last letter I sent you that I had met John again and we had resumed our relationship, to my parents' disgust. The persistent and relentless hounding and persecution of John and me by my relatives drove us away. First we went to London, where we got married in the local registry office. But we were tracked down and nearly murdered by my own kith and kin! Then we went to Canada, where we lived for two years before we managed to get permission to live in the US. We have been here for nearly six years now. We have two children, a boy and a girl. John is an IT consultant, and I am a full-time teacher at our local school.

I can't get over the news about you. Now that we are both compatriots, who knows, we may meet again some day! I would certainly love to hear from you at least. It's been a decade since Istanbul! The last words you whispered in my ear: "We'll always have Istanbul". I still remember them like it was yesterday; what about you? Please do drop me a line.

So long, and God bless.

Love, Zaf x x x x

Jonathan was pleased to hear from Zaf, as he had always feared something untoward might have happened to her after her last letter to him. He wrote a brief letter back, thanking her for getting in touch, and said that he was very pleased that things had worked out for her and John in the end. He also told her that he planned to stay in the US, but his business interests were in Afghanistan, so he would be travelling between the two countries for the foreseeable future. He also said that he too still thought about Istanbul and couldn't believe it had been ten years. "We were so young then!" he wrote, and wondered what the next ten years would be like. He wrote that he planned to work hard, and to try and achieve something before he got married and had a family himself. He closed by wishing her and her family well.

He considered inviting her to his reunion party, but then he decided it wouldn't be right, now that she was married with children. Besides, his heart now belonged to Eva.

VIII

By the time the party was nearly upon them, Jonathan had seen Eva Nowak for lunch several times, and they had also gone out in the evenings many times. One evening he had invited her to dinner at home with the family, and everyone had been pleased to meet her, especially his mother, who had made sure that Eva realised she was well liked and welcome in their home.

The party was due to start a little after noon on the Saturday. All the preparations had been made and while the guests were arriving, beautifully prepared canapés and champagne were served. Some two hours later, one of the butlers whispered to Jonathan that there was a woman who was trying to gain access to the party, but her name was not on the guest list.

Not expecting anybody else, Jonathan asked the butler, 'Did she give her name?'

'She said to mention "Julia" to you, Sir.'

Jonathan was taken aback; that was potentially ominous. Suddenly he was in an unexpected and awkward predicament and did not know how to deal with it in such an environment. He told the butler that he would attend to her shortly, and went to find his parents. He really didn't know what to do – she had not been invited and couldn't have known about the party. She must have found the Everests' home address and come on the off-chance of finding and confronting him. He didn't think, after the rejection letter he had written to her, the meeting would be amicable.

His mother, unknown to Jonathan, had read Alisha's letter herself, and had formed the opinion that the woman was besotted with him. She didn't think, from his reaction to the situation, that he had done anything other than write a polite rejection letter, and suggested to Jonathan that he go to see her, but with one of the security guards in case of trouble. She said he should explain to her that they were having a private party and that it was not a good time to visit.

A couple of minutes after he had gone, Greta found Eva and told her that Jonathan might need some moral support, as he had been called down to see an old girlfriend who had turned up uninvited.

When Jonathan and the bodyguard went downstairs, Alisha was standing in the drawing room. She looked very smart. She had taken off her scarf, and her shiny, wavy hair hung down to her shoulders. She still had a slender and shapely figure, and looked very beautiful. As soon as she saw Jonathan she rushed towards him with a broad smile and tried to embrace him. He gently held her back and her smile died. He said, 'You shouldn't have come here alone, Alisha. You are a married woman, and you really shouldn't be here.'

'Don't you want me?' she demanded. 'I need to hear you say it!'

'Alisha, it's been five years and a lot of things have happened – to both of us.'

'Just tell me this: why did you give me up so easily? Why didn't you try to win me back? Didn't you love me? Didn't you? Tell me!' she shouted.

'Forget about the past,' he tried to reason with her. 'We have both moved on. Please leave. You must forget about me and go home to your husband,' he pleaded with her.

'I came to ask for your forgiveness; you were right, we should have talked. I married the wrong man. I don't love him! I still love *you*, and I want to be yours forever! I don't want to go back to him!'

'Listen, Alisha, I don't love you,' Jonathan said. 'Besides, I am now a Christian, so please, go, and forget this ever happened.'

That, on top of everything else, was the final straw. That he had not fought to keep her five years ago had been unbearable, and his rejection now had destroyed her, but giving up Islam was the final insult. She sensed fury and disgust building up inside her and she screamed at him, 'How could you turn me down? And worse of all you have committed apostasy; it's religious treason, you disgusting creature! You deserve to die like the infidel that you are!' In a state of frenzied hysteria she pulled the gun out of her bag and pointed it menacingly at Jonathan.

'Come on, Alisha, calm down. Don't do anything stupid,' Jonathan said in a calm voice.

The security guard had pulled his gun out and was pointing it at Alisha. 'Release the weapon, ma'am! Do it now!' he shouted, as the door into the room opened and Greta and Eva charged in.

'What's going on?' Greta asked, as she took in the situation.

'Who is she, Jonathan?' Eva asked.

Alisha looked at the two women momentarily; then swung her head and faced Jonathan, her eyes burning with rage and yelling, 'I'll tell you who I am – I am the judge and executioner,' as she fired her gun.

Simultaneously, the security guard fired his weapon. Both Alisha and Jonathan fell down.

'No! No! No!' Greta screamed in horror.

'Oh! No! Oh my God!' cried out Eva. Both she and Greta rushed over to Jonathan, who had knocked his head as he fell and lay on the floor, unconscious and bleeding from a gunshot wound in his chest.

'Call an ambulance, quickly!' Greta ordered the security guard, as she sat on the blood-stained floor and cradled her son.

'He's alive,' Eva muttered, feeling for a pulse.

'She meant to kill him – kick her gun away from her and see if she's still alive,' Greta said to Eva.

'She's semi-conscious and muttering something – "Infidel" and "Allah" it sounds like – but I think she is seriously wounded. She must have realised she would be shot and yet she went ahead and attacked him.'

Emily, who had been talking to one of her cousins upstairs among the guests, had seen Jonathan and the security guard pass by, and had also seen her mother and Eva following soon after. She had wondered what was going on and, having an inquisitive mind, she had not been able to resist the temptation to go and find out what was happening. She had excused herself, left the room and headed downstairs. When she was halfway down, she had heard shouting, followed by gunshots. She had rushed the rest of the way to the drawing room and had seen her mother and Eva bending over Jonathan, whose chest was covered in blood.

She then rushed back upstairs, burst into the room where the party was being held, found her father and brother and said to them, 'Dad, Alex, come quickly! Jonathan has been shot!'

By the time Edward and Alex arrived, many other guests had gone downstairs and the room was nearly full. Everyone was wondering and worrying about Jonathan, and asking who the woman was and why she had shot him.

When Evelyn Withers, one of their guests, saw Jonathan and Alisha covered in blood, she cried out, 'Let me through, I'm a doctor!'

The crowd parted and she rushed to Alisha, who was semi-conscious and bleeding from her chest and mouth. She tried to help her but soon realised there was nothing she could do for her, so she simply tried to comfort her, saying, 'The ambulance is on its way, dear, hold on.'

Choking on her own blood, Alisha managed to confide, 'He didn't love me enough and I loved him too much. It ruined my—' The sentence was left unfinished as she passed out.

Among the guests were the two TV reporters who were going to interview Jonathan later on. They turned on their remote cameras, broadcasting the scene, live, to the world. As soon as Edward realised, not long after the ambulance had departed, he stopped their broadcasting, but by then the horrific images had been seen by millions.

"Breaking News!" the newsfeeds read. "Jonathan Everest, abducted as a baby twenty-six years ago by the Taliban and Al-Qaeda, and only recently reunited with his genetic parents, has just been shot. So far it seems that the shooter was a married Arab princess in her twenties who was known to him. She gained access to the house, where a disagreement between the two ended in her firing a single shot. A security guard on the scene then shot the princess, who did not seem to be in her right mind. They were rushed to the hospital, where both are believed to be in a critical condition. Speculation appears to be rife as to whether this was a Muslim extremist act of revenge following Jonathan's conversion from Islam to Christianity, or the work of a woman scorned."

Greta and Eva went to the hospital in the ambulance with Jonathan. Edward said he would follow them with the rest of the immediate family and Dr Omar once their guests had been settled and dispersed.

When they reached the hospital Jonathan was rushed into surgery, but Alisha was pronounced dead on arrival. A nurse explained to Greta and Eva that Jonathan needed an operation to stop the internal bleeding, and took them to a private waiting room where they could stay until the surgery was over.

Greta and Eva waited there in a state of severe anxiety. It seemed to last forever; time passed at a crawl and there was still no news. At long last, after several hours, the surgeon came to speak to them.

'He lost a lot of blood but we have managed to stop the bleeding now and his condition is stable. He was very, very lucky: a fraction further to the left and the bullet would have severed a major artery – he would have bled out within minutes. Anyway, I'm delighted to tell you that there is no reason now that he shouldn't make it. With rest, and good care, he should make a full recovery and not be any the worse for his experience.'

'Thank God for that. What a relief!' Greta exclaimed. 'Thank you, doctor. Can we go and see him now?' she asked.

'Yes, you can, but he's still unconscious. The anaesthetic won't wear off for an hour or so yet.'

Greta called her husband and told him the good news. He was relieved to hear it and said that he was on his way with the rest of the family and Dr Omar.

Eva and Greta waited by Jonathan's bedside for about an hour before he came round, as the surgeon had predicted.

He opened his eyes and, after struggling to focus, he whispered, 'What happened? Where am I?'

'You're in hospital, Jonathan. You've been shot but you are going to be all right,' his mother assured him.

'Yes, my darling, you will be fine!' Eva added, with a big smile despite the tears running down her cheeks.

He managed to smile back at them, and squinted to see the others who were standing in the background. Slowly he recognised them and closed his eyes, feeling happy to be alive, and with the only people in the world that now mattered to him.

THE END

Lightning Source UK Ltd.
Milton Keynes UK
UKOW02f1159061114

241161UK00001B/51/P